THE
SECOND
WIFE

BOOKS BY SHERYL BROWNE

The Babysitter
The Affair

THE
SECOND
WIFE

SHERYL BROWNE

bookouture

Published by Bookouture in 2019

An imprint of StoryFire Ltd.

Carmelite House
50 Victoria Embankment
London EC4Y 0DZ

www.bookouture.com

ISBN: 978-1-78681-655-9
eBook ISBN: 978-1-78681-654-2

To my son, Drew, for painting such a vivid idea for this book that it simply had to be written!

PROLOGUE

I'd never imagined myself succumbing to a state of emotional abandonment where I lost all rational thought, my sense of identity. Lost sight of me. It happens gradually, subtly and insidiously, until you really do believe the madness is 'all in your mind'.

I know from experience that my passing from this life into oblivion won't take long. My limbs flail instinctively as I slip into what will become my watery grave. The water is cold, much colder than the surface air. Hypothermia will set in quite quickly as my body constricts surface blood vessels to conserve heat for my vital organs. My head begins to throb as my heart rate and blood pressure increase. I can hear it, the strange whooshing, gurgling sound, which isn't the water around me but the sound inside me. My muscles tense suddenly and I shiver uncontrollably. My lungs, bursting within me, scream at me to draw air. Once I do, of course, my lungs will fill and I will be gone. My hope is that my core temperature will drop rapidly and that my wasted life will fade to black before that happens.

My tears of regret mingle with the murky water as my thoughts ebb and drift. It isn't snapshots of my past life that flash before me. The images that will fade with me are of them together, bodies entwined, tongues seeking each other's – languid, sensual movements as they seek to pleasure each other, gaining satisfaction from the knowledge that I'm forced to watch. I truly believe she reached the height of ecstasy as she turned her smiling face towards me and whispered, 'It's all in your mind.'

The other women, I see them too, with their confused expressions, their bewilderment and deep disillusionment, which soon give way to fear as realisation dawns. They're trapped. Butterflies in bell jars, they continue to flutter until their colours fade and their fragile wings crumble to dust.

My dog, offering me unconditional love whatever my mood; I see him, patient and loyal on the hall rug, waiting for the familiar thrum of my car engine, my key in the door. I will miss him. I hope they'll look after him. Be kind to him.

Pain and sorrow turn to wisdom in time. You should have been more vigilant. Those were her last words to me. I wish I had been.

CHAPTER ONE

REBECCA

PRESENT

The service started and ended with Elgar's 'Nimrod', a beautiful, moving piece. Rebecca guessed it would be a popular choice for funerals. She couldn't help thinking it wouldn't have been Nicole's choice though. More likely she would have chosen Vaughan Williams' 'The Lark Ascending', with its solo violin reflecting the flutters and soars of the bird in flight. If any music ever evoked the rolling green hills of the English countryside, it was this piece, Nicole had once said. They'd been nowhere near the countryside at the time. They'd been lying on Nicole's bed in the poky room they'd shared, having pigged out on chicken and chips and Neapolitan ice cream at the local Berni Inn. The crumbling Edwardian property they'd lived in had since been demolished to make way for a retirement village, but the pub was still there, not far from where they'd lived, on the Hagley Road into Birmingham. Rebecca had noticed it while driving out from New Street station, heading for the motorway that would bring her here, to the little stone-built Norman church in Worcestershire to say goodbye to the woman who'd been the other half of her as she'd made her first forays into adulthood. They'd been inseparable at university and had stayed in touch, although less frequently lately – time and geography widening the distance between them. Rebecca still couldn't believe she was dead. Much less how she'd died.

Suicide.

Rebecca was struggling to believe that Nicole, the flame-haired, eighteen-year-old free spirit who'd whirled into her otherwise mundane student existence like a tornado, had taken her own life. Nicole had had a zest for living. She'd wanted to embrace all the world had to offer, experience everything. Bohemian in her choice of clothing, eschewing spaghetti-strap crop tops for ethnic print dresses, and with a rare, fragile beauty that belied her determination to tackle anything from abseiling to deep-sea diving, she would dance at the nightclubs until Rebecca dropped, dance barefoot in the rain at the festivals in the park. More talented than her by far, Nicole was going to ascend like the lark, obtain her fine art degree and exhibit at the Tate, the Birmingham Art Gallery and all the best London galleries. There would be no holding her back. She wasn't overtly feminist but despised any institution that would define a woman as unequal to, or weaker than a man, thus prevent her achieving her ambition. Marriage hadn't been on Nicole's agenda – not for her some man to tame her and tie her down. She wouldn't be shackled. Love had changed all that, of course, igniting hitherto unexplored passion inside her.

She'd fallen heavily the first time she'd married. After that relationship, one which had left her emotionally and physically broken, Rebecca had never imagined her friend would fall so easily in love again. She glanced to where Nicole's second husband was standing at the open graveside. Smart and immaculately turned out in his black suit and overcoat, Richard Gray was a handsome man: tall and broad-shouldered; dark hair with wisps of silver at the temples, which was always unfairly complimentary on a man. Rebecca could understand the attraction. Nicole had been besotted with him, singing his praises. He was conscientious, caring, kind – a liberal thinker, she'd gushed in her first excited email regarding the new man in her life. He clearly doted on his daughter. Rebecca noted him reaching to squeeze the shoulders of the girl next to him: Olivia, his grown-up daughter, whom she recognised from the photographs Nicole had sent her.

Rebecca had been wary for her friend, initially. A year on from her divorce was no time at all in which to recover, to find herself again after a painful marriage to an abusive, cheating man whose mission in life had been to clip Nicole's wings and stop her flying free. Nicole had quieted Rebecca's fears, assuring her that she would recognise misogynistic traits from fifty miles away, and at the first sign – even his insistence on ordering her meal for her – she would run for the hills.

She'd been damaged. Like a lark beating its wings against the bars of its cage until it has no strength left for fight or flight, she'd been injured. Rebecca had assumed that, despite her first horrendous marriage, or maybe even because of it, Nicole had seized her new chance at life, at love, with both hands and determined to live it.

Nicole and Richard had soon married, making Rebecca wonder whether Nicole might have been keen to try again for the baby her first husband had so cruelly robbed her of. Rebecca's son had badly broken his leg the evening before the wedding, so she hadn't been able to make it back from her own home in France, but she'd wished her friend well, praying that this new man was everything she believed him to be. He had been, apparently, though Rebecca was aware that they'd been beset by problems once they'd moved into the house they'd purchased in the tiny village of Marley. She'd been relieved to receive Nicole's last email. She'd said she was still working, thinking of exhibiting in the village hall – landscapes in watercolours, which had surprised Rebecca. Nicole had always painted in oils – huge, bold, abstract colours.

She'd been shocked to receive the email from Richard, informing her of Nicole's death, of the sudden, swift demise of her mental health after her mother had passed away and of her eventual breakdown.

How had it happened? How had the strong woman she'd known – a woman who'd had the strength to survive all she'd endured, despite thinking herself weak – been so vanquished by life? Could grief really drive a person so deep into depression that they would do something so drastic?

Rebecca supposed it could. She'd felt as if she'd lost part of herself when her husband died. The rawness of loss diminishes eventually, but the pain is always with you, a tidal wave of grief when you least expect it. But she doubted it was that alone that had driven Nicole to such a dark place. More likely, as worn down and confused as she was by other events, it was a more gradual decline. Had Richard been aware of how much she'd been struggling?

Realising that she was staring at the man, yet seeing only the swirling, swollen waters of the River Severn, Nicole's hair rising like flame-coloured seaweed above her as she sank silently to its muddy depths, Rebecca averted her gaze.

He was devastated. Rebecca swallowed back a knot in her throat as he turned away, wiping a hand over his face and heaving in a breath as if to contain his emotions. People stepped respectfully aside to permit him to pass. No one moved to follow him, apart from his daughter. Catching up with him at the periphery of the small crowd, Olivia slid an arm around his shoulders, and then stepped in front of him.

Feeling she was intruding on his grief, Rebecca looked away as they walked slowly together back towards the church. Despite her misgivings, it seemed that Richard had loved Nicole very much.

After waiting for the crowd to disperse, she crouched to place her own flowers at Nicole's graveside: a simple arrangement of early golden daffodils. 'Beside the lake, beneath the trees, fluttering and dancing in the breeze.' Wiping a tear from her cheek, she quoted the Wordsworth poem they'd both been so fond of, and which they'd quoted to each other while lying on their backs making castles in the sky one warm spring day. 'Fly high little bird,' she whispered. 'Know that a little piece of my heart flies with you.'

Giving herself a moment, Rebecca was surprised to see Richard's daughter hurrying back towards her. 'Sorry, I didn't mean to intrude,' Olivia said, noticing Rebecca dabbing at her eyes as she got to her feet.

'You're not,' Rebecca assured her. 'Sorry.' Wiping a hand under her nose, she rummaged in her bag for a tissue. She was sure she'd stuffed an abundant supply in there before leaving home.

Olivia smiled and quickly produced a tissue from her own bag. 'We wondered whether you were coming along to the house,' she said, handing it to her. 'Dad wanted to have a word with you, but… well, he was a bit too emotional, to be honest.'

'I know. I could see.' Rebecca blew, and offered her a small smile of her own. 'Quite understandable. I meant to approach him myself. It's clear he loved her a great deal.'

Olivia nodded sadly. 'He did. It took him a long while after Mum died to find someone he truly cared for. I think he was a bit scared, to be honest. You know, of giving his heart again, only to lose the person he loved.'

'Oh God, of course. I'm so sorry, I'd forgotten.' Rebecca was immediately sympathetic. 'When did she die, your mother?'

'Oh, ages ago now.' Olivia waved a hand, as if she were long over her loss. 'When I was five. I still miss her, but…'

Seeing the sadness in her eyes, Rebecca guessed that was the truth. Such a loss would be the hardest of all to truly get over. Her son – now almost twenty, she could hardly believe – had been just ten years old when his dad died. It had destroyed Rebecca to watch Sam's little heart breaking, knowing there was no way she could fix it.

'The pain never goes away, but it gets easier with time.' Olivia reached to squeeze Rebecca's arm, as if it were she in need of reassurance. Rebecca herself felt very much in need of reassurance, right then. She wanted to know that she hadn't failed Nicole when she'd needed her. If only she'd managed to sell her house and move back to the UK sooner, she might have been able to be there for her.

'You will come, won't you? To the reception at the house?' Olivia asked, her eyes searching hers hopefully. Striking eyes, Rebecca noticed, somewhere between amber and brown. Tiger's eyes.

'Yes.' She nodded. 'I'd love to.' Truthfully, she wondered if she could bear to see the empty house, where there would be only the ghost of Nicole, but she needed to. She needed to see where she'd lived, whether she'd ever truly made it her own. She certainly needed to talk to Richard Gray, the man with whom Nicole was supposed to be turning the house into a home.

'Excellent. Dad will be really pleased. I know he'd like to find out more about you.' Moving to thread an arm through hers, Olivia walked with her back to the path.

'About me?' Rebecca eyed her curiously.

'About the things that Nicole and you got up to in your wild youth,' Olivia added, giving her arm a conspiratorial squeeze.

'Oh dear.' Rebecca laughed. 'I suspect I'd better leave out the eyebrow-raising bits.'

'Ooh, no, please don't,' Olivia implored. 'If you think it will make Dad smile, go for it. It would be nice to see him smile again. What should I call you, by the way? Do you prefer Rebecca, or…?'

'Becky. Though Sam has labelled me Becks, as I apparently dribble a mean football.'

'And I'm Liv to my friends,' Olivia offered. 'Who's Sam?

'My son. He's coming up to twenty now.'

'Really?' Olivia looked at her in surprise. 'Gosh, you must have had him young?'

'True.' Rebecca smiled. The girl was aiming to flatter, but she accepted it gracefully. 'He's actually here in the UK at university. His girlfriend is at the same uni, so inevitably he spends more time here than in France.' Would Sam mind her sharing these personal details, she wondered? Probably not. He'd been a bit coy about it at first, but when Laura had come to visit and declared herself as besotted with Sam as he was with her, he'd whooped like a big kid and almost shouted it from the rooftop.

'It would be lovely to meet him. If you're holidaying here, we should get together and...' Olivia stopped, her expression clouding over, as if she'd forgotten that the common link between them no longer existed.

Aware of how awful that feeling was: the momentary forget-fulness, followed by the overwhelming sadness when you recall that someone you care for is no longer with you, Rebecca felt for her.

'That might be nice.' She smiled but didn't commit – though it would be an opportunity to learn more about Richard Gray.

'Oh. Have all the funeral cars left?' she asked, wondering how Olivia was travelling as she noticed the limousines gliding away from the church.

'I told Dad to go on to meet the guests. I thought I'd grab a lift with you,' Olivia explained. 'Assuming you don't mind?'

Assuming she was going, Rebecca thought, which Olivia must have done. But then, she had been Nicole's closest friend. 'No problem,' she assured her.

They walked in silence for a while. Then, 'She said she was painting again.' Rebecca fished a little as she mulled over Nicole's last email. 'About to exhibit?'

'That's right,' Olivia confirmed. 'Landscapes in watercolours. They're still up at the village hall. We could take a look later, if you like?'

'No oils then?' Rebecca enquired casually.

'No.' Stopping at Rebecca's car, Olivia sighed sadly. 'It's a shame really. Some of the canvases she brought with her were quite good, but she didn't want the mess in the house, apparently.'

Really? Rebecca arched an eyebrow as she unlocked the doors and climbed inside. That didn't sound at all like Nicole, whose philosophy after her first marriage had been not to worry too much about the housework on the basis it would still be there tomorrow.

CHAPTER TWO

NICOLE

PREVIOUS YEAR – APRIL

Dear lovely Becky,
Are you sitting down? No, of course you won't be. It's three o'clock in the morning. You will be sleeping, whereas I'm finding sleep as elusive as time itself. You're not going to believe this, but I've met someone! A male someone, obviously. And, yes, I know, I said I would never trust another man ever again, but the thing is, I do trust him, Becky. I really do. We've only been going out for a little over a month, but we have so much in common; I feel as if I've known him all my life. He's a widower, and everything looks-wise that really should have had me barricading my heart: tall, dark and handsome, got a little of the hair-greying-at-the-temples thing going on. In short, classically drop-dead gorgeous. I know you'll think I'm seeing him through the same rose-tinted spectacles I first viewed the bastard ex through, but the thing is, he's conscientious, a liberal thinker and genuinely caring. He lost his wife five years ago. He nursed her for a while and was devastated when she died. There's still a lingering sadness in his eyes whenever he talks of her. He's a single father. His daughter's grown up – twenty-two – but he

*obviously dotes on her, and she on him, which did endear him
to me, I must admit. I've only met her once. She seems lovely.
He had her when he was very young, which I suppose made the
loss of her mother all the more poignant. He's also modest, can
you believe, seemingly completely oblivious to his head-turning
attractions. He was actually nervous about asking me to have
a coffee with him. He'd thought I would turn him down flat,
he said. I was at the Ikon Art Gallery with Peter – you know,
the lecturer I used to work with at the art college years ago?
You met him a couple of times – and when Peter dashed off,
perpetually late as he always is, Richard approached me. I was
viewing the current contemporary exhibition: transformation
of materials and found objects. I was a little puzzled by one
exhibit and Richard and I started chatting, and… I digress.
What I'm trying to say is we clicked, immediately. We got
talking and one thing led to another, as they say. Obviously,
it wasn't my body he was after, saggy boobs and soft belly not
being something men generally lust after, but – brace yourself – I
gave it to him anyway.*

Have you recovered from the shock yet?

*Now, before you imagine I've been seduced by a gigolo,
I can assure you I haven't. My father's meagre inheritance
and the settlement from the marriage is all tied up in my
house and studio anyway, so he'd be sadly disappointed if
his aim was to be a kept man. However, it isn't, I'm relieved
to report. He's financially secure, lives in a great sprawling
house in Worcestershire (he's thinking of selling, which is a
shame – it has glorious views over the river) and he drives
a Jaguar XF Sportbrake, I think he said it was. And, in
any case, it was me who did the seducing. Richard has been
behaving like the perfect gentleman ever since we started
seeing each other, his kisses passionate, but never overstepping
the mark. Well, there's only so much temptation a woman*

*can take, and I'm afraid tonight my will to resist dissolved.
I know! She whose confidence was reduced to nil by the
control freak misogynist bares all and has sex with a man.
My mind's still boggling, too. And my skin is still tingling.
Seriously. Richard might have been caught by surprise by
my wantonness – pleasantly so, he told me when we cuddled
afterwards. Repeat: cuddled! – but he rose to the challenge
admirably. He certainly knows how to please a woman. As
in, we reached a very fulfilling mutual climax approximately
an hour ago and he's currently sleeping as I lust. Thus my
urgent need to drag myself back to bed.*

*I'm attaching a photo. No! Not of him naked. It's one I
took earlier while we were out lunching. Let me know what
you think.*

Much love and huge hugs,
Nicole. X
*PS Sorry I haven't written for a while. I promise to keep in
touch now I've caught my breath.*
PPS I'm an ignorant pig! Let me know all your news, too!

Nicole hurried back to her bedroom with the two glasses of
San Pellegrino Sparkling Limonata she'd fetched from the fridge
to find Richard stirring. She hoped he wouldn't mind that she'd
grabbed his shirt to pad downstairs in. She didn't imagine for a
second that she exuded the sexual allure of, say, Cameron Diaz, but
it was infinitely more flattering than her usual night-time attire:
a washed-out old onesie that resembled a pair of long johns, and
which even the postman had raised an eyebrow at.

'Ah, there you are,' Richard said, hitching himself up on his
elbows and looking her over so enticingly that Nicole felt her cheeks
flush down to her décolleté. Being fair-skinned really did have
distinct disadvantages – her face advertising her embarrassment
being one of them. 'I thought I might have frightened you off.'

'It's my house,' she reminded him, depositing a perspiring glass on his bedside table. 'I'd hardly run away, particularly with a red hot lover lying in my bed.'

'That good, hey?' Richard chuckled, catching her hand as she moved away.

'Sizzling,' Nicole assured him, at the risk of over-gushing. 'You appear to know my body better than I do.'

Richard ran a lustful gaze over her. 'My wife and I had a mutually satisfying relationship,' he said, the smile in his eyes fading – as it would, thinking of her. 'You've just reminded me how rewarding that can be. Come back to bed.' Clearly making an effort to dismiss his understandable sadness, he tugged her gently towards him. 'We have plenty of time until morning.'

'Now there's an offer a girl can't resist.' Nicole smiled, her eyes feasting on his torso as he threw the duvet back and patted the space she'd vacated. He really was unbelievable in every sense of the word: kind; attentive in and out of bed; attractive – most definitely that. Shamelessly, she stared at his chest, which was pleasingly toned and taut but not too muscular. He liked to keep himself fit, he'd said. Nicole was so glad that he did.

Her gaze strayed to his lips, which were full, but not too sensual on a man, and were now curved into a languid smile. She felt her cheeks heat infuriatingly again as she recalled where those lips had been – caressing her skin, her breasts, her nipples so slowly it was almost painful. Leisurely exploring every inch of her body.

After years of enforced celibacy in her marriage, she hadn't known what to expect when she'd abandoned her resolve to steer clear of men forever and decided to sleep with him. Awkwardness, she'd imagined. And she'd hoped that that awkwardness wouldn't be too excruciating when his hands found her breasts; that she wouldn't turn him off.

She needn't have worried. As unselfish in bed as he was out of it, Richard had soon shooed away the ghosts that had climbed under the duvet with her. There hadn't been fireworks. Mercifully, no frenetic fumbling or thrusting either; none of the urgency that comes with first embarrassing sexual encounters of youth. He'd known instinctively where to touch her, how to touch her. Whispering softly, he'd encouraged her to relax, to trust him, while he'd led her on a journey of beautiful sensual discovery, taking her places she'd fantasised about but never imagined she would reach with a man. Her orgasm, when it came, was like a warm, exquisite ripple flowing right through to the very core of her. She'd never experienced that before. Never imagined placing herself, naked and vulnerable, in the hands of a man. When the misogynist ex had withdrawn from her sexually – one of his control games, she now saw, designed to deprive her of the child she'd so desperately wanted – she'd felt as desirable as cold tapioca. Worse, self-conscious and ashamed of her body, as if there was something fundamentally wrong with her that she could be physically repulsive to a man. So unattractive he preferred to pay for sex with other women, she'd eventually learned. The cruel fact of which he'd got an extra sadistic twist from by insisting it was, 'All in her mind.'

She'd blamed herself for his cheating on her, just as she'd blamed herself for everything. She'd had no regard for herself in the end, only a self-loathing hatred that she could have been so pathetic, allowing someone to control her, subtly at first and then ultimately. Financially, sexually, he'd stripped her of everything. She had a long way to go to trust herself again completely. But she really did feel she could trust this man, who'd showed her how to love again, how to accept that she was attractive enough to be loved. He'd given her back her self-esteem.

'You're thinking,' Richard admonished her, his forehead creasing into a mock scowl as he realised her mind was wandering. Squeezing her hand, he tugged her a little more persuasively towards the bed, sitting up to meet her as she allowed herself to plop down on to it. 'Banish all thoughts of him,' he said firmly, placing an arm around her and drawing her to him. 'Think about it: if you're wasting even a single thought on him, then he's still wielding his power over you. Don't give him the satisfaction, Nicole. Be here, in the moment, with me.'

Nicole looked up at him and saw the kindness in his eyes – ice-blue eyes, almost the colour of the midwinter sky, yet not cold. They were burning with desire. The misogynist had worn that same look at first. His desire, though she'd little known it then, had been to control her. Richard's was to make love to her, to suppress her doubts and quiet her fears. There was an ocean of difference between them.

'You're right,' she said, her lips drawn irresistibly to his. She was glad she'd confided some of her secrets to him, relieved she'd been brave enough to. Richard had told her that's what she was. 'A strong, brave, beautiful woman, with a mind of her own,' he'd said, and then pulled her gently into his arms and held her. That's when she'd known she could love this man, that she would be safe with him.

'I always am,' Richard said, an amused edge to his tone. 'Do you think she'd approve?' he asked, nodding towards the photograph of her mother on the bedside table.

'Lord no. She'd be mortified, finding out her wanton daughter was fornicating with a man out of wedlock!' Feeling herself blush up to her hair follicles, Nicole reached to turn the frame around. She'd forgotten she was there, looking piously on. 'Do you know, I think she actually resents the fact that I managed to extricate myself from the kind of relationship she had to endure with my father. S-e-x was definitely a dirty word in the house I grew up in. God forbid a woman should actually enjoy it. I think she even resents the fact that I'm an only child, therefore her sole living heir. I'm sure she'd rather leave all her money to local animal charities – if she actually liked animals, that is.'

Truthfully, Nicole felt a good degree of resentment, too, that her mother hadn't been there when she'd so desperately needed her. It was hard to accept that the woman had expected her to endure the abuse she'd suffered at the misogynist's hands simply because he was her husband. She might have escaped sooner if she could have gone back home for a while, if her mother's attitude hadn't been that she'd made her own bed and should therefore lie in it until the life was sucked out of her. She might have been able to save her unborn baby.

'In which case, I suggest we make sure we're as shocking as possible,' Richard murmured, a mischievous glint now in his eyes as he closed his mouth over hers.

His far-too-tantalising tongue seeking hers, Nicole suppressed painful thoughts of her dear, lost child, and succumbed easily to his comforting embrace. His foreplay this time was less leisurely, but every bit as considerate and sweet. She'd been far from a virgin when she'd married the misogynist, but now she felt almost as nervous as one, embarking on this unexpected new relationship. Richard sensed it. That had to be special didn't it? She couldn't be wrong about him. She had been a victim, yes, though it had taken her too long to realise it. In her youth she'd been strong – determined not to be labelled or boxed. She would be strong again. She would fly again.

'You're beautiful,' he whispered, finding her mouth with his and sliding into her with a degree of urgency. 'I want to show you what you do to me. You have all the power, Nicole. See?'

He slowed his pace, gazing into her eyes. They were making love with the lights on. Nicole felt almost orgasmic at the very thought of it – that this good-looking man was gazing down at her, making love to her, seeing something beautiful.

'Stay with me, Nicole. Let me help you see you can make decisions. That you can be all that you want to be.'

*

Nicole cried afterwards, a single tear spilling on to his chest as she rested her head there, listening to the strong thrum of his heartbeat.

They stayed like that for a while, cocooned under the duvet, listening to the first optimistic birdsong as night gave way to day. 'Can I ask you something?' she ventured, circling one of his nipples gently with a finger.

Richard squeezed her closer. 'Anything,' he said.

'You never said…' She hesitated. 'How did your wife die?' Feeling Richard's arm tense around her, Nicole held her breath, hoping she hadn't elicited painful memories for him.

'Suicide,' he said quietly, eventually. 'At least, that was the conclusion of the coroner. She'd mixed her medication and alcohol. She'd taken her car keys before I realised she'd gone out, and…' He stopped, his voice catching.

Stunned, Nicole glanced up at him. 'But I thought you said…'

'She was ill? She was.' Richard took a deep breath. 'Multiple sclerosis. She watched her mother struggle with it. It's not strictly hereditary, but she obviously had a genetic susceptibility to the disease.'

'Oh God, that's awful.' Nicole's heart ached for him.

'It was, for her. The effects are different for everyone who has the disease, but Emily couldn't live with the prospect of what might happen.' He paused, his gaze on the ceiling, his hand softly stroking Nicole's back. 'To be honest, I suspect she thought I couldn't live with it. I wish I'd been able to convince her I could.'

'Don't blame yourself,' Richard,' Nicole urged him gently. 'You can only do your best in a marriage. Remember, that's what you told me.'

'That's right, I did.' Meeting her eyes, Richard smiled. 'I try not to. It's just… sometimes it creeps back to haunt me.'

Nicole nodded. 'How did your daughter cope? She must have been devastated.'

'She was. She's strong though. Resilient. Probably stronger because of it, if that doesn't sound odd.'

Like I used to be. Nicole hadn't been confident as a child, but when her father had died – ironically, the man the bastard ex had turned out to be a replica of – she'd grown wings. Felt free, for the first time, to be the person she was inside. It was as if the shackles had been taken off. She no longer had to try to be perfect, which she was never going to be in her father's eyes. He'd wanted her to join the family firm. As if she could ever be a fulfilled as a solicitor. He'd wanted her to be less of a dreamer. He'd wanted her to dress differently, to learn to cook, to find a good man; to put her in a box and slap a label on it. She'd applied for the degree she wanted the day after his funeral. Perhaps she had had a victim mentality, after all. Perceiving herself as stronger, yet sadly lacking in confidence underneath.

'It doesn't sound odd at all,' she assured Richard. 'Quite the opposite, in fact. I think Olivia and I will get on.'

'I know you will.' Richard squeezed her closer. 'Can I ask you a question, Nicole?'

'Anything.' She laughed, snuggling into him.

'Marry me?'

CHAPTER THREE

REBECCA

PRESENT

Standing on at least an acre of land and approached via electric gates, the period property Nicole and Richard had purchased together was magnificent. Coming through the door to find everything dazzling white, Rebecca wasn't sure whether she should leave her shoes in the hall, which was at least as big as her lounge.

Following Olivia's lead, she kept her shoes on – though she was tempted to take her weight off her heels lest they leave scuff marks on the expensive looking tiles. The whole house was immaculate, she realised, passing through a spacious sitting room furnished with contemporary stone leather sofas. It was truly beautiful. She did wonder, though, whether one might dare use the clinical-looking kitchen for anything as messy as actual cooking.

It was also a little perplexing. Given a choice of period proper-ties, Rebecca was certain that Nicole would have gone for more of a farmhouse feel, with original cross-beams, inglenook fireplaces and wood-burning stoves. Nicole had been excited about moving into the house, however, telling her how Richard had called it their blank canvas, how they were going to make it into something beautiful and individual. Rebecca hadn't doubted she would. Her friend's choice of decor had always reflected her artistic nature:

scatter cushions, mixed colours, patterns and textures everywhere, with no attention to rules. The room they'd rented together in their student days was stuffed full of second-hand prizes found at the Birmingham rag market, but it all came together somehow, creating unconventional, comfortable chaos.

She'd followed her heart in the little house she'd bought after her divorce too, her decor as diverse as she was, with pillows adorning odd pieces of furniture, rugs across the floors, bold colours on the walls. It had been homey to the point of messy, but it was Nicole. This house just wasn't. But then, Rebecca supposed a project of this scale would take time, careful planning, professional decorators.

'Rebecca?' a male voice said behind her, causing Rebecca, who was now gazing through the patio windows at the swimming pool as she recalled the content of some of Nicole's correspondence, to almost jump out of her skin.

Composing herself, Rebecca turned, and found herself taken aback. Up close, Richard Gray was more good-looking than she'd realised. Almost a head taller than her, with high cheekbones and a strong jawline, he was definitely classically handsome. Rebecca wondered if Nicole had been tempted to paint his portrait. His eyes would be hard to capture. Ice blue in colour, they were striking – utterly mesmerising. So much so, Rebecca almost didn't notice the hand he held out in greeting.

What exactly did he do for a living, she wondered. He was clearly wealthy. Nicole had mentioned he was in the property development business, and that they had decided to pool their resources to buy a place together of their own. She doubted her friend's assets would have amounted to a quarter of the value of this property, though, which had to be worth over a million pounds. Nicole had also been quick to mention he'd insisted on her keeping some cash for herself in a separate account. For her own peace of mind, he'd apparently told her, which Rebecca had conceded was very caring of him.

'Richard,' she said, relaxing her face into a smile.

He smiled back, his eyes narrowing slightly as he studied her, his gaze so intent it was almost unsettling.

'It's so nice to finally…' They both started together and stopped awkwardly.

'Meet you,' Richard finished, dipping his head in a small gesture of contrition. 'Under far too tragic circumstances, unfortunately,' he added, taking hold of the hand Rebecca eventually remembered to offer him. 'I wish it could have been any other way. I know Nicole would have loved to have you visit.'

Her eyes instantly filling up, Rebecca dropped her gaze. Nicole had asked her to visit once, not long after she'd married. Rebecca had made plans to visit Sam who was renting a room near his university in Warwickshire and had promised her a guided tour of the area. Feeling worried about the strange email Nicole had sent her from her honeymoon, she'd been desperate to talk to her face-to-face. And then Nicole had texted her, saying Olivia had been taken ill. She should have ignored it. Pretended she hadn't seen it and come anyway. 'I wish it could have been different too,' she whispered. 'I intended to visit sooner, but…'

'Life has a habit of intervening when you're busy making plans,' Richard finished sympathetically.

And death. Feeling a tear spill on to her cheek, Rebecca reached to wipe it away. 'Sorry,' she said, looking back at him. 'I keep thinking I've got these in check, but…' She shrugged hopelessly.

'They creep up on you.' Richard's smile was understanding. 'No apologies necessary. I've cried my fair share too. I think it's allowed.'

Rebecca nodded, but still she felt bereft, as if she'd deserted her friend when she'd desperately needed someone. 'Where's Bouncer?' she asked. Nicole had adopted an abandoned mongrel from her local rescue centre once she'd set up house on her own. Her loyal little man, she'd declared him, who would love her unconditionally and who would be her only male companion henceforth.

'In kennels,' Richard supplied. 'Just for today,' he added quickly, clearly noting her alarm. 'They both are – my dog and Nicole's. I thought, with people coming and going, they would be less stressed there.'

Rebecca felt a flood of overwhelming relief. Nicole would have been devastated to think that Bouncer was caged again and pining for her.

'Come and have some food,' Richard suggested, nodding towards where people were congregating in what appeared to be a formal dining area in the largely open-plan ground floor of the house. The furniture, all glass, chrome and white, was as pristine as everything else. 'It's been a long morning and I imagine you haven't had much time to eat.'

'Thank you, but I'm not very hungry, to be honest.' Rebecca smiled graciously.

'A small wine, perhaps? I have an excellent Château Bourgneuf breathing.'

'I'm not sure I'm familiar with that one.' The Travelodge she intended to stay in wasn't far, but she didn't want anything too strong, since she was driving.

'It's a Merlot-based wine,' Richard supplied. 'Nicole's tipple of choice.'

'That would be lovely,' Rebecca said, holding eye contact with him, though she wished he wouldn't look at her quite so intently. 'Just the one though.'

'Excellent.' Richard's smile widened. 'You know, you can always stay over if you'd like,' he offered, taking her gently by the arm and leading the way. 'We have plenty of spare rooms.'

Should she? She hadn't actually booked the Travelodge yet, but she didn't want to impose on his grief.

'I doubt Nicole would want you spending the night in a soulless hotel,' Richard said, seeing her hesitation. 'Your staying here is no inconvenience, I promise. I know Nicole would have wanted you to.'

Rebecca nodded. He was right. Nicole would have hated the idea of her going off to a hotel. At least here she would be closer to her friend, while her thoughts were only of her, as inevitably they would be. Plus, it would give her chance to get to know the man Nicole had loved a little better, which Rebecca felt she needed to. 'Thank you,' she said. 'It's very kind of you.'

'No problem,' Richard assured her.

'It's a wonderful property,' Rebecca commented, gazing around as they walked. 'Almost like a show home.'

'We liked it,' Richard said, with a nostalgic sigh. 'Nicole was happy here, I think.'

Rebecca nodded, conceding that most people would be, providing they had an army of staff. 'I can see why. It's very spacious. I love the open-plan design.'

'Me too.' Richard followed her gaze around. 'I prefer not to be boxed in. I find it too…'

'Claustrophobic?' Rebecca finished, as he searched for the right word.

'Something like that.' Richard smiled. 'I suppose it comes from my work being largely outdoors. Nicole indulged me, I think.'

As she would. Being caring by nature, Nicole would be inclined to do that, Rebecca knew. 'It must be hard work to keep it so… sparkling though,' she ventured.

Richard chuckled at that. 'It does rather sparkle, doesn't it? Mostly down to Nicole's hard work, I have to admit. Not being quite as house-proud as she was, I suspect I'm going to have to get a cleaner in now.'

'Nicole would have abhorred the idea,' Olivia put in, drifting across to them from the table. 'She preferred to do the housework herself, for some unfathomable reason.'

Someone approached to offer their condolences and Richard looked away. Rebecca glanced between father and daughter, now stunned. Were they talking about Nicole? *Her* Nicole, who had despised housework? Or 'women's work', as her father had labelled it. She'd hated that her mother had run around after him, that her controlling first husband had expected Nicole to do the same. Hated herself for becoming so cowed that she'd done it.

Life was too short, she'd said, when she'd finally broken free of him. People could take her home as they found it. Yet, this house was almost surgically clean. Had that been a symptom of her illness, Rebecca wondered. One which Richard might not have realised was?

CHAPTER FOUR

NICOLE

PREVIOUS YEAR – APRIL

Slipping out of bed quietly in order not to wake Richard, Nicole paused for another admiring glance at his torso. Draped in her patchwork patola silk bed throw, one arm thrown across his forehead, he looked every inch a heavenly body. A shudder of pleasure ran through her as she recalled what he'd done to her body. Nicole sighed blissfully and tiptoed towards the door. Her efforts to be quiet were somewhat thwarted when she tripped over one of the many scatter cushions that they'd tossed to the floor, but still he didn't stir. The poor soul was obviously exhausted.

'Shhh.' Pressing a finger to her lips, she beckoned Bouncer – so called because he hadn't stopped bouncing since she'd brought him home from the rescue centre – to follow her. Even he appeared to be in love, racing manically around and then snuggling up with Richard's golden retriever the first time the two dogs had met. The fact that Wanderer was also male hadn't deterred him. Nicole had thought they might fight, but no. It was true love.

Smiling contentedly, she crept downstairs to let Bouncer out into the garden and then came back up, stopping by the second bedroom-cum-office to check her emails. She wasn't surprised to see one from Becky. Nicole hesitated before opening it, crossing her fingers and hoping her best friend didn't think she'd completely taken leave of her senses.

Dearest Nicole,

Are you mad? No, don't answer that. Just tell me one thing... Did you let him pay for lunch?

Love and hugs,

Your slightly shocked best friend, who is now in need of another lie-down.

xxx

PS Write soon – so I know he's not a mass murderer!

Oops, poor Becky. She clearly thought she'd parted company with her sanity. Sensing she needed some reassurance, Nicole sat down to send a quick reply before making breakfast. She had no intention of serving Richard breakfast on a regular basis, but she'd decided he had earned it.

Dear prostrate best friend,

He's not a mass murderer! And, what's more, he doesn't snore! In answer to 'the did I allow him to pay for lunch' dilemma, he offered, but understood when I declined. He said, and I quote, 'because you see it as controlling?' I think he scores on that point. In answer to your first question, I think I might be. I've just agreed to marry him. Suggest deep breaths before replying. Off to make breakfast.

Love you loads.

Nicole. X

PS Understand completely and forgive you for questioning my sanity.

Pausing in the bathroom after brushing her teeth, she pinched her cheeks to give them a bit of colour. God help her, she was behaving like a love-struck teenager. Nicole padded downstairs, humming 'Ave Maria' softly to herself, which she and Richard had agreed they absolutely had to have at their wedding. She quite fancied 'Can't Take My Eyes Off You' by Frankie Valli and The Four Seasons for their first dance. She hadn't run that by Richard yet, but it would definitely be appropriate.

Stopping mid hum as she walked into the kitchen, she found she actually couldn't take her eyes off him. He was scrambling eggs. Bare-footed and bare-chested – since she was still wearing his shirt – he was making breakfast. Nicole blinked bemusedly. She hoped he didn't regret his hasty proposal, once he'd had time to think about it. She would have no alternative but to man-nap him and chain him up in her art studio.

'Hi.' Looking up, he smiled when he saw her. 'I'm assuming you like eggs? You had them in the fridge.'

'Absolutely,' Nicole assured him, smiling delightedly back. 'Especially when prepared by my own personal Adonis.'

Richard laughed out loud. 'I think you may need spectacles,' he said modestly, reaching to flick the coffee machine on. 'And you might not be quite so delighted when you taste them.'

'Oh, I will. Trust me.' Nicole petted Bouncer, who was right by Richard's side in hopes of food – suddenly man's best friend rather than hers – and then hitched herself on to a stool at the kitchen island. She propped her head on her hands and watched him – well, stared at him, astonished. Was it possible she had gone gaga? That she was imagining this appetising man making himself at home in her kitchen, cooking actual food after making spectacular love to her for half the night and then asking her to marry him?

'Suits you,' he said, nodding towards her as he dropped bread into the toaster.

'What?' Nicole asked, hardly able to believe that she didn't feel guilted into jumping up and taking over. He was plainly all the therapy she'd needed: a normal man who didn't have to make her feel inadequate in order to feel better about himself.

'The shirt.' He gave her a wink. 'It looks like you've laid claim to it, in which case I'm going to be driving home half naked.'

'Now *that* would definitely stop traffic.' Nicole's gaze travelled lustfully over him. 'I am rather attached to it.' She sighed and resisted pressing the collar to her nose to breathe in the scent of him – a subtle blend of cedarwood and orchid and essence of man. 'I'll let you have it back though, if you insist.'

At that, Richard downed his kitchen implements, folded an arm across his chest, pressed a thumb to his chin and waited.

Flushing furiously, Nicole laughed. 'Not *now*, fool.' Her eyes boggled at the mere thought of it – her parading around the kitchen in nothing but her knickers. If the postman caught a glimpse of her through the window, he'd have a heart attack and die on the doorstep.

'Damn.' Richard sighed disappointedly. 'I quite fancied working up an appetite over the kitchen island.'

'Richard!' Nicole gawked at him. 'You're terrible.'

'I know. But irresistible with it.' Richard winked and went back to his task.

Most definitely that. Nicole was tempted. Very. But, no. She wasn't ready to reveal all of herself in broad daylight.

'So, where do you fancy for the honeymoon?' he asked her, turning to wham the eggs into the microwave, Bouncer following his every movement.

Honeymoon? Nicole wasn't sure she was ready for that either. Was she *really* doing this? 'I'm not sure. I… hadn't really…' *Assertive*, she reminded herself. She had to make decisions now. It was the only way forward. She'd promised herself that she would never hand power over to a man again. 'Somewhere exotic?' she ventured.

'Barbados?' he suggested, glancing back as he set the timer for the eggs – looking very proficient, Nicole noticed. He'd done this before. 'Or Thailand maybe? If you're after beach and culture, South East Asia offers the perfect combination of sun, sea and cities.'

Nicole looked at him in wonder. 'It sounds perfect,' she said, trying not to let her jaw drop too heavily on to the counter.

'Excellent.' He smiled at her approvingly. 'Have you given any thought to where we might live yet?' he asked her, whisking up the coffee jug.

What? Nicole felt as if she'd been caught up in a whirlwind, but not in a bad way – a heady, giddy, exhilarating whirl of happiness. She hadn't felt like this since she'd been accepted for her fine art course and found the freedom to paint.

'No, not really. I, um…' she stammered. Lying next to him, naked in her bed, did he really imagine she had been able to think of anything but him? 'Have you?'

'Some,' he said. 'I'm selling my property, as you know, so I suppose we ought to be thinking about it.'

'Because it has too many memories.' Nicole immediately felt for him.

Nodding, Richard smiled sadly. 'I think a fresh start is best anyway, don't you? The last thing I imagine a woman would want is to live with the ghost of her husband's former wife.'

Nicole goggled at that, not quite able to believe a man could be so intuitive.

'Ideally, I'd like us to buy somewhere new, somewhere that's ours,' he went on. 'Given all you've been through, though, I'd understand if you wanted to keep your house.'

Nicole stared at him, dumbfounded. She never remembered to do the lottery, but she felt as if she'd won it anyway. She hadn't even considered where they would live, but… Finding somewhere that was theirs, chosen together – as in, she got to share in the choosing – had to be the right thing to do. She couldn't allow him to take on more than his fair share of the financial burden though. If they were going to do this, then all things being equal in a marriage – which was the way it should be – shouldn't she be contributing too?

CHAPTER FIVE

REBECCA

PRESENT

Having decided to take up Richard's offer to stay, and Olivia's subsequent offer to drive her to the village to view the exhibition, where she could see Nicole's latest work for herself – and judge whether she'd painted them with the passion she'd once had – Rebecca had accepted a small wine and was currently watching Richard Gray circulating the room. He still looked devastated, an intense sadness in his eyes, though he smiled stoically, as occasion demanded, and chatted easily to the people gathered to mark his wife's passing.

The two women he was talking to now were a little over-affectionate, Rebecca noted, one hugging him for possibly longer than was necessary, the other reluctant to let go of the hand she was squeezing.

Dipping his head charmingly, Richard excused himself after a suitable pause and turned to pick up two empty wine bottles from the table.

Rebecca couldn't help but feel amused as she watched him walk towards the kitchen, catching Olivia's eye as he went. She glanced in the women's direction and then rolled her eyes heavenwards. A bottle in each hand, Richard shrugged – not smugly, as a man who was aware of his attractions might, but contritely. He certainly had some endearing qualities. Rebecca could see what Nicole had seen in him.

Realising people were beginning to depart, she tore her gaze away from him, lest she make him feel self-conscious, and walked across to help Olivia, who was starting to clear things from the table.

'Thanks, Becky.' Olivia smiled appreciatively as she collected up glasses and plates. 'We had caterers in for the food, but Dad said he'd see to the clearing up.'

Rebecca glanced at her, surprised.

Olivia noted the look. 'He's actually always been quite handy around the house,' she said, with a conspiratorial smile. 'Quite a good cook, too, but don't tell him I said so. He'll only get big-headed.'

Another endearing quality, Rebecca mused, following her through to the kitchen. It only added to the mystery. From what she could tell, Richard Gray appeared to have genuinely cared for Nicole. He also appeared to be gracious and charming. From Nicole's initial sparkling description of him, Rebecca had expected him to be, to a degree. But the fact that he seemed genuinely so… she hadn't expected that.

Noticing Richard following them through, Rebecca deposited her crockery on the work surface and lingered as Olivia returned to the dining area.

Richard smiled as he saw her. 'Thanks,' he said, running a hand tiredly over his neck.

'No problem,' Rebecca assured him. 'Standing idle is not something mothers find easy to do.'

'You have children?' Richard looked at her, surprised.

'Yes,' Rebecca eyed him curiously. Had Nicole not mentioned that?

Remembering how heartbroken Nicole had been when she'd lost her baby at almost full term, Rebecca felt a stab of sadness.

She'd been desperate for a child after that, not to replace the little girl she'd lost, but because she'd been so desperate to love and be loved in return. Rebecca had been quietly relieved when Nicole failed to conceive again, able to see what her friend couldn't: that her then husband was slowly making her world smaller.

'No, she didn't. Sorry,' Richard shook his head, his expression contrite. 'It's just that, from what Nicole told me about you, I got the impression you were single and… I'm possibly digging myself a bigger hole here, aren't I?'

Rebecca couldn't help but laugh at his obvious embarrassment. 'No, don't worry. Nicole wouldn't have mentioned a husband. He died, sadly, when my son was young. So, yes, I am single.'

'I'm sorry.' Richard nodded sympathetically. 'I know how difficult that must have been.'

Rebecca nodded in turn. 'It was. More so for my son, but he survived, despite having me for a mum.'

'Because of you, I've no doubt,' Richard said, appraising her quietly. 'How old is he, if you don't mind my asking?'

Rebecca didn't. It was always the first question people asked when women mentioned they had children. 'Almost twenty,' she supplied.

Richard widened his eyes. 'Sorry,' he said again. 'For some reason I assumed he was younger. Your husband was obviously a cradle-snatcher.'

'Not quite.' Rebecca smiled. 'So, how's it going?' she asked him, indicating the dining area.

'That's the last of the guests gone,' he said, with a sigh. 'Now begins the hard part, I suppose.'

Drawing in a breath, he glanced down, seeming lost in his thoughts for a second, and then gathered himself and headed towards the dishwasher.

Rebecca watched him stacking dishes expertly into it, everything in the right place, sharp knives facing downward in the cutlery basket. He obviously wasn't a stranger in the kitchen.

'You're a natural,' she observed.

'What, at loading the dishwasher?' Richard smiled wryly. 'Yes, I always got full marks there.'

'Oh, I thought it wasn't your thing,' Rebecca said, attempting to sound casual. 'The housework, I mean. It's just that Olivia said Nicole preferred to do all the housework herself, and you said you'd have to get a cleaner in now, and I...' Realising she sounded as if she were judging him, Rebecca trailed off.

'Wondered whether I felt it wasn't my responsibility?' Richard finished astutely. 'No, I never thought that. Having nursed my wife for a while, I'm very much aware of how hard running a house is, trust me. I tried to do my share here, but Nicole was... Well, if I took on a job, she would do it again anyway. She was almost obsessive about it. To be honest, I started to worry about her mental health soon after we were married.'

Sighing heavily again, he paused and glanced at the ceiling. 'I wish we'd never bought this place. I swear she could see every speck of dust. I wish to God I'd made her go to see the doctor sooner.'

He had noticed then? Realised it might possibly be more than fastidiousness? Seeing his anguish, which really did seem genuine, Rebecca stepped towards him, hesitated briefly and then placed a hand on his arm. 'I'm sure you did everything you could,' she said kindly. 'It must be terribly difficult for you, losing two women you cared deeply about.'

Richard nodded. 'They say it gets easier with time,' he said, insurmountable sadness in his eyes as he met hers. 'I'm not sure it does. I still think about Emily, what I could have done differently. And now, after losing Nicole in such a tragic, senseless way, I know I'll be doing the same all over again. If only the river hadn't been flooded. I might have stood a chance, if I could have stayed down longer...'

Running a hand through his hair in frustration, he stopped.

He'd gone in after her. That was a fact. Cold prickled the surface of Rebecca's skin as she imagined the gut-wrenching panic, to say little of the physical trauma, he must have endured while submerged under fathoms of icy water, trying hopelessly to find her. Rebecca had arrived ready to judge him. She'd had him labelled a bastard. Now though? From all angles, it seemed that he wasn't. Still, though, she wondered why such a caring and intuitive man hadn't been able to save Nicole before she'd gone into the water. But she reminded herself that, in reality, no one can fix someone in so much mental anguish, make their demons go away. All he could have done was be there for her, listen to her. And Rebecca didn't know that he hadn't.

CHAPTER SIX

NICOLE

PREVIOUS YEAR – JUNE

The little stone-built Norman church in the heart of Worcestershire was absolutely perfect. Being divorced, the best Nicole had hoped for was a blessing after the civil ceremony. She couldn't believe that the vicar had agreed to marry them. He recognised, he'd said, that some marriages fail for all sorts of sad and painful reasons, and he could see that she and Richard were very much in love. The fact that Richard hadn't let go of her hand the whole time they'd sat talking to him had helped. It was all happening quite quickly, but she did love him, absolutely, and if some of her friends – not that she had many left, after the bastard ex had banned her from seeing them – couldn't make it at short notice, then it wouldn't be the end of the world. This was her future, her happily ever after, and Nicole intended to grab it with both hands. Becky, bless her, had said she would try her best to take some time off from the college she taught at and travel from Montrésor the day before. Nicole hoped she could swing it. If there was one person she wanted to witness her wedding, it was Becky. Though she hadn't been able to see much of her either, she was more like a sister than a friend – the family that Nicole didn't really feel she'd had growing up. She felt a pang of guilt when she thought of her mother. But then, she'd made her bed too, hadn't she? Nicole visited her occasionally, rang to check she was well, but conversation beyond that didn't come naturally.

She wasn't entirely sure about the house they were viewing though. It was so… white. She'd been thinking of somewhere more homey, somewhere with cross-beams and wood burners, and possibly an outhouse she could use as a studio. Richard, however, was smitten. 'So what do you think?' he asked her, once they'd seen every room.

'Well…' Nicole started, and then stopped, noting the hopeful look in his eyes.

'It has some fantastic views,' Richard pointed out, nodding towards the magnificent patio windows, which ran the entire length of one wall.

'It certainly does.' Nicole couldn't help but be taken by the panoramic view before her, revealing the rolling Worcestershire countryside in all its verdant glory. 'I'm not sure about the actual house though,' she ventured. 'I mean it's beautiful, but it's a bit…'

Searching for the right word, she faltered, and then steeled herself to be what she should be – confident and assertive. Richard wasn't the misogynist. He was—

'White?' he finished, his mouth curving into a knowing smile.

Understanding. He was so on her wavelength, he was finishing her sentences. They were destined to be together. There was no doubt about it. 'Very,' Nicole agreed, relief flooding through her. 'Imagine the mess the dogs would make, coming in from the fields on to those tiles.'

Smiling, Richard wrapped an arm around her shoulders and drew her to him. 'That's what I thought when we first walked in,' he said. 'But then, I thought that maybe we could see it as a blank canvas. Somewhere we could truly make our own.'

Nicole hadn't considered that. Looking around, she imagined huge abstract paintings adorning the walls, oriental rugs on the floors and bold colours on the walls, and started warming to the idea. 'It's a thought,' she said, glancing up at Richard, which was a fatal mistake. The instant he locked those mesmerising blue eyes on hers, she felt drawn to him, like metal to a magnet.

His lips were a breath away from hers when Olivia burst into the sitting room behind them, forcing them apart like a thunderclap. 'Isn't it fabulous?' she gushed enthusiastically. 'Have you seen the swimming pool? It's totally *amazing*. I'm thinking barbecues on the patio and lazy Sunday afternoons. And the bedrooms! There's five of them! And they all have en suites.'

Glancing apologetically at Nicole, Richard smiled amusedly. 'I take it you like it?'

'Like it?' Olivia gawked at him. 'It's to *die* for. Please say you love it too.' She glanced hopefully between them. 'Nicole?'

Richard turned his gaze towards her, his expression a mixture of enquiring and hopeful.

Still, Nicole wasn't sure, not least about the price tag. Over one million pounds? Surely that was madness? 'Can we afford it?' she asked him uncertainly.

Richard took a breath. 'Truthfully, it would mean we'd have to pool our resources initially to buy it for cash, thereby securing a good profit up front – with the proviso I pay a lump sum into your account as soon as I make my next sale, that is. But as I have a cash buyer for my house, then, yes, I think we can. It has to be your decision though, Nicole. I don't want you to make any wrong ones and then regret it.'

His brow creased in concern and he looked at her searchingly.

Nicole glanced from him to Olivia, who was almost bursting with excitement and obviously willing her to say yes, and relented. Richard was a property developer. He knew the builder and had therefore been given the option to buy it at less than the value before it went on the market, he'd said. In the long term, he could make a substantial profit from this. Plus, it was clear that he loved the house, which was located close to the village he'd previously lived in. She couldn't say no because of her own insecurities. She hadn't bargained on Olivia, whose plans to flat-share with a friend had apparently fallen through, being with them, but the house was certainly spacious enough for three people without them falling over each other. It might actually be a convenient short-term arrangement for Richard, since Olivia was also his personal assistant. 'I think I can work with it,' she said finally, smiling back at Richard.

'Yesss!' Olivia whooped and swooped towards Richard, throwing her arms around him and planting a kiss on his cheek. 'I *love* you,' she said, turning to practically skip back out the way she'd come.

'And clearly has a rather enthusiastic way of showing it,' Richard said, glancing embarrassedly at Nicole.

'Definitely.' Nicole laughed. She couldn't resent Olivia wanting to grab her own bit of happiness. The girl had lost her mother, under terribly tragic circumstances, and she wouldn't be with them forever. She had plans – ambitions to work in London, a house-share with another friend who had recently secured a job there.

Meanwhile, she *could* work with this. Glancing around again and seeing the vast white walls with a new eye, thanks to Richard, Nicole nodded determinedly. She could make this into a home with a heart.

CHAPTER SEVEN

REBECCA

PRESENT

'Did she not have a studio here?' Rebecca asked Olivia as she slipped into a pair of jeans and a sweater. Now that she was staying, she was glad she hadn't stopped off at the Travelodge on the way, as her overnight bag was still in the boot of her car. Feeling the need to get back in touch with Nicole, the person she'd become and the environment she'd lived in, she'd decided to amble around the village for a while after visiting the exhibition. Rebecca was no stranger to exploring places on her own, often walking around the beautiful village of Montrésor in her lunch hour, strolling from the college to the Café de la Ville or the crêperie, taking in the exhibition at the Halles des Cardeux on the way or simply enjoying the views. Sometimes she preferred the simplicity of solitude – craved it, in fact, after hours spent in the energetic company of students. Rebecca felt she needed that now: some quiet time alone with her thoughts.

'She did use one of the upstairs rooms for a while,' Olivia said, glancing at her in the mirror as she touched up her make-up. 'She was worried about the paint fumes wafting through the house though. She flecked paint on one of the walls, too, and then worried about that. Dad told her it didn't matter, that they could paint the wall over, but she was adamant it was too messy a hobby for the house.'

Hobby? Nicole's art was never a hobby. It was who she was. Or it had been. Her first husband had stolen that away from her, along with everything else that defined her, but Nicole had taken it back up with fervour once she'd broken free of that prison. She'd just started to sell again when she met Richard. Two of her first contemporary colour-filled canvases had sold instantly at a group exhibition at The Brick Lane Gallery in London. There was no way Rebecca could believe that Nicole would ever have referred to her work as a hobby. She hadn't quite been able to believe that Nicole had proposed to work in a bedroom either. Given the amount of money being spent on the house, she'd assumed an art studio had been factored in. Nicole had said it was just a temporary thing when she'd asked her about it, that the studio – which would have been extremely important to her – was on her to-do list. It never had happened though, had it?

'Do you mind if I take a look?' she asked. 'Just out of curiosity.'

Glossing her lips, Olivia glanced again at her. 'No,' she said, turning towards her after a second. 'There's not much to see though. Just a few paintings Dad brought up from the garage. I'm not sure what they're supposed to be. They seem… Well, a bit depressing, to be honest.'

Perplexed, Rebecca followed Olivia into the furthest room at the end of the long galleried landing. Her heart squeezed inside her as her gaze fell on the canvases stacked against one of the walls. These hadn't been produced by the Nicole she'd known. Reminiscent of Goya's black period – debilitating illness and impending death driving him to the darkest regions of his mind – these paintings seemed terribly pessimistic. A predominance of swirling dull greens and greys, they were in stark contrast to the bright, optimistic strokes of light and colour Nicole had always favoured. Rebecca felt a cold chill run through her, as if someone were treading lightly over her grave. Was this work a reflection of her mental health, the inner demons she must have been struggling with as she'd spiralled into deepest depression? Why on earth hadn't Nicole reached out to her in those weeks preceding her death? Rebecca had been juggling like mad. With the sale of her own house imminent, she'd been looking for somewhere to temporarily rent until end of term, but she would have found a way to be there for her. She would have dropped everything. She should have made it clearer to Nicole that she would.

Going over Nicole's messages and emails in her mind, Rebecca was subdued on the way to the village. Richard was also quiet, she noticed, seemingly miles away as he drove.

'Okay, Dad?' Olivia asked him, reaching to place a hand on his arm.

Richard nodded. 'Just thinking.' He glanced sideways at her. 'You know.'

Olivia gave his arm a squeeze. 'Difficult not to, isn't it?'

'Definitely.' Richard drew in a long breath. 'Rebecca?' He met her eyes in the rear-view mirror. His were full of concern, she noticed. 'How are you doing?'

Rebecca smiled. 'Coping,' she said. 'Lost in my own thoughts, too, to be honest.'

Richard smiled back understandingly. 'If you need to talk…' he offered.

'Thank you,' Rebecca said, and then, feeling conflicted, turned her gaze to her window. She hadn't known what to expect when she'd met him – certainly not that he'd be all that Nicole had claimed. Yet, he appeared to be.

'Would you like me to pick up the dogs?' Olivia asked him as they pulled into the small car park at the end of the high street.

'I could always go out again once we get back. Or pick them up tomorrow. You seem too distracted to be driving.'

'No. Thanks, but I'd rather pick them up now.' Richard seemed adamant. 'They'll be pining. Bouncer will need some reassurance. I think Nicole would have wanted me to make sure he wasn't too distressed above everything else.'

She would have. Rebecca swallowed back a small lump in her throat.

'What about you, Becky?' Unbuckling her seatbelt, Olivia twisted to face her. 'Would you like some company at the village hall? Or would you rather be on your own?'

Well, that was definitely astute. The girl could clearly read people well. 'If it's okay with you, I think I would rather be on my own.' Rebecca smiled gratefully.

'No problem.' Olivia smiled warmly back. 'I'll have a browse of the library and then pop in to see one of my friends. She's only five minutes outside the village. I'll see you at the café in, say, a couple of hours? It's about halfway along the high street. You can't miss it.'

'Perfect,' Rebecca said, climbing out.

'See you later.' Richard offered her a small smile as he climbed out alongside her. His expression was concerned, Rebecca noted.

Nodding, she smiled back and set off through the pretty streets towards the village hall, which was a short walk from the church where Nicole's wedding had taken place, only to be tragically followed by her funeral.

There was no one manning the door to the hall, she found. Obviously, they were unconcerned about anyone stealing the paintings, which were marked up for sale at around fifty pounds. They were good – subtle light and reflection depicting the muted tones of the Worcestershire landscape. But the very fact that the colours were muted just wasn't Nicole, whose work had always screamed vibrancy. There were many studies of the River Severn, again in muted, swirling tones: studies of the actual water rather than the surrounding landscape, all of which seemed disturbingly prophetic now. How long had Nicole stared into that cold, foreboding water, Rebecca wondered. What had been going through her mind?

Growing more perturbed, Rebecca moved on, perusing the animal portraits it seemed Nicole had also taking to painting, including one of Bouncer curled up with a golden retriever – Richard's, presumably – which made her smile, albeit sadly. Surely she must have been content when she'd painted that?

Approaching the next frame along, Rebecca's step faltered. Moving closer, she squinted hard at the painting, which depicted a little lark on the perch of a huge art deco birdcage. It was bleeding. Rebecca's heart skittered against her ribcage as surely as the bird had flapped fearfully at the bars of its cage. A single blood red teardrop fell from the very tip of its wing.

CHAPTER EIGHT

NICOLE

PREVIOUS YEAR – JULY

Hearing her phone beep as the duetting piano and violin drew their rendition of 'Ave Maria' to its beautifully evocative close, Nicole winced and scrambled to retrieve the phone from her bag.

'Sorry,' she mouthed at Richard, who turned to scowl at her as she muted it. A mock scowl. Nicole knew she hadn't ignited an anger that would quietly smoulder until he could vent in private, as her former husband would have done, reminding her how useless she was, what an embarrassment she was. She'd never imagined she would feel safe in a man's company ever again. Yet she did in Richard's. It felt good. As if, after years being slowly suffocated, she could finally breathe again. The fact that he was undeniably handsome was a definite bonus. God, he looked gorgeous in his tailored grey suit and blue tie. She couldn't wait to get him on honeymoon and unwrap him.

Waiting until the musicians were duly applauded by the small gathering they'd invited back to the house for the reception, Richard rose from his seat and walked around behind her. 'You look good enough to eat, Mrs Gray,' he whispered huskily in her ear, causing her insides to melt, and then moved on past her to talk to Peter, her ex-work colleague, with whom he hadn't yet had the chance to exchange more than a quick word. Richard knew of him, but the two men had never met properly, Peter having left the Ikon Art Gallery before Richard had 'plucked up the courage' to come and talk to her that first time.

Seeing that Richard was already breaking the ice and shaking Peter by the hand, Nicole took the opportunity to retrieve her phone and check the text, which she guessed would be from Becky. Nicole had been gutted that the one person she cared most about in the world, apart from Richard, couldn't be here. She was also upset for Becky. She must have been so shocked upon hearing that her son had been in a road traffic accident, just as she was about to leave for the ferry. Mercifully, Sam had sustained no more than a broken leg, but naturally Becky hadn't been able to make it.

Opening the text, Nicole smiled. Modern technology could sometimes be an annoying intrusion, but it meant they were able to communicate, even with an ocean between them.

How did it go? she'd texted. *Get back when you can. I want details, assuming I'm not texting the runaway bride?*

Typical Becky. Nicole's smile widened. In an exchange of serious emails regarding the purchase of the house and her impending wedding, Becky had warned her that she might be making the second biggest mistake of her life. Nicole couldn't blame her for thinking Richard sounded too good to be true. She'd had to pinch herself several times. If only Becky could meet him, she would see in an instant she had nothing to worry about.

Rings are on fingers. Sun is shining. Man is hot! First dance shortly #nottherunawaybride Will get back with goss!

She typed her reply quickly and then went to join Richard.

'Ah, Nicky, looking utterly gorgeous.' Peter squeezed her into a firm hug as she approached him. 'If I may say so?'

'You may.' Nicole laughed and hugged him back hard. She was so glad he and his son had been able to come. She'd lost touch with all of her friends, apart from Becky and Peter, while miserably married to the misogynist, meaning most of the guests were Richard's or Olivia's. Peter had kept in touch via email, access to which she'd only ever had when she snuck off to the library, the one place the misogynist had let her visit on her own, because he'd found it boring. Even then, she'd had to take the phone he'd provided, which had a tracking app on it. Back then, Peter would regularly ask her if she would reconsider going back to the college where she'd taught the evening art classes – she'd inspired the students, he'd said. It had been out of the question, of course. He might as well have asked her to fly to the moon.

The misogynist had found out about her secret correspondence, inevitably. Nicole had never been able to hide anything easily. She felt it afresh, the cold fear clenching her stomach as she'd turned away from the PC to find he'd been standing behind her. It had been there then, the fury burning silently in his eyes. His fingers had bitten painfully into her flesh as he'd taken her by the arm and 'escorted' her out, smiling charmingly at the librarian as they went. Strangely, the cracked rib she'd sustained when he'd been 'forced to reprimand her for her deceit' had hurt less than him calling her a whore and spitting in her face.

Goosebumps prickling her skin, despite the summer heat, Nicole shook off the memory. She wouldn't let it spoil her day. He'd stolen her life. She had it back. Henceforth, she would make new, happy memories with a man who wanted her because he loved her, not because he couldn't bear anyone else to want her.

'Seriously, you're looking stunning, Nicky,' Peter cut through her too-depressing reminiscing. 'Obviously the new man in your life is good for you.'

She followed his gaze towards Richard, who, though still standing with them, now seemed distracted, glancing across the patio to where Olivia seemed to be enjoying Peter's son's company. Zachary appeared somewhat awkward, Nicole noticed, flushing profusely as Olivia took hold of his hand and led him to the buffet table. Nicole remembered him as a shy boy, from the few times Peter had brought him along to their evening art classes. She wasn't surprised that he was embarrassed by the attentions of someone as head-turningly beautiful as Olivia.

'He is good for me.' She turned back to Peter rather than stare at the poor boy and embarrass him further. 'The best thing that's happened to me in a very long time.'

Nicole did actually think she looked better lately, more her old self, with the sparkle back in her eyes and some colour to her cheeks, which definitely improved her pale complexion. Finding the dress had been a nightmare though. With little time to shop, she'd decided on an oyster silk slip dress from a local store, which fitted rather too snugly; but, miraculously, she wasn't too bothered how she looked. Richard had never once looked her over with a critical eye. She was sure he never would.

'As long as he appreciates you,' Peter said, glancing again at Richard, whose gaze was still on Olivia. She appeared to be feeding Zachary a slice of quiche. Poor Zach looked as if he might choke on it.

'Oh, he does. And I appreciate him, too.' Looking teasingly back to Richard in hopes of drawing him into the conversation, Nicole smiled. Richard's attention, however, was still on Olivia and Zachary.

Nicole shrugged good-naturedly. He was rather protective of her, having been her sole carer since her mother died. 'Do you fancy a top-up?' she asked Peter, nodding at his almost empty wine glass.

'Better not. I'm driving. Time I went on to soft drinks, I think,' Peter declined regretfully. 'It's a fabulous house,' he commented, glancing around. 'Not quite the kind of property I imagined you in, but classy.'

'Too classy for me, you mean?' Nicole raised an eyebrow in amusement.

'Definitely not that.' Peter gave her admonishing glance. 'You could outclass royalty, Nicole, trust me. I just couldn't help noticing it's a bit…'

'White?' Nicole suggested.

'Soulless, I was going to say.' Peter smiled, looking relieved that she obviously wasn't about to take offence. 'In need of a Nicky boho makeover.'

Nicole laughed. 'Which it will have,' she assured him. 'We're thinking of it as our blank canvas, aren't we, Richard?'

Richard was still watching Olivia and Zachary, who were now heading towards the open patio windows. 'Liv?' he called curiously. 'Bored already?'

Stopping, Olivia turned towards him. 'Swimming costume,' she shouted over the sounds of the band tuning up, indicating her body with a sweep of her hand, which definitely had one or two male heads turning. 'Can Zach use one of yours?'

'Zach, swimming? As in, baring his body in public?' Peter glanced in surprise at Nicole.

'He must be getting over his shyness,' Nicole suggested.

'So it would seem.' Peter's look was a mixture of bemused and amused.

Richard's seemed to be one of agitation, Nicole noticed, puzzled. 'No problem, help yourself,' he said eventually, his smile rather tight.

'Sorry.' Kneading his forehead with his forefinger and thumb, he turned to Nicole at last. 'It's just that Liv already has a boyfriend.'

'She does?' Now Nicole was surprised. She hadn't seen any evidence of one.

Richard nodded apprehensively. 'They've been going out a while. He's been away at uni, but he said he'd drop by sometime today. I'm a bit concerned, as you can imagine.' Moving closer, he slid an arm around her. 'Apologies for seeming distracted, Peter. Can I get you some more wine?'

'No more for me, I'm afraid,' said Peter, declining again graciously. 'I think I might need to go and grab some food to soak up what I've already had. Catch you later, Nicky.'

'Sorry,' Richard apologised again, as Peter went across to the buffet table. 'I was being a bit overprotective. I need to let her grow up and live her own life, I suppose.'

'Which won't be easy, having been a single parent.' Nicole understood. Any father would worry about his daughter – particularly such an attractive daughter.

'No,' Richard conceded, with a sigh. 'But then, I have my own life to live too now, don't I?' He eased her towards him. 'I believe this is our dance, Mrs Gray.'

'Oh heck.' Dropping her head to his shoulder, Nicole tried to still her nerves. 'I haven't danced in so long, I'm sure I've forgotten how.'

'Just close your eyes and hang on,' Richard said softly. 'I'll make such of mess of it, all eyes will be on me, trust me.'

Nicole laughed and held on tight, as she intended to forever.

The lead singer hadn't got further than the opening line when a high-pitched scream from inside the house caused the music to die.

Pulling away from her, Richard paled.

'Stop!' Olivia screamed. 'I said no! Get *away* from me! Dad!' she sobbed. '*Dad!*'

'Jesus Christ!' Richard ran.

CHAPTER NINE

REBECCA

PRESENT

Shaken, Rebecca swallowed back her tears as she left the village hall. She was positive that the painting had been as much a message as any typed in black and white. What on earth had gone on that Nicole had felt unable to convey it but through her art? Despite her best attempts to spot the flaws in Richard Gray that she'd imagined Nicole couldn't see, she hadn't yet found any. He seemed genuinely deeply caring, not the kind of man who would cause Nicole to recoil into herself, to feel trapped or threatened all over again.

Wiping a hand across her cheek, she walked slowly back to the churchyard. She needed some alone time before meeting Olivia and Richard at the café. Some space to try to get her conflicting emotions in some sort of order.

Wondering again at how quickly the wedding had taken place, about why they'd chosen to live in such a grand house – or rather why Nicole had, thereby relinquishing the funds from her own house, which Richard had at first said she shouldn't – she followed the meandering path which took her past the church towards Nicole's plot, and then stopped and stepped back into the stone arch of the doorway. Richard and Olivia had also come here, it seemed, and not to reflect in quiet contemplation. They appeared to be arguing: Richard's back was towards her, and Olivia's body language was animated, her voice not as subdued as it should be, given their location.

'We can't!' Rebecca heard her shout. 'It's too soon!'

Richard said nothing, raising his hands instead, as if despairing, and then half turning to walk away.

'It's too soon! You know it is!' Olivia called after him.

Richard stopped. Even from a distance, Rebecca could see him drawing in a tight breath. Slowly, he turned back to face her. 'I have to, Liv,' he said tiredly. 'The new development isn't going to build itself. The builder's gone bust.'

'But how?' Olivia glared at him, somewhere between tearful and angry. 'There must have been some indication they were in trouble. You're a property developer. You should have known.'

'Yes, well, the way things escalated with Nicole…' Richard stopped and massaged his temples. 'I took my eye off the ball, Liv. I didn't foresee this happening. If I had, I could have done something about it. I'm sorry, but what else am I supposed to do? I have to cut my losses and free up funds to employ another contractor. It's either that or I'm stuck with half-renovated properties I can't sell on.'

'But we said we'd take some time – at least give ourselves the chance to breathe and take a holiday. And now this! It's not fair,' Olivia cried.

Rebecca hardly dared breathe. He *wasn't* financially secure – or at least not as affluent as appearances might have people believe. Her heart palpitated at that realisation. Clearly, he had money worries, with no available funds he could immediately put his hands on to rescue whatever venture had gone wrong. Was that truly because he'd been so preoccupied with Nicole's illness he'd taken his eye off the ball?

Olivia seemed to be extremely upset: wrapping her arms about herself and dropping her gaze. Transfixed, Rebecca watched as

Richard faltered for a second before going back to her. Sliding an arm around her, he spoke quietly and then eased her closer, nestling her head on his shoulder and stroking her hair with soft, soothing strokes as she gave way to tears.

Despite this clear display of tenderness, Rebecca felt a prickle of apprehension run through her. She had some information – glimpses into their relationship, provided by Nicole's correspondence – but even with that knowledge, knowledge that Richard and Olivia plainly weren't aware she had, she couldn't know for sure what had happened. She needed to talk to him, get to know him better, before asking the questions she needed to, which would seem like accusations unless asked in the right context.

She needed to spend more time here. Once her house sale was complete, she'd been intending to rent until she could find somewhere suitable to buy, so it would seem a natural thing for her to stay at a hotel in order to view properties available for rental. There were so many things unresolved in her mind; she couldn't just leave it. She simply couldn't rest until she'd fulfilled her unspoken promise to Nicole to establish all the facts.

Seeing Richard turn around again, Rebecca almost stepped back, but then, realising he couldn't fail to see her, she stopped. 'Sorry,' she said, trying not to appear too flustered. 'I saw you two were deep in conversation and thought I should give you a minute.'

Coming towards her, Richard nodded and smiled. His look was wary, though, as if he knew she couldn't have failed to have overheard.

'It was lovely to finally meet you,' Rebecca said, as Richard walked her from the house to her car the next morning. 'I wish it could have been sooner. Things might have been different…'

'If only?' Richard picked up intuitively, as she trailed sadly off. 'There are always *if onlys* in life, Rebecca. Always *what ifs*. I haven't stopped questioning myself since it happened, haven't stopped wondering what I might have done differently. My head tells me I couldn't have done anything differently. My heart, though – that's a whole other story.'

Rebecca nodded understandingly. 'Did her GP not refer her to someone?' she asked, still not able to understand why she hadn't received expert help.

Sighing heavily, Richard ran his hand over his neck. 'He did, apparently. It came out at the inquest. Nicole obviously decided not to pursue it. I offered to pay for a private psychiatrist, but…'

'But?' Rebecca urged him, as he hesitated.

Richard met her gaze, nothing short of agony now in his eyes. 'She thought I was trying to control her.' He shrugged hopelessly. 'I don't think she ever really recovered enough from her abusive relationship to trust me completely. I wish I could have convinced her that she could. That I wasn't anything like that bastard. *Christ*, what I'd give to get hold of him. Show him what it's like to be mercilessly bullied.'

Rebecca closed her eyes. He *had* known her – or at least that much about her. 'No, she would always have borne the scars,' she said, swallowing back a tight knot in her throat as the caged lark came to mind. Nicole's first husband had clipped her wings. She'd been too broken to fly free again. Was that what she'd been trying to convey in that sad, lonely painting?

'Apologies for the language.' Clearly contrite at his display of temper, Richard glanced down and back.

'Don't be,' Rebecca said, not blaming him for that in the least. 'He was. A complete bastard. Sadly, they do exist.'

Richard's jaw tightened. 'Evidently,' he said, reaching to open her door for her as Rebecca pressed her key fob. 'Sorry about the conversation you overheard yesterday too,' he said, broaching the subject Rebecca had assumed he must have been reluctant to in front of Olivia.

'Not a problem,' Rebecca assured him, climbing into her car. 'It's really none of my business.'

'Still, it was bad timing, to say little of the location.' Richard sighed regretfully. 'My only excuse is that I'm not thinking straight. I shouldn't have announced to Olivia that I was going to sell the place out of the blue. I had a property deal go wrong. Nothing that can't be remedied – I have other properties I can sell, funds overseas I can release – but since I'm not sure I can live here without Nicole… Though Olivia clearly needs a little more time, so…'

'No apologies necessary, Richard, honestly.' Rebecca said reassuringly.

'We should keep in touch,' Richard suggested. 'Just in case anything comes up. And to talk, if either of us feels the need to. I'm not sure what your plans are, but if you're thinking of holidaying in the UK, then you're more than welcome to stay here.'

'I'd like that,' Rebecca said. 'I'm selling my house in France at the moment, and I still have some things to tie up, so I'm not sure quite when I'll manage, but, yes, I'd love to come and visit. Thank you.'

'I'll look forward to it.' Richard's smile was warm. 'It really would be great to have some company.'

'Then I'll definitely take you up on your offer. Meanwhile, you have my email address. Take care, Richard. Make sure to look after yourself as well as your daughter.'

'I'll do my best,' Richard promised. 'You take care too, Rebecca,' he urged her. 'Drive carefully.'

Rebecca started the engine and pulled away. An enigma, definitely, she thought, watching him through her rear-view mirror as he slid his hands into his pockets and watched her go. One she needed to fathom.

CHAPTER TEN

NICOLE

PREVIOUS YEAR – JULY

'Richard? *Richard!*' Apprehension knotting her stomach, Nicole raced for the stairs – and then froze halfway up as she saw Zachary being roughly manhandled from Olivia's room by Richard.

'You perverted little bastard!' Richard seethed, his expression murderous, his face close to Zachary's, who looked utterly petrified.

Locking his elbow tighter around the boy's throat, with his other hand he wrenched Zachary's arm high up his back and shoved him hard against balustrade. *Oh dear God!* Was he going to throw him over it?

'Zach?' Peter was close behind her. 'What…? *Christ almighty!*' Mounting the stairs, he pushed past her to get to his son. 'Let him go,' he warned Richard, who now had his hand gripped around the back of Zachary's neck, forcing him further over the rail. The boy's face was puce and he was gasping for breath.

'Richard, *please.*' Clutching the banister, Nicole hurried after Peter. 'Stop!' she begged. 'Richard!'

Richard didn't acknowledge her. His face twisted with rage, his focus all on Zachary, he didn't even appear to hear her.

'For God's sake!' Peter stepped further towards him, followed by another man striding urgently after him. 'Let him go!'

Reaching to grab a fistful of Richard's shirt, Peter attempted to drag him away. The other man flung an arm around Richard's chest. Neither of them could budge him. Richard's gaze was fixed on Zachary, his eyes as dark as thunder. It was as if something had snapped inside him.

Nicole's blood ran cold.

'Richard, let him go!' she screamed. '*Richard!*' She reached him just as the other man succeeded in pulling him backwards, both men colliding heavily into the wall behind them.

'I'm going to *kill* you, you snivelling little son of a bitch,' Richard snarled, jabbing a finger past the man who was now struggling to restrain him.

'What *happened?*' Nicole cried, moving in front of Richard as Peter grabbed hold of his terrified son.

Richard seemed to see her at last, the fury in his eyes abating for a second as he scanned her face.

'Richard?' Her heart banging against her ribcage, Nicole caught hold of his shoulders. 'Talk to me. Tell me what he's done. Richard, *please…*' She trailed off as Olivia appeared on the landing, stepping tentatively from her room.

Clutching the front of her torn dress to her breasts, her hands shaking, mascara wending a watery black track down her face, she looked towards Richard. '*Daddy,*' she said shakily, her voice that of a child's.

'Isn't it perfectly fucking *obvious* what he's done?' Richard's voice was hoarse. 'Call the police, Nicole.'

Oh God, no. Surely he hadn't…? Nicole's gaze shot towards Peter.

His face draining of all colour, Peter met her eyes for a blood-freezing second. 'Not Zach,' he said, swallowing hard and looking back to Richard. 'He couldn't have.'

'*Couldn't have?*' Dragging his forearm across his mouth, Richard stared at him incredulously. 'He very nearly did!' he bellowed. 'For

Christ's sake, someone call the bloody police, or I swear to God, I won't be responsible for my actions.'

'Daddy, no! Leave him. Please!' Olivia protested tearfully, as he attempted again to get to Zachary.

'What?' Richard turned disbelievingly towards her.

'I don't want the police involved. It's your wedding day. I—' Choking back a sob, Olivia stopped.

'It doesn't matter what *day* it is, Liv,' Richard said, his voice catching. 'The bastard tried to—'

'I don't want them here. I just want him to go.' Olivia backed away, slipping back to her room, as Richard attempted to move towards her.

'For *fu*...' Dragging in a tight breath, Richard turned his gaze to the ceiling. 'Get the bastard out of here,' he growled. 'Now!' And you.' He spoke angrily to the man who was still holding him back. 'Get out of my way. I need to go to my daughter.'

Shocked to the core, Nicole stood rooted to the spot, torn between following Richard and Olivia or going to Peter, who looked as if his whole world had come crashing down. He'd had full custody of Zachary since he was three. He lived for his son.

'You should go,' she said gently, stepping towards him.

Tightening his grip around Zachary's shoulders, clearly too dazed to speak, Peter simply nodded.

Nicole looked to the young man who was visibly trembling beside his father. His face was as white as chalk, his eyes wide and terrified. 'I didn't...' he stammered. 'She asked me to help her with her zip. I didn't...'

'How is she?' Nicole asked, when Richard finally came down to the kitchen.

'Traumatised,' Richard said, his expression taut, his voice tight. 'Have they gone?'

Feeling responsible, Nicole nodded sadly. 'Everyone has. They thought it might be prudent. I'm so sorry, Richard.'

Richard didn't say anything immediately, drawing in a breath instead and going to flick the kettle on. 'Not your fault.' His back still towards her, he shrugged after a second. 'I hope you'll understand, though, that I'd rather Peter didn't come here again, with or without his son.'

Swallowing hard, Nicole nodded again. That was another friend she'd lost. She could hardly blame her husband, though – not this time. 'Did he…? Did Zachary actually…?' She hesitated, uncertain how to ask how far things had gone. She still didn't know. When she'd tapped on the door earlier, Richard had said that Olivia needed some time.

'What, hold her down and rape her?' Richard finished angrily. 'No, not *actually*. Undoubtedly, if they'd been anywhere remote…'

'And Olivia's sure he didn't think…?' she continued awkwardly. And then immediately wished she hadn't, as Richard turned to face her.

'Are you serious?' He studied her, astounded. 'Did you *see* her? Did you not *hear* her, Nicole?'

'Yes. I mean, no. I… That's not what I meant, Richard,' she said falteringly. She hadn't meant anything. She was simply trying to understand what *had* happened. 'I just wondered whether he—'

'Misread the signals?' Olivia interjected, from where she was standing behind them, her face bereft of make-up and looking so young and vulnerable that suddenly Nicole's heart broke for her. 'Not unless he's deaf, Nicole,' she said, her eyes filling up. 'Even then, I imagine me trying to fight him off might have been a subtle indication, don't you?' Her expression disappointed, she swiped away the tears now cascading down her cheeks and turned to fly back to the stairs.

'Liv!' Giving Nicole a despairing glance, Richard went after her. 'Liv, wait.'

'I'm all right!' Olivia called back, her voice full of emotion. 'I'm going to take a bath.'

Dragging in a terse breath, Richard stopped.

'I'm sorry,' Nicole blurted. 'Truly, I am, Richard. I didn't mean to sound as if I was doubting her. I was just trying to understand what happened. You never said, and I… I just wanted to understand, that's all. I hoped she might feel able to confide in me. I want to be her friend, not her enemy.'

Richard didn't answer. Dragging a hand agitatedly over the back of his neck, he seemed reluctant even to look at her.

And Nicole cursed her stupid mouth. Why hadn't she thought before opening it? What was the *matter* with her? 'Richard?' She stepped towards him.

Still, Richard didn't answer, and Nicole turned away, not sure what to do other than to give him the space he clearly needed.

Standing alone on the patio a minute later, she looked up to the sky, where dark clouds were now ominously gathering, and blinked hard against her own tears. The misogynist had enjoyed making her cry, calling her weak and pathetic, even when she had lost her beautiful, innocent baby. Her hand went involuntarily to the empty, soft round of her tummy. She didn't think Richard ever would, but she didn't want him to think she was feeling sorry for herself.

Staying like that for a second, she didn't realise Richard had followed her until he slid an arm around her. 'I'm sorry, Nicole,' he said. 'I realise this has been an ordeal for you, too. I shouldn't have raised my voice. Please accept my apology.'

Nicole almost wilted with relief – that he didn't hate her, that he didn't blame her. She hadn't expected him to, but… old ghosts would always haunt her. 'You were angry. You'd every right to be,' she assured him, relaxing a little with his comforting arm around her.

'Not with you.' Richard eased her closer. 'I don't know what to do.' He tugged in a tight breath. 'I can't leave her here on her own. Not now. Not like this.'

He was talking about the honeymoon, Nicole guessed. They were due to leave later that night. 'I know.' Composing herself, she turned towards him. 'It's just a thought,' she said tentatively, 'and you might think it's a mad one, but could she come with us? We'd have to change our flights and the hotel booking, but it might do her good to get away from things for a while.'

Looking up at him, Nicole waited, not sure what Richard's reaction would be.

Her heavy heart lifted when Richard, after studying her curiously for a second, leaned in to press a soft kiss to her forehead. 'I think she would love the idea,' he said, looking immensely relieved. 'And it would be a load off my mind. You're a special person, Nicole. Do you know that?'

'If a little clumsy.' Nicole smiled weakly. 'I really am so sorry about what I said. I honestly didn't mean it to sound the way it did.'

Richard smiled reassuringly. 'I'll go and ask her,' he said.

Reaching to squeeze her hand, he turned back to the house, leaving Nicole surveying the remnants of her wedding day.

They never had had their first dance.

CHAPTER ELEVEN

REBECCA

PRESENT

Relaxing outside the Café de la Ville, Rebecca was indulging in her favourite pastime – sampling the excellent *tarte tatin* washed down with Aperol lemonade – whilst people-watching. Seeing a young couple, obviously in love, stroll by hand in hand, she smiled nostalgically and savoured the last mouthful.

Realising it was time to go back to work, she sighed regretfully. It was a beautiful day – they were heading for a heatwave. Calling reluctantly for the bill, she checked her phone while she waited. She felt it every single time she did: a stab of intense sadness, knowing there would never be another email or text from Nicole. She hadn't deleted her details from her phone. She didn't think she could bear to do that.

Two new messages, she noted, both from Sam regarding the upcoming holidays. Sam had decided to stay in the UK this year, to spend more time with Laura. He'd suggested that Rebecca might like to book a hotel in Warwickshire – if she was at a loose end, he'd said diplomatically – and they could spend some time together. It was a nice idea. Laura and she got on, but Rebecca suspected that more than a few days might be overstaying her welcome. With the house sold, she'd decided to contact Richard

Gray instead and take up his offer of a holiday. She'd explain that she would be looking for somewhere to rent in the UK whilst house-hunting, thereby informing him that she would be moving back to the UK. Richard didn't know it yet, but Rebecca intended to see much more of him. The lark in the cage had haunted her dreams every night since she'd arrived home. She knew she wouldn't sleep soundly until she'd unravelled what had happened to her dear friend. It had been almost three months since the funeral and still she felt the loss inside her like a tangible weight; still she couldn't believe Nicole was gone.

Rebecca checked her emails and blinked in surprise. Had the man been reading her mind? 'Just a thought', the subject line of Richard Gray's email read. Feeling a prickle of something – nervousness? – wash over her, Rebecca opened it.

Dear Rebecca

I hope you won't mind me contacting you. Sadly, with the house now up for sale, I find that it's time to start thinking about Nicole's belongings. Her art meant so much to her, and I can't bring myself to simply dispose of her materials. There are also her canvases (there are more stored in the loft – I'm not sure you saw those), along with the watercolour paintings. The exhibition was left up out of respect for a while, which was kind, since the villagers didn't know Nicole that well, but it seems the space is now needed for a new exhibition. I was wondering, therefore – and please do say so if you'd rather not; I'm not easily offended – whether you might like to spend some time here at the house and help me go through them, selecting anything you might like to keep for yourself. The weather is glorious – and will be for a while, so we're told – and the swimming pool sits unused. Your son would be welcome, too, of course. As I say, it was just a thought, as you mentioned you might like to stay, so please feel free to say no. To be honest, I'm feeling the loneliness of being alone and would welcome the opportunity to talk about Nicole with someone who knew her, possibly better than I did.

I hope you are well and had a safe journey home.

Kindest regards,

Richard.

PS Whenever suits you would be fine.

Well, that was a guaranteed incentive. He would know she wouldn't want Nicole's things – her canvases, treasured paints and brushes being disposed of. Checking her watch, Rebecca responded immediately.

Dear Richard,

Thanks for your email. I've just been idling outside a café in my lunch hour and now find myself in danger of running late. Please excuse the short reply. Yes, I would love to visit and would welcome the chance to go through Nicole's art things – they were very dear to her. My own house has recently sold so I'm flexible re timings. I'm not sure what Sam's movements are, however, so will get back soonest.

Hope you are as well as you can be.

Best,

Becky

With a combination of relief and apprehension running through her, Rebecca pressed send. Finally, here it was: her chance to step into Nicole's world, to view her friend's life from the inside. What might she find behind the unblemished white walls?

CHAPTER TWELVE

NICOLE

PREVIOUS YEAR – JULY

Shielding her eyes against the scorching Balinese sun, Nicole watched as Richard and Olivia made their way to the pool bar after a lengthy swim in the pool. They had asked her to join them, but Nicole hadn't realised how athletic they both were, leaving her struggling to keep up. They were also competitive with each other, which she found a touch exclusive, which was silly. They had a whole history together that didn't include her. And in any case, exposure to the sun while in the water would do her pale complexion no favours. In her teenage years, she'd learned the painful way that she would never achieve the sort of all-over golden glow that Olivia effortlessly seemed to.

Pulling her knees up so that her vulnerable toes were adequately shaded, Nicole sighed, despairing of herself. As if she was competing with Olivia physically. Richard loved her the way she was; she didn't doubt that. Still though, lying alongside Olivia's lithe tanned body, every bare inch of her own milk-white skin slathered in sunscreen, lest she end up looking like a boiled lobster, Nicole couldn't help feeling the tiniest bit... Well, she definitely didn't feel like a bronzed goddess.

Deciding to console herself with another moreish cocktail, she caught the pool attendant's eye and ordered a Bali Bali, which had a dash of everything in it: cognac, dark rum, gin, citrus fruits and passion fruit syrup. It was probably hugely fattening, but also scrumptiously delicious. Returning the waiter's beaming smile, she settled down to enjoy her book, glancing occasionally towards Richard and Olivia. As she watched, Olivia slipped from her stool at the pool bar back into the water with the agility of a well-oiled sea lion. Seconds later, she bobbed up, smoothed back her blonde braids and then scooped up armfuls of water with which she proceeded to drench Richard.

Richard was after her in a flash, sliding slickly into the water as Olivia squealed and splashed around to swim away. With Richard in close pursuit, she headed to the far side of the tree-fringed pool. Nicole was glad that Olivia was enjoying herself after everything that had happened, but she hoped they didn't disappear for too long, as they'd done yesterday. She understood that Olivia needed time with her father, but she had felt a bit lonely, left on her own for so long.

Feeling a tug on her toe a while later, Nicole stirred woozily. 'You're exposed,' Richard said, looking very much like a bronzed god, silhouetted hazily against the sky and smiling down at her.

'Oh *hell*.' Realising she was indeed exposing large expanses of herself to the merciless sun, Nicole jumped up and dashed for the cover of the nearest shaded lounger. 'I must have dozed off,' she said, blinking, feeling disorientated. 'What time is it?'

'Around three,' Richard said, collecting up her towel and sunscreen and carrying them over to her.

'Three o'clock.' Nicole boggled. She'd been asleep for over an hour?

'One too many cocktails?' Richard enquired, eyeing her with amusement.

'Obviously.' Nicole winced and eased a strap of her swimsuit away from the livid red skin on her shoulder. 'Where's Olivia?' she asked, glimpsing around and seeing no sign of her.

'Taking a shower,' Richard said, squeezing sunscreen into his hand. 'Turn around,' he instructed. 'I'll do your shoulders and back.'

Oh, *that* was nice. Nicole closed her eyes as she felt his firm hand glide across her hot flesh, immediately soothing it – and arousing her. It was a strange honeymoon, in that they hadn't yet managed to make love. Having Olivia in the adjoining room was rather off-putting. Bearing in mind why she was here, they'd both felt it somehow inappropriate.

'So, what have you been up to?' she asked him, melting into his touch.

'Just walking,' Richard supplied, continuing to smooth the cream over the contours of her back in soft, sure strokes. Nicole felt her pelvis dip, her breasts tingling with yearning. 'Along the beach. Liv needed to talk. I didn't think you'd mind.'

'I don't.' Nicole assured him, her back arching as he gently traced the bare length of her spine. 'Not really. I do miss you a bit though, when you go off.'

Richard paused, his hand at the small of her back. 'I'm not exactly "going off", Nicole. I'm just walking – with my daughter.'

He sounded defensive, Nicole realised with alarm. 'I know.' She twisted to face him. 'It's fine. I just…'

'Just?' Richard prompted her, when she trailed off under his questioning gaze.

'Nothing.' Nicole felt her cheeks flush. 'I suppose I thought it would be nice if we could find some time to be alone together, that's all.'

Nodding, Richard pondered for a moment and then got to his feet. 'She needed to talk, Nicole,' he said quietly, collecting up his own towel and wiping the cream from his hands. 'Under the circumstances, I thought you of all people would understand.'

Nicole looked at him, bewildered. 'I do,' she said quickly. 'I just thought that maybe we could—'

'I'm going up to shower.' Richard cut her short, his expression disappointed as he swept his gaze over her. 'I'll see you later.'

'Richard?' *Oh no.* Nicole's heart plummeted. She'd done it again. 'Richard, wait.' She jumped to her feet, hastily tugging her straps up as he walked away. 'I didn't mean…'

Letting her herself tentatively into their room, Nicole found Richard pouring himself a drink from the minibar. A scotch, it looked like, despite the fact that it was the middle of the afternoon. Dropping her things on the bed, she walked across to him. 'I do understand, Richard,' she said softly, placing a hand on his arm. 'Of course I do.'

Richard took a sip from his glass. He didn't look at her.

'I know Olivia will need to talk, and that she probably won't feel comfortable talking to me. I can't begin to tell you how sorry I am about what happened. It's just that you've been out walking together a few times now, and in the evenings too. I don't mind – honestly, I don't. I only thought it might be nice if you and I could find some time to…' Nicole stopped, her eyes drifting towards the balcony, where Olivia had obviously been sitting. She couldn't have failed to hear her.

'I don't think Dad thought he needed to ask your permission,' she said, stepping through the patio doors into the room.

'He doesn't,' Nicole said quickly.

Olivia said nothing, folding her arms across her breasts and looking at her judgementally instead.

'That's not what I meant, Olivia,' Nicole said kindly, stepping towards her. 'I seem to be saying all the wrong things. I—'

'Yes, you *do*,' Olivia said pointedly. 'You know, I really can't believe you would be jealous of him spending time with his own *daughter*.' Her expression contemptuous, Olivia shook her head and then flounced past her to the door.

'Jealous?' Stunned, Nicole spun around after her. 'I'm not jealous, Olivia. Why on earth would I be?'

Olivia faced her. 'I don't *know*,' she snapped angrily. 'Because you want him all to yourself, presumably.'

'Liv, don't.' Richard moved towards her as Nicole looked in bewilderment between the two of them. 'That's not fair. It was Nicole who suggested you come with us.'

'Not fair?' Olivia gawked at him. 'If you ask me, *her* as good as calling me a liar, preferring to believe her friend's disgusting son, who tried to *rape* me, is what's *not fair*.'

Nicole felt the blood drain from her face. 'I did *not*,' she refuted. 'Olivia, please believe me. I was just confused about what exactly had happened. I didn't doubt that you—'

'She's trying to turn you against me!' Olivia cried, jabbing a finger in Nicole's direction. 'That's what she's doing. Trying to drive a wedge between us – and you can't even see it!'

Whirling around, Olivia yanked open the door and flew tearfully out of the room.

'Olivia!' Richard started after her. 'Dammit,' he muttered, coming back to grab up his phone and his key card.

'I didn't believe Zach over her,' Nicole said, a sick feeling settling in the pit of her tummy as she tried to remember what she had said. 'I never meant to imply that. I—'

'But you did imply that.' Richard glanced at her in frustration as he strode back to the door. 'And now this. And you wonder why she's reluctant to talk to you?'

'But I didn't mean to!' Nicole protested for the umpteenth time. 'I swear I didn't. I don't understand why you would think that I would.'

'I know.' Pausing, Richard sighed despairingly. 'Look, I can't do this now, Nicole. I need to go after her.'

'Anyone I know?' Richard asked, coming out on to the patio a good hour later.

'Becky, my friend in France,' Nicole said, her eyes fixed on the text she was keying in.

Dearest Becky, I sooo wish you were here. Instead, I have Richard's daughter for company on my honeymoon, and I seem to have upset her irretrievably. Will fill you in later. I live an interesting life, don't I? Lol. Miss you! LOVE, Nicole. X

She pressed send.

'Not your friend Peter, then?' Richard asked, a sarcastic edge to his tone, which surprised her.

'Not Peter, no,' she said, now feeling extremely defensive and close to tears herself. 'I do want to keep in touch with some of my friends, though. If that's all right with you, of course?' The last came out equally sarcastically. She couldn't do it again – creeping around meekly, living in fear of causing offence.

Glancing from her phone to her, Richard studied her inscrutably for a second, and then sighed heavily. 'Of course you do,' he said, his shoulders deflating as he ran a hand over his neck. 'I'm sorry. Obviously, I feel concerned about any of this becoming general knowledge, for Olivia's sake, but it's none of my business who you text. Ignore me.'

Nicole answered with a small nod. He wasn't jealous then, which was a good thing. She'd seen first-hand how destructive that emotion could be. He was merely protecting his daughter, as any father would.

'How is she?' she asked, as he walked across to look out across the tropical paradise they were fortunate enough to be in: rich greenery everywhere, spilling over balconies, tumbling through gardens, and coming to rest on the pure white sands of the beach. It was truly beautiful. How was it that they suddenly seemed so utterly miserable?

'Better,' he said, and paused. 'She needs me, Nicole. I know it's difficult for you, particularly as the… person concerned is the son of your friend, but I have to be there for her one hundred per cent right now.'

'I know.' Nicole so wished she'd suggested they postpone coming away. It might have been better for all of them if Richard had been able to spend time with Olivia at home. 'Look, why don't you and Olivia go out for dinner together tonight? She'd probably rather that than…' She trailed off, worried she might put her foot in it again by suggesting Olivia wouldn't want her there.

Richard glanced uncertainly at her. 'I can't leave you in a hotel room on your own, Nicole. It's supposed to be your honeymoon.'

Nicole couldn't help but smile wryly at that. 'I'll be fine,' she assured him, glad that he cared. 'I thought I might have a wander around the hotel. I haven't seen the temple yet, or the lily pond and water features. They're beautifully lit up at night, apparently.'

She didn't add that she would quite like to wander around hand in hand with her husband, just the two them. But then, Richard and Olivia had probably already seen the various sights the hotel had to offer.

'But what will you eat?' Richard turned to her, his forehead creased with worry.

'Um, food?' Nicole suggested. 'I'll get something at one of the bars, or order room service and indulge myself in our lovely spa bath – with wine, of course.'

Richard's mouth curved into a smile. 'I wouldn't mind indulging you in our lovely spa bath,' he said, moving towards her and finally bending to kiss her. Ridiculously, Nicole felt even more like crying. And then she almost did as Olivia appeared on the adjacent balcony, before his lips had even grazed hers.

Seeing Olivia's scowl as she looked across, Nicole nodded discreetly in her direction and eased away from him. 'You'd better get ready,' she said, kissing his cheek instead.

Once Richard had gone off with Olivia to the beachfront restaurant, Nicole went down to reception and enquired after the use of the PC the hotel had available for customers to use. She would have a stroll around the hotel, but she'd decided to write to Becky first, and she wanted to send an email, rather than text her. Since it would be a lengthy one, she'd decided a keyboard might be more comfortable. She wouldn't want either of them thinking she was sharing personal things behind their backs, but the fact was, she was now feeling excluded. She understood why, to a degree, but that Olivia was being so hostile towards her wasn't making her feel any better. She hoped they could get past this, that Olivia could accept that she hadn't been incredulous of her telling of events, just confused, and that they could eventually become friends. For the moment, however, in the absence of her husband, Nicole needed someone to talk to. Someone who knew her. Someone she could safely confide in, and who wouldn't judge her.

Settling down in the little room that housed the PC, Nicole checked her phone first. Sure enough, Becky had replied to her text, short and to the point: *Darling Nicole, what on earth is going on? Does Richard not realise three's a crowd? Get back soon. Am concerned.xxx*

Nicole picked up her laptop and began to email.

Dear lovely Becky,

Sorry! I didn't mean to worry you. Sorry, also, that I haven't had the chance to get in touch sooner. I've been a bit busy trying to work out how I actually came to be on honeymoon with Richard and his daughter. As you might have gathered, she's here in Bali with us. In the adjoining room, in fact. Not quite the romantic getaway I'd envisaged.

There was a little incident before we left. Well, actually a bloody great whopping incident, which was terribly upsetting. I hardly dare write it down, for fear I'm making a judgement without all the facts, but… it seems Peter's son attacked Olivia in her bedroom. Richard intervened, thank God, before things were as awful as they could have been, but needless to say it was traumatising for Olivia. I didn't help the situation, I'm afraid. In the confusion afterwards, I was asking Richard whether Zachary might have misunderstood why Olivia was taking him upstairs, and Olivia overheard. It was a completely stupid thing to say. I was honestly only extremely confused, but… needless to say, I'm not flavour of the month as far as Olivia's concerned.

Anyway, Olivia was adamant she didn't want to go to the police, and given the situation and how distressed she was, we thought it better she wasn't left on her own. Thus my current gooseberry-like status. Richard's having to spend time with her – talking a lot, walking a lot, keeping her company in the pool (she's a better swimmer than I am). I have him for the rest of my life, and it's hardly his fault. He's stuck between a rock and a hard place, concerned and distraught for Olivia, but also equally concerned for me, which proves how caring a man he is.

I know I don't really have to ask, but please keep this between the two of us. I would hate it if Olivia or Richard thought I was sharing this with anyone, to say little of Peter.

Please don't worry either. All is well, I promise. It's probably not a good idea to liaise about this via text, by the way – I'd die if R or O glimpsed any exchanges. I really just wanted a shoulder. I'll fill you in more when I get home. Meanwhile, I actually wish I was there, with you!

Loads of love and big hugs.

Nicole. X

After sending the email, Nicole waited awhile, looking out of the window and listening to the soft sounds of paradise: flowing water, Balinese music, wind chimes, all manner of birds, crickets and frogs. She breathed in the unique smell: smoke and spice, incense and oil and the heavenly scent of natural flowers. She needed to take an abundance of photographs. It would be rich inspiration when she got home.

Should she have a massage tomorrow? This was something else she hadn't envisaged doing alone. Blow it. She would, she decided. She needed to be content with her own company. And Richard would probably be relieved she was finding something to do, rather than being needy of his attention too.

Nodding resolutely, Nicole gathered up her bag, determined to find to somewhere to dine, albeit on her own, when Rebecca pinged back a reply.

Dearest Nicole,

Oh God, how awful! I know Olivia will be traumatised, Richard too, but this was also traumatising for you, Nicole. I understand you probably can't exchange emails now, but please look after yourself. Remember, wherever you are, I'm always here.

Email or call me as soon as you get home. I need to know you're okay.

Much love, sweetheart, and huge hugs back.
Becky
xxx

PS Am thinking about selling the house. Will talk more when you can.

CHAPTER THIRTEEN

OLIVIA

PREVIOUS YEAR – JULY

She'd been drinking. Coming into Nicole's' room, Olivia immediately noted the almost empty wine bottle on the table. Drowning her sorrows, obviously. *Oh dear. Poor Nicole.* Olivia wandered across the room, helping herself to Nicole's bedtime candy treat from the pillow as she plopped down on to the bed.

Standing by the window, Richard, worried father, and now equally worried husband, glanced in her direction and then turned his attention back to his phone, a scowl knitting his brow as he tried Nicole's mobile number again.

'Anything?' Olivia enquired, kicking off her flip-flops and lying back to suck languidly on the creamy coconut delicacy.

Richard sighed and shook his head. 'Nicole, can you call me back please?' he spoke apprehensively to her voicemail. 'It's late. I'm concerned. Extremely. You shouldn't be wandering around in a strange place on your own.'

'You sound like *her* father,' Olivia observed, as he went across to the minibar.

'I'm worried about her,' Richard said, not sounding overly impressed as he poured himself a whisky and knocked it back. 'You're not exactly going easy on her, Liv.'

Olivia noted the agitation in his tone. 'Well, *excuse* me,' she said huffily, peeling herself from the bed and walking to the balcony.

Richard sighed behind her. 'Look, this isn't easy on either of us, Liv. We have to at least try to—'

'You can stop worrying.' Olivia said wearily, glancing back at him. 'She's out there.'

'Thank God for that.' Now sounding relieved, as Olivia supposed he would be, Richard hurried to join her. 'Where?'

'There.' Olivia nodded towards the lily pond.

'Oh Christ.' Seeing Nicole was circumnavigating the pool, her arms outstretched as if she thought she could fly and with a definite weave to her walk, Richard clamped his eyes shut and then spun on his heel. 'Stay here,' he instructed, heading for the door. 'I don't want her upset any more.'

And miss all the fun? He had to be joking. Olivia gave him a head start, then skidded across the bedroom, stuffed her feet back into her flip-flops and followed him.

Hanging back once they reached the periphery of the seating area around the pond, she watched him approach Nicole, who was now standing still and gazing down into the water. God, she was pissed out of her brains.

'Nicole, what are you doing?' Richard asked, approaching her carefully.

Nicole didn't answer, inching further forward instead, teetering precariously close to the edge.

'Nicole! *Jesus!*' Richard sprang into action and grabbed his troublesome new wife around the waist before she fell in. With the amount of booze she'd consumed and no skill in the water whatsoever, she'd sink like a stone. Olivia sighed. She would definitely frighten the fish in that flowery kaftan thing she insisted on wearing. Honestly, the woman had about as much dress sense as she had backbone, which was precious little.

'What in God's name are you *doing?*' Richard demanded, yanking Nicole backwards and whirling her around to face him.

Nicole blinked as he took hold of her shoulders, looking guilty, as she perpetually did. Olivia really was growing bored with her. She was no challenge whatsoever. She had no idea how *he* was putting up with her.

'Just walking,' Nicole said, her expression now one of bemusement.

'Walking?' Richard shook his head in exasperation. 'You were right on the edge! You were about to fall in.'

'I was not,' Nicole protested indignantly. 'I was making a wish. I toshed a coin in.'

Definitely pished. Olivia rolled her eyes.

Relaxing his hold on her, Richard stared at her. 'You're not supposed to, Nicole,' he said, working to keep his tone calm. 'There's a notice. See?' He pointed towards it. 'There are very expensive coy carp in there.'

Nicole squinted in the direction he was pointing. 'Oh,' she said. 'I didn't see it.'

'Clearly.' Richard moved to take her by the arm. 'Just come in, Nicole, will you? It's way past midnight.'

'It was only a little coin,' Nicole said defensively. 'I'm sure the fishes won't mind.'

'Fish. No, I'm sure they won't.' Richard's tone was now rather strained. 'Though the management might. Come back inside, Nicole. Please.'

Nicole didn't move. 'But the band's shtill playing at the barbecue on the beach,' she slurred, waving her hand vaguely over her shoulder.

Whoops. Noticing Nicole swaying on her feet, Olivia's mouth curved into a smirk. Someone was going to have an almighty hangover in the morning.

'Even so, we need to go inside, Nicole,' Richard repeated. 'This is getting a little embarrassing.'

At that, Nicole yanked her arm from his grasp and dug her heels in. 'I am *not* embarrassing,' she said, her chin jutting defiantly.

'I didn't say you were.' Richard stopped and turned to face her. 'I said this—'

'Yes, you did!' Nicole eyed him angrily. 'I'm not deaf. And I'm not horrible either. It's *you* who's being horrible.'

'Nicole, could you please just stop,' Richard said tersely.

'Do you want to know what I wished for? Do you?' she asked, sounding tearful, which was most definitely going to be embarrassing.

Blowing out an exasperated sigh, Richard plunged his hands deep into his pockets.

'I wished that I knew what I'm supposed to have done wrong!'

'You've done nothing wrong, Nicole,' Richard assured her, with remarkable patience, considering. 'Can we discuss this inside, please?'

'I must have done!' Nicole apparently wasn't going anywhere. 'Why else would you suddenly be treating me as if I don't exist?'

'Nicole, I'm not. I'm simply trying to do what's best for—'

'But you are! You're spending more time with your daughter than with me. This is supposed to be our honeymoon. We're supposed to be making mad, passionate love, and you're—'

'Nicole, that's enough!' Richard raised his voice. 'This is childish! You know damn well why I need to spend time with Olivia. Now, you can either stay out here and make a complete fool of yourself or you can come inside. It's up to you. I've had enough.'

With an agitated tic tugging at his cheek, he turned to walk away, leaving Nicole looking disorientated and very foolish.

Ha! Olivia thought, heading smugly back after Richard. Did the ridiculous woman really imagine he would take her side over his traumatised daughter's? But then, she supposed she couldn't blame her for thinking he might. She was supposed to be his wife.

Oh. She stopped as Richard ground to a halt, turned on his heel and walked back to where Nicole was now quietly sobbing.

CHAPTER FOURTEEN

REBECCA

PRESENT

It was a sweltering summer's day when Rebecca pulled on to the long, pebbled drive to Richard's house. It truly was magnificent; the glass and white-walled façade of the property practically shimmered in the distance. Still, though, it wasn't the kind of house she'd ever imagined Nicole choosing to live in.

Stifling an overpowering sense of sadness, she drove on, parking the car at the front of the house and spilling out of it to see Richard emerging from the front door. Wearing tailored cotton chinos and a short-sleeved white linen shirt, he looked not the least bit fazed by the heat.

'Rebecca… Becky. I'm so glad you could make it,' he said, smiling broadly and coming around to the boot to help her with her bag. Rebecca didn't decline the offer; she was sure she might pass out if she didn't get some shade soon.

'Is your son not coming?' he asked.

'Sam and Laura are visiting Laura's parents in Birmingham on the way,' Rebecca explained as she followed him into the house. 'I just hope Laura's ancient car doesn't expire in the heat.'

'The joys of student life,' Richard empathised, dropping her bag by the stairs in order to fend off two bounding dogs, who, judging by their manically wagging tails, were happy to see him.

And her, it seemed. 'Bouncer!' Rebecca laughed, bending to greet Nicole's adopted dog, a scraggy but endearing little mongrel. The animal emitted a pathetically excited cry and then, not knowing who to greet first, scrambled frenziedly around in a circle.

'Bouncer, down!' Richard commanded.

'Aw, he's fine,' Rebecca assured him, crouching to the dog's level and getting a face full of tongue for her efforts.

'If a little over-exuberant.' Richard shook his head good-naturedly and took hold of Bouncer's collar, gently steering him towards the kitchen. 'Basket, Bouncer. You too, Wanderer.' He pointed them both there.

Rebecca couldn't help but smile. She doubted the two dogs would have been so instantly obedient if he hadn't enticed them with treats fished from a jar on one of the work surfaces. Maybe it was a functional kitchen, after all.

'I imagine you'll want to go and freshen up,' he said, once the dogs were settled. 'I thought a cold drink might hit the spot first, though.'

'Oh, it definitely would.' Rebecca nodded gratefully.

Richard smiled and headed for the fridge. 'So, what do you fancy? I have some cold beer, Pimm's – on ice, of course – and soft drinks. Or perhaps you'd prefer tea or coffee?'

'Pimm's sounds divine,' Rebecca said appreciatively. *A gentleman and a good host.* Despite the endless questions rattling around in her head and her initial assumptions about him, with the dogs here and Richard less formal than he'd been the first time she'd met him, Rebecca had to concede that the place felt more homey, more like somewhere Nicole could have made her own, had things not started to go awry almost before the ink was dry on her marriage certificate.

'I know it's not exactly the holiday you might have planned,' Richard said, extracting a jug of Pimm's that was so cold from the fridge it was perspiring, 'but I hope you can relax a little while you're here.'

'I'll do my best.' Accepting the glass he offered her, Rebecca sipped thirstily. She didn't normally drink alcohol this early in the day, but he was right, it absolutely did hit the spot.

'Excellent.' He looked relieved. 'I hope you've brought your swimming costume. I think you'll need to cool off after five minutes out on the patio.'

'I have,' Rebecca assured him. She wasn't entirely sure she wanted to bare herself in it, but it was as much as she could contemplate wearing in this almost tropical weather, and she could wear her loose sarong with it. Also, she needed to appear relaxed, because she very much wanted Richard to relax in her company.

'Great.' He smiled, now looking pleased. 'I'll put this in the outdoor fridge, along with some wine for later.' He walked towards the sitting room and the patio doors, and then stopped and turned back. 'But I'll show you to your room first.'

Shaking his head, as if despairing of himself, he smiled as he passed by again to put the jug back in the kitchen fridge.

'Thank you.' She offered him a smile back, noting that he seemed far from relaxed – more nervous, in fact. Did he know she would be assessing him?

'My pleasure.' He glanced awkwardly down and back again, his striking blue eyes coming to rest on hers. There was still a deep sadness there, Rebecca saw, searching his face carefully.

'I'll go up and get changed,' she said, after a moment, in which Richard seemed to have drifted off somewhere.

'Right, yes. Sorry.' He pressed his fingers to his forehead. 'My mind keeps wandering. Going over things, you know?'

Rebecca nodded. She did know. Several times she'd found herself only half listening to her students and colleagues, endlessly wondering what had happened and how.

'I thought we'd have a barbecue later,' he said, heading to the hall. 'Assuming that's okay with you?'

'More than.' Rebecca was grateful for sustenance of any sort after her journey. 'But you mustn't feel you have to cater for us, Richard. We're all perfectly capable of shopping and cooking, including Sam. Trust me, he doesn't get waited on at home.'

'We were barbecuing tonight anyway.' Richard stepped back to allow her to go up the stairs before him. 'Nothing fancy. Steak and salad, or veggie burgers for any non-meat eaters.'

'Perfect,' Rebecca said, thinking that he actually did seem perfect – on the surface, at least. *What went so wrong, Nicole?* Rebecca knew things had gone on between these blank walls that Richard and Olivia weren't likely to open up about. Had Nicole's final despair been anything to do with Richard's handling of events, his attitude towards her, his treatment of her? Or had it been nothing to do with him, and he was exactly what he seemed? A caring man, still struggling with his grief and as confused as she was as to why Nicole had chosen to end her own life.

Richard was crouching down by the side of the pool when Rebecca ventured out on to the patio – talking to Olivia, who was in the pool, she realised.

Noticing Rebecca, Olivia gave her a wave and twisted to glide under the water, surfacing three yards or so later. Clearly at home in the water, she swam like a fish. Rebecca was immediately reminded of Nicole's email, the one she'd sent from her honeymoon, which had shocked her to the core. She'd wondered at the time about one point in particular: Nicole's fear of 'making a judgement without all the facts'. Rebecca had sympathised with the girl, but hadn't Nicole been entitled to the facts? If not from Olivia, who'd apparently taken umbrage at Nicole's comment, then from Richard? Nicole had been his wife, after all.

Nicole had called her, once she'd got back to the UK, as she'd promised she would, but even then, she still hadn't been sure about the exact details of the attack. She'd been concerned about trying to mend fences with Olivia, concerned about Zachary and Peter. Most of all, she'd been concerned for Richard, who'd found himself torn down the middle. He'd been amazing, Nicole had told her: there for her, even though it was impossible for him to take sides; caring, as he always was. But how concerned had he truly been when things had escalated thereafter? Had he been there for her then? Cared for her then?

Shielding her eyes from the sun, Rebecca looked towards Richard as he stood up and walked towards her. His shirt open at the front now, under the almost blistering heat, he looked more at ease – genuinely pleased she was here. Genuine. He'd almost drowned trying to save Nicole, she reminded herself. No matter how many times she pondered it, what had happened simply didn't make sense.

'Okay?' Richard asked, his forehead creased in concern.

'Yes.' Rebecca shook herself and mustered a smile. 'Just thinking.'

Richard nodded. 'I never stop,' he said, a noticeable swallow sliding down his throat. 'I wish she'd felt she could confide in me. She did at first, but then… I go over it and over it, but I still can't work out why she suddenly felt she couldn't.' He shrugged sadly.

And Rebecca stared at him, confounded. Was he saying he hadn't realised the extent of Nicole's distress? If not, why not? Had Nicole, fearing his disillusionment or disapproval, glossed it over? Up until her last email, she'd maintained that he was a caring, thoughtful man. But would such a man truly have been that blind to her emotional pain? Unless, of course, Nicole hadn't seemed particularly distressed in the days prior to her death? It was possible that the way she'd chosen to end her life might not have been as impulsive as it seemed. That she might have made her decision before that fateful day and felt somehow lighter for it. That thought landed like a cold stone in Rebecca's chest.

CHAPTER FIFTEEN

NICOLE

PREVIOUS YEAR – AUGUST

It was almost too pristine to use as an art studio. 'What do you think, Bouncer?' she asked her loyal little man, who was sniffing the now bare floorboards. He sat down, looked confusedly up at her and emitted a soulful whine.

'Yes, that's what I thought.' Nicole smiled and stroked his soft, silky head. 'We can work with it, though, hey, boy?'

Sighing, she looked around the upstairs room she'd chosen as a studio and decided to make a start by pinning a selection of the photographs she'd taken in Bali, some of which she'd had blown up, to the stark walls. These would be her inspiration – something that had been sadly lacking since they'd returned from their honeymoon that wasn't. The vibrant red, gold and white of the sacred Barong masks, with their black bulging eyes, and the verdant green of the tropical foliage would be the basis of her colour theme downstairs. She'd decided on large canvases, three of them, which would bring much-needed colour to the long sitting room wall. For their bedroom, she was thinking of white sands and blue seas: colours to evoke a sense of calm. It was coming together – in her mind, at least.

Pondering using Indonesian batik fabric for the cushions and bed throws, she headed downstairs to make the first of many trips to her car for her art supplies, Bouncer on her heels.

Olivia was still lounging on her bed as Nicole passed her room for the third time, lying on her tummy, her feet raised behind her, bobbing to some tune or other on her phone. Thinking better of asking her for a hand, since Olivia now only bothered to speak to her when Richard was around, Nicole left her to it, and made a fourth – and hopefully final – trip down again.

Finally, with everything brought up from her car, she went to the garage to fetch the blank canvases she'd already stretched over their frames. Propping one against her new studio wall, she turned to open her art box and was greeted by the familiar smell of oil paints, linseed oils and thinners. She took a deep breath, feeling soothed. It would be all right, she assured herself. Richard and she would get back on track soon. As Richard had said, Olivia was hardly going to recover immediately from her ordeal, thus her reluctance to socialise very much, which meant she was always home. Nicole tried not to feel put out about it. It was just a temporary thing, as was Olivia's inability to sleep. She was wandering about at night, which meant that Richard and she were uncomfortable with any close intimacy. She did wish, however, that Olivia didn't have an uncanny knack of popping up every time Richard and she tried to steal even a kiss.

It wasn't Olivia's fault. She was a young woman who'd lost her mother, she reminded herself. Yes, it was a while ago, but still her loss would be painful. It had occurred to Nicole that, despite their getting along initially, Olivia might feel she was competing for her father's affection now he'd remarried. Things would work out. Olivia just needed some time. And Nicole really needed to work off her frustration. That in mind, she set about priming the canvas with PVA glue, which would seal the fabric and allow her brushes to flow more freely. Nicole wanted flow – lots of it.

After applying one thin coat, she went to make a quick coffee, leaving the glue to go tacky before she gave it a second coat to ensure a good seal. She was heading back into the room, mug in hand, when Olivia said behind her, 'Oh my God, what is that smell?'

Nicole jumped, cursing silently as her coffee slopped over the sides of the mug. She placed it carefully on to the work table she'd set up and turned around. 'What smell?' she enquired, smiling pleasantly.

'In here.' Her hand under her nose, Olivia screwed up her face as if encountering something putrid. 'It's like dead fish – and it's wafting everywhere.'

'It's just glue,' Nicole said, surprised. She couldn't smell anything. But then, she was probably used to it.

'Glue?' Olivia gawked. 'But isn't that poisonous, inhaled in quantity?'

'I shouldn't think so,' Nicole said, her smile now on the tight side. 'It's just wood glue. The sort they use for furniture.'

'Well, it's foul.' Olivia scowled. 'You shouldn't be using it indoors.'

Nicole's heart sank. Surely she wasn't going to spoil this for her too? 'I'll close the door,' she offered. 'And open the window. Perhaps you should open yours too?' she suggested. 'It's quite warm outside.'

Her scowl deepening, Olivia folded her arms. 'I hope this isn't going to be a regular thing,' she said moodily.

Stunned, Nicole simply stared at her. Did the girl really dislike her that much? She was trying to understand her outbursts: Olivia would be highly emotional, possibly blaming herself for what had happened, wondering what she'd done to invite the abuse inflicted on her. Nicole had been there. She was trying to give her space, not to criticise her or make her feel uncomfortable or do anything to make her feel she wasn't welcome here. But now *she* was the one feeling uncomfortable, creeping around for fear of upsetting anyone. And, actually, it wasn't on.

'It's my home, Olivia,' she pointed out, holding her gaze determinedly.

Olivia, however, didn't flinch. Her amber eyes narrowed; she seemed equally determined to outstare her. 'You should keep that dog downstairs, too,' she said smugly, as Nicole, sensing all-out war, eventually looked away. 'I'm allergic to dogs' hairs.'

But not to Wanderer, over whom Olivia fussed regularly. Nicole's heart plummeted. Disbelieving, she watched as Olivia strolled back along the landing, a slow smile curving her mouth as she turned to close her bedroom door.

The penny dropped resoundingly. She was doing it deliberately. This was nothing to do with her emotional trauma. The girl was getting some kind of kick out of this. She was clearly trying to cause friction between Richard and her, and possibly trying to make life so intolerable that Nicole would leave. Well, Nicole had news for her. Summoning Bouncer, she clenched her teeth hard and slammed her own door. If the gauntlet was down, then she would bloody well fight. No more creeping around, trying to make herself invisible. She'd done enough of that in her life. This was her house, and she'd do what she damn well liked in it.

Grabbing the primer, she set to with gusto, giving her canvas its second coat of PVA. Olivia would just have to hang her scheming little head out of the window, wouldn't she? With any luck, she'd fall through it, Nicole thought bitchily, and then felt immediately guilty.

CHAPTER SIXTEEN

REBECCA

PRESENT

'Becky!' Olivia called delightedly, hoisting herself lithely out of the pool and smoothing her hair back, making Rebecca feel immediately frumpy in her black M&S Secret Slimming swimsuit. Wearing a miniscule bikini that consisted of three strategically placed silver triangles, the girl definitely looked hot.

'I'm so pleased you could make it,' Olivia gushed, and flew across to greet her.

So it would seem. Rebecca tried not to mind as the girl pulled her fiercely into a wet hug.

'Oh, sorry.' Realising she was dripping all over her, Olivia pulled away, grabbed a towel from the lounger and proceeded to dab at Rebecca's breast area, which was slightly embarrassing with Richard looking across from where he was mixing more drinks at the minibar. 'I'm a bit overexcited,' Olivia confided. 'It's just so fabulous to have some female company. I mean, Dad tries, but it's been a bit…'

She trailed off as Richard came across with two perfectly presented glasses of Pimm's, complete with lemon slices and mint sprigs. 'Miserable?' he suggested.

'Boring,' Olivia said tactlessly, now using the towel to pat herself dry.

Richard's mouth twitched into an embarrassed smile. 'I'm obviously not very good company,' he said, his eyes drifting briefly down as he handed Rebecca her drink.

'Not surprisingly. It's early days yet.' Olivia redeemed herself, smiling sympathetically as she wrapped an arm around him and gave his shoulders a squeeze. 'The thing is though, Dad, you're a man,' she teased, planting a kiss on his cheek. 'Completely incapable of discussing anything remotely interesting.'

Richard looked at her in amusement. 'Such as?'

'Fashion, make-up… men.' Olivia gave Rebecca a conspiratorial wink.

At this, Richard rolled his eyes skywards. 'Clearly I need to work on my conversational repertoire,' he said, shaking his head as he walked back to the bar.

Watching him, Rebecca felt a pang of sadness. His efforts at light-heartedness were an obvious act. The rest, though – the underlying grief that emanated from him, the captivatingly charming persona – was all that an act? Rebecca knew that she'd wanted it to be, that she'd needed to blame someone for Nicole's death, but she still hadn't been able to convince herself that it was all fake.

'Is your son not coming, after all?' Olivia asked. She was now sitting on the lounger, sweeping her hair up and tying it artfully into a knot.

Rebecca sat on the lounger next to her, rather than stand around looking spare. 'He's on his way. He and Laura decided to—' She stopped as something that sounded remarkably tank-like reached her ears. 'Oh dear. I think he might have arrived.'

Obviously also hearing the commotion, followed by the distinct sound of an engine backfiring, Richard winced as he came towards her. 'How ancient did you say that car was?' he asked her.

'Very.' Rebecca jumped up, joining him to walk around the house towards the drive. 'It's a Volkswagen Beetle. Much loved. Unfortunately, still possessing most of its original parts, not that reliable.'

'Ah.' Richard nodded understandingly.

'Sam's an old car enthusiast?' Olivia asked, hurrying to join them.

'No, his girlfriend Laura is,' Rebecca said. 'She fell in love with the car when she saw it on a garage forecourt apparently. It's yellow. Her pride and joy.'

'Oh, I see.' Olivia nodded, her brow furrowed. 'I didn't realise his girlfriend was coming too.' She looked momentarily perturbed. 'Ah well, the more the merrier, I suppose. We can have a party on the patio.'

Brightening, she skipped on ahead of them, reaching the drive first. 'Sam!' she cried, plainly as delighted to see him as she had been with Rebecca. 'It's so lovely to meet you.'

Seemingly unaware of Laura standing at the driver's side of her beloved car, Olivia proceeded to squeeze Sam into a firm hug. 'It'll be so cool to finally have some company my own age around the place,' she enthused, giving him another squeeze before easing away. Sam looked rather embarrassed as he took in her skimpy bikini, Rebecca noted.

'And you must be...?' Olivia looked curiously towards Laura, oblivious to her unimpressed expression as she banged her car door shut and came around to join them.

'Laura,' she replied, also taking in the minimal clothing Olivia was wearing. By contrast, Laura – a petite, natural-looking girl, who tended not to wear make-up and didn't tolerate sun well – was wearing a floral maxi dress with a shirt over it, and possibly felt overdressed in Olivia's company. She was also clearly put out by Olivia's exuberant greeting of Sam.

'Sam, hi,' Richard said, defusing the awkwardness, thankfully, as he walked across to them. 'Nice to meet you.' He smiled, extending his hand.

'You too,' said Sam, shaking hands. 'Thanks for the invite. It's a fabulous property. I couldn't help noticing the tennis courts as we drove in.'

Richard looked him over with interest. 'Do you play?'

'As often as I can,' Sam said enthusiastically. Athletic by nature, Rebecca guessed he was keen to get a game in while he was here.

'Excellent.' Richard looked pleased. 'We'll have to organise—'

'Oh fab,' Olivia interrupted, locking her arm through Sam's. 'We can play doubles. It's been ages since we had anybody decent to play with.'

'Er, great,' Sam said uncertainly. 'As long as Mum fancies a game? Laura doesn't play.' Shrugging at Rebecca, he turned to give Laura an apologetic smile.

Olivia also glanced in Laura's direction – a tad superiorly, Rebecca thought. 'Oh, that's a shame.' She sighed exaggeratedly. 'Never mind; she can be umpire. Now, come on,' she said, steering a bemused Sam towards the back of the house. 'You absolutely have to try a Pimm's. Dad's already mixed some. It's to die for.

'You too, Laura,' she called, throwing her a smile over her shoulder. 'You must both be about to combust, travelling here in that old thing.'

CHAPTER SEVENTEEN

NICOLE

PREVIOUS YEAR – AUGUST

Nicole waited nervously as her phone rang out. She hoped he would pick up – and that Olivia wouldn't come floating downstairs at the crucial moment. It was strange that, since the girl couldn't seem to tolerate her, she would appear wherever Nicole was in the house, always wearing the same expression – something near contempt. Except when Richard was around, of course, then she was sweetness and light, bordering on childlike. Nicole did wonder whether she had some sort of Oedipus complex. She worked with her father. Nicole actually had no idea what she did as his supposed personal assistant, other than go out with him to viewings. She didn't seem to do much else, and she was home more often than not. She lived with him. She wasn't too old to be living with her father by today's standards, but she seemed unnaturally close to him. It was because she'd lost her mother, Nicole had first thought, but now didn't know what to think. She wished she dare ask Richard about Olivia's relationship with her mother, and whether it had been a difficult one, but she guessed that would be misconstrued, the way things currently were. Richard would be naturally protective of his daughter – more so after the awfulness on their wedding day. She dreaded to think how he might react if she were to suggest

Olivia might benefit from counselling, which, of course, would seem to confirm the girl's accusations that she was trying to 'turn him against her'.

Thinking he wasn't going to answer, she was about to cut the call when Peter picked up. Thank God. Nicole had wondered whether he would ever speak to her again. As it was, his tone was cool, which wasn't surprising. 'Nicole,' he said formally. He'd always called her Nicky. 'How are you?'

'Fine,' Nicole lied, and faltered. 'Actually, I'm not that fine, to be honest, but that's not why I've called. How's Zach, Peter? I've been really worried about him.'

She heard Peter's sharp intake of breath. 'So concerned you haven't called until now?' he replied pointedly.

Nicole felt immensely guilty. 'I meant to,' she said. She had, but she hadn't known how. 'I wanted to. I… it was awkward, Peter. You must see that.'

'Obviously.' Peter's tone was caustic. 'He's coping. Trying to get on with his life. Thankfully the lying bitch didn't press charges.'

'Peter!' Nicole was shocked. She'd never known Peter to be anything but a soft-spoken, gentle man. 'You can't accuse her of *lying*. Something happened, clearly. I just—'

'Nothing happened!' Peter's voice went up an octave. 'Nothing that wasn't staged – for God knows whose benefit. Zachary is *gay*, Nicole. Do you understand? And before you go down the "confused about his sexuality" route, he's not. We talked about it some years ago. He's not inclined to walk about wearing a badge declaring he's homosexual, but he is. It's a fact. I have no idea why someone would do what she did to him, but that girl needs help. Serious help.'

Gay? Stunned, Nicole tried to assimilate this new information.

'I have to go.' Peter's voice was tight with anger.

'Peter, wait!' Nicole said urgently. 'Why didn't you say something? Why didn't Zach say something? I don't understand.'

Peter went quiet for a second. 'It wasn't my place, Nicole. That's something for Zach to share. But he didn't really get a chance, what with your *husband's* hand around his throat, did he? Here's the thing, Nicole. Would people have believed him? Or would they have judged him anyway?'

Nicole didn't answer. She wasn't sure she could get the words past the sharp lump in her throat.

'I really have to go. Look after yourself, Nicky,' Peter said, more subdued. 'And, Nicky…' He hesitated. Nicole sensed his awkwardness. 'Just remember I'm here if you ever need me. Okay?'

Her heart banging against her ribcage, Nicole promised she would and ended the call. She believed him. In her heart, she'd always believed Zach would never do what he'd been accused of. Feeling sick to her soul, Nicole sat on one of the kitchen stools and tried to get her disorientated thoughts in some sort of order. What should she do? Olivia really did need help. She was ill. Surely, she must be? Did Richard know? Was that why he was so tolerant of her? Why she worked with him? Had that been at Richard's instigation, in order to keep her close, or Olivia's?

She had to speak to Richard. She couldn't do nothing. If Olivia's allegations had gone further, Zach would have endured so much humiliation and pain. Peter was right. Other people wouldn't necessarily have believed he was gay, or that his sexuality meant he wasn't capable of such an attack. Lawyers and police would have delved into his personal life in intimate detail. He could have been arrested, charged. But it wouldn't have gone further, would it? Olivia had never intended it to. It was obvious, now. Her aim had been twofold: to draw Richard's attention back to her; and to ruin the wedding day and, subsequently, the marriage.

It seemed absurd. Said out loud, it would sound as if she were being totally irrational. Was she? Was it possible that she was getting everything out of proportion? A headache threatening, Nicole massaged her temples and debated what she should do.

She jumped as she heard Richard's car on the drive. She had to get to him first, speak to him quickly, before Olivia monopolised his attention. Ask him… No, *tell* him: they needed to go out together. Alone. Tonight. Nicole had tried to be patient with Olivia. She'd almost convinced herself that the animosity between them was her fault. But it wasn't. She'd done nothing to warrant this sustained hostility, and she wouldn't lie down and take it. Not again. This time, she *had* to fight back.

Hearing Richard's key in the lock, she headed for the front door, trying to quell the panic churning inside her. She needed to be calm, to give him no hint of what she wanted to talk about until they were alone. With Olivia hovering, as she perpetually was, she would stand no chance of talking to him in the house.

The door opened just as she reached it. Nicole breathed in hard and arranged her face into a smile. 'Evening,' she said brightly, and then, needing to feel the solidity of his body close to hers, she stepped towards him, threading her arms around his waist.

Richard seemed taken aback, tense for a second, and then he relaxed into her. 'To what do I owe the pleasure?' he asked, his mouth close to her ear.

'No reason. I just wanted to remind you that I love you,' Nicole said, looking up at him. 'I thought… hoped… you might fancy going out tonight, just the two of us.'

Glancing towards the stairs, Richard looked doubtful. 'I have some work to do, Nicole. I'm sorry, I—'

'I've booked a table,' Nicole said quickly. 'I probably should have rung you first, but I thought you wouldn't mind if I took the initiative. I haven't done that in a long time. Anything spontaneous in a relationship, I mean. I didn't dare. I always got it wrong, but I thought…' Trailing off – feeling guilty, but not quite lying – Nicole waited.

Richard searched her eyes, indecision in his own, and then his mouth curved into an understanding smile. And Nicole's heartbeat slowed to somewhere near normal. It would be fine. They would talk it through – work out a way to help Olivia. It wouldn't be easy, but she would be there for him. For Olivia, too, because he would need her to be. Because, in time, Olivia might need her to be.

'In that case, I would love to go out with you,' Richard said softly.

'Thank you.' Tears pricking her eyes, Nicole buried her face in his shoulder and hugged him tight.

And then instantly tore herself away, as Olivia rasped breathlessly from the landing behind her, '*Daddy.*'

'Liv?' Richard's gaze shot towards her. '*Jesus Christ!*' His face blanching, he moved past Nicole to bound up the stairs. 'Where's your inhaler?' he demanded, grabbing hold of Olivia's shoulders and frantically scanning her face.

'Olivia!' He almost shook his daughter as she clasped a hand to her chest, nothing escaping her mouth but an audible wheeze.

Dumbstruck, Nicole watched as Richard smoothed Olivia's hair back and attempted to calm her. 'Nicole!' he shouted. 'Call an ambulance!'

Jolted into action, Nicole flew for her phone as Richard swept Olivia, who was now gasping for breath, up into his arms.

Blundering after him, Nicole attempted to relay the situation as best she could to the emergency services. 'She's not breathing properly,' she said, feeling terrified now, as she followed Richard into Olivia's room. 'I don't know. I…'

'Asthma!' Richard said tightly. Nicole looked towards where he sat on the bed, an arm around Olivia, supporting her, as she clearly struggled to draw breath. 'Tell them it's an emergency.'

The emergency operator heard him. Nerves and nausea making her head swim, Nicole mumbled her thanks as they assured her an ambulance was on its way. Richard looked close to tears as he glanced desperately around the room. 'There!' he yelled suddenly, causing Nicole's heart to leap into her mouth. 'The inhaler.' He nodded towards where it was lying on the floor next to Olivia's dressing table.

Flying across the room, Nicole snatched it up, prised off the top, and handed it to him.

His hands were shaking. *Oh dear God.* Nicole swallowed hard.

'It's okay, baby,' Richard murmured, his face deathly pale as he turned his attention back to Olivia. One arm still supporting her, he pressed the blue tube gently to her lips. 'Here we go, sweetheart. Breathe it in for me, baby, will you?'

Clearly panicking, Olivia appeared not to hear him.

'Come on, Liv. We've been here before. You can do this.' Richard kept his voice calm, though Nicole could hear the constriction in his throat. 'One long breath in, yes? And then hold.'

Her stomach knotting inside her, Nicole prayed silently as he pressed the canister down, and then thanked God when Olivia finally took a breath, sucking the lifegiving medication into her lungs.

'Good girl.' His face flooding with relief, Richard moved the inhaler away, a bead of perspiration sliding slowly down his cheek as he waited for her to breathe out, and then quickly offered the inhaler again. 'One more, Liv. For me, yes?'

Richard waited for Olivia to take another inhalation and then, appearing to hold his own breath, he pressed the canister again.

'Better?' he asked her, studying her face intently as her wheezes abated and her breathing became deeper and slower.

Nicole stepped apprehensively towards them. 'Is she all right?' Her voice came out a petrified whisper.

'She will be.' His eyes filled with fear, Richard glanced briefly at her and then turned his attention back to Olivia.

'Sorry,' Olivia croaked raggedly. 'I couldn't find my inhaler. It wasn't on my bedside table. I started to panic. I—'

'*Shhh.*' Richard eased her closer to him. 'It's fine. You're fine. You did good. Well done, sweetheart.'

Swallowing hard, he held her close, and then eased back and lifted her chin to look at her. 'Do you know what triggered it, Liv?'

Olivia dropped her gaze and then looked hesitantly back at him, then towards Nicole. 'The fumes,' she said weakly. 'The glue and the other chemicals. I told Nicole I was asthmatic, but…'

'*What?*' Nicole gasped, disbelieving. 'You did *not*, Olivia.' She looked in bewilderment between them.

Richard simply stared at her.

'She didn't,' Nicole insisted, fear rising inside her. 'I wouldn't have dreamed of priming my canvases indoors if…' She stopped, realising that that's exactly what she had done. 'She said she didn't like the smell, and that she was allergic to dogs' hairs, but she didn't say—'

Seeing Richard's face darken, his expression a mixture of incredulity and anger, Nicole stopped. He didn't believe her. He thought… Dear God, what was he thinking?

Richard looked away. 'Will you be okay?' he asked, turning back to Olivia.

He squeezed her hand when she nodded timidly, then got abruptly to his feet. His expression was inscrutable, Nicole noted, as he walked towards her. *The quiet before the storm; before the insults and venom spew forth.* Her heart beat a violent rat-a-tat in her chest. Nicole closed her eyes. *Richard isn't him.* She clamped her mind down hard on thoughts of the misogynist, of the malice that would spark in his eyes before his hand shot out. Richard wasn't him. He wouldn't condemn her. He wouldn't despise her. He *wouldn't*. 'I think we need to talk,' he said, his tone devoid of any emotion as he walked past her to the door.

Nicole glanced in Olivia's direction before following him. She simply smiled. Like a cat that had got the cream.

CHAPTER EIGHTEEN

REBECCA

PRESENT

Watching Sam and Olivia dive into the pool in perfect synchronicity, Rebecca turned her gaze towards Laura, feeling for her. Laura attempted to keep her gaze fixed on her book and failed. After glancing at the two, who were now racing each other to the end of the pool, she closed the book and climbed off her lounger.

'I think I'll go and make sure we're unpacked,' she said, smiling half-heartedly in Rebecca's direction.

'Do you want a hand?' Rebecca offered, thinking she might need an ear.

'No.' Laura forced another smile. 'I thought I'd take a quick shower and reapply my sunscreen while I'm at it. Thanks all the same, Becky.'

'Good idea,' Richard said, shielding his eyes against the sun as he looked up from his lounger. 'I think I might need to cool off myself soon.' He nodded towards the pool.

Laura's smile was a bit wan as she turned for the house.

'She seems like a nice girl,' Richard observed, as she disappeared through the patio doors.

'She is,' Rebecca confirmed, tempted to join her anyway. It was obvious Laura did feel put out – and possibly pale in more ways than one in comparison to Olivia, whom Sam was paying too much attention to. In fairness, Olivia seemed determined to monopolise him. But still, Rebecca should have a quiet word with her son. He wasn't an unfeeling person – far from it. He was caring and very aware of not treating women disrespectfully, having been brought up solely by her, but unfortunately that made him a little naive to women's wiles sometimes. And to the fact that he attracted women's attention. She was biased, obviously, but with his toned muscles and blonde good looks, he was definitely a magnet.

'She seems shy,' Richard commented.

'She is a bit,' Rebecca said, looking back to where Sam and Olivia were now splashing about with each other in the water. 'I think that's what Sam loves about her,' she added, glancing sideways at him. Was Richard aware that his daughter was flirting with Sam? Apparently not. She watched him as he gazed across the pool, seemingly miles away.

'Olivia seems to have recovered well,' she ventured, broaching the subject around which Nicole's troubles appeared to have started.

Richard's gaze came back to hers. 'Sorry?'

'Olivia. She seems to have recovered well from her ordeal.'

'Oh, yes. Yes, she has. She was devastated at first. She was very fond of Nicole. Her death was traumatic for her, but she seems to be doing okay now.'

Rebecca nodded. 'Actually, I was thinking more about the awful event on your wedding day,' she clarified tentatively.

'Ah.' Richard picked up his beer and took a large slug. 'Nicole told you about that then?'

Rebecca noted his uncomfortable expression. 'Out of concern,' she said. 'She was worried for her. For both of you. As she would have been.'

Sitting up, Richard faced her. 'She was.' He sighed and ran his hands through his hair. 'She was really supportive of her. It wasn't easy for Nicole either, as you can imagine, but we got through it – Olivia did – with Nicole's help and some counselling.'

Rebecca glanced again at Olivia. She certainly seemed to have recovered. Rebecca hadn't got the impression she'd been receptive to any help Nicole had tried to offer, however. 'She didn't want to report it though?'

Richard shook his head. 'I wanted her to, to be honest, but Olivia was adamant she wouldn't, for Nicole's sake.' Turning his attention to his beer glass, he reached towards it, manoeuvred the glass full circle on the table and left it where it was.

Rebecca read the body language. This was clearly something he wasn't comfortable discussing. 'Tell me about yourself,' she said, changing the subject. She wondered whether she should contact Peter. Both Richard and Peter might think it was none of her business, but given that it had been the catalyst to the circumstances of her dear friend's death, Rebecca felt that it was. 'I gather you're a property developer, but I've no clue what that actually involves.'

'That's right.' Richard smiled distractedly. 'Buying and selling property, put simply.' He reached for his beer again, this time taking a smaller drink of it.

'What? Private property?' Rebecca asked, reaching for her own drink.

'Some,' Richard said, appearing to relax a little. 'Commercial property mostly.'

'So how does it work? I mean, do you just buy buildings and sell them on at a profit?'

Richard smiled. 'It's not quite that simple,' he said. 'I wouldn't make much of a profit if I bought properties at market value. I buy older properties, some historical, in need of repair, do them up and then sell them on. The secret is to identify a buyer and suggest he could buy the property at a lot less than the market value if he buys direct from me before it goes up for sale.'

Rebecca knitted her brow. 'So you have a ready buyer identified before you even make the purchase?'

'That's the gist of it, yes. For example, I might buy at, say, two hundred thousand, spend maybe twenty thousand on necessary repairs, and sell at two hundred and eighty.'

Rebecca was impressed. Aware that Richard knew she'd overheard his conversation that day at the cemetery, she wondered whether impressing her with talk of money had been his intention or he was simply talking shop. She couldn't help but wonder about the ethics of such a transaction either. Wouldn't it exclude other interested buyers?

'Surely there's red tape though?' she asked him. 'Planning permissions to obtain, that sort of thing?'

'Yes, usually.' Richard clasped his hands in front of him and glanced down. 'And no, I don't resort to bribes. Where there are large sums of money, there are always going to be wheelers and dealers, dishonest people. I consider bribery and corruption far too risky. I have my family to consider, after all. Sadly, that now consists only of my daughter.'

He looked back at her – a long, penetrating gaze. 'So, do I pass?' he asked. 'Or do you still consider me a bit dodgy?'

Rebecca was taken aback, both by his forthrightness and his apparent honesty. 'I didn't,' she protested, laughing embarrassedly. 'I don't.'

'Good.' Richard narrowed his eyes briefly, and then smiled more easily. 'I don't need to resort to illegal activity, Becky,' he assured her. 'I was distracted for a while, naturally, and I do still have some figures to juggle to cover my losses, but my business acumen is good. I suppose you could say I'm lucky at gambling, unlucky in love.'

The look now in his eyes was heartbreaking. Rebecca did have cause to want to judge him, and Richard was aware of that. It had all happened so fast. Nicole had been doing so well until he'd come into her life. He'd swept her off her feet, seduced her. Because he'd fallen in love with her? Or might he have had 'figures to juggle' then? That thought had already occurred, but still, Rebecca couldn't make it add up. Nicole, who'd never wavered from her belief that Richard was anything but a kind, caring man, had been comfortable financially, but not wealthy, as Rebecca was. Had Nicole shared that information with him? He must think her reasonably well off, with her own house in France. Would she try to seduce her, she wondered? Perhaps she should be the one to do the seducing? The thought of his hard body pressed close to hers wasn't an unpleasant one. But what then? What if Richard Gray was all he seemed to be: a charming, heartbroken man who'd just lost his wife? If he turned her down, would she have her answer?

'So, do you trust me enough to share a little about yourself?' Richard asked, as she deliberated. 'How you came to live in France? Whether you have someone in your life?' Locking his eyes on hers, he studied her intently. 'Or is that too personal?'

CHAPTER NINETEEN

NICOLE

PREVIOUS YEAR – AUGUST

Once the paramedics were satisfied that Olivia had received the right medication and was out of danger and breathing normally, Richard saw them out and then walked straight past Nicole, who was hovering uncertainly nearby.

Going across to the far side of the kitchen, he stood with his back to her for a long, agonising moment.

Nicole waited, apprehension twisting her stomach. She'd learned in the past that silence was her safest option: the best way to avoid the full wrath of her first husband's vileness for whatever imagined crime she'd committed. She'd sworn she would never do that again. Yet she had no idea what to say. What could she say that would make Richard believe she hadn't done anything with malice in her heart? That she would never, ever dream of causing harm to Olivia in such a calculated way? There was no way to tell him that she suspected it was Olivia who was trying to harm her. To do that would be to fall into the trap, to be seen by Richard as the one making ridiculous allegations. That was what Olivia wanted, she was sure of it.

Sighing heavily, Richard finally turned to face her. 'I'm sensing some resentment, Nicole,' he said, massaging his forehead tiredly. 'I think I'm going to need some help understanding what's going on.'

Nicole felt relief surge through her body. Closing her eyes, she thanked God that he could see it, too. 'She seems to hate me,' she said quickly. 'Ever since the incident on our wedding day. I'm not sure why – whether she holds me responsible in some way – but she clearly resents me. Every time we're together, she interrupts on some pretext or other.' She glanced over her shoulder, half expecting to see Olivia standing behind them, despite the apparently debilitating asthma attack. 'Everything I do seems to cause a problem for her. I have no idea…'

Seeing Richard's incredulous expression, Nicole trailed off. He hadn't meant Olivia's resentment of her, she realised, cold trepidation creeping through her. He thought *she* was resentful of Olivia. He truly did.

'She lives here, Nicole,' he said, his tone terse. Nicole couldn't fail to see the flash of fury in his eyes. 'And what you did today *did* cause a problem. A quite considerable problem. She could have died, for Christ's sake!'

Nicole's stomach tightened like a slip knot as he moved towards her, fear born of years being on the receiving end of a man's explosive temper causing her to step instinctively back.

At this, Richard stopped. 'You really do have some issues, don't you, Nicole?' he said, his expression one of astonishment.

She had issues? 'I didn't *know!*' Nicole protested vehemently. 'I had no idea she suffered from asthma. She never said. *You* never—'

'She told you she has allergies!' Richard pointed out, running his hand agitatedly through his hair. 'Did you not think that might include poisonous fumes?'

'To dogs' hairs!' Nicole countered, hating herself for her weakness as tears sprang to her eyes. She'd *sworn.* She'd promised herself she would never let a man reduce her to tears again. 'Yet you have Wanderer, a long-haired golden retriever! How was I supposed—'

'Who stays downstairs,' Richard reminded her. 'She was trying to *talk* to you, Nicole, but you obviously weren't listening.' His face taut with anger, he glanced at the ceiling, and then, 'This is useless,' he said, striding past her, causing Nicole to flinch.

'Richard!' Nicole stopped him. 'This is wrong. *All* wrong. You *know* me. You know I would never do anything as awful or careless as Olivia is implying.'

Tugging in a breath, Richard stayed where he was. 'The thing is, I don't know you that well, do I, Nicole?' he said eventually, his tone more subdued as he turned back to face her. 'I do know my daughter is asthmatic though.'

He searched her face for a long, soul-crushing moment, then shook his head and turned away.

'Richard, please…' Nicole tried. 'You *have* to believe me.'

Richard paused. 'It's probably best if we discuss this further when emotions are less fraught,' he suggested, after a second. 'Meanwhile, I'm sorry, but Bouncer needs to stay downstairs in future. And please do something about those lethal fumes.'

Watching him walk away, Nicole felt disorientated, as if the ground had been ripped from underneath her, leaving her freefalling into space. Bouncer followed her everywhere. He was like her little shadow. She looked across to where he sat in the middle of the kitchen, his tail thumping nervously on the floor, his huge, chocolate-brown eyes beseeching. He'd slept on her bed in her own house. Richard knew how she'd struggled, after moving here, even to leave him downstairs at night. She'd only been able to because he'd had Wanderer for company.

And now it seemed he was banned. As was she – from intimacy with her husband, from her art. Olivia thought she was winning. Nicole felt something harden inside her. Well, she was wrong. Being married to the misogynist had taught her the art of survival. She would play the game. She would bring the canvases down and work in the garage if need be. She would vacuum every dog's hair and speck of dust from the house.

Marching to the utility room, she grappled the vacuum from the cupboard, cursing as she caught her shins on it. Heaving it upstairs, she avoided looking at Olivia as she passed her bedroom, though Olivia was watching her. Nicole could sense her eyes on her, like a cat choosing its moment to pounce.

Hearing her put her music on speaker, Nicole took some small pleasure from turning the vacuum on and making as much noise as she could while she worked.

Finally, everything free of dust and largely non-existent dogs' hairs, including curtains and blinds, she switched the vacuum off and dragged it back to the landing, realising that Olivia was on her phone as she did. Not being inclined to eavesdrop – and in favour of getting her art materials out of the house to the sanctuary of the garage, where she could at least vent some frustration through painting – Nicole turned back to her short-lived studio. And then stopped.

'She won't last long,' she heard Olivia say assuredly. 'She's so needy, it's pathetic.'

Nicole's blood froze in her veins. *Her.* She meant her.

Bitch. Walking back to the large, airy room she'd intended to work in, Nicole surveyed the canvas she'd already swept with broad strokes of vibrant reds, greens and whites. She was trembling, she realised. Because of *her.* Biting back the cry of rage rising inside her, she snatched up a large bristle brush and slashed it through the still-wet oils, again and again, diagonally, vertically, horizontally, over and over, finally swirling the paint into a vast grey-green sludge.

Her anger eventually abating, her energy depleted, Nicole paused, her chest heaving. She was giving her what she wanted. Giving in to destructive emotion, which could only lead to argument. Now Olivia wouldn't have to work at destroying her marriage. She would simply sit innocently by and watch gleefully while Nicole destroyed it herself.

*

Covered in paint after heaving her materials and canvases to the garage, Nicole sat on the floor amongst a chaos of canvases and texted Becky. She needed to hear a voice of reason.

Dear lovely Becky, do you think there's part of me that's fundamentally selfish? I ask because Olivia seems to think I'm driving a wedge between her and her father, so I can keep him all to myself. I'm not, or at least I didn't think I was. She's also accused me of trying to poison her with fumes while I was priming my canvases. She's asthmatic apparently. I didn't do anything intentionally. Though I'm tempted. In short, we're not getting on. At all. As I don't get on with my mother and the misogynist said no man could ever live with someone as vile and self-centred as me... I'm beginning to wonder, is it me?

Hearing the side garage door open, Nicole looked up to see Richard coming in bearing a mug.

'Hey,' he said, offering her a small smile as he came towards her. 'I brought you a coffee.'

Nicole felt like ignoring him, but then, wouldn't that behaviour be as childish as Olivia's? She was older – more mature, supposedly. Right then, she felt like weeping like a baby.

'It has some brandy in it. The good stuff,' he tried. 'I thought you could use it.'

Realising her reluctance to meet his gaze, Richard parked the mug on the floor and then crouched down, clasping his hands in front of him. 'I don't blame you,' he said, 'for what happened with Olivia, or for not speaking to me. I've been an idiot. I was worried about her – terrified, for a while there – but that's no excuse for blaming you. Can you forgive me?'

Nicole glanced up and, seeing the sincerity in his eyes, very nearly burst into tears.

'You can take a swing at me if it'll make you feel better.' He smiled sheepishly.

Nicole felt her mouth twitch in response. 'I don't do violence,' she said, doing her best to look haughty.

'I think your canvases might beg to differ,' Richard pointed out, glancing around him at the bedlam that was the garage floor.

'Only to inanimate objects.' Nicole winced inwardly. Had she really done all this in a temper?

'I'll make sure to keep moving then.' Richard's smile reached his eyes, at last. 'Incidentally, I know it's a bit of a cliché, but did anyone ever tell you that you look gorgeous with green paint all over your face? Like an adorable little leprechaun.'

Nicole laughed. 'Twit.' She sniffled and glanced hastily around for something with which to wipe her face and her nose.

'Sleeve?' Seeing her predicament, Richard offered his smart shirt sleeve.

'You're bonkers.' Nicole wiped an errant tear from her eye with the cuff of her jumper.

'So they tell me.' Richard reached out, grazing a thumb across her green-painted cheek. 'Come back inside, Nicole,' he said softly. 'We can sort this lot out—' Hearing a frantic scraping at the door, he stopped.

'Wherever his mistress goes…' Richard shook his head good-naturedly. 'I'll go and take him in, lest we end up with a camo-print dog. Back in a sec.'

Giving her a reassuring smile, he pulled himself to his feet and headed off to rescue Bouncer.

Just so you know, Richard's being really supportive, despite being torn down the middle. Can't help feeling sorry for him, poor soul. Will fill you in more soon. LOVE U. Nicole. X

Quickly sending a second text, hoping Becky wouldn't worry too much about her first, Nicole scrambled up, grabbed her coffee and went to join Richard. She wasn't sure about the adorable little leprechaun bit, but he really was lovely. She could understand him being so worried, but he didn't have it in him to be anything but caring and kind.

She wouldn't let Olivia spoil this for her. That girl – no, woman – had underestimated her if she thought she wouldn't fight for her man. She would stay standing. She would bide her time until she'd gone. If there was one valuable thing she'd learned from her first marriage, it was how to do that. Curiously, she'd had no sense of guilt when she'd made up her mind to watch and wait, squirrelling bits of money into the bank account her husband had had no knowledge of. Her many trips to the hospital had allowed her the little freedom she'd had to do that. The private investigation company had provided the evidence of his nefarious activities with the women he'd paid. Michael – misogynist, abuser, murderer of women's spirits – had gathered she was serious, that she would fight back with whatever she had, when she'd posted that evidence to him the day after she'd left him – along with the client list obtained from his PC. Michael, a financial advisor, had realised that many of those clients, some wealthy older women who'd followed his investment advice, wouldn't be overly impressed with his habits.

CHAPTER TWENTY

REBECCA

PRESENT

After a week at Richard's house, and with the heatwave predicted to last at least another week, Rebecca was feeling more at ease with him. He'd helped her go through the canvases Nicole had left behind in the garage and the spare room, handling them reverently, though he was as aware as she was that they were expressions of sombre moods and not reflective of the Nicole that Rebecca had known – not even when she'd been at her lowest, during her first marriage.

Rebecca had decided to keep one: a smaller canvas which at least had a ray of hope, a splash of yellow amongst the grey. Several of the watercolours, along with Nicole's art materials, she'd decided to keep, including the one of Bouncer and Wanderer together, some of the Worcestershire landscape and a couple of prophetic water studies. The caged lark – she would keep that, too. Nicole had felt trapped. The painting clearly showed that. It had been a cry for help. Rebecca felt sure that Nicole had been communicating through her art what she'd felt unable to with words. She'd been scared when she'd painted it, Rebecca sensed it. Whether of shadows in her mind or of real people, Rebecca didn't know, but she wouldn't rest until she had answers.

Reflecting on the last week, in which Richard had been nothing but amiable and courteous, she debated what her next move should be while gathering greens from the fridge to make up a salad to accompany the pasta she was making for dinner. She was checking the ingredients of the pasta sauce – and sneakily feeding lumps of cheese to Bouncer and Wanderer – when Sam, Laura and Olivia came downstairs. Sam and Olivia were carrying rackets, Rebecca noticed – obviously about to take advantage of the slightly cooler evening air and play tennis. 'Remember to take some water,' she suggested, as the three headed for the patio.

'Got it.' Olivia stopped fussing over Wanderer and waved a bottle of water in her direction.

'Damn. Forgot my book. Have to have something to entertain me while you two are grunting on court,' Laura said, about-facing to go back to her room.

'Excuse me,' Olivia huffed indignantly. 'I do no such thing. It's Sam who makes all the piggy noises.'

'Ha, ha,' Sam replied dryly, and then called after Laura, 'You don't have to come, Laura. It's probably a bit boring for you.'

Laura stopped. 'But I want to,' she said, sounding piqued. 'I like watching you play.'

Evidently hearing the hurt in her tone, Sam went after her, his expression contrite, as well it should be. It seemed to Rebecca that Laura was beginning to feel like a gooseberry. Sam needed to be aware that Olivia was hogging too much of his time – deliberately, it seemed.

Collecting her own drink, Rebecca followed Olivia out, thinking she might take a dip in the pool. Hearing Olivia talking to Richard as she was about to step out on to the patio, however, she hung back a little.

'Can't say I blame her for wanting to keep her eye on him,' Olivia said, idly plucking an olive from the dish that was already on the table.

'Liv…' Richard gave her an admonishing glance.

'What?' Olivia's eyes grew wide with innocence. 'I've no idea what he's doing with her anyway. If you ask me, it's Laura who's boring. She doesn't play tennis, doesn't want to swim. I mean, this bookworm thing might look all Brontë-ish and romantic, but really? She wants to sit under the shade of the oak tree rather than swim in the pool with her hot boyfriend or cool off on the patio with a cocktail? Weird, in my opinion.'

'You weren't asked for your opinion though, Liv, were you?' Catching her eye as she helped herself to another olive, Richard nodded towards where Rebecca had decided to make her presence known.

'Shoot!' Spinning around, Olivia almost choked on the olive. 'Sorry, Becky,' she said, an embarrassed flush to her cheeks. 'I didn't realise you were there.'

'Obviously,' Richard said drily.

'Apology accepted. It might not be a good idea to let Sam or Laura hear you though.' Rebecca smiled, quietly wondering what Olivia might be up to. It might be nothing, of course, but Rebecca knew she wasn't all sweetness and light like she pretended to be. The girl definitely had the hots for Sam, which was worrying. Sam would have to be on his guard.

'All set?' Olivia asked, as Laura and Sam reappeared. Laura was looking happier, with Sam holding firmly on to her hand. They'd kissed and made up then. That was good.

'Yes, thanks.' Smiling, Laura indicated her book, while Sam gave his mum a slightly sheepish look. The two headed after Olivia, who was leading the way around the house to the tennis court. Keen to be gone, Rebecca suspected, after putting her foot in it.

'I'll put the pasta on when they get back,' she said, sitting down on the lounger next to Richard.

'Perfect,' Richard said. 'Meanwhile, how about we indulge ourselves with a pre-dinner drink?'

'I'd love one.' Rebecca sighed blissfully and settled back. 'Something long and cool would be lovely.'

'Chilled wine?' Richard suggested, downing his book and getting to his feet. 'Vodka orange? G and T? With ice and a slice, of course.'

'He knows me too well.' Rebecca smiled. 'G and T please. Not too heavy on the G though, unless you like congealed pasta.'

'Love it.' Richard smiled back and relieved her of her empty orange glass. 'Sorry about Liv's thoughtless comments. She can be a little tactless sometimes.'

Rebecca nodded. 'It's forgotten. We can't be responsible for everything they do.'

'No,' Richard mused as he went to play bartender. 'We sometimes need to remind ourselves of that.'

'It really is a beautiful house. It's such a pity you have to sell,' Rebecca commented, watching him preparing the drinks with practised expertise. He was the perfect host, and very easy on the eye. She'd enjoyed watching him in the pool. His torso was athletic, lean and muscular, his skin tanned a perfect shade of copper. It would be no hardship having sex with the man. Could she go through with it though? He'd certainly given signals he was interested: his hands lingering longer than necessary while applying her sun cream; an unmistakeable glint of desire in his eyes when she'd twisted to face him, catching him unawares. But even entertaining the idea of intimacy with him felt like the biggest betrayal of Nicole. She had to know, though, how far he might go, whether, knowing her financial situation, he would push for more. She could be wrong, horribly wrong, but she still couldn't believe he was as perfect as he seemed.

'I don't have to sell.' Richard came back with the drinks. 'It's just that the house now seems…'

'Empty?' Rebecca supplied.

'Very.' Richard smiled sadly. 'So, tell me about your house. Didn't you say you'd recently sold it?'

'I have, finally,' Rebecca said. 'I'm aiming to move back to the UK as soon as I can now, particularly with Sam wanting to settle here. I'll miss the cottage though. It's pretty and very unusual; not the kind of property you'd find here. A troglodyte dwelling.'

Richard looked bemused. 'A what?'

'Dwellings dug into the slopes and rock faces of the landscape,' Rebecca explained, picking up her phone from the table, selecting a photo and handing it to him. 'They started out as cave-like dwellings, but they're a little more luxurious now.'

'So I see.' Richard scanned the photo of the renovated three-bedroom cottage which overlooked the river, impressed. 'It's beautiful. Worth a fair sum, I imagine. God, sorry...' He looked quickly up at her. 'I didn't mean to pry. It's the property developer in me.'

'You're not after my money then?' Amusedly, Rebecca narrowed her eyes.

Richard smiled ruefully. 'No, I'm not after your money.' He swept his gaze over her, then his eyes came back to hers. His look was intent and meaningful, and he lingered for a long, penetrating moment, causing every inch of Rebecca's skin to tingle.

Flustered, despite her assurances to herself that she was in the driving seat, Rebecca looked away. How was it, she wondered, that those arctic-blue eyes which emanated such deep sadness could also smoulder with such tangible longing?

'You've no family in France then?' he asked interestedly.

Rebecca shook her head. 'My parents had me late in life,' she said. 'I lost them when I was quite young.'

'I'm sorry, Becky,' Richard said quietly. 'That must have been difficult.'

'It was.' Rebecca nodded and searched his face. His expression was earnest.

'No sisters or brothers?' he asked.

'No. I was an only child. Thus my troglodyte dwelling, bought with the money my parents bequeathed me. It was a fair amount, allowing me to buy it in cash.'

Finishing her drink, Rebecca swished the ice around in her glass and glanced down at it, leaving Richard to ponder.

'And you wanted to stay in France after you husband died?' he asked, after a contemplative moment.

'I did. Going home would have felt like leaving him behind. Does that make sense?'

'It does. Perfect sense,' Richard said. 'Another?' He nodded at her glass.

'Please. That definitely hit the spot.' Rebecca smiled, feeling more at ease. Then he reached for the glass and his fingers brushed hers, sending a ripple of sexual tension up the entire length of her spine.

'Good,' he said, his mesmerising gaze again holding hers as he got to his feet. 'He was French then, I take it?' he asked, leaving Rebecca in a state of shock as he went back to the bar.

This was ridiculous. She'd had relationships with men since her husband had died. But always with men she'd considered safe. Men who she'd grown to know rather than plunge into relationships with. This man seemed to be stripping away her ability to consider anything but what his firm body would feel like next to hers. Was this how it had been with Nicole? Had she too been spellbound by his sexual chemistry and irresistible charm?

'Your husband,' he prompted, watching her as he fixed the drinks. 'I assume he was French?'

'Yes,' Rebecca said quickly, attempting to get a rein on her emotions. 'I met him on a mad weekend in Paris, drinking wine and viewing galleries with Nicole. He wanted to paint my portrait and he ended up proposing.'

'I like his style. He obviously knew a good thing when he saw it.' Richard nodded approvingly as he returned with the drinks. 'So, you were swept off your feet by a starving artist then?'

'Well, not exactly starving, thanks to my money,' Rebecca said, dropping a further hint regarding her own financial situation. 'But yes, he would have starved for his art. He was driven, passionate. His work was very evocative – life studies, mostly. Nicole adored it.'

'I imagine I would, too. Particularly life studies of you,' Richard said, holding on to the glass as he passed it to her, the insinuation this time clear. As if he were testing the waters.

Destabilised, Rebecca took a sharp breath. 'I think I'll cool off,' she said, taking the glass. She felt him watching as she placed the glass on the table and slid off her lounger.

Several lengths of the pool later, and feeling more in control, Rebecca swam to the ladder and heaved herself up. Richard walked across to her as she reached the top rung.

'I brought you a towel,' he said, his gaze travelling languidly over her, an implicit question now in his eyes as they came back to hers.

'Thank you.' Rebecca reached for the towel and then took a faltering step back as he stepped closer.

'Careful!' Richard said, his arm encircling her waist as she teetered, yanking her bodily towards him. There was no escaping his eyes then, or the hardness of him and the frisson of primal desire inside her.

Plainly reading what was in her eyes – she couldn't hope to hide it – Richard leaned towards her, seeking her mouth with his, parting her lips so softly that Rebecca felt something beyond physical dissolve inside her. His kiss was slow, deep and passionate, his tongue finding hers, exploring her, tasting her. Warning herself to be very careful of this too attractive man, Rebecca tentatively reciprocated, and then grew bolder as he responded eagerly.

Stopping to catch his breath, he looked into her eyes and then pressed his forehead to hers. 'I want you, Rebecca,' he said, his voice low and husky. A wave of white-hot desire surged right through her.

CHAPTER TWENTY-ONE

NICOLE

PREVIOUS YEAR – SEPTEMBER

In her mother's kitchen, Nicole stowed the provisions she'd bought and then made her another cup of tea. She wasn't sure what had prompted her to visit. She wasn't here by invitation, or because she'd fancied dropping by for a chat. They'd never done that, her mother blaming her 'rebelliousness' – as she'd termed Nicole's desire not to kowtow to her father's will – for the misery and violence she herself had suffered at his hands. Their tenuous mother–daughter relationship had been irretrievably fractured the day Nicole had gone to her for help and her mother had closed the door in her face. Nicole had lost her dear baby girl shortly after that. She'd told herself she hadn't needed her since then.

Lydia, though, clearly needed her. She certainly needed help of some sort. It had taken ages for her to answer the door. When she had, finally, Nicole had been shocked to find not the formidable, house-proud woman she once was, 'too busy doing what needs to be done to waste time on pipedreams and nonsense', but someone so thin and drawn that she looked feeble. The house was still clean – God forbid the woman ever stopped cleaning; or rather, Nicole's father forbid she ever did – but it was no longer so sterile that you could eat off the floor.

Taking the tea through, Nicole placed it on the occasional table next to the armchair and then gently shook her mother's arm.

Lydia woke with a start, her eyes unfocussed for a second before they settled on Nicole. And then they were more resigned than relieved. Still, at least she didn't look disappointed, her normal expression whenever Nicole had been around before.

'I've made you some tea,' she said, nodding towards it. 'I've brought you a chocolate digestive, too.'

'Thank you,' her mother managed, heaving herself up in her seat, glancing at the cup and then sighing in despair. 'Honestly, Nicole.' She glowered up at her. 'You've dribbled tea in the saucer. It will be soggy now. I can't abide soggy biscuits.'

No? Well, you'll just have to like it or lump it then, won't you? Nicole forced a smile. Her mother might look frail, but her tongue was in perfect working order, and as acerbic as it ever was. 'I've brought you some soups and microwavable meals,' she said. 'There are some in the freezer and some in the fridge. All easily digestible: mash and fish, that sort of thing.'

Lydia sniffed, but didn't turn her nose up at her offerings. Since her fall in the garden, when she'd damaged her ankle, she hadn't been able to get out to shops. Nicole had taken her to the doctor's and stocked up her cupboards. She would organise some home help and a gardener – Lydia's garden with its pretty orangery was her pride and joy – but there wasn't a lot else she could do, other than check up on her. They simply didn't have that much in common any more. They never really had.

'I'll get off then,' she said, as her mother munched on the chocolate biscuit, which wasn't so soggy that she would turn her nose up at that either. 'I have to feed Bouncer.'

'Yes, off you go. You obviously have important things to attend to,' Lydia said pointedly, and took a sip of her tea. 'I hope you're attending to your new husband's needs,' she added, the implication being that Nicole's slovenliness was why her first marriage had failed. If only she'd realised, Nicole thought cynically, that she could have hung on to her man if she'd worked harder at pleasing him. Perhaps by not 'whimpering pathetically' when he'd punched her in the stomach, or getting up off the floor quicker to serve him his dinner?

'He's not complaining, Mother,' she said, her smile more of a grimace as she collected up her handbag. She'd been feeling guilty that she hadn't seen much of Lydia since extracting herself from her first marriage. Now she remembered why she hadn't.

'He's treating you well then?' Lydia enquired, clinking the cup into the saucer as Nicole turned to the door.

'If you mean is he abusive, then no, he's not.' Nicole didn't turn around. She doubted she would be able to hide her contempt, given the indifference of that comment. 'He's kind and attentive, and extremely loving,' she imparted, getting some satisfaction as Lydia's cup clinked loudly this time. Her heart fell, though, as she wished there was a little more loving in their relationship. The truth was, they'd hardly dared to touch each other since coming back from their disastrous honeymoon, for fear of Olivia overhearing. With Olivia seemingly prone to asthma attacks whenever Bouncer was in the vicinity, Nicole had taken to keeping their house so clean you actually could eat your dinner off the floor. Richard clearly didn't feel relaxed there, and had taken to working longer hours, but Nicole was damned if she was going to make Bouncer sleep in the garage, which she'd given up working in, as the light was so poor. And she would most definitely *not* take him back to the rescue centre, which she was sure was Olivia's aim. Nicole hated herself for thinking it, especially when faced with Olivia's wheezing and panting, but she did wonder, particularly since she always seemed to make such a fuss of Wanderer, whether some of her symptoms weren't feigned.

She didn't dare suggest that, though. As she'd promised herself she would, she was biding her time instead, praying Olivia would get one of the many jobs she was applying for and leave. Or else that she would do something that would tear the scales from Richard's eyes. Meanwhile, God help her, Nicole was becoming so fastidious about cleanliness that she was in danger of turning into her mother.

'You should bring him round,' Lydia suggested.

'Yes, possibly,' Nicole said, picking up her jacket, which she'd amazingly gotten away with not hanging up, from the arm of the sofa. *Not*, she thought.

'I'd like to meet him, Nicole,' Lydia said, as she headed for the hall and the front door. 'I know you don't think I care, but I do. I would like to see you settled with a good man before I die.'

That stopped Nicole in her tracks. 'Maybe,' she said, ridiculous tears pricking her eyes. 'I'll mention it to him.'

Should she bring him, she wondered, letting herself out. While she wasn't sure she wanted Richard to meet Lydia, who would no doubt embarrass her in his presence – hinting that if only she'd given the misogynist children, forgetting the child he'd caused her to lose, then her husband would have been happy and fulfilled – she would like her mother to see that a normal, kind man thought her worthy of his love. That it didn't come with a caveat that she attend his every whim, no matter how demeaning or painful. That she had to change who she fundamentally was.

She was pondering whether to mention her visit that evening when Richard came home. He looked tired. Nicole knew the tension between Olivia and her was stressful, but she wished he would come home more. 'Hi.' She smiled, switching the vacuum off.

Richard offered her a small smile in return. 'Hi,' he said. 'Still at it, I see.' He nodded at the vacuum.

'Dogs' hairs,' Nicole explained, as the furry culprits who'd had the effrontery to shed them bounded from the kitchen to greet him.

His look turning from one of patient resignation to pleased, Richard bent to give them a fuss. Both of them, Nicole noticed, reminded why she loved him. He was everything the misogynist hadn't been: a caring man who was trying to do his best for everyone around him. He loved Bouncer as much as she did. He would never see any harm come to him. He was simply trying to do his best. He believed his daughter had been attacked, in the worst possible way, and he had to be there for her, as any good, loving father should be. He was trying to be there for her, too – Nicole knew he was. It was tearing him apart. She needed to reach out to him, be there for him, even if meant tolerating the situation with Olivia a little longer.

'Good day?' she asked him.

'Busy.' He smiled wearily. 'You?'

'An odd one,' Nicole admitted, parking the vacuum under the stairs. Any hairs she'd missed would have to wait until morning. Olivia had gone out, which she rarely did, bypassing Nicole with barely an acknowledgement. She'd been on the phone to Lydia at the time, checking that she'd eaten something. Hopefully, she wouldn't find cause to have an asthma attack when she got back tonight. 'I decided to go and see my mother.'

'Oh?' Depositing his briefcase on the floor and shrugging out of his jacket, Richard eyed her curiously, as he would, knowing that she and her mother didn't exactly get on.

'She's not well, so I'm thinking I might have to see a bit more of her. Not that I particularly want to.'

'She needs care then?' Richard asked, following her through to the sitting room.

'More keeping an eye on, really,' Nicole said, going to the drinks table to fix him a whisky and herself a large wine, which she felt she'd earned. 'She had a fall. She couldn't get out to the shops and she hasn't been eating properly.'

'Couldn't she shop online?' Richard suggested, accepting the whisky gratefully.

'She doesn't have a laptop.' Nicole said, with a roll of her eyes. Richard looked surprised at that.

'Technology passed her by a bit, sadly. She didn't work,' Nicole explained. Having a job, in her father's estimation, would have meant his wife having a life of her own, and possibly even an opinion, which would have been intolerable. 'I'm organising some home help for her, someone to cook her meals and do a bit of cleaning, but I think I'll have to pop in now and then until she's on her feet.'

'And are you okay with that?' Richard asked, a concerned frown crossing his face, reminding her again that she had a good man, one she intended to hold on to, despite his daughter.

Nicole took a gulp of her wine, feeling nervous about mentioning that Lydia had invited him to visit. She didn't want to put him on the spot, and she'd hardly painted a picture of her mother as someone he would particularly want to meet. Plus, he was so very busy with work. 'She asked about you,' she said lightly. 'She said she'd quite like to meet you.'

Richard swished his drink contemplatively around his glass. 'Do you *want* her to meet me?' he asked, his expression uncertain as he looked back at her.

Nicole was taken aback. 'Of course,' she said. 'I can't wait to show you off. What woman wouldn't want to? You're gorgeous and generous and caring and…' She trailed off, thinking she might be overdoing it a bit.

Richard mouth twitched into a smile. 'You forgot sexy.'

'And that.' Taking in the toned, tanned length and breadth of him, temptingly packaged in his grey business suit, Nicole sighed wistfully. 'Definitely that.'

Richard took a step towards her, placing his glass down on the long chrome and glass coffee table, which had been meticulously dusted. Studying it for second, he turned his attention back to her, his expression troubled. 'So, you do still find me desirable then?'

What? Nicole's eyes boggled at that.

'It's just that… Well, you know, you seem to have been keeping your distance, and I thought that maybe you… didn't.' He stopped, shrugging awkwardly.

Incredulous, Nicole stared at him. 'Are you mad?' She laughed. 'I thought that *you* didn't want to. With what happened with Olivia, I mean, and her being here.'

Still, he looked unsure. A man like him, who knew exactly how to please a woman? Nicole could hardly believe it. 'I desire you so much, I'm about to explode with frustration,' she said.

Clearly confounded, Richard studied her for a second, and then his mouth curved into a deliciously slow smile. 'In which case, I think I might need to do something to help you release it,' he said, his eyes gliding over her body before coming to rest meaningfully on hers. 'It may require the removal of certain items of clothing. Shall we?' He nodded towards the bedrooms.

Nicole felt nervous, ridiculously, as he followed her upstairs. It wasn't yet dark, and she preferred no light – or, at least, subdued light. She still wasn't sure she was ready to reveal all of herself in broad daylight. How on earth was she going to undress right in front of him?

Richard didn't give her the chance to ponder her dilemma for too long. Closing the door behind her and sliding across the lock, he moved purposefully towards her, yanking off his tie, popping buttons and tugging his shirt over his head as he did.

His eyes growing purposeful, he reached out and slid the straps of her dress slowly over her shoulders, then the straps of her bra. Nicole caught a breath in her throat as he slid the garments further down, exposing her breasts. Instinctively, she moved to wrap her arms about herself.

He caught them, lowering them back to her sides. 'Don't hide yourself, Nicole,' he said softly. 'Never be embarrassed in the company of a man. You're an exceptionally beautiful woman.'

He cupped her face in his hand. Nicole turned her cheek to his touch, her desire spiking as he dragged a thumb over her lower lip.

'Your face, your body… you're beautiful,' he assured her, sweeping his gaze down over her then looking back at her, a flash of heat now in his eyes.

She held her breath as he peeled her clothes further down, freeing first one foot of the restricting garments and then the other. Wordlessly, he kissed his way back up her body. Then, his eyes on hers, a smouldering intensity now therein, he stood and guided her towards the bed, taking hold of her arms and urging her to lie down. 'Beautiful,' he repeated, his gaze never moving from hers as he eased her legs apart. Nicole wasn't beautiful, she knew that, but seeing herself through his eyes, she almost believed that she was.

Lowering himself over her, he scanned her face, as if looking for confirmation. Then, finding what he needed, he pressed himself into her, thrusting deeply. And again. Slowly increasing the pace, building the momentum, until he felt so incredibly deep, he filled her to the brim. She felt full, physically and emotionally. She whimpered as he picked up the tempo, thrusting still deeper and deeper, with fast, sure strokes. She wanted him to. She needed him to.

Nicole undulated under him, raising her hips to meet him, matching him, thrust for thrust, pushing her tongue deep into his mouth, biting his lips, breathing into him. Dragging her fingernails down his back. Her muscles clenching around him in one flowing contraction, her climax exploded with such ferocity that she sobbed out his name.

His eyes smouldering above her, Richard thrust one last time, and then, with a throaty moan, he came. She felt his release. Felt a drop of sweat fall on to her forehead. His breathing was ragged. He closed his eyes, exhaling hard, his beautiful dark eyelashes brushing his cheeks.

'Sorry,' he murmured. 'I, er… It was a bit rushed.' He smiled and kissed her eyelashes. 'We'll take it more slowly next time.'

'It was perfect,' she assured him, revelling in the novelty of climaxing with a man, let alone a man who cared whether she did.

Richard laughed. 'Roll over on your side,' he said, the mischievous glint back in his eye as he lay down beside her. 'Tuck that gorgeous bottom into me and I'll be ready to go again in no time.'

'You're bad, Richard Gray,' Nicole scolded, turning to nestle into him. *Bliss*, she thought, wanting to preserve these few precious moments before Olivia came home.

'I know,' Richard said, finding her ear under her mad mess of hair and brushing it with his lips. 'See what you do to me?'

'I thought we were spooning,' Nicole said after a second, realising he was perched on his elbow, studying her.

'We are.' Richard settled back behind her, encircling her waist and pulling her close. 'I was just wondering about your mother.'

'Oh.' Nicole's blissful contentment evaporated. 'What about her?'

'I'm sensing you're worried about her,' Richard said thoughtfully. 'You hardly ever mention her normally.'

Nicole was quiet for a minute. Then, 'She looks very frail,' she admitted, her guilt that she hadn't visited her more often resurfacing, though she wasn't certain she should feel that way.

Richard kissed her shoulder. 'Not good news,' he said.

'No.' Nicole sighed, lightly tracing the hairs on the arm he had wrapped tightly around her. 'She said she wanted to meet you before she died.'

Richard squeezed her tighter. 'I'm sorry, Nicole,' he offered. 'That must be difficult, particularly with unresolved issues between you.'

Nicole nodded. 'It is. Do you think I should see her?'

Richard hesitated. 'I think you have good reason not to want to, but, to be honest, I don't think you would be able to live with yourself if you didn't.'

He knew her so well. Nicole marvelled at how comfortable she felt right now. She wished it could always be this way. That Olivia would go away and live her own life. She was young, but Nicole really did feel as if she didn't want her father to have a life. 'You're right,' she said. 'I wouldn't.'

'Be kind to yourself, though, Nicole. Don't let yourself be emotionally manipulated by her.' Richard warned. 'You should take the opportunity to make sure her affairs are in order, too.'

'I hadn't thought about that,' Nicole said pensively.

'I didn't think you had, being so selfless.' Richard sighed, pseudo-despairingly. 'You might feel you're being mercenary, but it's actually pragmatic, if you think about it. Long-term care costs money. As well as which, in my estimation she owes you.'

He was right. Nicole had told herself she didn't care if her mother left her money to some obscure charity, but she supposed she did. It would confirm that Lydia didn't care about her at all. Then there was the issue of the cost of care. 'She has plenty,' she said. If her father had done nothing else for Lydia, he'd left her well provided for. 'And her house is worth a fair amount.' At least five hundred thousand, Nicole thought. The Georgian property was desperately in need of refurbishment, but still, it would fetch a tidy sum. Enough to make sure Lydia was comfortable if she should need more care.

'Let me know if you need help finding someone to organise her estate,' Richard said, pressing a light kiss against her hair. 'You'll need someone who's trustworthy.'

Normally Nicole wouldn't dream of texting someone regarding her love life, but Becky was her best friend, and probably the only person in the world who would understand why her heart was beginning to feel whole again.

Dear lovely Becky, all is well! We made love! Spectacularly! Richard's currently downstairs fetching some chilled wine, so I'll keep this short. Just wanted to reassure you that he's there for me. He was as confused as I was about the distance between us. And as desperate, it seems. Hope you're okay, my lovely. We have to meet up soon! Much love, Nicole. X

Becky texted smartly back: *Dearest Nicole. Did he live up to expectations?*

Yes. And he's about to live up to them again shortly.

Go easy on him. xxx

CHAPTER TWENTY-TWO

REBECCA

PRESENT

Rebecca closed her eyes as he pulled her towards him. His kiss was urgent this time – deeper, more sensual. His hands were in her hair, gliding down her back, everywhere.

Rebecca caught a gasp in her throat. With Nicole barely cold in her grave, she'd wanted to know how far he would go. She'd been testing him, searching for facets of his character that would… what? Cause a woman to slide into such a deep depression that she would take her own life? Nicole had been stronger than that. She'd grown stronger. There had to be more – something above and beyond the familial feud she was aware of. She'd baited him, wanting him to make a move on her sexually, needing to know what his next move would be; whether he was what Nicole had so quaintly termed a 'gigolo'. But now she was in dangerous waters. She wanted him. Wanted this. It was as if the electric charge between them had ignited something primal inside her. Her breasts tingled in anticipation as he traced her neck with his lips, his hands now sliding the straps of her swimsuit over her shoulders. She had to stay in control. She had to go through with this in order to establish whether his seduction of women had an agenda, but she couldn't allow her emotions to become embroiled, no matter how perfect a front he presented. And if he was what he seemed, what then? She would find out. She had to.

'Not here,' she whispered, her voice tinged with fear, of being discovered, of this.

Richard scanned her face, his expression a mixture of frustration and obvious relief that she hadn't said 'not at all'.

'There.' He nodded towards the pool house, which wasn't particularly spacious but was situated away from the main house and therefore adequate for purpose.

Taking her by the hand, he led her that way. Checking over his shoulder, clearly as concerned as she that they might be seen, he guided her in before him, closed and locked the door, pulled the blind and flicked on the light. Then he turned, his eyes dark and intense as he swept his gaze over her. Wordlessly, he stepped towards her, one hand going behind her head, his fingers entwined in her damp hair, the other tugging aside restricting clothing as he urged her back against the cold tiles of the wall.

With his hands cupping her face, his kiss was tender yet possessive. She smelled sweat and chlorine, felt the nearness of him, the firmness of his flesh overwhelming her senses. His tongue found hers as he pressed himself closer. Did he have no sense of guilt at all? Of shame? Did she?

His own breathing heavy, he paused, easing his face away from hers. There was a flicker of doubt now in his eyes: a question. Guilt: it was there.

Closing her eyes, Rebecca nodded her answer.

'You're beautiful. I want to see you. Look at me, Rebecca,' he murmured hoarsely, bringing his mouth back to hers. 'Let me see you.'

Rebecca did. Difficult though it was not to close her eyes, she watched him, looking at her as he entered her. Aware of her sharp intake of breath, he paused again, checking that she was okay. She smiled her reassurance, part of her glad that he had, another part of her sad that she was unashamedly testing him.

Richard smiled, withdrawing from her and thrusting slowly into her again. Stroking her hair from her face, he locked his eyes on hers and increased the pace, moving with deep, sure strokes.

Sliding his hands up her body, weaving them through her hair, he kissed her hungrily. 'Tell me when, Rebecca?' he whispered. 'Come with me.'

'Now,' she cried, a tear escaping her eye as a white-hot spasm clenched her muscles around him, followed by another, and Richard groaned throatily and jolted inside her.

'Christ,' he muttered, exhaling hard and resting his forehead against hers. 'Okay?' he asked her, concern now clouding his magnetic blue eyes.

'Yes, I…' Her emotions hopelessly confused, despite her promise to herself not to allow them to be, Rebecca glanced away. She'd wanted to dictate the pace while allowing him to imagine he was. Now, she wasn't sure who was leading whom. How dark would the dance grow?

'We shouldn't have,' Richard said, his tone full of obvious regret. '*I* shouldn't have.' Dropping his head to her shoulder, he swallowed hard.

'It was wrong,' Rebecca breathed, wanting to hold him and, equally, to push him away.

Richard's gaze came back to hers. 'Then why did it feel so right?' he asked her, an agonised look now in his eyes, as if he needed her somehow to absolve him.

CHAPTER TWENTY-THREE

OLIVIA

PRESENT

He really should have taken the time to make sure the blind was properly drawn. Her cheeks feeling hot, Olivia walked quickly away from the pool house. God forbid Sam should have walked past. He would undoubtedly have been shocked to see his mother behaving like a complete whore. And boring Laura, who was probably saving her virginity, to poor Sam's frustration, would have been traumatised for life after witnessing such a display of wantonness.

She hadn't imagined Rebecca would be able to resist for long. He was a good-looking man. With his height and undeniably attractive physique, women also perceived him as strong, but he wasn't. He was weak. He fell in love too easily. Rebecca, though, was wary, no doubt conflicted by notions of loyalty. And precisely because of that, she would enjoy him all the more: her dear, recently departed friend's husband, who was now her lover.

Watching Richard emerge from the pool house – clearly thinking it prudent they leave separately – Olivia bit into the apple she'd fetched from the kitchen and licked her lips with the pink tip of her tongue. *Bittersweet.*

Catching sight of her, Richard walked across, his expression guilty, as it would be.

Smiling when he reached her, Olivia decided to tease him a little. 'So, what have *you* two been up to? Anything interesting?' She took another languid bite of her apple.

Searching her eyes, Richard smiled awkwardly. 'Just talking,' he said. 'Getting to know each other a little better.'

Olivia arched an eyebrow. 'Oh yes?' She smirked, and then looked past him to where Sam and Laura were coming around the side of the house. 'It's a good job Sam didn't walk by while you were "getting to know each other". He might not approve.'

Richard glanced in Sam's direction and then looked back to her, his eyes holding a warning.

As if she would say anything to Rebecca's son at this delicate time in their budding relationship and ruin everything. Honestly, she wasn't completely naive. He knew her better than that.

'Hi.' Coming across to them, Laura still hanging on to his hand like a needy child, Sam smiled warmly. He had a gorgeous smile. Perfect teeth. Olivia was tempted to offer him a bite of her apple but guessed that Laura might be put out by the obvious symbolism. 'Where's Mum?' he asked, scanning the patio.

'In the pool house, cooling off,' Olivia supplied.

'She's taking a shower after her swim.' Richard smiled embarrassedly.

'She got a bit hot and sticky in the pool,' Olivia added, and twirled around to head back to the house. 'I'll put the pasta on,' she called back. 'Don't want Becky getting all flustered because she got distracted and forgot, do we?'

'I'll give you a hand,' Laura offered, but not sounding particularly keen, Olivia detected. It was a shame, really. The girl was to be pitied for her obvious lack of sexual allure, possibly more than Sam was. Clearly she would feel inferior in her company – more so without Rebecca around to protect her delicate sensibilities.

Nonetheless, Olivia enthusiastically accepted her offer. She didn't want Sam thinking she was a bitch, although he was obviously turned on by the fact that she had a bit of spark. Boring Laura was so wooden, she practically blended in with the trees she insisted on reading her silly books beneath.

Delegating her the job of chopping the onion, garlic and peppers, rather than get crap under her nail extensions herself, Olivia attended to the job of watching the pan of water boil for the penne, pausing in her efforts to beam Sam a smile as he came in with Richard. 'Do you want to grab a red wine, Sam?' she asked him, indicating the wine rack. 'I think you and Dad prefer red, don't you?'

Sam eyed Richard enquiringly.

'The Cabernet Sauvignon's good.' Richard nodded towards it.

'Cheers.' Sam smiled. 'Laura and I will go into town and get some wine for when we next eat in,' he offered, heading across the kitchen. He really was a catch, Olivia thought: caring and conscientious, and way too sexy for boring Laura.

'No need. We have plenty,' Richard said. 'Actually, Sam, while your mum's not here and I've got you and Olivia together, do you think I could run something by you?'

Selecting the wine, Sam looked back at him, his brow furrowed curiously. 'Shoot,' he said.

Richard now definitely looked awkward, like a nervous school-boy, which was rather endearing. 'I, er, wondered if either of you would have any objections if Rebecca and I…' He stopped, clearly searching for the right words.

Fucked? Olivia mentally supplied, smiling interestedly.

'That is, I wondered it would be okay with you, Sam, if I asked Rebecca out to dinner?'

Aw, how old-fashioned. Olivia smirked with amusement in Richard's direction, which he did his utmost to ignore.

Taken aback, Sam stared bemusedly at him, while Laura almost chopped her fingers off. Olivia guessed the poor girl was aware of the chemistry between her and Sam, and was wondering whether she might have just heard the death knell sound on her relationship. It was obvious that Laura couldn't wait for the holiday to be over so she could keep him all to herself. Alas, Olivia would be seeing much more of him now. Of course, she would have to remind Sam that they wouldn't actually be related. She had a feeling Sam might have principles, unlike his mother.

'I know it's soon after my wife…' Richard went falteringly on, 'but… well, we like each other, and…' He shrugged and stopped.

Sam nodded in contemplation. 'I noticed you two seemed to be getting along,' he said. 'I don't have any objections, as long as you're sure you're ready for a relationship?'

He eyed Richard questioningly. Olivia had to admit she was impressed by his thoughtfulness.

'Ahem.' Rebecca – decently attired in her sarong – coughed from the doorway. 'Thank you, Sam,' she said. 'And do I get any say in this?'

'Damn,' Richard muttered, no doubt realising he'd been presumptuous. Massaging his forehead, he turned to Rebecca and mouthed 'Sorry' in her direction.

Rebecca's expression was admonishing, but Olivia noted the amusement in her eyes.

Hooked, definitely. Olivia gave Laura a wink and slid the pasta into the water.

CHAPTER TWENTY-FOUR

NICOLE

PREVIOUS YEAR – OCTOBER

Nicole hadn't been sure the local art shop would take any of her paintings. The oils on canvas they might have been interested in displaying, but the landscapes in watercolours she'd taken to painting while she searched for an alternative studio… She'd imagined they would have those in abundance, produced by local artists. She was pleasantly surprised, however.

'These are really good,' the owner, Isobel, enthused, already halfway across the shop to put Nicole's study of the swirling woodland mist, entitled *After the Rain*, on display in the shop window. It was a painting she had embarked on in one of her more contemplative moods – largely contemplating whether she'd been misinterpreting Olivia's antagonism towards her, and whether she might have misjudged her because she actually was jealous of Richard's obvious love for his daughter, in which case that did make her a selfish, insecure person.

'I'm experimenting with watercolours at the moment,' Nicole said, her confidence boosted by the woman's obvious enthusiasm. 'My stepdaughter suffers with asthma and she's allergic to the fumes from oil paints, so I'm having to look for a studio, rather than paint at home. I am quite pleased with these, though.'

'Ah, Olivia,' Isobel said, glancing curiously at her and then back to the painting to straighten it on its hook. 'Yes, Emily said she had certain allergies. Emily's perfume set her off apparently, and then various household cleaning products. Such a nuisance.'

Did they? Nicole hadn't had any complaints regarding those yet. She sighed. 'It must have been a real worry for Emily, especially when Olivia was a baby. She's suffered with it all her life, so Richard tells me.'

'Well, yes, Emily was worried about her.' Again, Isobel gave her a look that Nicole couldn't quite interpret, and then, satisfied the painting was straight, came back across the shop. 'But Emily wasn't—'

The door jangling open stopped her mid-sentence. 'Five minutes.' Isobel gestured to the man who came in. 'My husband, come to take me to lunch,' she explained to Nicole. 'Have to grab the opportunity while I can.'

'Ooh, wouldn't do to keep him waiting then.' Nicole smiled and gathered up her belongings.

'I'm worth waiting for, hey, Mike?' Isobel addressed her husband.

'Absolutely. I'd wait forever, my lovely.' Mike smiled and gave Nicole a wink. 'I often do.'

Isobel gave him a flat smile.

Nicole laughed. 'I'll leave you two to it,' she said.

'Come back later.' Isobel stopped her as she turned for the door. 'If you're looking for somewhere to paint, there's a room at the village hall. It could probably use a coat of paint itself, but it has French windows, so lots of light.'

'Really?' Nicole turned back, delighted. 'That would be fantastic. How much would it cost?'

'Well, I'd have to have a few words in the right ears, but – only if you're interested, of course – we were thinking of reviving the art classes,' Isobel said. 'Just for local people. These paintings of yours really are excellent – you're hugely talented. I was wondering whether you might be interested in maybe holding the class?'

Nicole bristled with pride. She'd adored teaching at the college – which seemed like another lifetime ago now, in a time when she actually did feel more confident – and it would certainly be a way to spend some time out of the house and away from Olivia. 'I'd love to,' she said, feeling almost tearful.

After arranging to meet Isobel later, Nicole left feeling buoyed up by the thought of using her oils as well as the friendliness of Isobel and Mike. One or two people in the village, she'd noticed, had given her curious looks, as if she were an oddity. Nicole supposed she was, in the way that newcomers always were to a village. The woman in the café had stared at her so hard before asking whether she was Richard Gray's new wife that Nicole had wondered whether she'd had something worse than a milk moustache on her face. The woman had looked surprised when Nicole had confirmed she was. She'd been about to comment more when the woman had mumbled, 'Congratulations,' not over-effusively, and then twirled around to go and talk to someone in the kitchen. She probably fancied him, Nicole had concluded. Richard was quite the catch, after all. He no doubt had one or two female admirers.

Still, she could deal with it. Richard loved her, and she'd never once seen his eye stray in another direction. Running the art class would be the perfect icebreaker: giving her the opportunity to get to know people, and for people to get to know her and realise she was no threat. She'd thought she might be nervous at the prospect of teaching again, so useless had she been made to feel by her first husband, but she was actually looking forward to the challenge.

Lighter of foot, she called in to Baby Steps, the 'all things babies' shop, to pick up the stair gate she'd ordered, and then she checked her watch – and made a mad dash for her car. Where had the time gone? Richard would be waiting. Not to take her to lunch, unfortunately, but to meet her mother. Nicole prayed he didn't spend five minutes in Lydia's company and end up viewing his wife through her disappointed eyes.

Arriving at her car on the high street to find herself blocked in – barely an inch to spare either way – Nicole started to panic. It took her a whole twenty minutes to find the owner of one of the cars blocking her, and even then, halfway through his lunch in the café, he took his time.

God. She was hopelessly late now. Nicole tried Richard's number as she drove, only to get his voicemail. Having taken time out of his work day, he was not going to be pleased. Pressing her foot down, Nicole drove faster than she should for the first part of the journey, and then cursed as she met traffic.

Finally arriving, almost an hour late, she found Richard's car parked outside her mother's house, but no sign of Richard. *Hell.* He was inside. By now, he'd probably be put off her for life. Lydia would no doubt be regaling him with tales of her wild youth and failed marriage – with a few misconceptions as to why it had failed thrown in – whilst looking frail and lonely, having been abandoned for so many years by her uncaring daughter. All of this she would do to make *sure* Richard was put off.

Parking haphazardly, Nicole scrambled out of her car, grabbed the shopping she'd bought to stock up Lydia's cupboards, and then let herself in with the key she'd been entrusted with. *Breathe.* Nicole deposited the provisions in the kitchen and then braced herself and walked to the living room door, where she stopped and listened – and then did a double take. Lydia was laughing. Nicole shook her head. She couldn't remember seeing her smiling, let alone actually laughing. What's more, Richard appeared to be chuckling along too.

They were getting on?

Nicole eased the door open and stepped in, looking first at her mother, who had a tissue pressed to her chest and whose eyes were sparkling with merriment, then to Richard, whose gaze shot to hers.

'Nicole!' Sounding pleased to see her – to Nicole's relief, since she was so terribly late – he got to his feet to take hold of her hand and kiss her cheek. She'd thought he would be annoyed, with every right to be. He'd had a busy schedule this morning, viewing one property and overseeing works on another, he'd said, meaning he might be hard pushed to get here himself. Yet here he still was, apparently getting along like a house on fire with Lydia.

Wonders never... Nicole smiled. 'Sorry about the time,' she said. 'I forgot I had to pick the baby gate up, and then I found my car blocked—'

'Baby gate?' Lydia interjected, staring at her in surprise.

'Stair gate,' Nicole quickly amended, lest her mother get on to that subject.

She hadn't told Richard that she'd lost a child. How she'd lost her. He would have wondered why she hadn't left her monster of a husband immediately. Nicole hadn't known how she would explain, at first, that her strength and her sense of self-worth had been so depleted she hadn't known how to. That, knowing what he would be capable of if she reported him, she'd been too frightened to. She'd intended to tell him, once she'd realised Richard wouldn't think any less of her, but then events, particularly with Olivia, had overtaken her. She would speak to him, soon, she decided. She would have to, before her mother did.

'It's to keep Bouncer downstairs. Richard's daughter's allergic,' she explained. 'I see you two are hitting it off.'

'Indeed we are.' Lydia's eyes drifted fondly back to Richard. 'He's hilarious. And such a gent. He's changed the bulb on the landing and tuned my radio in. I'd hold on to this one, if I were you, Nicole.'

'Yes, Mother,' Nicole said flatly. 'So, what's so funny?' She arched a curious eyebrow at Richard.

'Him, naked in a lift,' Lydia supplied, fanning herself with her tissue as she dissolved into another fit of laughter. 'Stopping on every floor!' She was so overcome, she could barely get the words out. She'd have a heart attack if she wasn't careful.

Nicole boggled at Richard, who now looked the tiniest bit embarrassed.

'Construction company prank, back in my apprenticeship days,' he explained, with an awkward shrug. 'My workmates decided it would be amusing to leave me in the lift with my hands and feet tied and stop the lift on every floor.'

'But that's not funny.' Nicole stared at him aghast. 'That's bullying.'

Placing an arm around her, Richard squeezed her shoulders. 'I got over it,' he assured her.

'And didn't bear any grudges,' Lydia felt compelled to add.

Yes, well, it's difficult not to bear grudges when you've been bullied your whole life, Nicole would have liked to say, but she didn't. 'I'll go and make some tea,' she said instead.

'No need,' Lydia said. 'Richard's already made one. We discussed the lovely new apartment I'm moving into over a digestive, didn't we, Richard?'

'We did.' Richard smiled, his eyes travelling to Nicole, who was now staring at him with her mouth agape.

Her mother moving into an apartment? This was news to her.

'They're luxury apartments,' Richard went on. 'Much sought after, and closer to where we live, which would make it easier for us to visit. I told Lydia that, if she was interested, I could secure her one. She's having a think about it, aren't you, Lydia?'

'I most certainly am,' Lydia said, now looking at him in adoration. 'This place is far too big for me to keep. And it will free up some money. I might even go on a cruise or two.'

'Live it up a bit, hey, Lydia?' Richard gave her a mischievous wink. 'Why not? You've earned it.'

'Most definitely.' Lydia glanced pointedly at Nicole.

'I have to get back to work,' Richard said, taking hold of Nicole's hand again and giving it a squeeze. 'I've brought Lydia's file down for her, so she can go through the various paperwork with you.'

Leaning in to kiss her, he held her gaze meaningfully. Then he turned to Lydia, bending to kiss her cheek, at which Lydia blushed like a schoolgirl.

'Bye, Lydia.' He smiled and squeezed her hand. 'It was lovely to meet you. I'll call again soon. Meanwhile, take care of that ankle. And shout if you need any help with that paperwork. You have my number.'

CHAPTER TWENTY-FIVE

OLIVIA

PRESENT

'So, will you marry him, do you think?' Olivia asked, as Rebecca applied the finishing touches to her make-up, preparing to go out to dinner with Richard. She actually did look quite beautiful, with her lustrous dark curls pinned into a loose up-do, which accentuated her high cheekbones and long, slender neck.

'*What?*' Rebecca stopped halfway through her application of lip gloss: soft coral. It suited her full lips, especially with her tan. Olivia could quite see why Richard would be particularly taken with her.

'We hardly know each other, Liv.' Rebecca laughed incredulously. 'Why on earth would you think that either of us would be contemplating marriage?'

But she did know him, in the biblical sense – thoroughly, judging by the moans of ecstasy that had emanated from his bedroom last night. Rebecca had thought Olivia was out, and with boring Laura having dragged Sam back off to Warwickshire, lest he be tempted elsewhere, it seemed she'd accepted Richard's invitation to explore each other further.

'Because he's falling in love with you,' Olivia said, as if it were perfectly obvious. 'He's bound to ask.'

'But, why would he?' Rebecca's huge mocha-coloured eyes were filled with confusion. 'I know we're... seeing each other, but he's still going to be grieving, Liv. It's far too soon for him to be considering a serious relationship, let alone getting married again.'

Pausing, Rebecca smiled, as if humouring her; as if now she'd had sex with him, she knew him better than she did – which was rather naive, in Olivia's opinion.

'Are you not serious about him then?' she asked, holding her gaze.

The woman was immediately flummoxed by that, as Olivia had suspected she might be. She could hardly confess that she was only interested in fucking her father, after all. Olivia doubted that was the case, though. She might be attractive but she wasn't getting any younger. Richard was good-looking, eligible. He could have his pick of women of any age, of which she would be aware.

Her brow furrowing, Rebecca pondered her answer. 'Well, yes, I hoped we might see more of each other,' she said, eventually, 'but I hadn't really thought about anything in the long term.'

She would be now though. She would be experiencing a little flutter of panic, Olivia fancied, thinking she might do well to get her skates on and bag him before someone else did.

Nodding, she did her best to look thoughtful. 'Can I be honest with you, Becky?'

'Yes,' Rebecca said, turning to give Olivia her full attention. 'Please do.'

'If he's made...' Olivia hesitated, glancing awkwardly down and back. 'If you and he have made love, then he *will* be taking it seriously, Becky. Really he will. Because he's good-looking, people make assumptions about him, but he's a one-woman man. He always has been. He – how can I put this? – has principles, I suppose you'd call them. I call it old-fashioned, but...' She stopped, reading Rebecca's expression interestedly. She was soaking it up. Olivia supposed women of a certain age would.

Taking a breath, as if reluctant, she went on. 'His parents never married,' she said, glancing over her shoulder, as if worried about confiding. 'His father treated his mother abysmally, womanising and drinking and getting abusive when he did. He left her, my gran, with nothing when he died. Dad looked out for her – financially, I mean. I think he thought she'd be relieved that his father wasn't around any more, but she just couldn't cope – with life, with anything. It was a self-esteem thing, I think. She started drinking herself and… well, Dad was broken-hearted when she died so suddenly.'

Rebecca's eyes widened in alarm. 'Oh God,' she said, paling visibly. '*How?* I mean, I had no idea. How did she die, his poor mother?'

Painfully, probably. Olivia sighed inwardly. She really did wonder sometimes at how easily women allowed their emotions to rule their heads. Rebecca was clearly lapping all this up.

'A heart attack. Dad was there at the time,' she said, with a soulful sigh. 'He was devastated. That was the first time I saw him cry. He made a promise to himself then, I think, never to treat a woman the way his father had treated his mother. He treats women respectfully, Becky. That's why I think he will ask you at some point, not because he thinks he should, because you two… you know… but because he *is* falling in love with you. He won't want to lose you. But if you're not serious about him… I just thought you should know – for my Dad's sake, I suppose.'

'I see,' Rebecca said, the furrow in her brow deepening as she tried to digest the news that she might lose him, a caring prize of a man, the kind she wasn't likely to meet again in her lifetime. Olivia could almost see the cogs going round. Yes, she would be struggling with her conscience out of loyalty to her best friend. But Nicole was dead, when all was said and done. She was hardly going to claw her way out of her grave and scratch her eyes out.

CHAPTER TWENTY-SIX

REBECCA

PRESENT

Thinking about all that Olivia had said, the information she'd fed her, Rebecca tried to quell her nerves as they dined. He'd chosen the venue: Brown's Restaurant at the Quay, a pretty location overlooking the bridge and the River Severn in central Worcester. The meal was fine cuisine and good service at its best. He was working to impress her, Rebecca guessed, dressed immaculately in a white linen shirt and cream chinos, which both offset his tan and highlighted his toned physique.

Why had Olivia told her about his parents? She'd seemed determined that Rebecca should have that piece of information, and whilst it might have been presented as consideration for Richard, it seemed to be more manipulation than matchmaking. And why would she want to marry him off again, when she'd had such a disastrous relationship with Nicole?

'So the highlight of your week was scouring the Birmingham rag market for bargains?' Richard asked, going back to their conversation about her student days, once the waiter had served their coffee.

Rebecca noted his expression: one of amused puzzlement, as if he couldn't think of anything less exciting. 'Not quite. Saturday night clubbing, or rather man-spotting, was the real highlight,' she said, a teasing look in her eyes as she bit slowly into her mint.

Trailing the tip of her tongue over her lips to mop up the chocolate, she noted Richard's gaze lingering. What was going through his mind, she wondered. What kind of future, apart from the immediate, was he really contemplating with her? No doubt she would find out. 'Nicole had an eye for a bargain though,' she went on. 'She could always make the most obscure thing into something beautiful.'

Richard's gaze came back to hers. 'I know,' he said, guilt flitting across his features.

'You've heard enough about me. Tell me about yourself,' Rebecca said, having revealed as much as she wanted him to know. Her relationships, beyond her marriage, she wasn't about to go into. 'About your childhood. Your parents. I know hardly anything about you.'

Now Richard looked awkward. Very.

'Oh dear, sore subject?' she asked, as he picked up a sugar spoon, fixing his gaze on it and twirling it pensively between his thumb and forefingers.

'Not really. It's just…' Richard glanced up. 'It wasn't great, my childhood. My father… Let's just say he wasn't the sort of man that should have fathered children. My mother never really got over their volatile relationship. She died suddenly; in front of me, actually. Heart attack.'

'Oh no. I'm so sorry.' Rebecca reached to still his hand. 'That must have been so awful. And you just a child.'

Richard drew in a breath and looked back at her. 'It was. Not something I find easy to talk about, to be honest.'

'No,' Rebecca said understandingly. 'Of course not.'

'As for the rest, nothing spectacular: comprehensive education, left school with not many qualifications and then went straight into the building trade. Luckily, I had a flair for figures and enjoyed the work, and the rest followed.'

Rebecca smiled, but she was only half listening. Her mind was on Olivia, and her claim to have witnessed Richard crying over his mother's death. 'Boy done good,' she said, realising Richard had stopped talking and was watching her.

'Eventually. Not so well on the personal front, unfortunately.' He shrugged sadly.

Rebecca squeezed his hand and eased herself to her feet. 'Ladies' room,' she said, nodding in that direction and then leaning to kiss him softly on the cheek.

Smiling at one or two fellow diners, she walked calmly to the toilets, though her heart was thrumming a manic beat in her chest. She needed to phone Sam. He'd mentioned something about swinging by on their way to a concert in Worcester. Rebecca wasn't sure they would , but she wanted to put him off nevertheless.

Richard surprised her when, having sent Sam a text when she couldn't get hold of him, she returned to the table. 'I'd like to offer to pay,' he said. 'However, I think Nicole deemed that to be controlling?' He smiled as he said it, as if he didn't quite get it, but understood why she would. 'How about a compromise? I pay for this meal, you pay for the next?'

'Done,' Rebecca said, still trying to make things add up in her head. Would he really have remembered that detail if he hadn't cared for her?

'How about a walk?' he suggested, taking her hand once the bill was settled. 'It's a beautiful evening.'

'That sounds like a plan.' Rebecca decided she would be glad of the exercise, to work off the wine and focus her thoughts on what her reaction should be if this was leading where she thought it might. 'Though I'll have to walk a fair way to burn off the chocolate-and-marshmallow brownie.'

'It was a bit moreish, wasn't it?' he smiled, opening the door and allowing her to go before him out of the restaurant.

'It's a lovely restaurant,' Rebecca said, surveying it from the outside. 'Intimate and cosy.'

Richard nodded. 'A bit too cosy for me, if I'm honest. I'm not great in confined spaces,' he added, as Rebecca glanced at him curiously. 'Got trapped in a lift once. Long story.'

'Ah, brave of you to admit it,' she said, amazed that he had. Some men wouldn't admit as easily to their vulnerabilities.

'What about you?' he asked her. 'Do you have any…'

'Phobias?' Rebecca finished, as he searched for the word. 'Not really. I tend to feel the fear and do it anyway.'

'I think I gathered that.' Richard smiled, his expression a combination of amusement and admiration as he looked at her.

They walked on in silence for a while, stopping as they neared the bridge to watch a gaggle of glorious white swans gliding ghostlike along the river. Rebecca's thoughts were inevitably on Nicole as she looked across the calm water, thinking of the secrets it held, the lives it had stolen. Where were Richard's thoughts, she wondered. Was he down there in the dark underbelly of the river with her? Or had he really moved on so swiftly?

He reached for her hand, after a moment. 'Shall we?' he asked, squeezing it gently and nodding them onwards.

Pulling her closer as they turned, he threaded an arm around her waist. Would he really propose to her, Rebecca wondered? As quickly as he had to Nicole, and so soon after her death? She'd expected he would at some juncture, but as she spent more time with him, his possible motives were becoming muddled in Rebecca's mind. Knowing what she knew, it seemed almost inconceivable, but was it possible he *was* doing it for love? That he'd really played no part in the events that had led to Nicole's death? That he was a man who believed in love? If that was so, wouldn't that make him as naive as he was supposedly perfect?

'You'll be leaving to go back to France soon,' Richard said quietly.

Rebecca nodded. 'I have things to tie up. Furniture that needs to be sold, as well as organising storage of anything I want to keep. Plus, I still have to find somewhere to rent here, at least in the short term, until I find the right property to buy. I think I'll start looking around properly once I'm back in the UK.'

'And will that be soon?'

Rebecca hesitated. 'Do you want it to be?'

'Very much,' Richard said, tightening his arm around her.

'Why?' Rebecca asked, as they slowed their walk to a stop.

Richard didn't answer immediately, turning towards her instead. His eyes were dark and intense as they searched hers. In the light of the streetlamps, Rebecca saw a flicker of uncertainty therein. 'Because you're fantastic in bed,' he said, with a nervous smile.

'Thank you for the compliment.' Rebecca mock-scowled. 'I think.'

'Because I like being with you,' Richard amended, his look back to serious.

Rebecca smiled. 'Likewise.'

'Would you consider something while you're away?' he asked her.

'As in?' Rebecca eyed him quizzically.

'Rather than rent somewhere, would you consider staying at the house? I've decided to take if off the market,' he rushed on, before Rebecca had a chance to answer. 'There's plenty of space for storage, too, if you need it, and… it seems to make more sense than hunting for a property to rent, which presumably you'd have to do online, which might be risky. I thought it might be more convenient, and I, er… Well, I hoped you might consider it.' Stopping, finally, he shrugged hopefully.

Rebecca raised her eyebrows in surprise. 'Richard, are you asking me to move in with you?'

'Yes, I think I am,' he said, his expression also one of surprise. 'Actually, I definitely am,' he added, with a resolute nod.

'But…' Rebecca shook her head bewilderedly. 'It's so soon after…'

'Losing Nicole,' Richard finished, his expression apprehensive as he searched her face. 'I know, and I realise it might seem as if I don't care, as if I don't miss her, but…' Running a hand over his neck, he glanced at the skies and then back to her. 'Looking out over the river just now, I wondered what she would think.'

His thoughts had been of her, then. 'And what conclusion did you come to?'

'That she would be glad – happy for me – that it's you I've found myself falling in love with.'

Dumbfounded, Rebecca said nothing.

'I love you, Rebecca,' he said, his eyes a shade darker as he reached again for her hand. 'I don't want to lose you. I'm not sure how you feel, but if, by any chance, it's the same, will you consider staying with me?'

CHAPTER TWENTY-SEVEN

LYDIA

PREVIOUS YEAR – NOVEMBER

Taking it steadily, Lydia made slow progress up the cellar steps. She shouldn't have ventured down here with her ankle still not properly mended, but she'd wanted to fetch a decent wine to offer Richard over lunch. It was the least she could do after all he was doing for her. She'd thought she would die in this mausoleum of a house, which she'd once loved. Sadly, it held too many bad memories now: recollections of her hellish years spent in purgatory with a man who was a tyrant. Nicole had thought she'd had problems in her first marriage. She should have tried living with her father, Lydia had once told her, forgetting for a moment that she had. Nicole had claimed that her first husband was the same as her father – a bully, she'd called him, a misogynist. Lydia had never quite understood why he'd earned that label. All men could be a bit controlling, after all. It was in their natures as the providers. Nicole should have counted her blessings, in Lydia's opinion. Her husband had always been attentive, as far as she could see: phoning her to make sure she'd arrived and what time she would be home, if she visited on her own – although such occasions had been rare. He'd always seemed happy to accompany her anywhere. He hadn't been violent or dismissive of her, as far as Lydia knew.

Nicole had been unhappy though. Perhaps she'd never truly loved him, as Lydia had loved William. At least she had, for a while.

Richard had been a surprise. Extremely handsome and impeccably mannered, he was quite the catch. Lydia couldn't believe Nicole had managed to net him so easily. Not that she wasn't beautiful enough to bag such a man. She was. Nicole had been exceptionally pretty as a child, although her father had never thought so, considering her red hair to be an unfortunate affliction. She was so lacking in poise, though, and such a dreamer, appearing to have no sense of direction in her life. That only seemed to endear her to Richard, however, who'd obviously fallen for her, whatever her shortcomings. Lydia had been suspicious of him, at first. How could she not have been, given how quickly he'd swept Nicole off her feet? But then, having met him, she'd quite realised how he had – and why Nicole had grabbed him with both hands and raced him up the aisle. The man clearly cared about her and he was extremely successful, therefore with no separate agenda.

It was thanks to Richard that she and Nicole were now seeing more of each other. Lydia was sure that, without his interest in her welfare, Nicole would have visited as little as she could. She would have organised her some home help, she'd said as much, but Lydia doubted she would have been much in evidence herself. Richard had strong family values. He clearly adored his daughter, proudly showing off her photo and regaling Lydia with stories of her childhood. It was such a pity Nicole had never had children, which was clearly what had been missing in her first marriage. And it was a greater pity that, at thirty-eight, it was possibly too late for her to have children with Richard. But then Nicole herself had been a late arrival. After two miscarriages, Lydia had never imagined she would be pregnant at forty. And Richard hadn't seemed to mind that they might not have children together, when she'd tentatively enquired whether he would have liked to have had more. He would have loved more children, he'd confided, and but for the tragic illness his first wife had suffered, he might have had them. He was content with his life now though, he'd assured her, his smile so heartbreakingly sad that Lydia's own heart had melted.

The man was a gem, definitely. Nicole would do well to hang on to this one, whatever it took. Thinking she should perhaps make more of an effort to talk to her daughter, who rarely seemed to confide in her, Lydia heaved herself upwards, the last half of the steps like climbing a mountain – and then froze as she heard a distinct clunk in the hall. And then another. Her heart skittered against her ribcage. Someone was in the house. Lydia tightened her grip on the rickety stair rail, held her breath and clutched the vintage bottle of wine close to her chest.

'Lydia? It's me, Richard,' she heard from the hall, and breathed a considerable sigh of relief.

'Down here,' she called. 'I was fetching some wine to have with our lunch.' She waved the bottle as Richard appeared at the cellar door, looking perturbed. 'Unfortunately, it seems a lot further coming up than it was going down.'

'Lydia, you shouldn't be climbing stairs on that ankle.' Richard shook his head in despair. 'Let alone dodgy stairs,' he added, finding the loose rail as he came down to meet her.

'Another neglected repair, I'm afraid.' Lydia sighed apologetically as he tested it, the furrow in his brow deepening. 'I meant to get around to it, but time slips by so fast nowadays.'

Richard glanced at her and then back to the rail. 'I'll bring my toolbox next time,' he offered.

Such a gentleman. Lydia smiled wistfully. If only she had her time over again. 'No need,' she said, handing him the wine and taking hold of the arm he offered her. 'It will be someone else's responsibility soon, won't it? I expect the new owners will give the old place the tender loving care it deserves.'

'Even so,' said Richard, patting her hand as he assisted her up, 'we don't want you having another fall, do we? You've got some living it up to do, remember? On the subject of which, I've brought the papers for you to sign regarding the transfer of the proceeds of the sale. Once that's done, we can secure your apartment – and then book that cruise together.'

Lydia chuckled. *If only.* Such a charmer. And with a sense of humour, too. Altogether, a rare breed indeed. She so hoped Nicole realised how lucky she was. He really was worth his weight in gold.

CHAPTER TWENTY-EIGHT

NICOLE

PREVIOUS YEAR – NOVEMBER

'Hi,' Richard said, coming into the utility room, where Nicole was washing her brushes. Her watercolour brushes, that was, with not a whiff of fumes about, lest she be accused of deliberately trying to poison Olivia. She'd already taken most of her oil-based supplies to the room adjoining the village hall. It was perfect. And thanks to Isobel arranging for the rental to be waived in exchange for her teaching an evening art class once a week, she didn't even have to pay for the privilege of using it.

'Hi.' She smiled, turning her cheek to his kiss. 'Good day?'

'Not bad,' Richard said, bending to give the dogs, who were close on his heels, a fuss. 'I managed to pick up that property on the high street at a reasonable price,' he said, heading back into the kitchen.

'The one the Society for the Blind were going to put a bid in for?' Nicole asked him, thinking it a bit sad that they wouldn't now be able to make a bid.

'That's the one. It will make excellent private rental accommodation, once it's converted. Oh, and I saw Lydia on the way back.'

'Oh yes?' Wiping her hands, Nicole came back to the kitchen. Richard and Lydia had definitely bonded. But then, most people did with Richard. He was charismatic and easy-going. Certainly, most women would feel flattered by the attention of a charming, good-looking man, whatever their age. Nicole was glad Lydia was getting on with him. It meant Richard could pop in on the odd occasion in lieu of her. It had raised a niggling worry though. Because he had seemed to get on with Lydia so easily, Nicole was beginning to wonder if she herself was the one at fault, imagining people were out to get her. Was the hostility she felt towards her mother, towards Olivia, because she was being paranoid? Mind you, being paranoid didn't mean people weren't out to get you as well, did it?

'I found her halfway up the cellar steps, struggling to fetch wine, would you believe?'

'Oh Lord.' Nicole rolled her eyes. 'Typical Lydia. Once her mind's made up about something there's no talking her out of it.' Which is why, Nicole supposed, they'd eventually stopped talking about anything meaningful. As far as Lydia was concerned, she was to blame for the failure of her first marriage as much as she was to blame for her father's disappointment in her. There'd been no point looking for a shoulder where there was none. 'I hope you told her off. I dread to think what might have happened if you hadn't turned up.'

'I did, but diplomatically.' Richard smiled knowingly and went to grab the orange juice from the fridge. 'I dropped by with some information about the luxury apartment complex. Looks like she's definitely going to go for it, which will be a good thing. No more stairs for her to negotiate, at least. Did you manage to go through all her paperwork?'

'Finally,' Nicole assured him. 'Her house deeds and legal papers all seem in order. There was a copy of her will in the file, too. Looks like she hasn't disinherited me for some obscure charity yet.'

'Better keep on her good side then.' Richard winked and took a swig of his drink. 'I'll get it all checked over with a solicitor, make sure there's nothing we've overlooked. I know a guy who specialises in estate planning. Assuming you'd like me to, of course?'

'Good idea,' Nicole agreed. 'I think the solicitor Lydia uses is about to retire, or else already has. He was my father's solicitor. He's so old he's probably fossilised.'

Richard laughed. 'I'll get it sorted,' he promised. 'It's good news she's agreed to move, don't you think? Her being nearer, I mean, where we can better keep an eye on her?'

'It certainly is.' Nicole peered into the fridge in hopes of inspiration for dinner. She'd thought barbecued fish and salad on the patio, but it was looking a bit overcast now. 'She can't possibly see to the upkeep of that house on her own, and I'm worn out trying to keep this house clean, let alone hers as well.'

Richard walked across to place a hand around her waist. 'You don't have to keep it quite so meticulously clean though, Nicole.'

'No?' Nicole glanced towards the stairs, hearing Olivia cough, as was her wont lately, as she came down.

Richard removed his hand, tugged off his tie and headed that way.

'God, honestly, this stair gate thing is a real nuisance,' Olivia moaned as he reached her, causing Nicole to clench her teeth.

'It's easy enough to climb over, Liv,' Richard said.

'For you it might be,' Olivia huffed. 'I have to open it. I'm not sure how I'm supposed to do that when I've always got my hands full.'

Her hands were always full with her phone and her Coke, glasses of which went upstairs never to come down again. Nicole looked over to see Richard dutifully opening the gate for her. Or else shopping bags or make-up, suntan lotion… the list was endless. She had yet to see her carrying any implements that might be put to use cleaning the space she lived in.

'It's just a baby gate, Liv.' Richard climbed easily over it – since Olivia had impolitely closed it again, kicking it shut behind her with her foot. 'We'd have one if we had little ones around.'

Olivia rolled her eyes. 'But we're not likely to have little ones around, *are* we? Not while you're living with *her.*' Carrying on to the kitchen, she looked Nicole disparagingly over.

Feeling that like a low blow to the stomach –almost as painful as the one that had caused her to give birth prematurely – Nicole simply stared at her, stunned.

'Liv! That's out of order!' Richard said angrily behind her.

'*Sorry.*' Olivia pouted. 'I'm just stating a fact: you're not going to hear the pitter-patter of tiny feet other than her dog's, are you?'

Not happy at Richard having, for once, not taken her side, Olivia had decided to make a point of not eating with them. Nicole didn't care what she did. She was still in a state of shock. Why would she say such an awful thing? Was it *her?* Was she being oversensitive? Olivia was young, spoiled and clearly thoughtless. But she wasn't a teenager, someone whose horribleness might be blamed on raging hormones. She was a young woman. She must have known how hurtful her comments would be.

She clearly did hate her. Staring down at her plate, Nicole pushed her food around. She couldn't eat it. She doubted she'd be able to swallow it past the sharp lump in her throat. She'd always wanted children – desperately wanted children. Even after she'd woken up to her reality, the terrifying situation she'd found herself trapped in, she'd still craved a child. But how could she have contemplated getting pregnant again and exposing a tiny human being to the violent mood swings she'd discovered her husband was capable of? The doctor had explained that another pregnancy was unlikely to end in miscarriage; that although she had an incompetent cervix – wouldn't the misogynist have just loved it if she'd told him that: that it was her incompetence rather than his vicious blow that had killed her perfect baby? – there was a procedure they could carry out to make sure the pregnancy went full term. As long as she didn't do anything silly to overtax herself, everything would almost certainly be fine, he'd said, smiling reassuringly. Such as falling down the stairs. That was the lie she'd told them. She should have had her vile husband arrested. Even though he'd said he would come back and kill her as soon as they let him go, she should have given a statement and run. Thinking they would release him within hours, as they had once before, she'd been too scared to. She'd been stupid and pathetic and weak. She still was. And Olivia could sense it.

'You're quiet,' Richard observed, after a while. 'And that fish isn't faring too well.'

Coming back from a past she found so painful to dwell on, Nicole realised she'd stirred her food into a sludge. 'I'm sorry,' she whispered, downing her fork and looking up at him.

Richard cocked his head to one side, his expression concerned. 'For?'

'Everything,' she said, feeling incredibly sad, which made her feel even worse about herself. She had everything now to live for: a good man, a beautiful home, all she could wish for. Apart from Olivia.

'Look, Nicole…' Getting to his feet, Richard walked around to her, placed an arm around her shoulders and took hold of her hand. 'Whatever it is you imagine you have to be sorry for, you don't. It's me who should be apologising. What Liv said earlier was thoughtless and cruel.'

'It was.' Nicole glimpsed up at him and then back to her plate.

Straightening up, Richard sighed and plunged his hands into his pockets. 'I know it's difficult having her here, but I can't ask her to go, Nicole, at least not until she has a job and a place of her own lined up, not after all that happened.'

He was referring to the sexual assault, which Nicole had struggled even more to make sense of since speaking to Peter.

'Can you bear to put up with her a little longer?' Richard's voice was hopeful.

Nicole answered with a small nod. She wasn't about to tell him he had to ask his daughter to leave. It would only cause trouble between them, and then Olivia would win whatever unfathomable game it was she was playing.

But she couldn't leave it there. Hearing him talk of having little ones around, she had to ask him. Bracing herself, Nicole took a breath and looked up at him. '*Did* you want more children?' she asked him, searching his face. 'Do you?'

'Nicole…' He sighed again, heavily, and closed his eyes. 'I did once, yes. But now, I only want whatever makes you happy.'

Again, Nicole nodded, but her heart skipped a beat. If he had once wanted more children, then he must still, surely. Was it too late? She was thirty-eight now, but could she at least try? It would certainly be a wanted child if she succeeded. A child that might bind them together – and show Olivia that she wasn't the centre of his attention.

CHAPTER TWENTY-NINE

REBECCA

PRESENT

'Well?' Olivia asked, practically bursting with anticipation as she dashed from her bedroom to meet Rebecca coming upstairs.

'Let's just say we're making future plans,' Rebecca answered, with an enigmatic smile.

'Yesss!' Olivia flew towards her as she reached the landing, throwing her arms around her with such enthusiasm that she almost bowled her over. 'I knew it! You two are just made for each other. You only have to see the way he's been looking at you to realise he's falling in love with you. I'm so happy for you, Becky. It's just the best news—'

'Hold on.' Rebecca laughed, cutting her off mid gush, while discreetly extracting herself from Olivia's over-exuberant hug. 'We're just discussing my moving in here, Liv. We haven't made any concrete plans yet.'

Olivia's face dropped. 'But you will move in?' she asked worriedly. 'You have to. I can't possibly go off to my new job and leave Dad broken-hearted all over again.'

'You've got a job?' Rebecca was surprised. She'd gathered that Olivia had been looking for one, on and off, but she hadn't realised she'd actually got one.

'In Birmingham,' Olivia confirmed. 'I don't start for a couple of months, but I was thinking of flat-sharing with a friend, rather than commuting. I probably won't, though, if it means Dad's going to be on his… *Damn.* Sorry, that sounded like I was pressurising you. What I meant was, I can always postpone the flat-share for a while and take the train. It's not cast in stone yet.'

Rebecca studied her, wary of Olivia's overt concern for her father. It seemed almost as if Olivia were the parent. Richard and she would have formed a strong father-and-daughter relationship, she supposed, after her mother died, but she seemed rather overprotective of his feelings. 'There's a lot to think about, Liv,' she pointed out. 'I have to go back to France and sort out my affairs there, work my notice at the college. Then there's Sam. I'd need to talk to him, obviously.'

'So it's just the practicalities then?' Olivia's expression was hopeful.

'To a degree, yes, but…' Rebecca hesitated. Already her emotions felt compromised, her inability to find the flaws in the man and her physical desire for him clouding her judgement. She couldn't allow that to happen. 'I need to be sure, Liv,' she said carefully. 'Your father does, too. I shouldn't imagine either of us wants to be doing this for the wrong reasons.'

Olivia nodded slowly. 'You think he might be rushing into things?' she asked.

'I do, yes.' Again, Rebecca answered carefully. Having no reticence about a decision that would affect the rest of her life simply wouldn't be natural. 'He's barely had time to draw breath since losing Nicole, has he?'

'No,' Olivia agreed. 'But then, he wouldn't be doing this at all, would he, if he hadn't met you at her funeral.'

'True,' Rebecca conceded, guessing what might be coming next.

'I think it's fate.' Olivia sighed romantically. 'You both needed someone, and you both found someone. Under tragic circumstances, yes, but that doesn't mean your feelings for each other are any less true. You shouldn't feel guilty about falling in love, Becky. I doubt Nicole would want you to. She would be happy for you. She was that kind of person – caring and generous. She would hate it if she thought she was standing in the way of your future happiness.'

Nice little speech, Rebecca couldn't help thinking. She was sure Nicole would have been a lot happier if she were alive.

'You do love him, don't you?' Olivia said quickly, as Rebecca tried not to let her cynicism show.

'I think so, yes,' she said, giving the girl what she wanted to hear.

'Then you're not doing anything wrong. You're simply following your heart.' Olivia's expression was earnest. 'There's no point delaying what's meant to be out of some sense of loyalty, Becky. Life's too short,' she said, as if Rebecca wasn't aware of that fact. 'You two are right for each other. It's just so obvious from the outside.'

Rebecca smiled indulgently. It seemed Olivia was determined for this to happen, whatever she said. Strange that someone so protective of her father would be so eager to push him into the arms of someone neither of them really knew that well.

CHAPTER THIRTY

NICOLE

PREVIOUS YEAR – NOVEMBER

Pleased that two more people had signed up for her art class, thereby justifying her use of the room at the back of the hall as her studio, Nicole headed homeward, feeling all was right with her world. Well, as right as it could be, with Olivia still no closer to moving out.

Nicole was toying with the idea of suggesting to Richard that they set her up in her own little apartment. She'd need to learn to be independent, after all, if she was thinking about eventually living in London. She would have to broach that subject very carefully – get Richard on her side to sell the idea. She couldn't imagine Olivia going for it if she thought it was her suggestion. It would be an additional expense, but Richard might have a way of purchasing such a property cheaply through his contacts, thus making it a worthwhile investment. She'd talk to him about it, she decided, as soon as her mother had moved. Richard had already put Lydia's house up for sale, and the new apartment her mother was moving into would be ready soon, apparently.

Turning into their lane, she thought about the wonder of her mother agreeing to sell up and move so readily. Richard had said it was because she could see the sense of releasing the equity on the house, thereby affording her a bit of luxury. Personally, Nicole thought it was because she had been seduced by Richard's charms. She looked very fluttery-eyed and girlish whenever he visited.

Smiling, she turned into the driveway and noticed the electric gates were already open. *Strange.* They normally closed automatically, unless the manual override was employed. Perplexed, Nicole drove on through, rounding the bend on the long drive to the house – and then slowed, the ominous sweep of a rotating blue light causing her blood to freeze in her veins. *Oh God, no.* Panic rising inside her, Nicole stepped on the accelerator, sending grit and dust flying as she screeched up behind the ambulance parked right outside the house.

'Richard!' Scrambling from her car, she raced to the open front door. 'Richard!'

Seeing him descending the stairs, Nicole closed her eyes, relief flooding through her. 'What's happened?' she asked him urgently.

Richard didn't answer. His expression anguished, his complexion deathly pale, he barely acknowledged her as he continued on down.

'Richard?' Nicole looked past him to where two paramedics were manoeuvring a slim form on a stretcher down the stairs. Nicole's stomach dropped like a stone.

Richard dragged a hand over his face as he stood aside to allow the paramedics to pass to the front door.

'Richard…' Nicole caught his arm as he turned to follow them. 'Please tell me what's happened?'

'The bloody dog happened!' Richard snapped.

'Bouncer?' Nicole stared at him, uncomprehending. 'Richard, I have no idea—'

'He can get over the gate, Nicole.' Richard's expression was so furious that Nicole took a step back. 'That damn dog has to go!'

*

Richard was more subdued when he met her in the hospital corridor, the fury gone from his eyes, replaced by weary exhaustion.

'Is she all right?' Nicole asked, sick with apprehension.

Richard nodded. 'She will be.'

'Was it asthma?' She hardly dared ask.

Tugging in a breath, Richard shook his head. 'Not asthma, no,' he said, his voice thick with emotion.

Not asthma? Then why…? He'd blamed Bouncer. For what?

Richard scanned her face then looked away. 'She had an attack but she managed to get to her medication,' he said quietly. 'She rang me. She was upset, as she would be. I came back and… We argued – about the dog, things in general. She tried to take her own life, Nicole.'

He looked back at her, looking nothing short of tortured. 'I… I thought she was… *Jesus.*' He stopped, blinking hard as he glanced at the ceiling.

Dear God. Nicole felt nausea rise inside her. 'I'm so sorry, Richard,' she whispered, her heart booming a warning in her chest. 'I had no idea.'

'Don't be.' Dragging a hand over his neck, Richard sighed heavily. 'It's not your fault. If it's anyone's, it's mine. I lost my temper, with Liv and with you. I shouldn't have.'

Nicole glanced down. 'You were worried. Upset. You were bound to be.'

Richard fell quiet for a second, and then, 'About Bouncer…' he started hesitantly. 'I know you love him, Nicole, but I honestly can't see any alternative other than to—'

'To *what?*' Nicole snapped her gaze back to his. Bouncer was her *soulmate.* Her go-to guy. He'd been there for her when there was no one else. She couldn't…

'We have to think about getting him rehomed, Nicole. I—'

'How can she be allergic to him?' Nicole cried incredulously. 'To Bouncer's hairs and not to Wanderer's?'

'I don't know!' Richard raised his voice and then rubbed his forehead in frustration. 'The type of hairs, possibly?' he suggested, with a hopeless shrug. 'I really have no idea. It could take months of endless tests to try to establish what the cause of it is, and even then we might never figure it out.'

Nicole stared at him, horrified.

'Asthma can kill, Nicole,' he pointed out tersely. 'Olivia… she's got it into her head that I don't care. I do care. I care about *both* of you. I don't want you to have to get rid of your dog, for God's sake, but I can't go through this again.' He searched her face beseechingly. 'What do I do, Nicole? Tell me? What other choice do I have?'

Get rid of your bloody daughter! Nicole seethed silently.

CHAPTER THIRTY-ONE

OLIVIA

PRESENT

'So you're definitely moving in then?' Olivia asked, helping Rebecca extricate her luggage from the boot of Richard's car.

'It would certainly seem that way.' Rebecca nodded back to the Transit van, now trundling up the drive, which contained the various items of furniture she hadn't wanted to part with, some of which would be installed in the house and the rest stored in the garage.

Olivia had no doubt that Rebecca would marry him. It was only a matter of time. Who could resist, after all? Olivia looked Richard over as he climbed out of the car, and had to admit his charms were many. He would be a catch for most women, let alone someone of Rebecca's age. Mind you, she wasn't yet past her prime. Far from it, in fact. Sweeping an appraising glance over her prospective new 'stepmother', Olivia couldn't help but concede that. She was wearing her hair piled on top of her head again, she noticed, showing off her slender neck; and her legs, toned and shapely in flattering leggings, seemed to go on forever.

Richard was also quite taken, it seemed. Turning her attention back to him, Olivia saw that he was definitely acting like someone in love. He couldn't seem to take his eyes off her, running a lustful gaze over the woman. Rebecca, noting the not-so-subtle suggestion therein, reciprocated, her gaze suggestively gliding across the length and breadth of him.

Honestly, you'd think they'd show a little restraint in front of his daughter. 'Um, do you think it might be a good idea to do your sinning inside?' Olivia suggested. 'You'll be undressing each other on the drive in a minute.'

'Liv…' Closing the driver's side door, Richard shook his head, now looking slightly awkward, Olivia noted.

'What?' She blinked innocently at him and walked around to grab the last of Olivia's bags and close the boot. 'It's not like Becky's going to be embarrassed, for goodness' sake. She's a woman of the world. You're so old-fashioned sometimes, Dad. Sex is what people in love do.'

Glancing towards Rebecca pseudo-despairingly, she heaved the bags she was carrying towards the hall. 'I did warn you,' she said, as Rebecca came in behind her. 'He's a hopeless romantic and such a traditionalist; it really is embarrassing. Be warned, if he's done the deed and asked you to marry him, he's going to keep asking you until he wears you down.'

'He has asked,' Rebecca said, giving her a look somewhere between quizzical and amused. 'But only about ten times, if you count the text messages.'

'Definitely a man smitten.' Olivia sighed and fluttered her eyelashes theatrically. 'And are you weakening?'

Rebecca looked coy at that. 'I'm considering my options,' she said.

As if she had any. Olivia smiled. 'So, what will you do about your job?' she asked her, leading the way to the kitchen to play dutiful daughter and put the kettle on.

Rebecca dropped her handbag on the countertop and perched herself on a stool at the kitchen island. She really did have amazing legs. Olivia's eyes were drawn to them as she crossed one gracefully over the other. 'I'm not sure yet,' she said, reaching to unpin her hair and shake it free.

Olivia couldn't help but notice her breasts straining under her strappy vest top, firm and full. She didn't have any of that awful crêpe skin thing going on yet either, instead blessed with supple skin that tanned easily. She was so different to Nicole, Olivia couldn't help but wonder how they'd become such close friends. Opposites attracting, she supposed. Nicole had been a willowy, weak, needy thing, where Rebecca seemed to ooze self-sufficiency and confidence. She did hope Richard was aware that this was a woman with a will of her own.

'I work because I want to, not because I need to,' Rebecca said, gratefully accepting the tea Olivia offered her and taking a sip. 'I thought I might take some time out. I don't think it would hurt to indulge myself a little.'

'I don't blame you. Life isn't forever, is it?' Olivia reminded her. 'We should grab every chance of happiness while we can.'

With Richard making an appropriate entrance just then, she gave Rebecca a wink and nodded pointedly in his direction. Rolling her eyes, Rebecca shook her head amusedly and then reached into her bag for her ringing mobile.

'That will probably be Sam,' Olivia informed her, as Rebecca checked the number. 'I told him you were on your way from the ferry when he rang earlier.'

Picking up her tea, she smiled and turned for the door, leaving Rebecca gazing perplexedly after her. She would be a touch curious, wondering why her son would have rung her. Planting seeds now regarding her plans for Sam couldn't hurt, Olivia had decided.

CHAPTER THIRTY-TWO

NICOLE

PREVIOUS YEAR – NOVEMBER

Nicole's heart sank as she arrived outside her mother's house to find the 'For Sale' sign had been amended to 'Sold'. She'd been hoping to persuade Lydia to take Bouncer for a while – if not for her sake, then to impress Richard, whom she clearly adored.

She'd been reluctant to ask her. She didn't imagine Lydia would be cruel to Bouncer, but she doubted she would be very affectionate either. The alternative, though – to send him back to the rescue centre – Nicole couldn't contemplate that. Hearing his heartbroken, pathetic yelps as she walked away from him would kill her. Bouncer wasn't just a dog to her. He was her baby. The loyal, warm body she'd snuggled up to when her nights had been bleak and lonely. Her mind drifted to Rosie, her precious little baby girl. She would be five years old now, probably sitting here chattering away next to her... alive, if only Nicole had been stronger.

Determined to be strong now, she squeezed back a tear and picked up her phone. Becky would be fed up with her whingeing texts, but she had to talk to someone, and while Becky would probably despair of her handling of the Olivia situation, she would be there for her. Nicole wished she was more like her friend, who would never allow her life to be dictated in the way that Nicole was allowing Olivia to dictate hers. But what could she do in reality, other than wait it out? Could she really ask Richard to put her welfare above his daughter's?

Lovely Becky, whose shoulders are possibly weighed down with my burdens. Something awful has happened and I don't know what to think.

Nicole pulled in a shuddery breath and typed on.

Richard and Olivia argued, and Olivia made an attempt on her life. The thing is, it was my fault they argued. It was over her allergies and Bouncer, apparently. Poor Richard is devastated and I don't know what on earth to do. I'm not sure what you can do, but I very much needed an ear. So sorry to shock you with this, Becky. Much love, Nicole. X

Becky replied immediately: *Firstly, you can STOP blaming yourself. Secondly, and be honest, do you think it was a serious attempt?xxx*
Nicole took another breath and replied, simply: *No.* She didn't. In her heart of hearts, she really didn't.
Becky texted back: *Call me. As soon as you can.xxx*

Just about to see my mother. Going to ask her to take Bouncer for a short while before she moves. Will call after. Love U. X

Feeling better already for touching base with her friend, who understood why she was so full of self-doubt, Nicole squeezed back another tear and turned to stroke Bouncer's silky head. It was the only part of him that was soft, the rest of his coat being wiry and woolly and sticking out at all angles. It must be his fur that Olivia was allergic to, she supposed. Try as she might, though, to feel sympathetic towards the girl, Nicole just couldn't. She really didn't think her suicide attempt had been a serious one. She had no idea what she was going to do in the long term about the whole awful mess. For now, all she could do was try to borrow some time for her dog, and her mother was her only option, but it looked like she'd be moving to the new apartment Richard had organised for her sooner than Nicole had expected. What she would do once she moved…

'We'll think of something, hey, Bouncer?' Seeing the unremitting trust in his eyes, Nicole fixed a smile on her face and shook the paw Bouncer offered. She had no idea where to go from here if Lydia refused to take him. Maybe Becky would have some suggestions, she pondered, climbing out of the car and opening the passenger door, out of which Bouncer duly bounced. She would ask her when she called. She wasn't sure what Becky would think when she told her what she really thought about Olivia. Telling her that she thought she was a manipulative, scheming bitch who was doing her best to destroy her would sound barking mad. Was she? Was she getting everything horribly out of proportion because of her own insecurities? It would sound insane, after all, to someone who wasn't the target of Olivia's spiteful campaign; to anyone who'd ever met Olivia on a casual basis, in fact. The girl oozed sweetness and light whenever it suited.

She would write it all down, Nicole decided, bracing herself as she walked to Lydia's front door. It would be cathartic, if nothing else. She would write good old-fashioned letters and hold on to them until she was sure. At least then she would have a record, should she need one when things came to a head – which they would. Nicole was positive of that. If not by Olivia's instigation, then, so help her God, by hers.

Stopping at the door, she crouched down to give Bouncer a hug. 'It won't be for long, sweetheart. I promise I'll come and visit you every day,' she whispered, and then heaved herself to her feet to push her key into the lock.

'Only me,' she called, realising how late it was. There wasn't a lot of love lost between them, but she didn't want to give her mother a heart attack. Peering around the lounge door, expecting to find Lydia dozing, since the TV was still on, she was surprised to find her armchair empty. 'Lydia?' she called. She still wasn't quite able to address her as 'Mum'. She hadn't been much of one.

Heading for the kitchen, Bouncer padding along beside her, she stopped short when she found the cellar door ajar. Oh no, she hadn't ventured down there again, had she? Richard had said he'd found her in the cellar once, in search of vintage red wine from Nicole's father's stock, with which she'd obviously hoped to impress him. What on earth was she thinking, going down there this late in the evening?

'Lydia?' Nicole pulled the door wide and squinted into the darkness. She clearly wasn't down there but she groped for the light switch located inside the cellar door anyway, just in case.

'Stay, Bouncer,' she instructed him, stepping tentatively on to the wooden steps, lest anything eight-legged and hairy leap out at her.

It took a second for Nicole's eyes to adjust to the bright white light of the single bulb in the ceiling. It took another second for the horrific scene at the foot of the steps to register.

Oh God, no. 'Mum!' Nicole's scream echoed shrilly around the stone walls of the cellar. '*Mum!*' Blundering forward, she groped for the rickety stair rail. With her focus on her mother, her heart bursting, her stomach turning nauseatingly over, she didn't realise half of the rail was missing – until she found herself plunging downwards to land in the sticky red liquid surrounding Lydia's body.

Oh God, oh God. Shuffling closer, her mind recoiling, Nicole lifted trembling fingers to touch the gaping wound in the back of her mother's head. Fingers that were dripping with blood – she splayed them in front of her. Lydia's blood; her mother's brains spilled across the concrete.

'*Stay!*' Hearing the clattering of claws on wood, she turned to bellow at Bouncer. 'Stay, baby,' she sobbed, slipping and slithering and sliding as she attempted to find some purchase with which to drag herself up.

She didn't feel the shard of glass, from the wine bottle Lydia had thought it so important to fetch, when it punctured her knee. Ice-cold terror was all she felt as she scrambled to get away. Retching at the smell – warm, metallic, vinegary – Nicole stumbled back up the steps.

Clutching Bouncer's collar as she reached the hall, the back of one blood-covered hand pressed under her nose, she went instinctively to the phone on the hall table. It wasn't there in its cradle where it should be. Lydia carried it about. *Had* carried it about. Lydia, her mother…

Dead.

It permeated her terror with sickening clarity. She'd died alone. Nicole pressed her hand closer, suppressing a wretched sob. She must have been terrified. So very, very frightened. She'd lived her whole life frightened. And now… Nicole didn't hate her for it any more. She loved her. And she'd never once said it.

Not once!

Why? Flying to the front door, leaving bloody prints in her wake, she fumbled it open and headed back to her car, where she'd left her mobile. What good was it there? *Useless.* She was utterly useless: too weak to defend herself against a bullying monster; and now too weak to fight a different kind of monster, who hid her malevolence beneath a thin layer of beauty. Incapable of looking after her own mother. What was the *matter* with her?

She jabbed 999 into her phone, but the knot in her throat threatened to choke her as she struggled to relay what she'd found. Nicole stopped talking.

'Hello, caller?' a concerned voice said in her ear as her heart slowed to a dull thud.

Narrowing her eyes, Nicole tried to make out the indistinct shape darting across the drive towards the orangery at the back of the house. An animal? A trick of the light: branches swaying in the waxy light of the moon?

No. *A figure*, crouching low. Nicole's heart stopped beating. She wasn't mistaken. She watched it dodge and weave and disappear into the trees. Someone had been in the house. Had Lydia fallen, or had someone... *pushed her?*

CHAPTER THIRTY-THREE

REBECCA

PRESENT

Rebecca had relented. She'd had no choice but to. He'd asked her to marry him several times in France – the final time just before they'd departed. She hadn't been quite sure what to think when he didn't broach the subject again in the five weeks she'd been 'living' with him. She hadn't been sure what she would do if he didn't. Propose to him, possibly? If this was a game, she needed to stay one step ahead of them, even if she didn't yet have all the facts. And if it wasn't? She would cross that bridge when she got to it.

And then she'd come down to breakfast this morning to find a wonderfully romantic proposal. His expression had been nervous as she'd walked towards the table, seeing immediately the rose petals he'd scattered there. He'd written the words 'I Love You' on a white paper napkin, a solitaire diamond ring serving as the 'o' in the word love.

There was a part of her that wanted Richard to live up to his image. A parent's love for a child, even an adult child, is unerring, Rebecca was aware of that. You feel their pain; you hurt when they hurt. Your mission in life is to protect them until they're strong enough to carve a path through life on their own. Sometimes you overprotect, close your eyes to their flaws. Could Richard's love for Olivia really have rendered him blind, though, to the hurt she'd caused Nicole?

Soon she would know. For now she was truly stepping into Nicole's shoes and walking in her footsteps, which had brought her here: to the lock at the junction of the Worcestershire Canal and the River Severn, the precipice over which her dear friend had stepped from this life into oblivion.

Drawing in a breath, Rebecca looked down at the depths of muddy, dark water, deceitfully still and calm in the lock below her. It was a wide-beam lock, allowing boats access to the river. She'd checked the information board on her walk up. This was one of the deepest locks in the country, she'd learned: twenty feet wide, ninety feet long and at least eighteen feet deep. And the drop between gate and water contained any number of fall-breaking, bone-crushing obstructions before a body would land.

Beyond was the river: in flood – fast-flowing and deadly. Nicole hadn't been a strong swimmer. If she'd stepped from the lock into the river's swirling black waters, she would have known she was embracing death. And Rebecca was no closer to knowing why. What unbearable pain she must have been suffering on that bleak day that had brought her to this.

'Afternoon,' a man said, passing by behind her. 'Someone looks deep in thought.'

Smiling distractedly, Rebecca glanced at him. 'I am. Miles away,' she said. Actually, she wasn't. She was down there with Nicole, feeling her weightlessness, the tightness in her chest, the ebbing away of hope, of life.

'Aye, it's the place to come if you need time to reflect,' he said companionably, pausing to amble across to her. 'I often do the same. There's something about the water that helps put things into perspective, I find.'

Rebecca smiled wryly at that.

'My wife used to say the same,' he went on nostalgically. 'She's gone now, bless her. There's never a day goes by I don't think of her.'

Rebecca looked more interestedly at him as he leaned an arm on the lock gates and gazed reflectively across the water. He was early seventies or thereabouts, with an open, ruddy face. She didn't miss the sadness in his eyes. 'I'm sorry,' she said. 'Her loss must have been difficult for you.'

He gave her an appreciative smile. 'She's at peace now. She was ill for quite a while. It was better she went when she did,' he said, his voice catching despite his assurances. 'I couldn't bear to think of her suffering.'

Rebecca nodded, understanding more than he knew. 'I was thinking about my friend,' she confided, somehow feeling safe to. 'She died here.' Swallowing, she contemplated Nicole's watery grave again, as if it would somehow yield the answers she sought. 'I'm not sure I've managed to get any perspective on why, but I feel closer to her here.'

The man straightened up at that. 'The red-haired lass?' he asked, his wizened forehead knitting in concern.

'Yes.' Rebecca turned curiously back to him. 'Did you see her?' There had been witnesses – two, apparently – who arrived at the scene after Nicole had gone under. Was he one of them?

'Heard it, more like. I live in the lock cottage just over the way.' He nodded towards it. 'Couldn't help but hear the poor bloke screaming for help.'

Richard.

'Frantic, he was.' The man shook his head sombrely. 'He'd already gone in after her by the time I reached him with my torch. Brave thing to do. I mean, I know he was acting on instinct, but there was a red danger alert that night. The river was treacherous.'

Rebecca stared at him, her heart rate spiking as she felt the fear Richard must have felt. That Nicole must have felt.

'He dived four or five times. Down there a long time too, he was. Came up spluttering water and empty-handed each time. Poor bugger, he was bloody heartbroken when the police finally managed to haul him out.'

Rebecca felt her own heart twist inside her. She'd been looking for flaws – flaws she felt had to be there. A motive, even. The traits that might have driven a vulnerable woman to take her own life though, were *they* part of Richard's make-up?

He could have died, too; that reality wasn't lost on her. The water would have been freezing: cold enough to cause his body temperature to plummet in seconds. Yet he'd gone under, time and time again. Were those the actions of a manipulative, unfeeling man, the kind of man Nicole would have taken her own life to get away from? Perhaps it truly was her depressed state of mind that had driven her here. Olivia had contributed to the despair she must have felt, that was irrefutable, but had Richard? Rebecca might never know. No matter how hard she stared into the water, she might never find answers.

Was it time to let it go, she wondered? To let Nicole go?

CHAPTER THIRTY-FOUR

NICOLE

PREVIOUS YEAR – DECEMBER

'Where is she?' Nicole demanded, sliding off her hospital trolley as soon as Richard walked into the cubicle.

'Mrs Gray, you need to stay still,' a nurse tried to encourage her back. 'We haven't finished stitching—'

'Where *is* she?' Pushing past her, Nicole screamed it.

Richard stepped back as she advanced on him, his expression bewildered. 'Nicole…' He took a second to recover himself and then moved towards her, gently taking hold of her arms. 'Where is *who*? You're distraught. You need to do as the nurse says, and then we'll—'

'*Who?*' Nicole laughed bitterly, struggling to break free of him. 'Your bitch daughter! Who do you *think* I mean?'

Richard said nothing. Dropping his hands away, his face chalk white, his eyes dark, he simply stared at her.

'She's not here. I've asked.' Nicole waved an arm vaguely around. Olivia had been admitted to hospital earlier, but apparently she had since been discharged. 'Is she at home?'

His expression stony, Richard didn't answer.

'Well?' Nicole glared at him.

Richard's eyes grew a shade darker. 'Yes,' he said tightly. 'She's at home. Where else would you expect her to be?'

Nicole matched his hostile gaze with one of her own. 'Nowhere *but* there, plotting and scheming,' she retorted.

A small tic spasmed in Richard's cheek; his eyes were dangerous. Nicole didn't care. Whatever he thought of her, she *couldn't* care. She could no longer say nothing for fear of angering or upsetting him. Her mother was dead! He couldn't bury his head in the sand and ignore *this*.

'Has she been there all the while?' she asked him, her gaze hard on his.

Richard narrowed his eyes, looking at her as if maybe she had taken leave of her senses. She hadn't! She was *not* imagining any of this.

'Since she was discharged?' she clarified. 'Has she been at the house the whole—'

'Yes!' Richard snapped. 'She'd not capable of going out! For Christ's sake, what the *hell* is this all about, Nicole?'

'Mrs Gray… Nicole,' the nurse said kindly, attempting to intervene, 'you really do need to let us attend to that wound, lovely. You're bleeding—'

'I'm not lovely!' Nicole turned on her tearfully. 'I'm horrible! Or at least his daughter is convincing him I am.' She swept her gaze back to Richard. '*Isn't* she?'

Shaking his head, Richard glanced warily at the nurse and then back to her. 'Nicole, I have no idea what's going on in your mind, but will you please allow the medical staff to attend to you? You're clearly extremely distressed. We'll talk as soon as we get home. *Calmly.* Okay? Just—'

'Yes, right,' Nicole sneered. 'Where no doubt Olivia will have an asthma attack at the crucial moment.'

'*Jesus!*' Sucking in a sharp breath, Richard eyed the ceiling. 'Nicole, you need to stop this. Now,' he said, stepping quickly towards her.

Nicole took a hasty step back. She'd had to hone her skills when it came to dodging out of a man's way. He might not want to hit her, but he wanted to catch her, to make her do what he wanted her to do: go home. Accept that Olivia had nothing to do with this? She wouldn't. She couldn't. 'How did she try to take her own life?' she asked, notching her chin up defiantly.

His look now one of open disgust, Richard laughed scornfully. 'This is unbelievable. You're ill, Nicole, clearly. You need help. Please let me—'

'*How?*' Nicole yelled.

'Sleeping tablets!' Richard yelled back. 'Prescribed when her mother died. Are you happier now for knowing? Are you getting some kind of kick out of crucifying me here, Nicole? Because you bloody well are.'

Nicole ignored that. 'No visible signs she attempted suicide then?' she said, her voice loaded with contempt. 'Did they take blood tests?'

'*What?*' Richard stared at her in astonishment.

'She was at the house,' Nicole informed him icily. It was her. She *knew* it was. No matter what kind of alibi Olivia had, Nicole was unshakeable in her belief that it had been her. 'My mother's house. When she died, your daughter was there.'

'This is utterly *insane*.' Richard looked at her as if she'd just punched him.

'I saw her!'

'She was with me, Nicole. She was with me the whole time.' There was no anger in Richard's tone now. Instead it was flat, emotionless. 'Whatever ludicrous imaginings you're having here, you've got it wrong.'

'She hates me!' Nicole cried as he turned his back on her. He couldn't walk away. He couldn't! Not this time.

'Right.' Turning slowly to face her, Richard sighed heavily. 'And presumably you also think she hates your mother, who she's never even met.' He scanned her face, his eyes deeply troubled. 'I seem to recall it was *you* who actually hated Lydia, Nicole.'

'I did *not*,' Nicole refuted, panic clenching her stomach. She needed him to believe her. She needed him to see. 'I didn't get on with her, but that didn't mean I—'

'Enough!' Richard interjected forcefully. 'You need help, Nicole.' He fixed her with a steely gaze. 'I'll be in the waiting room. Please let me know when you're ready to talk sense.'

CHAPTER THIRTY-FIVE

REBECCA

PRESENT

Letting herself in through the front door, Rebecca found Richard halfway down the stairs, hastily tugging on his shirt.

'Hi,' she said, arching an eyebrow as she noted his flustered expression. 'Are we getting dressed or undressed?'

'Dressed, unfortunately. I have to go back to work.' Looking her over regretfully, Richard hurried down. 'Liv's had me heaving furniture about.' He rolled his eyes good-naturedly towards the ceiling. 'Thus the hot and sweaty mess.'

'Hmm,' said Rebecca, her eyes full of deliberate suggestion. 'I'm thinking I could quite go for hot and sweaty.'

Richard's mouth curved into a mischievous smile. 'Later,' he growled huskily, snaking an arm around her waist and anchoring her to his hips.

'I hope that's a promise,' Rebecca breathed, the hardness of his body igniting the same primal desire she'd felt that first time on the patio. The man oozed a sexual allure that was fatal. That *had*, in fact, been ultimately fatal for Nicole. Rebecca felt her heart dip inside her.

'Most definitely,' Richard assured her, closing his mouth over hers. Then, '*Damn*,' he murmured, pulling away as Olivia padded barefoot down the stairs behind him – humming, Rebecca noticed, as if to announce her presence.

'Don't mind me,' Olivia said brightly, making insinuating eyes at her as she squeezed by, heading for the kitchen. 'Just carry on as if I'm not here… though preferably not in the hall.'

'Sorry,' Richard mouthed to Rebecca, shaking his head and reaching to fasten his shirt buttons. 'So,' he said, smiling despairingly as Olivia commenced clanging kettles and cups, making it obvious she was around, 'been anywhere interesting?'

'Just walking.' Rebecca shrugged evasively. 'Taking in the sights.'

'I was getting worried.' Richard glanced at his watch as he straightened his collar. 'Wondering whether I should send out a search party.'

'Sorry,' she apologised in turn, realising she had actually been gone for some while. 'I needed to do some thinking and I lost track of the time.'

'Not thinking about changing your mind, I hope?' Richard's gaze shot apprehensively to hers.

Rebecca noted the immediate nervousness in his eyes. For an assured businessman, he did vulnerable little schoolboy very well. 'No,' she assured him. 'To be honest, I was thinking about Nicole.'

Richard dropped his gaze. 'Oh,' he said, his eyes now troubled as they came back to hers.

'I was wondering how she would feel. About us, I mean,' Rebecca went on, watching him with interest and wondering how he would react to mention of the wife he'd so recently lost now that he was about to marry again.

Emitting a sigh, Richard nodded understandingly. 'Of course. Your emotions will be in turmoil, I imagine. You knew her though, Becky.' Smiling sadly, he reached to give her hand a reassuring squeeze. 'I doubt she would have begrudged you your happiness, if she was sure it was what you wanted.'

His eyes held a question as they searched hers, as if it were him who needed the reassurance. 'It is. It's just...' Rebecca faltered.

'Just?' Richard urged her, his eyes clouding with concern.

Rebecca hesitated. 'If you were thinking of a church wedding, then...' She paused, looking uncertain. She was going to go through with this. She'd made her decision. She couldn't walk away, nor did she want to. But there was no way she could stand in the same place Nicole had taken her wedding vows believing she would live happily ever after.

'God, no.' Richard wrapped his arms around her, drawing her to him. 'That would be far too painful, for both of us. You choose.' He brushed her cheek with his lips. 'Wherever. A hotel. The top deck of a bus. I don't care, as long as you're there.'

Rebecca laughed. I'm not so sure the minister would be happy about the top deck of a bus, but I'll check out some venues,' she said.

She would, she decided. She would go into the village. There was a little hotel there that might cater for small weddings. She could also pay a visit to the art shop, which she'd been meaning to check out. After noting some of Nicole's work on display in the window when she'd last been here, she'd wanted to go in, but the owners had been away on holiday. She supposed Nicole's works might have been taken down by now, but it would be an opportunity to introduce herself and talk to people who'd known Nicole. It was the owner of the art shop who'd encouraged her to take the evening art class, she recalled. She would certainly be worth speaking to.

CHAPTER THIRTY-SIX

NICOLE

PREVIOUS YEAR – DECEMBER

Watching Richard, who was agitatedly pacing in reception while on his phone – no doubt to the daughter he thought could do no wrong – Nicole chose her moment when his back was turned to slip out of the hospital.

Limping to her car, she found Bouncer curled up fast asleep on the back seat. Thanking God that she'd remembered to leave the window open a fraction – even though, in Richard's estimation, she'd lost her mind – she slipped into the driver's seat, at which Bouncer howled ecstatically and proceeded to bounce joyously around.

'*Shhh.*' After helping him scramble into the front passenger seat, where at least she could placate him, Nicole started the engine. Even if she could go home, to the house which didn't feel like a home, she couldn't go with Bouncer, could she, thanks to the bitch. *God!* Crunching gears, Nicole pulled out of the car park. Couldn't Richard see what she was doing?

She couldn't go back there at all, not now that she'd done exactly what Olivia had hoped she would, despite knowing he wouldn't believe her: she'd told Richard that she'd seen Olivia at her mother's house. She *had*. Richard had no right to tell her what she had or hadn't seen with her own eyes. She wasn't blind. She wasn't 'insane' either. It was *her* – that bloody witch in the guise of an innocent young woman – who needed psychiatric help.

Who knew what she might be capable of. It wouldn't be safe to go back there. Was Richard so blinkered that he really couldn't see what had been happening? Couldn't see that his daughter had systematically set out to destroy her from the day of their wedding? Why she was doing it, Nicole had no clue. Why would she have befriended her and then turned on her? Why would she pick on a defenceless old woman in order to hurt *her*? She'd killed Lydia. Whether by accident or with intent, she had. Richard must know she would never invent such a thing. But she also knew that everything she'd accused Olivia of sounded preposterous, like the ravings of a madwoman.

Which was exactly what Olivia wanted.

She needed to fight back. She *had* to. And she would be as vicious and as devoid of emotion as Olivia. Play her at her own game. In order to do that, she had to appear rational. She had to calm down and get someone on her side, since Richard clearly wasn't.

'It's okay, boy.' Nicole attempted to reassure Bouncer, who was panting worriedly and probably desperate for a wee. 'I won't desert you, my faithful little friend, I promise.'

Blinded by the tears now spilling from her eyes, potent tears of grief and rage, Nicole drove determinedly on towards the village. She had nowhere else to go. No one she knew that well – apart from Isobel, who might label her mad too. It was a risk she had to take. She just prayed that Isobel would understand why she was knocking on her door in the middle of the night. Prayed harder she would take pity on her and take Bouncer until she could think what to do.

Parking in front of the little cottage situated next to the art shop, Nicole eyed the darkened windows with trepidation. Isobel and Mike would be fast asleep. Everyone, bar her and Richard, would be sleeping at this hour – even Olivia, now that she imagined she'd achieved her aim. Not heavily enough, unfortunately, Nicole thought bitterly. She didn't believe she'd taken sleeping pills. Not for a second. Or, if she had, only enough to fool her father and the doctors, who would presumably have taken a blood test. She was a liar. A vile, evil, manipulative liar, fixated on her father and prepared to go to any lengths to make sure he had no one in his life but her.

Once she'd gathered who it was, Isobel unhitched her chain and pulled her front door open. 'Nicole?' she said, stunned to find her standing there. 'What on earth…?'

'I'm sorry to call on you so late,' Nicole stammered quickly, aware that, with blood still matted in her hair and all over her clothes, she must look like a deranged lunatic on the loose. 'It's just that—' Stopping, she heaved in a breath and tried hard to hold back the tears. 'My mother died.'

'Oh my God, Nicole…' Her face creasing with sympathy, Isobel reached for her, ushering her into the hall and causing Nicole's eyes to fill up all over again.

'I think Olivia killed her!' she blurted. Choking back a sob, she realised she had no hope of achieving the calmness she needed to.

'What?' Isobel stared at her, shocked, and then gathered herself and pulled Nicole close to her. 'Mike!' she called, as her husband stepped warily into the hall from the stairs behind her. 'Pour Nicole a brandy, please. And fetch the throw down off the bed, would you?

'Come on,' she said, steering Nicole towards their cosy lounge. 'Careful,' she added, noticing her limp.

Seating her in the armchair, she grabbed the throw Mike appeared with and wrapped it around her shoulders, then took the brandy her husband also offered. 'Sip,' she instructed, holding the glass for her. 'Small sips, and then take a breath and tell me all about it.'

Nicole gratefully did as she was bid, feeling the liquid burn her throat all the way down to her belly. It did little to warm her.

'Bouncer,' she croaked, wiping a hand across her mouth. 'Would you take him for me? Just for a while, until…'

Nicole trailed off, a fresh crop of tears springing from her eyes as she remembered that she didn't have a plan, had absolutely no clue how to even start fighting back. If Richard refused to believe her, she had nowhere to go, no one to turn to in the whole world, apart from Becky, who suddenly seemed a million miles away. Could she even go to the police, with nothing but accusations which her husband, Olivia's father, would dismiss as utterly ludicrous?

'Olivia's allergic,' she blundered on, trying to explain. 'She has asthma. I can't take him back to the rescue centre. I just can't. That's what *she* wants me to do. She doesn't care about anything or anybody. She won't give a damn if he ends up being put down. I doubt she even cares about Richard, but he's too blind to—'

'*Shhh,*' Isobel urged her, crouching down in front of her to take hold of her hands. 'Bouncer, where is he?' she asked, her eyes kind and understanding as they held hers, which only caused Nicole to cry harder.

'In the car,' she managed snottily. 'He desperately needs a wee.'

'I'll fetch him,' Mike said, exchanging worried glances with his wife. He was bound to be worried. They both would be, with an incoherent madwoman descending on them in the dead of night.

Isobel waited for Mike to disappear into the hall, and then, squeezing her hands gently, she asked, 'Nicole, what did you mean when you said you think Olivia killed your mother?'

Nicole noted her expression: wary, as it would be. Blinking at her tearfully, she took a shaky breath. She would think she was mad. How could she not? But she had to tell someone. She was right about this. She *knew* she was.

'She was there, outside the house. I'd already found my mother,' she began falteringly. 'I thought she'd fallen down the cellar steps – the banister was loose, you see – but when I went to the car to fetch my phone, I saw someone. I thought it was just a shadow at first, but then I realised it was a figure running away from the house.'

'And you think it was Olivia?'

'I know it was.' Nicole was adamant.

Isobel, though, looked incredulous. 'Did you see her face?' she asked her.

She didn't believe her. Would anybody? Even Becky, her best friend – would she believe her, or would she think she was as mad as everyone else seemed to? Nicole pressed the back of her hand to her nose. 'No.' She shook her head. 'It was too dark. But it *was* her. I'm sure it was.'

Isobel knitted her brow. 'But why would she—'

'Because she hates me!' Nicole insisted, repeating what she'd told Richard. 'She's trying to get rid of me. She was trying to get rid of Bouncer. That's why I had to bring him.' Her eyes shot to her dog as Mike brought him in, the only friend whose loyalty she could rely on.

His tail going around like a windmill, Bouncer immediately scrambled towards her and tried to jump up on her lap. Nicole hoisted him up, cuddled him close to her and tried again – in between hiccupping sobs – to explain. And the more she did, the worse it sounded. She really did sound completely insane. It was obvious Isobel and Mike thought so. Nicole could tell by the anxious glances they were now exchanging.

'It's the truth,' she said, looking desperately between them. 'All of it. I swear to God it is. She wants me gone, whatever she has to do to achieve it.'

Isobel scanned her eyes, and then, her expression troubled, looked away to stroke Bouncer. 'Does your husband know all this?' she asked, her gaze coming back to Nicole.

Nicole hesitated. 'Yes,' she said, tugging in a breath. 'He makes excuses for her. He feels protective of her, I think, because of her mother dying so tragically. It's still such a short time ago. I suppose that might explain why she does seem to hate me so much. She probably thinks I'm trying to replace—'

'You mean Emily?' Isobel interrupted.

Nicole nodded, glancing towards Mike, who frowned in consternation, and then checked his beeping phone and excused himself to the hall.

'But Emily wasn't Olivia's mother,' Isobel said, now looking confused. 'Emily chose not to have children, because of her condition. She said—'

Isobel stopped, pulling herself to her feet as Mike came back in – followed by Richard. Her heart sinking to the pit of her stomach, Nicole watched as he swapped cautious glances with Isobel and Mike before approaching her – carefully, as if she were some unpredictable creature he was mistrustful of.

Instinctively, Nicole shrank back. *Emily wasn't her mother.* She looked at him, utterly bewildered. Why had he told her that?

Seeing her reaction, Richard paused, and then he took another tentative step, finally crouching in front of her, where Isobel – in whom she thought she'd found a safe harbour – had been just a second ago.

'Nicole…' Richard spoke gently, his face wretched with worry as he reached for her hands. 'Come home, sweetheart,' he said, his voice hoarse. 'You can't stay here. We'll talk. Everything is going to be all right, I promise you it will.'

Nicole scanned his face. He had tears in his eyes – ice-blue eyes, the colour of the midwinter sky, yet still they weren't cold. Now, they were concerned, frightened.

Emily wasn't her mother. Nicole swallowed back her heart, which seemed to be wedged in her windpipe. Should she go with him? Or should she react in the way Olivia – and now Richard – clearly expected her to: unpredictably, like a woman unbalanced? She wouldn't, Nicole thought angrily. She *wasn't*.

CHAPTER THIRTY-SEVEN

REBECCA

PRESENT

Having visited the hotel and finding it unsuitable, Rebecca tried the heritage centre, which had a small oak-panelled room for hire for modest functions. She definitely wanted modest, but she doubted even this would be understated enough. Collecting up a leaflet after viewing the room, she decided to take the route past the church to the art shop, purchasing flowers on the way. She needed to sit a while in quiet contemplation. To talk to her dear friend, whose soul she hoped was dancing free on the breeze, not trapped somewhere like the purgatory her life must have become.

She found flowers already there when she arrived. Roses, just beginning to shed their petals and bow their heads earthwards. Richard's? She crouched to weed out the saddest. The petals he'd sprinkled so romantically on the table had been the same colour – a soft, dusky pink.

After placing her own flowers – delicate freesias, because Nicole had loved their sweet-smelling perfume – into the urn alongside the roses, Rebecca settled down on the grass beside the grave. She had no particular place to go, nowhere to rush to. But she was rushing. Into what, she wasn't sure.

Feeling suddenly adrift, she drew her knees up to her chest and studied the inscription, which Richard had chosen, on the pretty white headstone: 'If love could have saved you, you would have lived forever.' Were those the words of a man who would knowingly have hurt her?

The headstone itself was beautiful: a simple marble heart with a hand-carved dove of peace at the right-hand apex. Thinking of the broken little lark trapped in its cage, Rebecca's eyes filled up. The stone had been picked with care; she couldn't have chosen better herself. He truly did appear to have cared for her. So what was she doing here? If ignorance was a sin, then yes, Richard had been guilty of that, but what other crime was she absolutely sure he'd committed?

Sighing, Rebecca rested her head on her knees. *Tell me what to do, Nicole,* she prayed silently. *Should I go through with it?* Dearly wishing she could hear her voice again, laugh with her again, dance barefoot in the rain together, Rebecca's heart squeezed inside her – and then flipped in her chest as the church bells began to toll, as if in celebration of a wedding.

On finding no ceremony taking place when she went back – and no sign of anyone – Rebecca had to work at convincing herself it had been a bell practice. She walked from the churchyard, calling Sam on her mobile as she went. She hadn't told him yet. She would have to eventually, but that very much depended on things continuing as they were and arrangements being firmly in place. For the moment, with the unpredictable nature of things, she'd made up her mind not to. Sam and Laura were thinking of going off to Europe for a couple of weeks, in any case, which would give her a little time.

'Hi, how's it going?' she asked, when he picked up.

'Okay… ish,' Sam answered vaguely.

And a bit flatly, Rebecca thought. 'Decided on your holiday venue yet?' she asked.

Sam hesitated. 'No.' He sighed, after a second. 'I'm not sure Laura's up for it now. She's thinking of taking a holiday with her family.'

'Oh?' Rebecca frowned. Reading the inflection in his tone, put together with the fact that the two were usually inseparable – going everywhere outside of university together or not going at all – she sensed there was trouble. 'Everything's all right with you two though, yes?'

Sam went quiet for a second, and then, 'We had a bit of an argument,' he said, now sounding definitely dejected. 'Don't worry, it's cool,' he added, attempting to sound blasé and failing. 'We haven't split or anything. Laura just needs some space, that's all.'

Which meant Sam was in the doghouse. Rebecca felt for him. 'Do you want to talk about it?' she asked him carefully. Growing into what Rebecca considered to be a fine young man, Sam was putting away childish things. Once it had been cuddles at the school gates. Now, it was confiding in his mum.

Again, he went quiet. 'Some girl,' he admitted eventually. 'She's been texting me.'

Rebecca hesitated. 'As in sexting?' she asked him warily.

'Yeah, I suppose.' Sam sounded embarrassed. 'The thing is, they're totally out of the blue. I haven't, you know, done anything. I only ever replied to the first one, kind of jokily, and then I ignored them, but they just kept pinging in.'

'And Laura saw them,' Rebecca guessed.

'That's about the gist of it.' Sam sighed again, heavily this time. 'I suppose I should have deleted them, but… Anyway, I didn't, and Laura's having a hard time believing me. I can't say I blame her.'

'Do you want me to give her a ring?' Rebecca asked gently, her natural instinct being to want to make things right for him, which she couldn't, of course.

Sam laughed at that. 'Yeah, right. My mother ringing my girlfriend for me is going to make me look really macho, isn't it?'

Rebecca smiled sadly. She supposed he would be worried about his image. 'For Laura's sake as much as yours,' she clarified. 'She might want to talk. You never know, it might help.'

'Nah. Don't worry, we'll sort it out. Or not. I've told her I'm changing my number. I suppose I'll just have to wait now. I'll let you know how things go when we've talked more.'

'Do that,' Rebecca said. 'And call me if you need to – any time.'

'I will,' Sam promised. 'I'd better go. I have to be somewhere. Speak soon.'

He ended the call rather quickly. Rebecca pulled her phone away from her ear, an uneasy feeling creeping through her. Hoping Laura might call possibly? Rebecca hoped she did. They were both still young, with plenty of time yet for romance, but she knew Sam was in love with Laura. Might he have encouraged the girl who had been texting him, she wondered? God, might it be Olivia? The worrying thought occurred. Surely, she wouldn't? But Rebecca had a sneaking suspicion she would. In which case, she wasn't sure what to think. She'd never known Sam to be anything but respectful to women, having been brought up by a single mum. But then, she couldn't know everything about him, she supposed.

Making a mental note to call him back later, and to have a quiet word with Olivia, Rebecca stopped as she reached her destination. Goosebumps prickled the entire surface of her skin as she realised Nicole's paintings were still on display in the window. Richard had given permission for them to stay, presumably.

Taking a fortifying breath, Rebecca went in, the door jangling quaintly as she did so, giving her a sense of melancholic nostalgia. 'Hi.' She smiled at the woman behind the counter, who smiled warmly back. Rebecca half expected her to leap out and ask if she was interested in anything specific. Rebecca was, but like Laura, she felt she needed a little space.

Grateful when the woman turned back to her laptop, Rebecca browsed the various works of art, the proceeds of which, she noted, were to be donated to a mental health charity. Most were much the same as those she'd seen at the village hall, all in muted tones. There were more here, though, of the river: some of the swirling black depths of the river in flood, possibly at the very lock Rebecca had stood at.

'She's a local artist,' the woman offered as Rebecca stared at them, trying to read the mood behind them. 'Deceased, sadly,' she added. 'Thus the charity donation.'

Rebecca swallowed a jagged knot in her throat. 'I know.' She forced a smile. 'She was a friend.' A close friend, who hadn't felt able – or been able – to call her on the darkest day of her life. Tears pricked the back of her eyes.

'I'm sorry,' the woman said, coming across to her. 'Isobel,' she introduced herself, offering her hand. 'You knew her well then?'

'Rebecca,' she said, offering her own. 'Yes. Yes, I did. We met at university. Shared everything together… up until she married, at least.'

She felt Isobel watching her as she looked back at the paintings, wanting to decode them, wishing she could.

'Those were later works,' Isobel said, nodding towards the river studies.

'Painted when she was troubled?' Rebecca squinted at the almost angry swirls of the brush that depicted the swollen waters in flood.

Isobel nodded. 'They're beautiful and evocative, but definitely the product of a chaotic mind.' She sighed sadly.

'When did it start? Her illness?' Rebecca faced the woman, hoping for something, anything, that would allow her to believe there was more to this than that she got ill and then she died. There were just too many gaps.

Isobel scrutinised her thoughtfully, appearing reticent to divulge information, but then seemed to relent. 'I'm not sure,' she said. 'She was having some problems with her husband's daughter when I first spoke to her. Nothing too horrendous – some issue about the fumes from the oils she used setting off the girl's asthma, I think.'

'Olivia.' Rebecca nodded. 'I gathered.'

'You know her then?' Isobel looked surprised.

'Yes.' Rebecca glanced down. 'Richard and I have become friends since Nicole died.'

'Ah.' Isobel narrowed her eyes slightly, as if drawing conclusions.

'Is that why she started using watercolours?' Rebecca asked, wanting to avoid the subject of the exact nature of her relationship with Richard and concentrate on Nicole.

'I believe so, which was good for us,' Isobel said. 'She ran the evening art class, just for a short while, in exchange for which she used the room at the back of the hall as a studio.'

'Really?' Rebecca's eyes widened. She hadn't known about that. 'So she was painting in oils as well then?'

'She was. It was her passion, I think,' Isobel confirmed, chatting more easily now. 'There are still some canvases there. I did mention them to Richard. Some art materials, too. I've been wondering what to do with them. There's one canvas I'd like very much to keep, but… Perhaps you'd like to take a look sometime?'

'I'd love to,' Rebecca assured her, her heart rate kicking up at the thought that Nicole had been able to pursue her painting, which might have provided some outlet for her emotions. Not enough of an outlet though, clearly.

'Olivia was also allergic to Nicole's dog, apparently,' Isobel went on, with a heartfelt sigh.

Rebecca was aware of this, but it made no sense, considering Bouncer was there at the house. Olivia had never so much as sneezed. Perhaps she was now on appropriate asthma medication, Rebecca wondered. And yet, if it was asthma she was supposed to have, Rebecca had seen no signs of an inhaler.

'That was one of reasons she was so distressed on the day her mother died. She was distraught at finding her the way she did, but she was also terribly upset at the thought of having to rehome Bouncer. She was devastated, confused. Ranting, almost. She seemed convinced that Olivia was trying to get rid of her.' Isobel hesitated. 'She claimed she'd seen Olivia running from the house after she'd found her mother, which caused Richard considerable distress, as you can imagine, but…'

She stopped, eyeing Rebecca cautiously now, as if trying to judge how much to tell.

'But?' Rebecca urged, her heart palpitating now for different reasons.

'There was something… something she said when I first met her, and which she repeated that night. It might have been because of her general confusion, but…' Isobel's gaze flicked down and back. 'She seemed to think that the woman Richard was previously married to was Olivia's mother. She wasn't. Emily wasn't married to Richard for long. I didn't know her well, but well enough to know she never had children – because of her condition, she said. I did wonder why Nicole would have been confused about that.'

As Rebecca had known she had. She'd guessed something was amiss when Olivia had said her mother had died when she was five, which meant that this woman, Emily, who'd died five years ago couldn't have been her. She hadn't been sure what had been amiss then. Since, realising how manipulative Olivia was, she'd wondered whether the girl might be a psychopathic liar, changing her story to elicit sympathy depending on who she was talking to. Now, she was wondering: had Richard and Olivia failed to get their stories straight?

Who was Olivia's mother? Had he been married to her? This man who had 'principles', who was 'old-fashioned', liked to do things properly?

More importantly, where was she?

CHAPTER THIRTY-EIGHT

PREVIOUS YEAR – DECEMBER

Dear Becky,

Please forgive me for not being in touch, as promised. I've been meaning to call you but so much has happened. I'm in a state of utter shock, if I'm honest. All is not marital bliss here, you might have gathered. Olivia, it turns out, is not the vulnerable, pretty young woman that she seems, still struggling to come to terms with her mother's death. The woman Richard was recently married to, you see, wasn't her mother. There's obviously been some miscommunication between us; he must have had a previous relationship. I haven't had chance to discuss it with him yet. I intend to, though not in earshot of Olivia, who would love a confrontation between us. She clearly hates me (and it can't be because she thinks I'm trying to replace her mother, if Emily, the woman Richard was married to, wasn't her mother – do you see?). She's preventing me from painting. Trying to take my only friend in the world – apart from you, my lovely – away from me, claiming she's allergic to Bouncer. She interrupts any private moment Richard and

I try to find together, making communication between us impossible. Whatever excuses Richard makes for her (and I can't blame him for that – she is his daughter, after all), Olivia is a dangerous, scheming liar. She's trying to get rid of me, Becky, and I'm not sure what lengths she might go to. I'm bracing myself to write this – and I know you will definitely wonder about my mental state when you read it – but I think she murdered my mother.

I can't give you details. I'm writing this letter quickly while waiting for Richard to pick me up (I can't drive myself, as the antidepressants the doctor prescribed yesterday me are making me woozy). I've been to arrange Lydia's funeral this morning, and now I'm sitting in the little café on the high street, debating what to do. Richard didn't come to the funeral home with me. I didn't want him to. He doesn't believe me; he can see no wrong in her. I think he thinks it's me who hates Olivia. Though the truth is, hatred is all I can feel for her now. I can't be beaten into submission again, Becky. I think you are the only person who would understand why. I have to resort to her tactics and fight fire with fire…

Seeing Richard's car pull up on the road outside, Nicole paused, watching him through the steamy café window. He hesitated before climbing out, dragging a hand over the back of his neck, loosening his collar – looking stressed. He was obviously as bone weary with exhaustion as she was. Neither of them had slept much since the dreadful day of Lydia's death. Nicole wondered whether she would ever sleep again whilst under the same roof as Olivia. She hadn't mentioned her suspicions to the police, saying only that she'd seen someone in the vicinity of the house, but their investigations had so far come to nothing, and the doctor on call had concluded that Lydia's death was a tragic accident, which only added to her frustration. Richard had begged her not to badger the police to investigate further until they'd talked properly, which they hadn't yet. Nicole had no intention of broaching the subject with Olivia ever present in the house.

Stuffing the letter into her bag to finish later, she stood up as Richard finally climbed out of his car. Sighing heavily, he paused on the pavement, looking up to the heavens as if searching for answers, and then walked towards the café with his gaze fixed downwards. He looked like a man condemned, as if he were carrying the weight of the world on his shoulders. Nicole so wanted to ease his burden for him. But how could she? She couldn't close her eyes and pretend none of this was happening.

'Hi.' He smiled half-heartedly as she stepped out of the café. 'Have you eaten?' he asked her, sweeping his gaze over her.

His strong features were etched with such worry that Nicole had to look away. She couldn't bear it. This was breaking him, and little by little, it was fracturing her heart into pieces. 'A sandwich,' she lied. She couldn't eat. She simply couldn't swallow.

He nodded. He didn't believe her. Nicole recognised his despairing expression, the one he now seemed to wear permanently when he was around her. 'You need to eat more, Nicole,' he said, his eyes coming briefly back to hers. 'You're losing too much weight. It can't be healthy.'

Nicole supposed that this was better than the many less-than-subtle hints the misogynist had given her regarding her weight: that her clothes were too tight, unflattering – even when she'd been pregnant; that she was revealing too much breast, etc. 'I will,' she said, stepping past him as he came to her side, about to place his arm around her. She didn't miss the hurt in his eyes when she didn't allow him to.

Climbing into the car beside her, Richard glanced over as she buckled her seatbelt. He didn't speak. There was safety in silence, Nicole supposed. They drove for a while, each with their own thoughts, and then, 'Did you manage to get everything sorted out?' he asked her.

'As much as I could.' Nicole nodded, her throat tightening as she forced back tears that were too close to the surface. She'd discussed possible dates and talked about Lydia's life, looking for anecdotes, of which she sadly couldn't relate many. They'd talked about the type of service she might prefer and hymns Lydia had liked. She'd chosen the coffin. Through all of this she'd managed to keep the emotion reasonably in check, until the young funeral employee had asked her which address she would like the hearse to leave from. The funeral home, Nicole had finally confirmed, realising that, with Lydia's house sold, there was nowhere else. She wouldn't bring her anywhere near Richard's house and Olivia.

It was where she would scatter the ashes that had triggered the tears. She didn't have any idea, and it hurt to realise how little she'd really known her mother, how little they'd known each other. Lydia had loved her orangery, but Nicole couldn't bear the thought of leaving her there in the company of strangers.

'I wish you'd let me help you, Nicole. You shouldn't be doing this on your own.' Glancing at her again, Richard reached for her hand. Nicole didn't move it away, but nor did she tighten her hold around his.

Drawing a breath, Richard squeezed her hand briefly and then drew his away. 'Can we talk?' he asked, a hopeless edge to his voice. 'We need to,' he pushed, when she didn't immediately answer. 'We have to try, Nicole. We can't go on like—'

He stopped as his phone rang. From his sharp intake of breath, Nicole guessed who it was. 'I have to get this,' he said, his tone guarded. 'I can't ignore it after… with things the way they are.'

After her supposed attempt at suicide, he was struggling to say. Nicole didn't comment. To suggest that this is exactly what Olivia wanted – him at her beck and call, night or day – would only incite argument, which would help no one with emotions already running so high. She was surprised when he took the call on his hands-free. But then he had no other choice while he was driving, she supposed.

'Liv, hi,' he said, a wary edge to his tone. 'What's up?'

'Where are you?' Olivia asked, her voice sounding small and vulnerable, like a child's, rather than an adult's. Knowing exactly what she was up to, how skilfully she was playing Richard, Nicole felt anger rise in her chest.

'Not far away, sweetheart,' Richard answered, his tone reassuring. 'We won't be long.'

'Okay,' Olivia said uncertainly. 'Is Nicole all right?' she asked, sounding actually concerned, to Nicole's utter disbelief.

Richard's eyes flicked towards her. 'As much as she can be,' he said, his expression uncomfortable. 'We'll be back soon. Ten minutes at most.'

'Good.' Olivia's sigh of relief was audible. 'I'll put the kettle on,' she said kindly, causing Nicole to gasp. She really ought to get an Oscar, she thought bitterly.

Olivia looked worriedly from her dad to Nicole as they came in through the front door. 'I've made it strong and sweet,' she said, nodding towards the kitchen. 'I know it won't help much, but...' She gave her a sympathetic smile.

Nicole looked away. She had to. She was dangerously close to giving vent to her anger.

'Thanks, Liv,' Richard said, looking awkwardly between them. This was a terrible situation for him to be in. Nicole felt for him. But it wasn't of *her* making. He needed the scales peeled from his eyes. However painful it was, he needed to see his daughter for what she truly was.

'I'll leave you two to it,' Olivia offered nobly. 'I'll be upstairs if you need me.' She was looking at Richard when she said it, Nicole noted, hinting that she'd be there to help when he found himself under attack from his demented wife.

We won't, she was tempted to say, but she restrained herself. She waited until Olivia had gone up and was heading along the galleried landing to her room before walking to the kitchen of the soulless house that could never be a home.

Richard followed her. 'I'll pour the tea,' he offered, walking across to pick up the teapot, but then stopping and placing it shakily back down again.

Nicole watched as he drew in a long, ragged breath. '*Christ*, I can't do this,' he uttered wretchedly, pressing his fingers hard against his temples. 'Talk to me, Nicole,' he begged, his voice choked as he turned to her. 'Tell me what to do. I have no idea.'

Nicole searched his face. He looked utterly jaded, with dark circles under his eyes, fear *in* his eyes. She couldn't make it go away. Couldn't tell him everything was going to be all right, or pretend she was. It couldn't be. She couldn't be. Surely he must realise that? 'You could believe me,' she said simply, swallowing back her own tears.

'Christ!' Richard shouted, causing her to start. 'Believe *what*? Your ludicrous suggestion that my daughter had something to do with your mother's death?' He stared at her incredulously. 'It's insane! It's all in your mind, Nicole! And I have *no* idea what to do about it. *None.*'

'I am *not* insane! Or stupid, or vile or pathetic, or blind!' Nicole's tears sprang forth, every one of the hurts she'd suffered at a man's hands coming to the fore; every insult, every humiliation, causing her cheeks to heat up and her temper to flare. 'She's been manipulating me! Manipulating *you*. Making you think that it's all me, and it's *not*! It's—'

'Nicole, stop.' His face taut, Richard took a step towards her.

Nicole immediately backed away. 'No! Do *not* come near me!' She glanced over her shoulder, an instinctive reaction, for means of escape, and then back to him, a turmoil of emotions churning inside her – fear, grief, guilt and most of all fury. 'I won't lie down and take it. I *won't* be bullied, Richard. Not by you; not by anyone!' She broke off with a sob.

'What?' Richard looked her over, clearly bewildered. '*Jesus*, Nicole…' Sounding now more shocked than angry, he tentatively reached out to take hold of her hand. 'I'm not going to bully you or hurt you, I swear I'm not. I wouldn't. Please… just let me help you.'

Nicole flinched as he eased her towards him, but she didn't pull away.

'Come and sit down,' he said softly, wrapping an arm around her. 'Please,' he said, when she didn't move. 'You're upset. You haven't eaten. You're unsteady on your feet. Sit down. I'm concerned about you.'

Nicole allowed him to lead her to the breakfast table, where he guided her gently to a chair. Helping her down into it, he searched her face, his own pale and apprehensive, and then crouched down in front of her and clasped her hands in his.

'Nicole…' he started hesitantly, taking a deep breath. 'I've spoken to Olivia. She's aware she's been behaving unreasonably, but—'

'*Unreasonably?* Nicole stared at him in amazement. 'She's been an absolute monster. She *is* a monster.' Her determination not to discuss any of this while Olivia was in the house flew out of the widow. 'This isn't hormones. It isn't grief, or your daughter feeling a bit jealous because you have another woman in your life. She was at my mother's *house*, Richard. Why won't you—'

Nicole stopped, her heart ricocheting off her ribcage as Olivia appeared and promptly burst into tears.

Letting go of her hands, Richard got to his feet, his look now that of a man who didn't know which way to turn.

'I came to apologise,' Olivia blurted out. 'I didn't mean… Oh God…' Breaking emotionally off, she pressed the back of her hand to her nose. 'I'm so sorry, Nicole. I've been vile to you. An absolute bitch. I don't know why. It was after the thing with Zachary. I felt so… stupid and pathetic and weak. And when you didn't believe me, I… I just felt so lonely suddenly, and I…'

Richard went to her as she sobbed, huge tears cascading down her cheeks. Of course he would. No father would stand by and watch his daughter breaking her heart.

Nicole got warily to her feet.

'I wasn't at your mother's house, Nicole. I swear I wasn't. Dad was here with me. I would never do anything so awful as to scare an old woman. Please believe me this time, Nicole. Please don't keep thinking the worst of me. I can't bear it.'

Olivia looked into Nicole's eyes, her own beseeching. 'I wasn't there,' she repeated. 'If you can't bring yourself to believe anything else I've said, please believe it wasn't me you saw there.'

Stupid, pathetic, weak. Lonely. Nicole felt every one of those feelings. Were Olivia's words genuine? She was shaking, she noticed. Gulping back sobs now. Richard tried to comfort her, to hold her, but she wouldn't let him, stepping away instead and holding Nicole's gaze.

Seeing the desperation in her eyes, Nicole swallowed hard, her resolve wavering. Doubt clouded her recollection. She hadn't actually seen her. Not her face, anyway. Was it possible she'd convinced herself, just because she had wanted to believe the worst in her? She could have been wrong. Her emotions had been all over the place, even before she'd discovered Lydia. Her every instinct had screamed at her that it was Olivia she'd seen, but she might have been mistaken. And yet…

Emily wasn't her mother. Someone was lying to her. Her? Or him? Nicole looked at Richard, who was raking his hand through his hair in frustration, and then back to Olivia. 'When did your mother die?' she asked her bluntly.

Olivia looked startled. 'Eighteen years ago,' she answered, swapping puzzled glances with Richard as he handed her some kitchen roll. 'I was young.' Dabbing at her eyes, she turned back to Nicole. 'I can't really know how you feel, but I can sympathise. I'm truly so sorry about your mother, Nicole. You must be devastated.'

Nicole scrutinised her. Olivia thought she was asking because it was relevant to her own loss, rather than imagining some sort of conspiracy against her, which sounded ludicrous, even in her own mind.

'I'll go back up to my room.' Olivia said, after several seconds of awkward silence.

Richard stepped quickly after her as she turned to the hall. 'You don't have to, Liv,' he said, exasperation obvious in his tone.

'I know.' Glancing back, Olivia offered him a small smile. 'But I want to. I'm okay, Dad, honestly. I've promised a friend I would call her back about a flat-share anyway.'

Richard hesitated, plainly not knowing what to do for the best.

'Sit down and talk,' Olivia urged him. 'Nicole needs you right now.'

Watching her go, Richard shook his head, a kaleidoscope of emotion in his eyes as they came back to Nicole's. The impatience she'd thought she would never see there was all too apparent now. '*Do* you need me, Nicole?' he asked her, his throat tight.

Alone in their bedroom five minutes later, having made excuses to come up and wash her face, Nicole retrieved her unfinished letter to Becky from her bag. She could hear Richard's muted tones as he talked to Olivia in her room, checking his daughter really was all right. Again, Nicole couldn't blame him. He would need to get his own emotions in check, too, she imagined before facing his volatile wife.

Reading the letter, she deliberated whether she should start it over, pretend that her world wasn't crumbling around her. Would Becky, a single mum who worked full time, really want to contend with all this, to worry about it from a distance? Nicole was disinclined to post it as it was. Yet something was compelling her to send the unedited version. She couldn't shake the feeling that it wouldn't end here; that there would be some kind of awful confrontation. God knew where that might end. Nicole had no intention of backing down, not this time. Whatever happened, she needed to confide in someone, if only for confirmation she wasn't wicked, uncaring or mad. Becky would understand why she needed that. It was only Becky, her dear friend, who wouldn't judge her.

Olivia was in a terrible state when we got back, full of apologies. She more or less said the attempt she'd made on her life was because of my doubting her and the rift between us that followed. Richard obviously thought so too. He told me it was all in my mind: her vendetta against me, her manipulation of him, her having anything to do with Lydia's death.

I think I came close to hating him when he said that. But now, reading this back, realising how it sounds, I'm confused, wondering whether it might be. That I've been so damaged by my marriage to the misogynist, I'm seeing everything as manipulative or controlling. I'm not sure I believe that though – or Olivia. Rather than lay down the gauntlet and bring things to a head with Richard – which I suspect is what she wants – I've decided instead to act contrite. I need to marshal my defences, I think – quietly.

I'll write again with further news, my lovely. Please don't worry about me. I promise to remain on my guard. Hopefully we'll see each other soon and we can crack open a bottle and laugh about all of this. Oh, to do that: laugh like we did when we were young. If only…

Take care of you, sweetheart.

Until we meet, all my love and more.

Nicole. X

CHAPTER THIRTY-NINE

OLIVIA

PREVIOUS YEAR – DECEMBER

Richard had left the bedroom door ajar, so Olivia loitered on the landing. Eavesdropping on the woman's inane wittering somewhat relieved the tedium of having her around.

'Are you off out?' she heard Richard warily ask his troublesome wife.

'Just to Isobel's to check on Bouncer,' Nicole answered timidly. No doubt she was feeling contrite and riddled with guilt, contemplating the awful trauma she'd put his daughter through. 'He'll be wondering where I am.'

Oh, please. Olivia rolled her eyes sky high. *Hello? It's a dog, sweetie, not a fucking child.* God, honestly. She loved Wanderer, but Olivia didn't imagine he was human. The woman was so desperate to be loved she'd even settle for her mangy mongrel's mindless attempts at affection.

'Do you need to?' Richard asked her. 'This evening, I mean. I've just rung and spoken to her husband. Isobel has taken Bouncer out for a long walk, apparently. They're obviously looking after him well. We need to talk, Nicole. Properly. Just the two of us. We have to clear the air. Be honest with each other and—'

'Why did you tell me Emily was Olivia's mother?' she asked over him.

'Sorry?' Richard answered, sounding confused.

'Emily. You told me Olivia was devastated when she died.'

Richard laughed, a short disbelieving laugh. 'Yes, and so she was.'

'But I thought...' Nicole faltered. 'You implied that you'd lost your wife and—'

'*Implied?*' Richard now sounded bewildered. 'I did lose my wife, Nicole.'

Nicole didn't speak for a second. 'But I said Olivia must have been devastated when her *mother* died, and you...' She trailed off, obviously attempting to unscramble her muddled little brain. 'You must have been married before Emily and... I'm confused, Richard. I don't understand.'

'You and me both,' Richard said, a despairing edge now to his voice.

'I thought Emily was her mother, Richard,' Nicole babbled on. 'That she'd lost her more recently, that she might still be struggling with her death and that might be why she resented me. Don't you see?'

'No, Nicole I don't see,' Richard said bluntly. 'We've been through all this. Olivia doesn't resent you, or at least she didn't.' He sighed in exasperation. 'Look, Nicole, I didn't say – or "imply" – that Emily was Olivia's mother. As far as I recall, you asked me how Olivia coped when she died. I told you as it was. I never said Olivia was Emily's daughter.'

There was another long pause. 'Well, did I?' he asked, breaking the silence.

'No,' Nicole answered guardedly, 'but...'

'I said I'd had previous relationships. I never claimed to be a saint,' Richard said, with another long sigh. 'She left me, Olivia's mother, I did mention this, but... You *are* confused, Nicole,' he went on more kindly. 'It's perfectly understandable after all you've been through.'

Another silence followed, in which Nicole was undoubtedly soul-searching, examining her conscience and coming to the conclusion that she was every bit as vile as Olivia had hinted she was.

'She thought I didn't care about what happened to her,' she said eventually, sounding mortified. 'She really thought I didn't believe her, didn't she? That I was trying to harm her in some way.'

'It's not your fault, Nicole,' Richard said, his tone reassuring. 'We've all made mistakes, miscommunicated – not saying how we were feeling, possibly for fear of upsetting each other. Try not to feel guilty about any of this. It won't help.'

Well, that would make sure she did feel guilty – as guilty as hell, and so she should. Olivia nodded piously.

'I alienated her.' Nicole's response was tearful and muffled. He must be folding her into his manly arms, the needy cow.

'Come to bed, Nicole,' Richard said softly. 'Lie with me. We don't have to make love if you don't want to. I just want to be close to you.'

Urgh. This Olivia really did not want to listen to. Did he have to be so sick-makingly caring? It was enough to *make* a person bloody suicidal. *Hello? Devastated daughter out here in need of comforting.*

It had gone quiet now. Olivia sucked in a breath, an inch away from intervening. But no. She stopped, her hand hovering over the door handle. She needed to bring this whole thing to a swift end, she realised, and there was only one sure-fire way to do that.

Determined, Olivia went quietly back to her room.

CHAPTER FORTY

NICOLE

CURRENT YEAR – FEBRUARY

'It's a nice day for it,' Richard observed, pulling up in the car park that allowed access to a remote vantage point popularly used for viewing the River Severn bore. The tidal conditions weren't such that the waves would be able to form, but the surrounding landscape and wide, tumultuous sky made it the perfect place to capture the constantly shifting moods of the water.

'Perfect,' Nicole agreed, glancing out of her window. The weather was mild for February – ideal for painting. Since Christmas, which they'd hardly acknowledged with her mother's death, followed by the funeral, hanging like a shadow over them, she was finding her time alone, with nothing but the elements around her, quite cathartic. Some of the watercolour studies she'd undertaken, out alone in the crisp winter air, had made wonderful bases for oil-based paintings, inspiring her to spend more time outdoors painting in her preferred medium. And when the weather didn't allow, she could use the room Isobel had secured for her at the village hall and paint until her heart was content. It was the best of both worlds really. She wished that her heart was truly content.

Turning back to Richard, she offered him a small smile, wishing dearly that they could go back before the day they'd vowed to stay together forever, which was when events had started to conspire against them. Richard was trying to make things right between them, as attentive and caring as he'd always been, thus his offering to drive her here while her car was being serviced.

Nicole still doubted Olivia's explanation of her attempted suicide, heart-rending though it had been. She was more inclined to believe it was a conscious manipulation of her father. Richard had assured her that she shouldn't hold herself responsible for Olivia's actions, but there was something in the way he looked at her sometimes – an uncertainty in his eyes, a disillusionment almost – that hurt, more than he would ever know.

'You will be careful not to go to near to the edge, won't you?' Richard asked, worry etching his features as he reached to brush a strand of unruly hair from her face. Such a tender gesture, demonstrating, as he often did, that he still loved her. She so wanted to feel safe with him, totally safe, to be able to share her innermost feelings, as she once had. Why couldn't she bring herself to now? How was it she'd fallen from the dizzy heights of happiness to feeling unworthy all over again?

It was partly to do with her past, Nicole supposed, and the fact that she'd always felt that way to a degree. She needed to alter her thinking. Stop undervaluing herself and pessimistically waiting for the worst to happen. It wouldn't, unless by her very inability to believe in him, to believe that she was worthy, she made it happen.

'I will,' she assured him, covering his hand with hers and turning her cheek to his touch.

'The tide's high,' he said, his expression wary as he nodded towards the water.

'Because the river's in flood,' she pointed out. Like her heart, she thought: flooded with her love for him, and conversely with a fear of losing him. Her emotions seemed to be in a constant state of flux lately, like the river's tidal ebb and flow. 'You could come with me, if you like. Walk awhile?' she ventured, thinking it would be nice to spend some time together, talking about inconsequential things rather than the catalogue of catastrophes that had plagued them since they'd married.

'I'd like to...' Richard glanced through the windscreen, as if considering. 'Unfortunately, I can't.' He sighed, looking apologetically back at her, as two walkers ambled by. 'Maybe another time. I have a business property to view, and Liv wants to check out that studio apartment we found online. She seems really keen on this one. You never know: ours might be a house for just two people very soon.'

God, Nicole hoped so.

'In any case, I wouldn't want to interrupt the creative flow,' Richard added, his mouth curving into an indulgent smile as he leaned to brush her lips with his. 'Just promise me you'll be careful. You're not that strong a swimmer, Nicole.'

Seeing the concern in his eyes, Nicole felt a surge of warmth thaw the perpetual chill that had settled inside her. He would be worried, she knew, because she had ventured too close to the edge once, when Bouncer had charged into the water after his ball.

'I promise.' She smiled, glad that he cared enough to be so concerned, sad, for him, that he would probably always worry about losing the people he loved. Whether she'd meant it or not, in Richard's mind, Olivia had attempted to take her own life. Emily had succeeded, leaving him with sense of foreboding that would no doubt haunt him.

She'd wanted to capture this scene to complement the canvases she'd already decided were good enough to exhibit at the village hall, but try as she might to lose herself in the landscape, her mind kept wandering. As much as she tried to put it down to misunderstanding, she simply couldn't fathom why Richard had never mentioned he'd had a relationship before Emily. He'd been vague about it, once it was obvious she had misunderstood, saying no more than the woman had left him for another man and that she'd had no interest in being a mother. That had seemed very odd to Nicole. But then, perhaps the pregnancy hadn't been planned. Perhaps she hadn't even realised she was pregnant. Nicole's hand strayed to the soft round of her tummy.

Her thoughts drifted to her own mother – the woman who'd given birth to her and tried, in her own way, to care for her. They might have become friends, if only Nicole had stopped looking back. She would never forgive herself for refusing to forgive Lydia. Now, she had accepted that, by very nature of being human, she could never have been perfect. She couldn't stop imagining how lonely and scared she must have felt as her life ebbed away. Had Emily been lonely, she wondered now? When she'd felt her life was no longer worth living, had she been having the kind of day where thoughts made no sense and tears came for no reason, where the world was suddenly flat and grey and colourless? Dark days. Nicole had crawled through them recently, wondering what the point was. She felt stronger now. Her life had colour and meaning. She had a reason to live, if only she could stop being fearful of what the future might bring. Of Olivia and what she might be capable of.

Her behaviour of late had been tolerable. Still, though, Nicole felt she was watching her, waiting, coiled like a snake ready to strike. She was sure the war that had been waged against her wasn't yet over. She couldn't make herself believe that it was all because of that one single event on her wedding day. Nor, if she were totally honest, could she make herself believe that Richard hadn't been able to see some of Olivia's calculated behaviour. Perhaps he'd simply been blinkered by his love for her. Still, unsure just how dangerous the girl could be, Nicole was treading carefully, biding her time, as she had promised herself she would. For the sake of her physical and mental health, she'd worked at avoiding anything that might be confrontational, all sweetness and light, like

Olivia pretended to be. She counted the days, reminding herself it wouldn't be long until Olivia was living her own life and not dictating theirs. Because she was, still. Bouncer not being where he should be – lying on the hall rug, waiting for her key in the lock – was evidence of that. Nicole still wondered about the asthma attacks, which miraculously seemed to have ceased. She thanked God that Richard had finally agreed that getting Olivia her own apartment was a good idea. She would be gone soon, and then Bouncer would be able to come home and live safely in a house with 'just two people' who loved him.

CHAPTER FORTY-ONE

REBECCA

PRESENT

'Richard found her?' She stared at Isobel, incredulous. He'd found Emily suffocated in her own car? He didn't talk about Nicole's death or his valiant attempts to save her –Rebecca had thought he found it too painful – but why would he not at least mention something so profoundly affecting as finding someone dead, either to her or Nicole, which he hadn't as far as Rebecca knew.

'Apparently,' Isobel confirmed. 'It was in the local papers. Richard wasn't well known in the village then, but obviously people felt for him. It was just so awful.'

Rebecca eyed her quizzically. 'It was suicide though?'

'Definitely. She'd driven to the car park of the building she worked in. Taken a hosepipe with her, it seemed. It's just…' Stopping, Isobel knitted her brow. 'I don't know. I can't help wondering about the coincidences now.'

Of which there were many, Rebecca realised, her throat feeling suddenly parched.

'Obviously, Emily was depressed. Nicole was, too; she confided in me that she had days when the cogs of her brain just didn't seem to be working. Dark days, she called them, when everything seemed blacker than black. I think that was reflected in her paintings. I suppose I worry that it does all appear a little odd.'

Rebecca nodded slowly, trying to digest this latest piece of information about Emily. She needed to speak to Richard. Now. 'I should go,' she said, checking her watch and attempting a smile. 'I'm sorry to dash off, but I have somewhere I need to be.'

'Wait.' Isobel caught her arm. 'The painting I mentioned...' She hesitated, her eyes scanning Rebecca, appearing to measure her. 'I think you should see it.'

Rebecca stared at the large oil-painted canvas in awe. It was bright and light and full of life. Rather than Nicole's usual swirls of abstract colour which came together to create something evocative and inspiring, it was representational – photorealism at its finest. It wasn't a sad little lark this time, trapped by the bars of its cage. Meticulously painted down to the last detail, its graceful neck tall, its wings arched high, as if poised for flight, the glorious white swan was majestic in all of its elegant glory. Rebecca's gaze strayed to the water: pearlescent blue; pinpricks of light sparkling like jewels. It was so realistic you could almost reach out and touch it. This wasn't bleak and pessimistic. This was a portrayal of hope. These bright, optimistic strokes of light and colour had been painted by the Nicole Rebecca knew; certainly not by someone who thought they had no future worth living.

'When did she paint this?' she asked Isobel urgently, careless of the tears streaming unchecked down her cheeks.

'It was the last one she did,' Isobel said, her own eyes glassy with tears as Rebecca turned to her. 'There's something else,' she added. 'Something I think you should have.'

Searching her eyes uncertainly for a second, Isobel glanced down and then walked to the side of the canvas to ease the frame carefully away from the wall.

Rebecca waited, puzzled, while Isobel felt behind it, eventually retrieving something that seemed to have been secreted in the far corner of the frame.

'I found it after she died.' Hesitantly, she handed her an envelope, the handwriting on which was definitely Nicole's. 'It was addressed to you. It wasn't sealed, and I confess I read it.'

Isobel paused while Rebecca took out the letter and scanned the contents, her heartbeat slowing to a dull thud as she did so.

'It confirms some of the things I mentioned,' Isobel went on. 'I almost posted it on to you, but… I just didn't know what to think, whether Nicole would have wanted me to.' She faltered, her gaze anguished as she looked back at her. 'The thing is, you see, I did begin to wonder how much of it really was Nicole's imagination.'

Closing her eyes, Rebecca swallowed, and then she looked back to the letter. Two things stood starkly out as she reread it: *She's trying to get rid of me, Becky, and I'm not sure what lengths she might go to… He told me it was all in my mind.*

CHAPTER FORTY-TWO

NICOLE

CURRENT YEAR – FEBRUARY

Richard was home. Nicole noted his car parked on the drive as the taxi pulled up. He would be surprised to see her back early – she hoped pleasantly so. She'd stopped in the village to get something special for dinner, finally deciding on smoked salmon with prawns and a cream and lime vinaigrette, mainly because the supermarket had had a recipe that looked remarkably quick. She was going to talk to him, she'd decided. She would tread carefully where Olivia was concerned – she'd already decided that was her only realistic way forward if she didn't want her marriage to fail – but she wouldn't walk on eggshells any more. She had a future to look forward to. Richard did, too. They should celebrate it. Would he want to? Would he be as full of anticipation as she was?

Climbing out of the taxi, her optimism wavered. Of course he would. There she went again, full of uncertainty and maudlin self-doubt that most men would find impossible to live with. Richard had been very patient through all that had happened. He had come close to losing his temper, but he hadn't. Nicole had been on the receiving end of a man's explosive temper, and Richard wasn't that man. The only thing he was guilty of was being unable to see past his love for his daughter and recognise that she was fundamentally flawed. Nicole had no reason to doubt his love for her, and it was time she stopped.

Smiling, she paid off the taxi driver, bidding him keep the change – which was a fair amount and earned her a beaming smile – and then headed for the house. She was sure that Richard and she could get back to the easy relationship they'd had, once Olivia was living in her own little apartment. It wasn't located that far away, so Richard could visit her often. She would tell him that Olivia was of course welcome to visit, whilst quietly hoping that she didn't. And if she did, she would find that Nicole had put her stamp well and truly on this house, her house – and Bouncer would stay in residence. Olivia could like it or lump it. Meanwhile, she would continue as she was, being conciliatory to a degree, if need be. She would try to talk to her, offer her friendship – making sure that Richard saw the effort she was going to. If Olivia didn't want her friendship, then no one could accuse her of not trying. Nicole wouldn't cause any more ripples on the water during the short time Olivia was still here. It simply wasn't fair on Richard. The poor man had been torn down the middle. It was a wonder he hadn't moved out himself.

Letting herself through the front door, she bent to greet Wanderer. 'Hey, boy.' She smiled, stroking him under the chin and making a kissy face at him as he wagged his tail manically, looking incredibly pleased to see her – or rather the salmon. 'Not yours,' she scolded him, hoisting her carrier bag high out of reach. She hoped Richard had remembered to feed him. But he would have done. His love for the dog was obvious. He was always pandering to him and feeding him titbits he really shouldn't. He'd loved Bouncer too. She knew he felt terribly guilty about Bouncer having to stay with Isobel and Mike. At least they'd been kind enough to take him in. The situation could have been so much more upsetting if they hadn't.

It would all be water under the bridge soon. Bouncer would be home, and Richard and she would be able to concentrate on repairing the damage to their relationship. Their marriage wasn't broken. It was just a bit dented. Easily fixed, if she just stopped looking for reasons it should fail.

'How about we go for a nice long walk with Bouncer tomorrow, hmm?' she asked Wanderer, thinking the exercise would do them all good.

Wanderer's ears pricked up at that. Probably at mention of the word 'walk', but Nicole was sure he'd been pining for Bouncer. And some people thought dogs didn't have feelings. One only had to look into their soulful brown eyes to know that they did.

Nicole walked to the kitchen, Wanderer hot on her heels, where she deposited her bags and tugged off her jacket. All was quiet, she noticed. Extremely quiet. 'Is he listening to his music with his earphones on, Wanderer?' she asked the dog. Richard had taken to doing that a lot lately, no doubt trying to soothe away his troubles with Elgar or Brahms, those being his go-to classical composers when he needed to destress.

'Richard?' she called, checking the dining area as she headed for the sitting room.

No sign of him in there either. She glanced through the patio doors, though she wasn't expecting to find him out there. The evenings weren't warm enough for swimming.

He must be upstairs – showering, probably. Instructing Wanderer to stay, she went up, toying with the idea of suggesting to Richard that they have a second honeymoon as she went. Just the two of them this time, obviously. They might even find somewhere they could finally have that first dance. Or perhaps they could download the song, order champagne and dance in the privacy of their hotel room. It was a thought… a very enticing thought. Her mouth curving into a smile as her mind conjured up a pelvis-dipping fantasy of what they might do after they'd danced, Nicole pushed open the bedroom door – and her heart lurched to a violent stop in her chest.

She couldn't comprehend it at first. It was as if her brain simply refused to process what she was seeing in the full-length wardrobe mirrors on the opposite wall… in her bedroom… on her bed.

Nicole's stomach turned nauseatingly over.

Two naked bodies: copulating, fornicating… She closed her eyes, but still the image was there, emblazoned graphically on her mind… They were fucking as if their lives depended on it.

Feeling the room shift beneath her, the foundations of her life crumbling, Nicole wrenched her eyes open, only to meet the gaze of the woman Richard was pushing himself into, whose neck he was licking and kissing, whose breasts he was squeezing. Feral eyes. Narrowed, smug eyes. The cat that had got the cream.

CHAPTER FORTY-THREE

OLIVIA

CURRENT YEAR – FEBRUARY

'Go after her!' Olivia yelled, as Richard came back through the front door, looking defeated. 'Don't let her prang my fucking car!'

'Your *car*?' His expression one of wry amusement, Richard glanced up to where she stood, halfway down the stairs. 'You might do well to worry about police cars screeching up to the front door, which they might well be doing shortly. Might be an idea to put some clothes on, too – unless you're considering fucking the entire police force in hopes of a reduced sentence, that is.' He looked her half-naked body over contemptuously and headed for the stairs.

'Don't be fucking insulting,' Olivia huffed disgruntledly. 'And don't be bloody ridiculous either. What's she going to tell them, assuming she makes it and doesn't wrap my car around a tree first? That she found you fucking someone she thought was your daughter? Not likely to come blue-lights-blazing to arrest you for that, are they?'

'She fell down the stairs,' Richard pointed out exasperatedly. 'She's bleeding.' He looked down at the hall tiles, which were stained a stomach-churning red. 'Though Christ knows from where.'

'Not my problem, though, is it, since it was *you* who pushed her?' It was ammunition to use against him, should she need it

– and they both knew it. Olivia folded her arms across her breasts, eyeing him smugly.

'She fell,' Richard stated flatly. 'I need to get dressed.'

'You really are a stupid bastard,' Olivia growled as he attempted to squeeze past her. 'Why the *hell* didn't you get rid of her earlier, at the river? I thought that was why you'd driven her. One little push, that's all it would have taken, and she would have sunk into oblivion. How hard could it be, for fuck's sake?'

Shit! Olivia saw the flash of thunder in his eyes – too late to step away from him.

'Don't,' Richard seethed, clutching hold of her wrist, wrenching her arm upwards and forcing her back against the wall. 'Just don't, Liv,' he warned her, pushing his face close to hers. 'We play by *my* rules. No one else's. Got it?'

His gaze was intense, dark, an implicit warning therein. 'All right, all right.' Noting his unflinching fury, Olivia backed down. 'Look, I'm sorry.' Lowering her eyes demurely, she allowed her free hand to stray to his most vulnerable parts, which usually distracted him from his dark moods. 'I just thought—'

'Well, don't!' Digging his fingers hard into her wrist, Richard eyeballed her angrily. 'Thinking doesn't suit you,' he said, smiling languidly as he pushed himself closer, locking his mouth hard over hers.

Bastard, Olivia thought, nevertheless accommodating him as he as he forced her legs purposefully apart with his other hand. Olivia felt her pelvic muscles contract, her will to resist evaporating as his fingers explored with easy expertise. She was wet already at the thought of what he might have in mind. Anger-fuelled sex was guaranteed to be orgasmic; painful, but highly satisfying.

'Do it now,' she whispered urgently, dangerously near the peak of arousal. But Richard pulled abruptly away, turning to continue on up the stairs without even a glance.

'Bastard!' Olivia threw after him, stunned.

Richard didn't so much as flinch.

Massaging the welts already forming on her wrist, Olivia fumed inwardly. *How dare he?* He would be nowhere without her. Nowhere. Apart from behind bars. Did he honestly imagine he could have pulled any of this off without *her?*

Apart from actually fucking them, it was *her* doing all the hard work, manipulating his pathetic victims until they were as pliable as shit. *And then he does this!* Seething, Olivia followed him.

CHAPTER FORTY-FOUR

NICOLE

CURRENT YEAR – FEBRUARY

She was nearing Isobel's house when she saw his car. Facing the oncoming traffic, his sleek black Jaguar idled at the side of the road ahead of her, the low growl of its engine like a predatory animal stalking its prey. Sweat wetting the palms of her hands, Nicole slowed, and then clamped her eyes closed as he flicked his lights to full beam, white, bright lights, slicing across her vision.

He was waiting for her to climb out. Cold trepidation prickled the entire surface of her skin. He *wanted* her to climb out, to run, and then he would follow her and bowl her down like a skittle. He meant her harm. Her heart squeezed painfully inside her as she recalled how his kindness had turned to cruelty in an instant, his attractive features becoming savage, hostile and unflinching. Her every instinct screamed at her to stay in her car. His every instinct would be to quiet her, she was sure of it. She'd discovered him, stripped away the veneer to reveal the monster underneath, ignited a fury that far surpassed any she'd seen in the misogynist's eyes. Richard's eyes had been like ice-cold glaciers, midwinter blue, pools of pure hatred.

Splaying a hand in front of her face, Nicole squinted, and then dropped her gaze and reached for the gearstick.

He revved his engine.

Nicole's stomach cramped violently.

Please… God! Emitting a guttural sob, crunching gears jarringly, she rammed her foot down on the accelerator, reversed sharply and swung the car into a turn.

She mounted the pavement.

He rolled further towards her.

Fear wedged like a knot in her chest, Nicole bit hard on her lower lip, suppressing a cry of pain as the car thudded heavily back on to the road, and then she drove. Gripping the steering wheel tight, ragged sobs now escaping her, she pushed the car on, panic constricting her breathing as she watched the speedometer climb.

She had no phone. As she pictured her bag sitting in the kitchen where she'd left it, nausea rose debilitatingly inside her. No way to get help. She was completely alone. The police station was in the opposite direction, the direction Richard had been parked in. Had he thought she would go there? Swiping snot and tears from her face, she tried to focus. Her headlights were dim, the streetlights non-existent. Of course he'd thought she would go there. This was about much more than his incestuous, depraved sexual urges. She tried and failed to block out the image of him with Olivia, her gloating cat's eyes meeting hers in the mirror.

It had something to do with Lydia. Icy fingers trailed the length of Nicole's spine. *Everything* to do with Lydia. She'd seen someone – a figure darting from the house, silhouetted against the dark. It hadn't been an animal, a figment of her imagination. She'd seen it! *Why* had she let him convince her she hadn't? She tried to think, to get the disjointed cogs of her brain to go round. The luxury apartment. The purchase hadn't been completed. Her mother had died days before the papers were due to be signed. There had never been a luxury apartment. That certainty landed like a cold stone in her chest. That's why he was desperate to catch her – to stop her prompting any investigation. It was obvious. Blindingly obvious. How could she have been so *stupid*? So pathetic? So weak and utterly malleable?

Her eyes flicking towards the rear-view mirror, she saw the ominous sweep of his lights on the road as he rounded the bend behind her. He was catching up, closing the distance between them, pushing her on further. The road was narrow, potholed and bumpy, each rise and dip juddering painfully through her. She had no one to run to. Nowhere to go. Beyond this road, there was no more road, only a short dirt track, leading straight to the river.

Nearing the rudimentary car park, Nicole pulled to a stop.

He cruised up behind her, stopping four or five yards off, his engine back to idling. Waiting. Anticipating.

She wasn't going anywhere. He knew it. She'd driven herself into a corner. A strange sense of calm washing through her, Nicole made sure the letter she'd hurriedly scrawled to Becky was well hidden under the mat in the seat well – hoping that someone other than him might find it – and turned her attention to the water. She'd painted here, wanting to embrace the perfect tranquillity of this little oasis, fascinated by the turbulent waters as the canal locks drained into the swirling River Severn. The almost primeval feeling evoked by a lone heron swooping over the water had caused her thoughts to stray to Emily, and she'd contemplated how lonely and scared she must have been, how bleak and black her future must have seemed.

Now, Nicole felt she knew.

Despite her bubble of hope, she, too, had no future, it seemed. Richard had never intended her to have one. He'd told her to be careful not to stray too near the edge. Had it given him a kick, she wondered, warning her of her impending death? Wiping salty, slow tears from her cheeks, Nicole switched off her engine, drew in a deep breath and reached for her door.

Richard's movements were languid as he climbed out of his car. Wearing a dark T-shirt and fitted black chinos, both of which flattered his toned physique, it seemed that, even as desperate as he must have been, he'd dressed immaculately – or perhaps appropriately, to blend in with the night.

He really was extremely handsome, she thought, as his classically rugged good looks were caught in the beam of his headlights as he walked to the front of his car. A man who stopped hearts, quite literally.

Turning to face her, he didn't speak, waiting instead for her to say something, she assumed – scream accusations at him, become hysterical, weep.

She wouldn't do that. She wouldn't beg or plead or grovel. It would only make this moment more painful. She didn't want to leave this world sprawled at the feet of the man who had finally destroyed her.

Lifting her chin – wanting to preserve whatever dignity he might leave her – she spoke evenly. 'I'm sorry for your loss,' she said. Concise and to the point.

Richard cocked his head to one side.

'You're killing your unborn child.' Nicole enlightened him without emotion, though her heart bled inside her as painfully as her womb.

'*What?*' Emitting an incredulous laugh, Richard stared at her, uncomprehending. And then, 'You're... *pregnant?*' he blurted.

Possibly not any more... But Nicole felt no need to disclose that. She simply nodded instead.

'Jesus...' Quite clearly blindsided, Richard shook his head, raking a hand through his hair and glancing down as he tried to digest. Nicole's heart leapt frantically in her chest. It wasn't ready to stop beating. Not yet.

She knew the ground underfoot. It was dark, treacherously so, but she could negotiate the lock gates. Her mouth ran dry. Her adrenaline spiked. She'd be nimbler than he, quicker than he. And if she wasn't? The sun might not rise for her in the morning, but she had to try, for the life of the child who by some small miracle might still exist.

'Nicole!' Shaken out of his stupor, Richard started after her as she turned and ran. 'Nicole, stop!'

The lock gates straddling the river were wet, moss-covered and slimy, the narrow wooden shelf facilitating passage across them barely visible in the thin light of the moon.

'Nicole, for God's sake, don't go any further! Wait there!' he yelled, sounding as desperate as she as he clambered on to the lock gates after her.

Nicole heard him curse as he stumbled, felt the shudder of the huge gates beneath her. The last thing she remembered before her watery tomb enveloped her was Richard's hand clasping hers, his anguished cry as gravity tore hers away.

A curious sense of peace washing through her, she vanquished memories of them together, bodies entwined, tongues seeking each other's, as she sank into the water. Accepting the inevitable, too tired to fight it, her thoughts drifted instead to her loyal, bouncy little friend, who might not understand why his human had deserted him. *Please don't let him fret*, she prayed silently. *Please, God, let him spend the rest of his days with someone who loves him.*

CHAPTER FORTY-FIVE

REBECCA

PRESENT

Out of necessity, Rebecca stopped halfway along the high street after leaving the art shop. Visibly shaking, she pulled the letter Isobel had given her from her handbag, tears blurring her vision as she looked again at her dear friend's flowery handwriting, reading in every word how truly scared Nicole had been. And what had scared her more than anything was the thought that she was losing her mind.

Nicole! Why didn't you post it? Why didn't you call me?

Grief surged through her, leaving her weak in its wake, and she slumped against the shop window behind her. She hadn't realised she'd spoken out loud until a woman passing by cast a wary glance over her shoulder. Turning to face the shop, Rebecca looked angrily skywards and tried to get her tears in check. Olivia had been manipulating Nicole, she was in no doubt about that, but had she pushed her so far she had taken her own life?

And what about Lydia? What part had darling, deceitful Olivia played in her 'accident', which Nicole had been adamant wasn't an accident? What part had Richard, distraught father, caring husband and mediator, played?

Feeling as if she herself were losing her grip on reality, Rebecca felt an icy dagger of foreboding pierce her heart as her eyes came to rest on the properties for sale in the estate agent's window – and on one property in particular. Standing on at least an acre of land and approached via electric gates, the period property was magnificent. Richard's property. Richard and Nicole's house, the house he said he'd taken off the market. Yet here it was, up for sale. For a handsome profit, presumably, since he'd bought it before it went on the market. Nicole's money had gone into that house, which would now be in his sole ownership. In fact, all of Nicole's assets would have gone to him on her death, including the proceeds of her mother's estate.

She swallowed hard as another thought occurred, one that should already have occurred: that Nicole had possibly been insured. Very probably *had* been. Whirling around, Rebecca pulled her phone from her bag as she raced back towards the car park.

Selecting Peter's number, whom she'd tracked down at the college he'd worked alongside Nicole with, she didn't see the two women coming towards her until she'd almost collided with them. *Shit!* 'Sorry,' she mumbled, attempting to skirt around them.

'More haste, less speed,' one of them, a rosy-faced, rotund woman, said, smiling indulgently.

'What?' Rebecca glanced confusedly at her. 'Oh, yes. Sorry,' she repeated, stepping into the road to get by.

'Isn't that the latest?' she heard her say to the other woman as they walked on.

Rebecca froze, nausea twisting her stomach as she waited for the other's woman's reply.

'That's her,' the woman said, with a mournful sigh. 'Let's hope this one cottons on a bit quicker than the last one. There's something not right there. You mark my words. I'm not one to gossip, but…'

Rebecca knitted her brow, straining to hear as the woman muttered on, unfortunately out of earshot.

*

Sitting in his car, Rebecca waited for Peter to read the letter Isobel had given her, which outlined Nicole's terror on the day she'd arranged her mother's funeral, her fear, her confusion. She would have confronted Richard, Rebecca was sure. As scared as she was of what was happening around her, to her, she would have done that. He would have talked her round, tried to. Told her she was imagining it all. Almost feeling her dear friend's bewilderment, her pain, Rebecca's heart hardened to steel. 'I think you were right,' she said, as he refolded the letter slowly and handed it back to her, clearly shaken.

Removing his glasses, Peter kneaded his eyes with his thumb and forefinger. 'I know I was,' he said, his voice tight. 'Zachary didn't touch her, Becky. She was lying. It was obvious to me she had an agenda. If only I'd known *what*.' Cursing quietly, he tugged in a terse breath.

Thinking he might never breathe out, Rebecca reached for his free hand, giving it a comforting squeeze.

Squeezing hers lightly back, Peter replaced his glasses and nodded, trying to reassure her that he wasn't about to dissolve into tears. He had cried, when she'd first spoken to him. His voice had cracked, and though he'd tried hard to restrain himself, he'd had to end the call and ring her back.

'I tried to tell Nicky that there was no way Zach would have done something like that,' he went on, more composed. 'But...' He trailed off with a sigh.

'She wasn't hearing you?' Rebecca suggested. She had, though, she suspected. Just as she was feeling now, Nicole's instincts would have told her the scenario was all wrong. When Rebecca had read the email she'd sent her from her crowded honeymoon, she'd sensed it. 'I hardly dare write it down,' Nicole had written, 'for fear I'm making a judgement without all the facts, but... it seems Peter's son attacked Olivia in her bedroom.' It had been telling that she'd sensed she didn't have all the facts, that she'd said 'it seems'... Rebecca should have pursued it further.

'She could hardly disbelieve her new stepdaughter, could she?' Peter pointed out, laughing cynically. 'We spoke, afterwards, just once. I tried again to warn her that something wasn't right. Obviously, though, it would have sounded like I was defending my son – which I was, given the horrendous thing he'd been accused of. After that…'

'You lost touch,' Rebecca filled in, as he fell silent, clearly contemplating what might have happened if he hadn't. Nicole might still be alive, if only… Rebecca empathised completely.

'That's the gist of it, yes. Inevitable, I suppose. She wouldn't have wanted to be reminded of the unsavoury event that ruined her wedding day.' Peter blew out another heavy sigh. 'Thereafter, her life presumably revolved around the perfect man,' he went on, with a disconsolate shrug. 'Rather too perfect, in my mind, but I doubt Nicky would have been receptive to any criticism of him.'

Noting the bitter edge to his voice, Rebecca turned to appraise him. He was a good-looking man, his thin-rimmed glasses making him look studious, which he actually was. He wasn't overconfident, Rebecca could tell. Each time she'd met him before, he'd been quietly spoken and gentle in his demeanour. 'You loved her, didn't you?' she asked him carefully.

Peter hesitated, and then, looking slightly awkward, admitted, 'Yes, I did. Very much.'

Rebecca's heart ached for him. 'Did you ever tell her?' She pushed it a little, wondering if Nicole had turned him down – and if so, why. With their shared interests, Rebecca imagined the two would have been an ideal match.

Peter smiled embarrassedly at that. 'No. I wanted to, but I left it awhile, thinking it might be too soon after her divorce for her to be thinking about another relationship. We actually went out for lunch together, to celebrate her one year anniversary of freedom. That was day we visited the Ikon Gallery. I was willing myself to just do it, to ask her. And then…'

'Richard Gray came along,' Rebecca finished, feeling for him. How painful it must have been to watch another man steal her from under his nose.

'Mr Debonair himself. I should have pushed that bastard over the banister when I had the chance,' Peter growled, swiping the back of his hand over his mouth. 'So… What will you do about the letter?'

'At the moment, nothing,' Rebecca said. 'I need more than a letter written by a woman who both Richard and her GP will confirm was mentally ill. Absolute proof. Something he and his daughter won't be able to bullshit their way out of. There's no way I'll pull this off without it.'

Peter conceded her point with a nod. 'I have one of the items we discussed you might need,' he said, reaching into his jacket pocket and extracting a small package. 'It's frightening how easily available this stuff is over the internet.'

Rebecca peered beneath the wrapping, and then hastily rewrapped it and pushed it into her handbag. 'You did cover your tracks though?'

'I did. The PC is pretty much defunct anyway, so I wiped it and ripped out the hard drive.'

'Thanks, Peter.' Rebecca tugged in a relieved breath. She hadn't wanted to order this locally and make it easily traceable.

'My pleasure, trust me,' Peter assured her. 'Just be careful how much you use.'

Rebecca nodded. She intended to be. Extremely. She hadn't been sure Peter would be willing to help her when she'd spoken to him about her suspicions, but he had been. Knowing what she now did, how strongly he'd felt about Nicole, Rebecca understood why. Now he'd had absolute proof of the torture she'd gone through, she had no doubt she had an ally. Rebecca was relieved. She would need one.

'I've ordered the other items you asked for. They should be with me by tomorrow. 'I'll text you. Meanwhile, tread carefully, Becky,'

Peter warned her. 'You have my number. My hotel isn't that far away. I can be there in minutes if you need me.'

Driving up to the house with her head and her heart in turmoil, Rebecca was surprised to find Laura's car parked outside, which could only mean Sam and she were here. *Oh no.* This was the last thing she wanted right now.

About to call out as she let herself through the front door, she stopped, hearing raised voices coming from the kitchen. Female voices. What on earth? Dumping her bag, Rebecca hurried through to find Olivia and Laura in some kind of stand-off. Olivia, her arms folded across her breasts, looked po-faced. Laura, her arms straight by her sides and her hands clenched into fists, looked absolutely livid.

Rebecca glanced towards Richard, who stood back from the pair, splayed his hands and shrugged helplessly.

'Laura?' Guessing what this was about, Rebecca's heart dropped like a stone. 'Are you all right? Where's Sam?'

Laura, though, was apparently in no mood to answer questions. 'You're a liar!' she shouted instead, her furious gaze locked on Olivia. 'Sam would never do such a thing.'

'Right,' Olivia said, with a roll of her eyes. 'And you know this because Sam told you so, presumably?'

Laura's face flushed with anger. 'No,' she seethed. 'I know this because Sam prefers not to sleep with lying bitches like you!'

'Sticks and stones, sweetheart,' Olivia drawled impassively. 'The fact remains that Sam and I made love. By his instigation, I hasten to add, so there's really no point in coming here and acting like some sad little woman spurned.'

Choking back her disbelief, Rebecca stared at her in astonishment. What utter *rubbish*. Sam would never be so deceitful. Why in God's name would Olivia do this? And *why* had she set Zach up so cruelly? She could have destroyed his life. She certainly seemed to want to destroy Sam and Laura's relationship, and subsequently Rebecca's relationship with Richard – just as Nicole had suspected she'd wanted to ruin hers. She'd succeeded. Well, little did the girl know Rebecca had an agenda of her own. She felt anger settle like ice in her chest. Olivia might as well have bloody well *pushed* her.

'Ring him, if you don't believe me,' Olivia went on cattily, a challenge in her eyes as she boldly held Laura's gaze. 'I doubt he'll deny it if he knows you're standing here insulting me.'

'There's nothing *to* deny! You're full of shit, Olivia.' Laura wiped her arm across her eyes, trying very hard not to cry. 'It's not true. Any of it!'

'Whatever. Believe what you will.' Olivia sighed wearily, as if she was finding the whole thing tedious. 'Just a thought, sweetie,' she added, with a supercilious smirk, 'if you want keep your boyfriend interested, it might be an idea to make your next read *How to Please a Man Sexually*.'

'Liv!' Richard finally interjected. 'That's *enough*. I have no idea what's going on here, but—'

Laura stopped him, stepping forward to land a stinging slap across Olivia's face. 'You're disgusting,' she spat, looking her over contemptuously and then turning to walk away.

Stunned, Olivia stared after her. 'You *bitch*.' She recovered herself, peeling her hand away from her cheek and starting after her.

Richard was quicker, wrapping an arm around the front of Olivia's shoulders and holding her back. He'd damn well better, or he might need to hold *her* back. Rebecca fumed inwardly and went after Laura.

'I said that's enough!' she heard Richard shout angrily behind her. 'This needs to stop, Olivia, now!'

'*Laura!*' Rebecca caught up with her at the front door. 'Talk to me, Laura,' she beseeched her, desperate to know how this had come to a head, where Sam was. 'Please, tell me what's happened.'

Her shoulders heaving with obvious emotion, Laura didn't answer. Then, '*Nothing* happened!' she said, whirling around. 'That's the point, Becky. She's some kind of fantasist, or else just a spiteful, jealous cow. She's trying to split us up. I have no idea why. Sam's not interested in her. He *told* me he's not.'

The tears came then, anguished tears, streaming down Laura's face. Rebecca moved towards her, taking hold of her shoulders. 'Do you believe him?' she asked her.

Laura searched her eyes. 'Yes,' she said eventually, but she didn't look a hundred per cent certain.

'Your heart will tell you, Laura,' Rebecca said firmly, her own heart feeling as if it were folding up inside her. For Sam; for Laura. For poor, dear Nicole. 'You need to trust your instincts. I mean really trust them, Laura. They rarely lie to you.'

Nodding, Laura glanced down. 'I need to ring him,' she said quietly, her tearful gaze coming back to Rebecca's. 'We had a terrible argument. He was really upset.'

As he would be, Rebecca knew. She would need to ring him too, to offer a shoulder. And to ask him outright. She could never know all of him, but he'd never lied to her yet. She hoped to God he hadn't got himself ensnared in Olivia's web. The girl was venomous.

'He's bound to be,' she said. 'As are you. You have every right to be upset, Laura, and furious. I know I would be. If Sam is half the person I think he is, he'll respect that. In fact, I think he'll quietly applaud what you just did.'

Laura's mouth twitched into a small smile. 'I don't think he's ever seen me lose it.'

Rebecca smiled. 'It never hurts to keep them on their toes,' she said, giving the girl a much-needed hug. 'Look, say no if you want to, but why don't we go into the village and have a quick coffee? I can't let you drive back like this.'

Laura hesitated, and then, 'Okay,' she said, with a more assured nod.

'Good.' Breathing a sigh of relief, Rebecca grabbed up her bag. 'And don't worry, I won't use the time to defend my son. It's up to him to do the talking.' She hooked an arm through Laura's and steered her to the door. 'I have an ear, though, if you need one. Or else we can just indulge and eat cupcakes.'

Laura's smile brightened a little at that.

CHAPTER FORTY-SIX

RICHARD

PRESENT

'What the fucking hell were you doing, taking *her* side?' Olivia demanded, barging into the main bedroom after him.

Sighing agitatedly, Richard turned to face her. Her face set in scowl, she looked like a petulant child. She was acting like one, too. 'You screwed up, Liv,' he pointed out, less than patiently. 'If this was your best attempt at psychological manipulation, it was pathetic.'

'*What?*' Olivia gawked at him.

'It's not going to work,' Richard stated flatly, reaching to unbutton his shirt. 'You know the rules.'

'I was following the bloody rules!' Olivia eyeballed him furiously. 'Unlike you, who suddenly seems to be making them up as he goes along.'

Richard ignored her, reaching to unfasten his cuffs instead. What Olivia didn't get was that Becky was different to the others. Less needy. Not needy at all, in fact. She was strong and independent, which he'd found himself admiring. Intelligent, too. She had a way of turning conversations around and extracting information from him, rather than vice versa. He had a suspicion she would see straight through Olivia's mind games. He was thinking it might be more interesting to take his time with her. She was definitely a challenge. And, of course, she was pleasing in bed – adventurous, but setting boundaries. He liked that. He certainly liked the idea of gradually breaking those boundaries down.

'I was trying to drive a wedge between her and her son. To isolate her, which, if you recall, is rule number one. And as far as I'm concerned, it worked.' Olivia stood her ground, her hard expression reflecting her compassionless soul. It amazed Richard how women who were undeniably beautiful could appear so ugly when their true temperaments came to the fore. 'She's not likely to think her precious son is quite so perfect now, is she?'

'We discuss things beforehand,' Richard reminded her tersely. The fact was, she'd acted on her own, completely forgetting the all-important detail that he and Becky weren't yet married. 'Stick to a pre-planned agenda. That way we both know what we're doing. That display downstairs was amateurish.'

'*Agenda?*' Olivia planted her hands on her hips. 'What *agenda*? You're not making any plans. At this rate, you'll die of old age together. If you ask me, the only plan you have is to fuck her.'

Smiling scornfully, Richard shook his head. 'What do you suggest I do, Liv? Tuck her up in bed with a nice cup of cocoa? Not going to work, is it?'

Olivia's scowl deepened. 'I think you prefer her to me,' she said, her tone more subdued – tearful and definitely needy. An act. He could see right through her games, too. And, quite frankly, he was growing tired of them. Worse, he was growing irritated. If she thought she could easily manipulate him, she should think again – fast.

'I do what I do with a degree of enthusiasm because I have to. It's a means to an end, that's all.' Eyeing her narrowly, he decided he would need to do something about her, but not now. She, too, was a means to an end. She just hadn't realised it.

'So prove it,' Olivia challenged, looking him provocatively over as he tugged off his shirt. 'Make me come. Now,' she purred, moving towards him to run a sharp talon the length of his torso.

Her eyes – feral cat's eyes – held a promise, Richard noted. He could do anything with her that he pleased. Richard considered what manner of pleasurable things he might do, and then considered that that would be giving in to her manipulation. There was also the added fact that the prospect of sadomasochistic sex no longer seemed that appealing. 'I need to take a shower,' he said, looking her dispassionately over and turning away.

Olivia, though, was not going to be easily dissuaded. 'Perfect,' she said, following him to the bathroom.

'Alone.' Richard stopped her bluntly. 'I'm tired, Liv. Sorry.'

Olivia was silent for a second, but Richard was braced for the fireworks. 'You *bastard*.' Her tone was a mixture of astonishment and hurt.

'Correct,' Richard countered. 'But then that's what you like about me, hey, Liv?'

'You can't get it up, can you?' she sneered, behind him.

Richard hadn't been expecting that, he had to admit. 'Not always, no,' he conceded, his jaw tensing.

'Except with her,' Olivia added. 'You've fallen in love with her.' She laughed, a short disbelieving laugh.

Richard said nothing. It was an interesting notion, considering that the psychiatrist at the care centre in which he'd spent his youth had, after several sessions spent trying to establish the reason for his lack of empathy, concluded he had Emotional Deprivation Disorder. 'People who have been physically or emotionally abused by a caregiver in early childhood often develop a kind of protective shield that prevents them from being able to love other people on a conscious level,' the man had explained carefully. 'It doesn't mean you're inherently evil, Richard. Think of it more as stunted emotional growth.'

Richard had decided not to view it any particular way. It was what it was. There was no cure, no way to fix it. At least, he'd never found one. He was simply unable to feel love for another human being. The closest he'd come to such a phenomenon, in fact, was the affection he felt for his dogs. So what was it then, this inexplicable fascination he had for Rebecca?

'You stupid bastard!' Olivia jolted him from his thoughts. 'You'll jeopardise everything!'

'*Me* jeopardise everything?' Richard turned to face her, his voice tight with anger. 'You have your sights set on her son in order to satiate your ravenous sexual appetite and you accuse *me* of putting everything at risk?'

'Why the hell shouldn't I? He's a grown man!' Olivia yelled. 'At least he's young and virile enough to—'

'Enough!' Richard shouted. 'Sam is off limits!'

'Ha!' Olivia as good as laughed in his face. 'You might think you dictate the rules, Richard, but you do *not* get to dictate who I sleep with.'

'No?' Richard walked towards her, his temper spiking. 'Says who?' His eyes narrowed and his hand shot out to seize her by her poisonous throat.

Olivia's mouth curved into a triumphant smile as he pushed her back against the bedroom wall. 'So we *can* get it up now, can we?' she taunted, her hand going to his groin.

CHAPTER FORTY-SEVEN

REBECCA

PRESENT

Hearing Richard's whispered curses as he gave in to his urges, Rebecca pressed a hand to her mouth, attempting to quash the nausea rising inside her.

Let's hope this one cottons on... There's something not right there... She played the gossiping women's words over and laughed disbelievingly at her naive stupidity. It had been staring her right in the face. The girl – woman – didn't have an Oedipus complex, as Nicole had once confided she'd thought she had. She was his lover, his partner, one half of a depraved couple that preyed on single, vulnerable women. They'd planned it from outset, choosing Nicole specifically because she fitted the criteria, the most important of which was, of course, that she had assets, just as the women before her must have. Lydia had been part of their vile plan, too. They'd spun their web and reeled in their victims – terrified victims, who must have suffered nothing short of torture near the end.

This was what had finally driven Nicole 'out of her mind', pushed her to that dark place to die a cold, lonely death. Had she really intended to take her own life, that bleak night, or had she been assisted by these two sub-human creatures? Had Richard's brave attempts to save her – his grand finale – been *planned* in order to deflect suspicion away from him?

Evil *bastards!*

Fury unfurling inside her, grief for her friend lodged like a shard of glass in her chest, Rebecca moved quietly away from the wall she'd been leaning against. Outwardly composed, she walked calmly back to the stairs, leaving the cries of a woman in the throes of ecstasy behind her. *Enjoy, you twisted bitch.* They were made for each other, their deviant natures seeking the same perverse pleasures. They deserved each other. Deserved to rot in hell together for all eternity.

Gripping the banister firmly, she went down to the hall, where to all intents and purposes she had just arrived home. She knew the rules now. And she intended to play the game. Olivia was obviously becoming restless, growing jealous. She'd tolerated it, Rebecca imagined, because Richard had always come back to her bed. Torture and murder had clearly been powerful aphrodisiacs, fuelling their debauched sex. But, for Richard, the excitement was beginning to wane. He was growing bored with her – and Olivia knew it. She also knew she had power over him.

But so, too, did Rebecca.

CHAPTER FORTY-EIGHT

RICHARD

PRESENT

'*Christ.*' Coming into the kitchen to find Becky unexpectedly in there, Richard's heart almost skidded to a stop.

'Sorry, did I startle you?' She glanced across from where she was putting the kettle on.

'A bit.' Richard arranged his face into a smile and hastily buttoned his shirt. Breaking a cardinal rule, Olivia had marked his torso, about which he was not pleased. He'd caught her hand too late to stop her fingernails digging deep gouges into his flesh. He was going to have a hard time explaining those away. He should have broken her wrist, the careless bitch. 'I hadn't realised you were back.'

'I thought you might be taking a shower,' Becky said. 'I was about to shout up to see if you fancied a coffee.'

She turned to smile at him – and Richard breathed a quiet sigh of relief. It wouldn't have been the end of the world if she had discovered them together at this stage, he supposed. She would have told him what she thought of him in no uncertain terms, might possibly have slapped him. He had a feeling Rebecca wasn't the sort who would rant and scream and weep pitifully; she would be more likely to impart her thoughts succinctly and then leave.

Then he would just have to do what he'd done on previous such occasions: select someone new and start afresh – a depressing thought. He wasn't sure he had suddenly discovered what love was, but he liked having Rebecca around, which led to him to ponder how he would feel when she wasn't. Bereft, he suspected, which was definitely a new phenomenon.

'I'd love one, thanks.' Richard walked across to kiss her on the cheek, glad he'd had the foresight to have a quick shower before coming down. Rebecca wasn't stupid – far from it – and she would have noticed his dishevelled appearance. He really was going to have to curtail his activities with Olivia, which would undoubtedly make her more problematic. She was becoming extremely tiresome. 'So, how did it go with Laura?' he asked her, contemplating how best to deal with the issue of Olivia while fetching the mugs from the cupboard.

Rebecca sighed despondently. 'Not great,' she said, her expression troubled. 'I'm really furious with Sam. I mean, I can understand why he would be attracted to Olivia – she's probably much more his type than Laura – it's just… Laura's such a sensitive girl. I wish he hadn't lied to her. I thought I'd brought him up to have more respect for women than that.'

'He's young yet.' Richard smiled reassuringly, deposited the mugs and pulled her into his arms. 'He'll learn that lies are what hurt most, in time.'

Rebecca's look was still troubled as she glanced up at him. 'I hope so,' she said. 'We've had a few words, I'm afraid.'

'And you're upset.' Richard scanned her eyes. She was, he realised. She actually looked very upset, which caused him a pang of guilt – something that was extremely troubling to him. These emotions were new, and despite years of role playing, pretending to be like other men – better than other men – he had no idea what to do with them or how to act.

Rebecca nodded. 'I am a bit,' she admitted, mustering up a smile and pressing a kiss to his cheek. 'We've always been so close,' she said, easing away from him to attend to the coffee. 'And now he's gone off in a huff. Things are a bit strained between us, to say the least, which I do find quite sad. We've only really ever had each other, you see, so—'

'Oh no,' Olivia interrupted, appearing from the stairs. 'I'm so, so sorry, Becky. I didn't mean for any of this to happen. I swear I didn't.'

Rebecca glanced worriedly at Richard and then turned to where Olivia was standing, twisting the tissue she was holding into a knot and looking suitably distraught, to Richard's irritation. Interrupting private moments between him and whichever woman he was with was something they'd agreed she would do. But actually, this time, he would much rather she didn't.

'You must absolutely hate me,' Olivia went on tearfully.

Her expression a mixture of sympathetic and surprised, Rebecca went across to her. 'I don't hate you.' She laughed kindly. 'Why on earth would I?'

'Because I've been awful. I've acted like a complete slut,' Olivia blurted, actual tears springing from her eyes. 'Laura must be so upset. And now *you're* upset, and…' She twisted her tissue tighter. 'I wish I was dead.'

She was good, Richard thought, hiding his now immense irritation behind a tight smile. Running a hand over his neck, he watched agitatedly on as Rebecca gently lifted Olivia's chin, she having dropped her gaze ashamedly to the floor.

'Look at me,' Rebecca urged, searching her eyes meaningfully. 'You are not a slut. Having sex with someone doesn't make you that, Olivia. What happened between you and Sam happened. That you're upset about Laura is a good thing and actually makes you okay in my book. All right?'

'Really?' Olivia sniffled, her calculating cat's eyes innocent and wide.

Christ, she should get an Oscar. Richard shook his head scornfully.

'Really,' Rebecca insisted forcefully. And then, to Richard's bemusement, she kissed Olivia's cheek and eased her into an embrace.

Richard acknowledged another emotion he'd rarely encountered as Olivia locked eyes with his. Aware that she was trying to win Rebecca's affections, to compete with him, he felt jealousy tightening like a hard fist inside him. Also insurmountable fury, as he watched the scheming bitch give him a knowing wink over Rebecca's shoulder.

CHAPTER FORTY-NINE

OLIVIA

PRESENT

Oh dear. If looks could kill, she would be dead on the spot. Smouldering with repressed anger, his eyes were shooting red-hot daggers right through her. Smiling smugly, Olivia lingered awhile in Rebecca's embrace. *Mmm*, she smelled nice. Pressing her face to her long, slender neck, she made a great show of breathing in her enticing vanilla-and-rose fragrance, at which Richard raked a hand through his hair in frustration. Obviously he would be frustrated, as the realisation dawned that the power wasn't all his, that he didn't have sole control over the women. That he never had.

The first time he'd realised he'd be better off without his wife, he'd had to do nothing more than stand by and let events unfold, thanks to her. Her bitch mother had treated him like shit, thinking that because she'd bailed his business out of a hole and was privy to a few bribes he'd passed that she had a right to. She'd controlled him like a puppet: his finances; who they saw and when; whether they had children, which – already having one daughter who 'physically and emotionally drained her' – she didn't want.

They'd argued constantly, even when they fucked.

She'd felt Richard's pain when she heard the cow belittling him one night. Slurring her words, having downed enough wine to really lay into him, she'd been truly noxious, screaming at him because he'd obviously been unable to stop: 'I don't want your disgusting seed inside me!' Did she not realise what that would do to a man's self-esteem?

They'd been halfway through a door-slamming argument when her 'loving mother' had stumbled downstairs and clutched up her car keys, leaving to 'stay anywhere but with him'.

'You can barely walk straight, let alone drive!' Richard had yelled from the top of the stairs, trying to stop her.

Olivia had joined him on the landing. 'Let her go,' she'd told him, watching the drunken mess stagger out of the front door. It was an accident, but it set a precedent. At eighteen years old she'd become instilled in Richard's life. Posing as his daughter had been a masterstroke, making him 'safe' in women's eyes. *Her* idea. Not his. They'd been a team ever since – the financial rewards immense, the sex potent. Olivia intended to keep it that way. But allowing him to think he dictated all the rules? Belittling her because he was bigger, and therefore imagined himself stronger? No way.

He'd hurt her today, crossed the line, leaving her with visible bruising. He'd scared her. The look in his eyes had been cool and indifferent, bordering on contemptuous, as he thrust cruelly into her, uncaring of her back slamming against the door jamb. Once he'd finished, he simply walked to the en suite without a word and closed the door.

Unacceptable, Richard. Not fair play. Not on! She fixed her own eyes hard on his. She could crush him in an instant, rip the foundations of his luxurious life from underneath him. He bloody well knew it. *Ha!* She felt a small sense of triumph when he looked away first, clearly now seething with fury. Such a shame the poor man had no one to vent it on. She doubted Rebecca would be amenable to the kind of sex he would need as an outlet to his emotions. And if he thought he could take her whenever the need 'arose' in future, he could damn well think again. Olivia had other fish to fry, starting with Sam. She squeezed Rebecca a touch closer.

'I'll go back upstairs,' she said, smiling tremulously as she eased away from her. 'Give you two some space. I'll avoid seeing Sam as much as I can, obviously, until I move out.'

Surprised, Rebecca scrutinised her face. 'You're moving out?' she asked, her brow creased in concern. 'When?'

'In a couple of weeks. I'm going to flat-share in Birmingham with an old friend from school.' Olivia glanced towards Richard, who shook his head in cynical amusement. 'She rang me the other day,' she went on, for his benefit. 'The rent's really reasonable and I've already paid the deposit, so…'

Richard narrowed his eyes, clearly trying to work out whether she was bluffing. He would take her aside at some point, possibly even be nice to her while he tried to establish what was going on. If that didn't work, he would demand to know, as if he had some God-given right to control *her*, body and soul. Well, she had news for him.

'I hope this isn't because of what happened with Sam.' Rebecca looked worriedly over her shoulder at Richard, who quickly arranged his face to appear suitably concerned.

'I thought it might make things less awkward.' Olivia shrugged sadly. 'For Sam and for Laura, as well as you two. You never know, they might even get back together.'

'Oh, Liv… You don't have to do that.' Rebecca folded her back into her arms, giving her a firm hug this time. Richard's expression was priceless. 'Come on,' she said, stepping back to place an arm around her shoulders, 'let's you and I go upstairs and have a good chat.'

Hesitantly, Olivia nodded and sniffled, and then gave Richard a victorious look from under her eyelashes. *Touché.*

'Won't be long,' Rebecca assured Richard, steering Olivia towards the door. 'Sometimes we girls need a bit of privacy, don't we, Liv?'

Olivia smiled at her gratefully. 'Yes,' she said, fresh tears brimming in her eyes as they headed for the stairs.

'You shouldn't let something like this drive you to move out, Liv,' Rebecca said, closing the door once they were in Olivia's bedroom and turning to her aghast. 'I'd feel absolutely awful if you did.'

'Really?' Olivia asked, her expression all contrived uncertainty as she sat demurely on the bed.

'Really,' Rebecca assured her, taking hold of her hands as she sat down next to her. 'I'd miss you,' she said firmly, her huge brown eyes fixed earnestly on Olivia's. They really were quite beautiful, and seemingly full of tender concern. That was a first. Olivia couldn't remember anyone ever looking at her like that. She couldn't recall her alcoholic mother's eyes ever being focussed, let alone focussed on her.

Sighing despondently, genuinely, she dropped her gaze. 'I don't think my dad would miss me,' she said, her voice small.

'Of course he would.' Rebecca laughed, giving her hands a squeeze. 'He loves you.'

Olivia's eyes flicked cautiously back to her and then down again. 'I know. It's just…' She stopped awkwardly.

'Just?' Rebecca urged her.

Olivia took a breath and dropped her gaze lower. 'Nothing,' she whispered.

Rebecca was silent for a second, and then, 'Liv?' she said, reaching again to lift her chin. 'What is it, sweetheart?'

Swallowing, Olivia closed her eyes, allowing a slow tear to fall. 'He…' She hesitated, not wanting to seem too keen to tell secrets she shouldn't. 'Things are a bit… difficult between us sometimes,' she said. 'And I…'

She paused, appearing to be struggling with her conscience. 'I don't want to hurt his feelings, but… I don't know what to *do*.'

Catching a harsh sob in her throat, she allowed Rebecca to pull her close.

'Oh, Liv.' Rebecca emitted a heartfelt sigh and eased her head gently to her shoulder. 'You have a good cry, my lovely,' she murmured, stroking her hair soothingly as Olivia wept – masterfully. 'Men, honestly, they can be such a conundrum, can't they?'

Olivia nodded fervently and then cried harder.

'*Shush, shush.* Things will sort themselves out, Liv, I promise you they will.' Rebecca stroked her shoulders with soft circular strokes. 'Would you like me to speak to your father? Sometimes an outside perspective can—'

'No!' Olivia looked up, alarmed. 'No,' she said more quietly, quickly dropping her gaze again.

Rebecca didn't respond immediately; then, 'Well, if you're sure,' she said, sounding wary.

'It would only annoy him if he thought I'd told you things he made me promise not to,' Olivia said, sounding fearful.

'*Promise?* Liv, what things? I don't…' Rebecca stopped, breathing in sharply. 'Where did you get these bruises?' she asked, noting the blue-black marks on Olivia's arms.

'Just a fall,' Olivia mumbled, glancing embarrassedly back at her. 'Yesterday, in the shower.'

Her eyes clouded with suspicion, Rebecca looked far from convinced.

Perfect. That should put the cat amongst the pigeons, Olivia thought happily. Rebecca would demand to know what was going on. And then they would argue, which Richard wouldn't abide.

And then it would be bye-bye, Becky, and all would be back to normal.

CHAPTER FIFTY

REBECCA

PRESENT

Richard's agitation was tangible when they came down. He was sitting at the dining table with what looked like a whisky parked in front of him, and he twirled the tumbler pensively around between his thumb and forefinger. 'You've been a while,' he said, his eyes narrowed as he looked between them.

He definitely looked ruffled, Rebecca noticed with satisfaction, for a man normally so cool and collected. Olivia had merely hinted at what Rebecca knew to be half-truths and lies. The abuse was there, but Richard wasn't abusing his stepdaughter. They were in a mutually abusive relationship, their sadomasochistic highs fuelled by the thrill of the chase and the kill. Richard was worried, though. He'd overstepped the boundary, and now he was concerned that Olivia, too, might choose not to play by the rules.

'Sorry.' Leading the way in, Rebecca beamed a smile to put him at ease and reached to pet Wanderer and then Bouncer, who sniffed his way around her ankles, his scraggly tail wagging manically. At least someone was happy, she thought, making a mental promise to Nicole that he would always be.

'We got talking,' she said, walking across to drape an arm around his shoulders and kiss his cheek. Should she be worried he might be on to her? Was he aware that she knew Olivia was ready to strike back? No, she thought. The bastard was so arrogant he imagined that only he was clever enough to play puppetmaster. 'I think we put the world to rights, hey, Liv?' she went on, glancing at Olivia, who was now holding Richard's eyes with a defiant look.

'Definitely,' Olivia concurred, a languorous smile curving her mouth. 'I feel *so* much better for a good chat. Becky persuaded me to stay,' she said, blinking innocently. 'She said she would be heartbroken if I left because of what happened with Sam. She's sure he and Laura will get over it, aren't you, Becky?'

'I think so,' Rebecca assured her. 'And if they don't…' She shrugged sadly. 'Well, I suspect that maybe their relationship wasn't strong enough anyway.'

Richard's gaze flicked to hers. Nodding, he smiled inscrutably and lifted his glass, taking a sip of his drink and placing it back on the table. Studying it for a second, he turned it in a half circle, as if he wasn't quite satisfied with its position, and then looked back to Olivia, his expression contemplative, his ice-blue eyes darkening to grey.

And so it began, the seed of doubt twisting insidiously inside him. How frustrating was it, Rebecca wondered, that he couldn't voice his suspicions? Might it drive him to a volatile reaction, cause his façade to slip – even for an instant?

Apparently not. 'That's good. I'm glad you're staying,' he said, smiling again, though rather tightly. 'How about we all go out for a meal to celebrate? It might be nice after such a demanding day.'

'Oh God, I'm sorry.' Rebecca sighed apologetically. 'I'd love to, but I had a huge lunch today with Isobel. We succumbed to temptation and had profiteroles and ice cream for pudding. I honestly don't have room for another morsel.'

Richard glanced indulgently at her, then his gaze travelled back to Olivia. 'Looks like it's just you and me then, Liv.'

'Oh, um, I don't know.' Olivia looked flustered. 'I mean, I was going to ring my friend and let her know about the flat-share, and then I was going to wash my hair, and—'

'That can wait, surely?' Richard cut across her, his smile still in place and his gaze never leaving hers as he got to his feet. 'You wouldn't want to disappoint your father, after all. *Would you?*'

Rebecca noted the emphasis and the steely look now in his eyes. Olivia obviously did too, acquiescing with a reluctant nod. She wasn't yet ready to openly challenge him. Rebecca breathed a sigh of relief. 'That sounds like a lovely idea,' she said enthusiastically. 'It will give you two time to catch up without me hanging around. Meanwhile, I'll indulge and have that scented bath I've been promising myself.'

CHAPTER FIFTY-ONE

RICHARD

PRESENT

With classical music playing loudly as he drove, Richard worked to control his temper. Sadly, the beautiful melody did nothing to soothe him. Not this time.

'Richard! For God's sake, slow down!' Olivia yelled, bracing herself against the passenger door and the dashboard as he negotiated a series of sharp bends, the needle on his speedometer nudging up to a hundred. 'You'll kill us both! *Richard!*'

Ignoring her, Richard notched the volume up and forced his foot down another fraction.

Several treacherous miles further on, once he was finally able to get a tenuous grip on his emotions, he eased up on the accelerator and allowed the car to slow to somewhere near the speed limit.

She was scared. He glanced sideways at her. He wanted her more than scared. He wanted her terrified. Yanking the wheel hard left, Richard pulled off the road, plunging as deeply as he could into a wooded clearing, and then hit the brakes and skidded the car to an abrupt stop.

Olivia didn't move, not a muscle. Richard didn't look at her, killing the music and resting his hands on the wheel instead.

'What bullshit did you feed her?' he asked quietly.

'Why have you parked here?' Olivia's voice was barely a whisper. 'I asked you a question.'

'I want to go. I'm getting out.' Olivia fumbled to unclip her seatbelt.

Richard laughed contemptuously. Clearly, she didn't comprehend that he wouldn't let her go anywhere ever again unless she fucking well answered him. 'I said…' His hand shot out and he clamped his fingers tight around her neck. 'What did you tell her?'

'Nothing!' Olivia's hands went to her throat, trying to prise him off.

Richard dug his fingers in deeper. He would kill her, he swore he would, if one more lie fell from her viperish little mouth.

'You're trying my patience, Olivia. Severely,' he warned her, unclipping his own belt with his free hand and pushing his face up close to hers. 'Think again. And while you're at it, imagine what the foxes and rats will do to your delicate features if I leave you here. Tied up. Unconscious. Until the carnivorous fuckers start sniffing and licking and feeding, that is. Then the flies will move in. Can you feel them yet, Liv? Maggots eating away at your eye sockets?'

'Stop!' Olivia screamed. '*Please!* Stop,' she choked out a sob.

Were they real tears, Richard wondered? He never could be sure. 'Talk to me,' he said. 'And do *not* piss me about, Olivia. You really do not want to see me lose it completely.'

Olivia stared at him, her eyes wide with fear.

'Talk.'

Olivia hesitated, and then, reminded of his hand around her throat, blurted, 'I didn't say anything, I *swear*. It was just girl talk. Intimate stuff she probably wouldn't want to share with you.'

Richard took a minute to digest this, a stab of jealousy tightening his chest, closely followed by an almost suffocating sense of panic as he realised how vulnerable that emotion made him. 'Did she ask you anything?'

'About what?' Olivia stammered. 'I don't know what you…'

'You know very fucking well what I mean,' Richard growled.

'No! *Please…*' Olivia gulped painfully. 'Let go, Richard. You're hurting me.'

Richard studied her, taking in her tear-strewn face and her sensual lips, which had pleasured and taunted him in equal measure. His gaze fell to her slim neck. He could snap it in an instant. Like a pretty, fragile bird, her head would flop; devoid of life, her deceitful cat's eyes would be vacant. She would have no lies to tell, no truths to tell, no way to tell.

She would be nothing. *Was* nothing. Rebecca would have been trying to relate to her, that's all it was, for his sake. She was in love with him. And he…? His stomach clenched and his heart rate escalated, beating erratically with a combination of frustration and growing confusion, as he tried to assimilate feelings that were completely alien to him.

'Richard, I didn't… *Oh God…*' Olivia's voice came out a harsh croak. 'Richard, *please…*'

Was it possible? *Was* he in love with her?

'Richard!' As Olivia's voluble terror reached him from some faraway place, Richard shook his head.

'Stop…' Olivia gagged hard against his hand.

Richard snapped his gaze back to her. He was strangling her; choking the life out of her. Murdering a woman at the side of the road – his supposed daughter, whose body might be discovered by morning. Richard's rational thoughts permeated the thick red fog in his head.

It was too risky. He needed to be careful. He was *always* careful, planning everything meticulously, every last detail. This was clumsy, incompetent. A sure-fire way to lead the law right to his door. Swallowing back his bewilderment, Richard blew a ragged breath out – and relaxed his grip.

Olivia turned on him in a flash. 'What the fucking hell are you *doing*?' she rasped, one hand going to her neck, the other flailing out to land an ineffectual blow to his shoulder.

They were genuine, the tears. Richard smiled scornfully as she scrambled backwards away from him.

'I could *crucify* you, you bastard!' she spat, her expression livid, huge tears rolling down her cheeks. 'One word from me – just one – and you go to prison for life!'

Richard's smile slipped, his mind instantly reeling back to the stifling cupboard under the stairs his snarling mother had locked him in as a kid, the suffocating claustrophobia he'd felt, the absolute terror. *Bitch!* He was tempted – so sorely tempted – to finish the job and damn the consequences. But no. He wasn't about to let her goad him, any more than he'd let the whore who'd spawned him. Not until he was ready.

'Small flaw in your masterplan, Liv,' he said derisively, settling back into his seat. 'I go down, you go down with me.'

'You need me!' Olivia grabbed his arm as he reached to restart the engine. 'You *know* you do. We're a team. Together for life. You said we were!'

'Nothing's forever, Liv. Definitely not life,' Richard reminded her, looking pointedly at her hand on his arm and then to her face.

Olivia plainly got the message, unhanding him and shuffling away again. 'You really are in love with her, aren't you?' Her hands now massaging her neck – which Richard imagined would be rather sore – she scanned his face cautiously. 'I can't believe you're prepared to risk everything for one woman. Why? It's totally insane. And what about me? I love—'

'I'm not,' Richard said shortly, starting the engine and turning up his music to drown out her drivel. He needed to think. He was confused, conflicted – also a new experience. One thing he was now certain about, however, was that two women in his life was one too many.

CHAPTER FIFTY-TWO

REBECCA

PRESENT

Rebecca had no intention of indulging herself. She intended to utilise the time while Richard and Olivia were out to search for anything that might help her achieve her aim. Determined to leave no stone unturned, she decided to start with the outside, rather than have to offer explanations about why she was out there to Richard and Olivia, should they come back early.

Not even sure what she was searching for, she started with the garages, where she found nothing unexpected. Nicole had tried to paint here once – a place where there was so little natural light, it would have been positively gloomy. Been *forced* to paint here, Rebecca reminded herself. She'd gone from one prison to another, her spirit quashed, her self-esteem reduced to almost nil, broken and bruised. She'd found the courage to fight back, to escape the abuse of her first marriage – only to come here. This time she hadn't known how to fight back. She hadn't known who her oppressor was. She'd grown smaller and smaller. Trapped like the little lark in its grand art deco cage, she hadn't been able to find her way out.

They'd taken everything from her.

A hard knot of anger tightening inside her, Rebecca made her way to the pool house, the memory of his lovemaking, so urgent yet so tender, making her feel nauseous as she stepped inside. His words, guilty whispers, echoed off the tiled walls, sending a chill right through her. *You're beautiful. I want to see you. Look at me, Rebecca. Let me see you.*

We shouldn't have. She recalled his anguished guilt.

It was wrong. Rebecca felt her own; guilt that she'd enjoyed him. That for one insane moment, she'd almost been taken in by him.

Then why did it feel so right? His arctic-blue eyes had been full of incomprehension when he'd asked her that.

But it *had* been right. It had brought her here, to a place where she'd finally uncovered the heartbreaking truth. She couldn't help dear Nicole, but she could help the next woman he would drive to insanity and murder without compunction. Thinking with the fetid mind of someone not fit to be labelled an animal, resorting to the same evil tactics he used, she could play the game just as pitilessly as he.

Her brief search yielding nothing but ghosts, she went back to the house; a house with no heart, just like the person who owned it. There was no colour, none of the personal touches that would have made it a home. No permanency about it. Rebecca smiled wryly. It had been a prop, that was all. An illusion with which to maintain an image, which he sold beautifully.

Incredibly, the man slept at nights. She'd watched him. He slept like an angel, his undeniably beautiful features lending him an innocence that belied the pure evil that lay beneath. Walking into their bedroom, Rebecca's stomach recoiled, the fine hairs on her flesh rising as she recalled the soft caress of his fingers, his hard flesh next to hers, inside her. Shivering, Rebecca shook herself and headed towards the room adjoining the bedroom, which he used as an office. Pulling open drawers, none of which were locked, she searched quickly, finding nothing particularly incriminating. The paperwork therein was mostly property related. One property in particular drew her attention as she flicked through the schedules:

a warehouse originally, it had been utilised by a catalogue company and was now being converted to luxury flats for private rental. No doubt he'd purchased that at a knockdown price before it went on the market. Reminded of the apartment he'd supposedly secured cheaply for Lydia, Rebecca shoved the paperwork away and slammed the drawer shut.

Her anger intensifying, she turned to his laptop to find it password protected. She'd guessed it would be. But was Richard Gray careless enough to implicate himself in anything through online correspondence? Rebecca very much doubted it.

The filing cabinet yielded more – filed under 'I' for insurance, unbelievably. Rebecca almost laughed at the appalling temerity of the man. The sum assured on Nicole's life was enough to allow the bastard to buy his soulless house twice over. No doubt that would be deposited overseas. What floored her, however, was that Richard Gray appeared to have had no hand in taking out the policy. He wasn't even a co-signatory on the document. Rebecca did laugh then – a short, scornful laugh. He would have sweet-talked her into it, told her it was a necessary part of the house purchase or some such bullshit.

Think on your feet, Rebecca. To beat him you have to become him.

Going back to the bedroom, she pressed a hand to her forehead and turned full circle, wondering what it was she hoped to find. There had to be something she could use that would implicate him without question. Walking to the full-length fitted wardrobe, she wrenched the doors open in frustration. The cupboards were empty of women's clothes, apart from the few clothes she'd hung there. As was Nicole's dressing room. Richard had disposed of Nicole's clothes, taking them to the charity shop. Rebecca had told him it was a good idea. In reality, she'd wanted to punch him.

Steeling her resolve, she went to Richard's dressing room, breathing in the woody scent of his aftershave. She'd thought it pleasant once. Now it made her feel sick. His suits lined one wall, in smart dark blues and greys; all made to measure, she imagined. All props, too: clothes behind which he hid his true persona. Quickly, she ferreted through the pockets, finding nothing but a few property-related business cards. It was almost as if he didn't actually live in them but merely dressed up as occasion demanded. His shoes, mostly designer, were hardly worn and highly polished.

Pondering where else she might look, her gaze snagged on a pair of shoes at the end of the rail, unusual in that they did actually appear to be dirty. Thus his reason for resting them on top of a shoebox, she assumed. Picking one up, she scrutinised it more closely. They were damaged, and stained … as if they'd been submerged in deep water. Closing her eyes, Rebecca stopped breathing, a heavy compression against her chest, as if she too were slowly sinking into the dark belly of the river.

He'd tried to save her.

These were the shoes he'd been wearing.

This was the incomprehensible inconsistency. *Why* would he have put his own life at risk, searching for her until he had to be dragged out, if he'd wanted Nicole dead? Retrieving the other shoe, Rebecca examined it. Why had he kept them? Confused, imagining that she herself might be going mad, she was about to place the shoes back when something compelled her to look more closely at the box they'd been resting on. Smaller than the shoes, it couldn't have housed them. Was it one of Olivia's shoeboxes? Or Nicole's?

Curious, Rebecca placed the shoes aside, picked up the box and prised off the lid. Her blood froze. She recognised it immediately: Nicole's handwriting on the folded piece of paper inside the box – artistic, flowery, unmistakable.

A note addressed to her. It had obviously been written hurriedly – but that wasn't what was causing Rebecca's stomach to turn over. It was the pregnancy test that lay beside it.

Nausea rising inside her, Rebecca went back to the bedroom. Sitting shakily on the edge of the bed, she braced herself and unfolded the note, focussing through her tears to read it. It was just a few lines, but each word cut Rebecca's heart to the core.

Dear lovely Becky,

If I should die before we speak, please forgive me for being not keeping in touch as much as I promised I would. Please forgive me and love me, as I know you always have. Do you remember you once told me that sometimes we see only what we want to? My eyes were blind. Now, though, I see Richard for what he really is: a sick, twisted man, capable only of the incestuous relationship he has with his daughter.

I will see you again, dear Becky. I will watch over you while I wait.

Be happy. Don't miss me.

Wherever you are, a piece of my heart will always be with you.

Nicole. X

She'd been pregnant. Rebecca reached too late to wipe a tear from her face. It landed with a splat on the paper, causing the ink to bleed as surely as Nicole had bled inside her. She had seen them. Just as she had, Nicole had discovered them, fucking like animals. It was obvious from this that she hadn't realised that Olivia wasn't his daughter. She'd been carrying his *child* and she'd walked in on… *Dear God!* What must that have done to her?

Rocking to and fro, Rebecca clutched the letter to her breast, a low moan escaping her. She would have guessed then. In that soul-crushing instant, she would have known that the madness wasn't 'all in her mind', but all around her. That these two depraved individuals had used her – and why. That Lydia had been doomed to die the moment she'd met him.

When had she written this? Feeling Nicole's fear, her complete desperation, Rebecca tried to imagine when she would have hastily scrawled it. And where she'd left it, that Richard had been able to retrieve it. Might he have witnessed her writing it? Had she written it just prior to breathing in the rancid water that had killed her? In which case, he would have known exactly where to find it.

Retching, Rebecca clamped a hand to her mouth.

She must have been so, *so* terrified. So scared for her baby, the child she'd desperately wanted. Now Rebecca knew. Without a shadow of a doubt, she knew that Nicole hadn't intended suicide. No matter how confused and emotionally broken she'd been, she would *not* have obliterated her child's life by taking her own.

No, he hadn't tried to save her. He'd probably gone down to make sure she did in fact drown. Or else he'd found out very late in his depraved game about the pregnancy. Had he experienced a pang of conscience? Highly unlikely. Richard Gray wasn't capable of feeling anything.

Inhuman bastard! Rebecca's heart hardened to stone. She would have vengeance for her friend. If it was the last thing she did on this earth, she would see him rot in hell.

Attempting to calm herself, Rebecca squeezed her eyes closed – and then snapped them open as she heard a car approaching on the pebbled drive.

CHAPTER FIFTY-THREE

RICHARD

PRESENT

'You're back early.' Rebecca smiled down from the landing as Richard walked through the front door.

'Yes. Liv – she, er… wasn't feeling too well.' Aware that Olivia actually looked like death warmed up, Richard glanced guardedly up at Rebecca.

'Oh no.' Alarmed, clearly, Rebecca hurried down. 'Is she all right? Where is she?'

Richard nodded towards the kitchen. 'Grabbing some water. She'll be okay. It's probably a bug of some sort.'

Olivia reappeared then, a glass of water in one hand, which she undoubtedly needed, her other hand clutched to her throat. Richard gave her a point for initiative there, at least. She would have some make-up in her room that would hide any evidence come morning.

'Liv?' Rebecca looked her worriedly over. 'You look terrible. Is there anything I can do?'

Taking a sip of water, Olivia shook her head. 'No. It's just a sore throat,' she croaked. 'I think I'll go straight up though.'

'Good idea.' Her expression concerned, Rebecca watched her go. 'Do you need anything?' she called after her. 'A hot drink? I could warm you some brandy?'

'No. Thanks, Becky,' Olivia assured her weakly. 'Water's fine.'

Glancing at Richard, Rebecca followed her progress up the stairs and along the landing. 'Do you think I should take her some paracetamol or something?' she asked him. 'She sounds terribly hoarse.'

'Better not. She'll take a sleeping tablet, more than likely,' Richard said, looking Rebecca over. She looked pale, definitely troubled. Only about Olivia's health? He still wasn't convinced that Olivia hadn't started to lay the poison for him. Judging by her attitude lately, there was something going on in her scheming little head, of that he was sure. Rebecca seemed to be acting perfectly naturally though, smiling at him when he came in and meeting his gaze.

'Sleeping tablets?' The worried little furrow in her brow deepened.

'Prescribed by her GP,' Richard supplied. 'She didn't sleep well after… certain events. She still takes them occasionally.'

'The attack.' Rebecca nodded, a mixture of annoyance and despair flitting across her face. 'Poor Liv. Poor you. I know you worry so much.' Smiling sympathetically, she walked across to him. 'I hope she knows she's lucky to have you,' she said, kissing his cheek softly. 'We both are.'

Richard smiled self-effacingly back, his concern abating somewhat. 'So,' he said, snaking an arm around her waist and tugging her towards him, 'did you manage to get your bath, or did we spoil it by coming back early?'

She didn't look as if she had bathed, still dressed in the jeans and shirt she'd been wearing when he left. Jeans that fitted in all the right places, which were quite a turn-on.

'Sadly, no.' She sighed regretfully. 'I felt a bit off, to be honest, so I snuck a quick lie-down on the bed, and the next thing I knew you were coming through the door. I thought it might have been a touch of food poisoning from lunch, but now I'm hoping it's not Liv's bug. You'll end up with two women to nurse.'

'It would be my pleasure.' Richard brushed her lips with his as she looked up at him. 'Why don't you go and run that bath now?' he suggested. 'I'll come up with wine and oil your back.'

'Mr *Gray*.' Rebecca made eyes at him, feigning shock. 'Surely, you don't mean *just* my back?' Smiling enticingly, she leaned into him.

Richard felt a surge of desire run through him as the pink tip of her tongue parted his lips, combined with an immense rush of relief. He'd been worrying unnecessarily. Shame about Olivia's bruises, but she had brought it all on herself, he thought, pulling Rebecca closer, his hands trailing the length of her back as he took up her invitation and closed his mouth hungrily over hers.

CHAPTER FIFTY-FOUR

REBECCA

PRESENT

Richard's expression had been one of bleary-eyed surprise when Rebecca went back into the bedroom in her outdoor jacket to grab her handbag.

'Bit keen, aren't we?' Easing himself up on his elbows, he'd blinked at the alarm clock and then curiously back at her. 'Off anywhere interesting?'

'Dog walking,' she'd told him. 'One of the dogs has been ill during the night.' Rolling her eyes good-naturedly, she'd kissed his cheek and suggested he catch up on his beauty sleep. Richard hadn't suspected a thing.

It was no trial walking the dogs – quite the opposite, in fact. They were probably the best company she had right now. Wanting solitude, to be alone with her thoughts, Rebecca had inevitably arrived back at the secluded vantage point Nicole had painted from, the wind whipping her hair and her tears mingling with the slashing rain as she looked across the deep lock gates. Had Nicole attempted to cross them?

Her heart heavy, Rebecca stepped towards them. They were wet and slippery with moss. In the damp night air, Nicole's passage across would have been treacherous. Had he followed her onto them? Pushed her from there? Rocked the gates, knowing she would lose her footing? Or had he shoved her violently from the bank? Feeling her terror, Rebecca's stomach constricted painfully. She could see her face, looking back over her shoulder, pretty and fragile – petrified, as she tried desperately to get away from him. And she would have. She would have fought for the child growing inside her.

She would never have endangered that pregnancy. She'd been here because of him. Wherever he sent her sprawling into the water from, she'd died because of *him*. She *had* to do this. Fury burned white-hot inside her. All she had to use against Richard Gray were Nicole's letters. Letters written by a woman who was supposedly out of her mind. She needed more.

Distractedly watching a Canada goose, gaggle of young in tow, waddle along the bank on the canal side of the lock, Rebecca was pondering her next move when a male voice spoke quietly behind her – 'Rebecca' – causing her heart to skid to a stop in her chest.

'Bloody hell! Becky!' Peter moved fast, wrapping an arm around her waist and snatching her back from where she teetered dangerously close to the edge.

'Christ, sorry,' he said quickly, easing her into his arms as she turned. 'I should have called ahead. I must have scared you half to death. Are you okay?' he asked kindly, as Rebecca clung to him, trying to calm the riot of emotion inside her.

Rebecca nodded. 'Yes,' she managed after a second, her heart rate returning to somewhere near normal. 'I thought…'

'I gathered,' Peter finished, his expression a mixture of concern and anger. He knew exactly what she'd thought. 'Come on,' he said, giving her a reassuring smile, 'let's get back to the car park. This damn place haunts me.'

Rebecca knew that feeling. She thought about it incessantly. In her dreams, she saw it. And every time she did, she felt Nicole's pain all over again.

'Come on, boys.' Peter beckoned Wanderer and Bouncer. 'That goose will have you two for breakfast.' Tongues hanging excitedly, the dogs took one last uncertain look across the lock at the hissing goose, and then, clearly realising they were no match for it, turned to bound after them.

'How are you doing?' Peter asked, glancing worriedly at her as they walked.

'Coping,' Rebecca answered vaguely. 'You?' She looked him over searchingly as they stopped.

'The same.' Peter shrugged, glancing away and back. 'I still can't believe she's gone.'

Seeing the deep sadness in his eyes, Rebecca felt for him. He was a good man, caring enough to be here for her, taking time out from his life. He'd loved Nicole, but only ever from a distance. Like his son, Peter was shy. Too shy to have made the first move. Rebecca so wished he had.

'I've brought the other items we discussed.' Peter nodded towards his car. 'I didn't tell him what they were for, obviously, but I got Zach to look online for me. He's quite the technical whizz kid.'

'Aren't they all nowadays?' Rebecca smiled. 'Let's hope it works, for Zach's sake as well as Nicole's.' And Sam's and Laura's, she thought. They'd both been touched by this, as had Lydia and the other women whose lives had been over the day they met Richard Gray: Emily's. Whoever Olivia's mother was. More?

Peter opened his back-passenger door to retrieve an innocuous-looking carrier bag. 'Zach agreed with you,' he said. 'He reckons using a smartphone for voice recording from any distance would probably mean low-quality audio data. And being caught, of course.' He paused, his face now etched with worry as he searched hers. 'You will be careful, won't you, Becky? Call me selfish, but I really don't want to lose another friend.'

Rebecca reached to squeeze his arm. 'I will. I won't put myself at risk. I promise.'

Peter nodded, but he didn't look totally convinced. 'Just make sure to call me if anything gets out of hand,' he said. 'I'd be more than willing to step in and break the bastard's neck.'

'Which would mean you'd be arrested and I would lose a friend – someone I've grown very fond of,' Rebecca pointed out. 'Plus there's the fact that that wouldn't be painful enough.'

Not nearly enough, compared to what Nicole had endured, but Richard Gray might at least suffer some of the same psychological torment when he realised that he'd been ensnared in his own evil web and had no way out – bar one.

'No.' His thoughts clearly on a par with hers, Peter pulled in a terse breath. 'But immensely satisfying.'

'Granted,' Rebecca had to agree. 'If this doesn't work, I'll help you hold him down and we'll revert to plan B.'

Nodding, Peter smiled half-heartedly. 'We looked at several possibilities, but decided on this,' he said, fetching an item from the bag.

Rebecca examined it curiously. 'An air freshener?' her mouth twitched into a surprised smile.

Peter looked pleased. 'Good, isn't it? I've got three, just in case. It's voice activated. Over 140 hours' capacity, no flashing lights or beeping when recording, plus it's scented.'

'Perfect.' Rebecca was impressed. She'd imagined all sorts of obtrusive devices that would be technically beyond her. 'Clever you.'

'Clever Zach,' Peter reminded her. 'It's Windows and Mac compatible. You just need a USB cable to connect it to your laptop and a folder of recorded audio files will pop up.'

Rebecca's smile widened as he produced the USB cable from his bag. He really was nice. One of the good guys, thank God. Rebecca had begun to think they didn't exist, until she'd confided in him. 'Tell Zach thanks for me. And thank you, Peter. I think you've restored my faith,' she said, leaning across to hug the man Nicole should have fallen in love with.

CHAPTER FIFTY-FIVE

OLIVIA

PRESENT

Hearing a light tap on the door, Olivia eased her head up from the pillows she'd been propped up on all night. Lying flat had been impossible, her throat seeming to close up, causing her to gag. She'd hardly slept a wink. Richard's fault. All of it. Thinking he had a right to push her around, bully her, hurt her. He would be *nothing* without her. Still under the thumb of her drunken bitch mother, he would have been sexually starved, financially controlled and utterly humiliated. She'd been the one to make him see he had a way out – one that would make him a rich man. She'd planted the seed that had grown them a fortune. He couldn't have done any of it without her. Yet now he seemed to think he could just cast her aside. That wasn't going to happen. She *loved* him. He belonged to *her*! She wouldn't damn well let it happen!

Inching the door open, Rebecca peered around it and then came quietly in. 'Hi, Liv. I brought you some breakfast,' she said kindly. 'Just scrambled eggs. I wasn't sure whether you'd fancy anything much.'

Relieved it was her, though food was the last thing she fancied, Olivia leaned back on the pillows. 'Thanks, Becky,' she croaked, 'but…' Unable to continue, she stopped, swallowing back the razor blades that seemed to be lodged in her windpipe.

'Oh God, Liv, what on *earth*…?' Sounding alarmed, Rebecca deposited the tray on the dressing table and hurried across to the bed. She'd noticed the bruises, Olivia guessed, which would be livid now. As would Richard. Her hand went gingerly to her neck. She should have covered them up, but she'd felt so listless and depressed last night. It had been all she could do to climb into bed.

Her expression shocked, Rebecca sat carefully down beside her and reached to brush her hair from her face. 'What happened?' she asked, scanning her eyes worriedly. 'Who did this, Liv?'

It was obvious what had caused the bruises then. That wasn't surprising, given how mercilessly he'd dug his fingers in. He'd meant it. He really had wanted to hurt her. Picturing his face, his fury and callous indifference to the pain he was causing her, a potent mixture of anger and fear bubbled furiously inside her.

'Liv? Please talk to me, sweetheart,' Rebecca urged her.

Olivia hesitated, wishing she could, wishing there was someone in the world she could confide in, but how could she without implicating herself? Unless… She needn't tell her everything, need she? Thinking about it, confirming what the clueless woman already suspected could actually work to her advantage. Rebecca would be appalled. She wouldn't want to be in the same stratosphere as him, let alone a relationship, if she imagined he was an incestuous, deviant monster who took advantage of—

'Liv?' Rebecca kept badgering her, interrupting her thoughts. Olivia quashed her irritation. She'd need to play this carefully, appeal to the natural nurturer and mother inside her. *Yes*, this might actually work. And if it did, it would open Richard's eyes to the fact that this woman couldn't ever love him the way she did; that she would never stand by him the way she had. She would be repulsed if he came anywhere near her. She would confront him, tell him she was going to the police. It would be enough to scare him shitless. And then Richard would realise: *he* had to follow the rules. There would be no way he could talk himself out of it. He'd have no choice but to cut his losses and get rid of the bitch.

She would help him. She would be right by his side, where she'd always been. He would be hopeless without her. Richard never had liked being hands-on. He would realise just how much he did need her.

Got you Richard. You really should have been more in control. Olivia managed a smile. She didn't have to work too hard at it. 'It's fine,' she whispered hoarsely. 'I'm fine, Becky, honestly.'

Rebecca stared at her, incredulous. 'Liv... you're not *fine*. How could you possibly be? Please tell me who...?' She trailed off, her expression growing horrified as realisation clearly began to dawn. Olivia had gone out with her 'father'. She'd come back with him. There was only one conclusion she could reach. 'Not Richard? Surely to God, he wouldn't...'

Olivia said nothing. Silence, she considered, would speak volumes.

'Liv...' Rebecca lifted her chin. 'It *was* him, wasn't it?' Now Rebecca's tone bordered on furious.

Still, Olivia didn't answer, lowering her gaze ashamedly instead.

'*Why?*' Rebecca asked, her big brown eyes wide and bewildered. 'Why would he do such a thing? Tell me what happened, Liv. I don't understand.'

'I can't!' Olivia cried, tears springing forth.

'Oh, dear God...' Distraught, Rebecca took hold of her hands. 'Why can't you?' she asked, more softly.

Olivia kept her eyes lowered. 'Because.'

'Because? Please tell me,' Rebecca implored her.

'Of things he might say.' Olivia's gaze flicked guiltily back to hers. 'Things he might do. Things he's made me do.'

Her face blanching, Rebecca was quiet for a second, and then, 'I see,' she said.

Glancing up, Olivia noted the myriad of emotions now in Rebecca's eyes as she tried to process this: confusion, anger, horror. She would be making assumptions – obvious assumptions. Idiot woman. She was as malleable as he was.

Rebecca moved to place her hands on her shoulders. 'Look at me,' she said firmly.

Making sure to appear hesitant, Olivia met her gaze.

'Olivia, whatever it is he's coerced you into doing, you can confide in me, you know. I promise I won't judge you.'

Nodding timidly, Olivia wiped a tear from her cheek.

Reaching for her hands again, Rebecca squeezed them gently in her own. 'Has he been abusing you? Sexually?'

Olivia took a breath, for effect, then, 'Yes,' she blurted. 'I didn't know what to do. I feel so, *so* ashamed.'

Rebecca pulled her towards her. 'There is nothing to be ashamed of, Olivia. *Nothing*. Do you hear me? It's him who should be ashamed, the absolute… *bastard!*'

'I'm scared of him, Becky.' Olivia gave it her all, sobbing wretchedly into Rebecca's shoulder. 'Really scared.'

CHAPTER FIFTY-SIX

RICHARD

PRESENT

It had been bracing in the cool morning air, but an early swim had washed the cobwebs from his brain, sharpened him up. He'd slept too heavily, dozing off again after Rebecca left, which was something he never normally did. He'd finally woken feeling lethargic, a dull ache pulsating in the base of his skull, and experiencing a mild sense of panic that he wasn't on top of things. He was becoming careless, deviating from the rules, which might lead to mistakes, one of which could be fatal. He had to stay focussed and concentrate on his priorities, the first being how to deal with Olivia, who'd unwisely decided to remind him she could hold him to ransom. The second was his relationship with Rebecca and whether it realistically had any kind of future. Was it likely to last, given his past?

Walking into the hall, he found her coming down the stairs with a breakfast tray, the contents of which were still intact. 'How is she?' Looking appropriately worried, he asked after Olivia as he bent to give Wanderer and Bouncer a fuss, but both were still far too busy with the chews he'd given them earlier to be remotely interested in him. *Fickle creatures*, he thought, smiling tolerantly. They were actually anything but; faithful to the person they perceived as top dog to the last. Unlike humans. He'd learned very early in life never to place his trust there.

Straightening up, he pondered again the problem of Olivia and how best to proceed. He was beginning to think that having her simply leave might be the answer. She'd told Rebecca she'd be moving out, so it wouldn't raise too much suspicion he couldn't invent some story about if she suddenly upped and left. A shallow grave in the woods was out of the question though. He needed somewhere more permanent, where she might never be discovered. The new-build construction site just out of town, possibly? Once the foundations were down, it would be as safe a place as he could find. Wearing his high-vis vest and an appropriately coloured hard hat, which was easily obtainable, he would pass as part of the construction crew. It was a possibility, and definitely a safer option than any of his own renovation sites, which were too close to home. Richard smiled inwardly at the irony that the only person with whom he could discuss the feasibility of such a project was Olivia.

Rebecca smiled at him over her shoulder as she headed towards the kitchen. 'She's very sleepy,' she answered his concerned question about Olivia. 'You were right about the sleeping tablets. She took one late last night apparently.'

'Oh. She's all right though?' Richard knitted his brow and followed her through. She had taken a sleeping pill then. He'd obviously shaken her up quite badly. No more than she deserved.

'She will be,' Rebecca assured him. 'Her throat's very sore, but it's just a cold, I think. I left her tucked up under the duvet.'

'Do you think she should see a doctor?' Richard asked, trying to establish whether Rebecca had seen the bruising he had no doubt would be obvious this morning.

'I don't think so,' Rebecca said, scraping the untouched food into the bin. 'There's not much they can do for colds, is there? I've told her to let me know if there's any swelling.'

'Thanks, Becky, you're an angel.' Richard smiled gratefully. 'I'll go up and check on her in a second.'

'I wouldn't bother until later if I were you. She's pretty zonked out. I should think she'll sleep at least until lunchtime. She's all right though, honestly.' Rebecca reached to press a hand reassuringly to his cheek as he walked across to her. 'A day in bed will do her good.'

Richard nodded. 'You're probably right. I'll go up later. Take her some soup or something,' he said. 'That smells good.' He nodded to the coffee machine she was busy at.

'I have an urge for cappuccino.' Rebecca smiled. 'Do you fancy some?'

'Now there's an offer I can't refuse.' Richard stepped towards her, snaking his arms around her and nuzzling her neck. She smelled amazing: fresh spring flowers with a subtle blend of vanilla. Far more enticing than the coffee. Did he want to be without her? He felt it again, that painful tug at his heart he'd only ever felt once before: as a child whose spirit had been crushed when he'd discovered his murdered dog. A lot like Bouncer, a bedraggled stray, the dog had followed him home from school. His mother had 'got rid of the flea-bitten thing'. Digging in the mud at the bottom of the garden, he'd discovered how. He'd put away childish things that day and concentrated his emotions on basic survival, biding his time until he could make sure that bitch was stuffed deep into the worm-ridden earth.

He'd concentrated on survival ever since, in a world he didn't fit into. He'd had to. He'd acted his fucking heart out, trying to be human. The fact was, though, he hadn't met any humans he liked, until Rebecca. She was an enigma: feminine, yielding to him, yet strong. Her love for her son was powerful. Richard was sure that, if she had to, she would lay down her life for him. She fascinated him. And she frightened him, because he couldn't contemplate his future without her. Existing once more, which was all he'd ever done, rather than living.

He ached to feel what other people did, to be 'normal' – something he'd believed he wasn't, could never be, thanks to the crap the psychiatrist in the care home had spouted. He'd been wrong. If he took nothing else away from his relationship with Rebecca, he would take the knowledge that he was capable of loving. He'd just never felt safe to. Had never felt safe enough even to acknowledge the possibility. This was normal. This was safe, for the moment.

He eased her closer, needing to feel the warmth of her body next to his. 'You do realise you're doing terrible things to me?' he asked her.

Rebecca leaned into him as he peppered the nape of her neck with soft kisses. 'I just might, if you keep doing that,' she murmured. 'But *after* the coffee.' Pressing her hand to her mouth, she suppressed a yawn. 'I was up at the crack of dawn with the dogs, remember?'

'Hell.' Richard squeezed his eyes closed. 'I've given them chews. Do you think they'll be okay?' That was a stupid thing to do. He should have thought. He would hate to think he'd done anything to make the dogs ill.

'They'd better be,' Rebecca called as he went to check on them. 'Or you're on the next dog run.'

'No problem,' Richard said, reaching to stroke Wanderer, whose tail thumped manically. Delighted as he might be to see him, Richard doubted he'd part company with the now ragged chew easily, even for him.

'Do you want chocolate sprinkled on top?' Rebecca asked from the kitchen.

'Why not,' Richard said, thinking that chocolate was poor compensation for what he really wanted as he came back. Stopping, he watched, his undeniable desire for this woman spiking, as she licked her finger, collected up spilled chocolate powder from the work surface and then inserted it slowly into her mouth.

Christ. Now he knew what it was like to be human. Richard walked across as she repeated the procedure, catching her hand before it reached her lips. 'Do you realise how erotic that is?' he asked her huskily, his body responding to the primal ache in his gut.

'What?' Rebecca laughed, surprised. 'I was just…'

His eyes holding hers, she stopped. Richard lowered his head, closing his mouth over her finger, sucking it deep into his mouth, the chocolate – sweet and piquant – whetting his appetite. He wanted her. His free hand found the small of her back, easing her closer, hitching her to him. He wanted to taste her, every enticing inch of her flesh.

CHAPTER FIFTY-SEVEN

OLIVIA

PRESENT

Halfway down the stairs, Olivia stopped breathing. Every sinew in her body tensing, she gripped the banister hard. They couldn't be. She couldn't. She wouldn't. After all she'd told her? Hearing Richard utter in that throaty way he did – '*Fuck*' – the unmistakable guttural moan of a man close to coming – her man! – she knew with absolute certainty what was happening.

Swallowing hard against the bile rising like corrosive acid in her throat, Olivia carried on downstairs, her heart thrumming wildly with a combination of growing fury and curiosity as she came in full view of the sitting room doors.

Oh God, no. Her stomach lurched as she took in the scene before her with nauseating clarity. She was on top, the clever bitch. She'd taken her in, lulled her into a false sense of security, caressing her sorrow with soft-spoken sincerity.

Her hands were on his chest, stilling him, like a black widow spider over her mate. She was rising from him slowly, pausing, then sliding unhurriedly back down; languid, sensual movements. She was making him wait. The dominant in their shameless erotic dance, she was orchestrating their performance, soaring and ebbing to Elgar's 'Salut d'Amour', which was playing in the background.

Playing softly.

She'd wanted her to hear.

Seeing Rebecca lean towards him, her lips seeking his, her tongue duetting with his, Olivia's heart drummed a prophetic warning in her chest.

She wanted her to know. She was stealing him, taking him to new heights of ecstasy. Places he could never go with her. With her, he fucked: primal frenzied fucking to satiate his base desires. With this woman, he was making beautiful love.

She was taking him away from her. Taking her place.

One hand clutched to her stomach, Olivia pressed the other to her mouth as the woman who would replace her arched back up, increasing the pace, bringing him to the sweet kind of climax she'd always hoped to: something meaningful, bodies and souls entwined. They'd never had that. He'd only ever taken what he wanted and then left, leaving her hurting and lonely. She longed to feel their limbs entangled as they lay together afterwards, satiated, depleted, two bodies as one. In all the time she'd known him, Richard had never closed his eyes, allowed her to sleep safe in his embrace.

Rebecca turned her face towards her as Richard clutched her hips, anchoring her hard to him. Reading the words on her lips as the melody reached a crescendo, the pieces of her shattered life crashing around her, Olivia backed away.

In that agonising moment, she knew he'd meant to do more than scare her. He'd wanted to kill her. It had been there in his cold, unflinching eyes. She'd told herself he wouldn't, that it was more than he dared. She'd tried to convince herself that he wouldn't ever truly harm her, that he could never survive without her. That he was nothing without her. But the reality was that she'd never been safe with him. And now... It was she who was nothing without him.

CHAPTER FIFTY-EIGHT

RICHARD

PRESENT

'So, was that a yes to the chocolate?' Rebecca asked, smiling mischievously over her shoulder as she led him by the hand back to the kitchen.

Feeling dazed after their impromptu sex, Richard took a second to answer. He wasn't used to giving over control completely. He'd never been sure he would be comfortable with it. In fact, it had been exquisite, an experience beyond anything he could ever have imagined. How much had he missed out on, he wondered, since he'd been that tearful ten-year-old child who'd made up his mind that displays of emotion were weak?

'I think I might need it,' he said, leaning to brush her cheek softly with his lips as she veered off towards the coffee machine. 'It will play havoc with my diet, but…'

'You don't need to diet.' Rebecca laughed as she set about preparing fresh coffee. 'Your body is perfectly toned and firm' – she turned to give him a look loaded with suggestion – 'in *all* the right places. Trust me.'

Seating himself at the kitchen island, Richard smiled. 'Thanks for the compliment, but some of us do have to work at it, you know.' Watching her dip a finger into the chocolate, making eyes at him as she licked it off deliberately slowly, he found himself actually laughing. He still didn't know what these feelings were that he had for this woman, how she'd ignited something he'd thought didn't exist inside him, but he now knew for sure he didn't want to be without her. Sadness enveloped him – another feeling he'd experienced rarely as an adult. How would he keep her? He wouldn't, if the truth ever came out. He couldn't let that happen.

'Penny for them?' Rebecca said, carrying the coffee across to him.

'Sorry?' Richard's mind was back on the problem that was Olivia.

'You're miles away.' Handing him his coffee, Rebecca seated herself opposite him.

Richard took a sip. She'd gone overboard on the chocolate and added extra cream as well. It was good. 'I was just thinking that I wish things could have been different.' He sighed demonstratively. 'But then, as selfish as it might sound, I'm glad that they're not.'

'Nicole?' Rebecca asked, looking sympathetically at him over her mug.

Richard glanced awkwardly down and back. 'Yes,' he said, playing the role, though the sweep of remorse about the child she was carrying was all too real.

'She wouldn't have begrudged you your happiness, Richard.' Rebecca reached for his hand.

'No. I know.' Richard nodded sadly. 'She was a very special person.'

'She was.' Rebecca squeezed his hand tightly. 'Come on, drink up. I thought we might take the dogs out together before you dash off to your meeting this afternoon.'

'Good idea. I could probably use the exercise after all that lying back and thinking of England.' Taking a large gulp of his coffee, Richard watched her amusedly as she widened her eyes at his effrontery.

'Oh, *you…*' she said, leaning across to give his arm a playful punch.

'Hey, go easy.' Richard said, looking serious. 'That was very nearly a terrible waste of excellent coffee.' Smiling, he was draining the last of it when he felt suddenly light-headed.

Very light-headed, as if he might even pass out.

'I, er…' *think we might have to postpone*, he was trying to say, but he couldn't seem to make his mouth coordinate with his brain. 'I feel a bit…' Pausing again, he shook his head. He was definitely feeling dizzy, he realised, and now troublingly queasy. Had he eaten something? Feeling hot and clammy, definitely not well, he ran a hand across his forehead, scraped his stool back and got to his feet. He was sweating profusely. Either the central heating was notched up to some ridiculous level or he was coming down with something.

Swallowing, he swayed woozily, as the floor seemed to undulate beneath him. Pulling in a slow breath, he attempted to alleviate the sudden tightness in his chest. Panic creeping over him, he blinked hard and looked at Rebecca, his anxiety escalating as her smiling face swam in and out of focus. He cocked his head to one side as the wall beyond her shifted violently. *Christ.* He felt inebriated, as if he'd drunk a distillery…

His stomach tightening, Richard swiped at the perspiration tickling his eyelashes and shook his head as the room swayed nauseatingly around him. Attempting to stay upright on legs that were threatening to give way, he stumbled forward and groped for something to hold on to, only to succeed in knocking over Rebecca's coffee. As if in slow motion, he watched the dark contents spilling across the white work surface and sliding over the edge like elongated liquorice. Morbidly fascinated, he saw the gloop hit the floor, the mug spiralling sluggishly after it, finally crashing down to shoot slivers of ceramic in a hundred different directions.

What the…? The room revolving steadily now, Richard turned anxiously towards Rebecca, who was standing two yards or so away from him. Her eyes were wide, curious, mesmerised. Squinting confusedly at her, Richard swallowed hard and stepped towards her. She stepped back. *Cat and mouse*, he thought, as they repeated the manoeuvre. Richard tried another step, but his limbs refused to obey. His head reeled, his stomach churned, his instincts screamed. *Had she … drugged him?*

Why? With what? He felt as if he'd been hit with a sledgehammer. Was it lethal? *Jesus Christ.* Nausea crashed through him; his legs buckled beneath him. Richard dropped to his knees. Groaning, he dragged his hands over his face, tried to still the whirling room as it picked up momentum.

'Richard?' He heard Rebecca's voice from a distance. 'Oh dear, I do hope Olivia's bug isn't catching. Poor Richard. Are you feeling unwell?' she asked, her tone that of a mother mollifying her child.

He felt her move closer, fingers running through his hair, clutching his hair, yanking his head back. 'Trust me, Richard, you haven't felt anything yet,' she assured him, a whisper away from his ear.

With a sharp twist, she released her grip. Walked around him. 'Would you like to know why this is happening, Richard?' She came to stand by his side. 'I'll tell you, shall I, since you're obviously struggling to answer?'

One push was all it took. Richard keeled heavily to the side.

'I was getting a little fed up, Richard, watching you and your devious little sidekick play your game and not being invited to join in. I mean, that's just plain unfair, isn't it? Cruel, in fact, since you robbed me of…'

Her voice drifted in and out of his consciousness; broken sentences punctuated by the dull thud of his heart.

'…she was a good friend, a dear friend, and I've decided you need to make amends.'

Richard stopped listening. Warm cotton wool enveloping his brain, too enticing a blanket. He just wanted to sleep.

'Pay attention.' A vicious kick to the ribs forced his eyes open. Another, well aimed to his kidneys, before the owner of the heavy shoes walked a slow circle around him. Men's shoes.

Peter?

Unable to even summon up the spittle to swallow, Richard watched hazily as Rebecca lowered herself to kneel down beside him. 'We're playing a new game now, Richard,' she said, her tone the soft purr of a cat. 'I'm not sure you'll like it.'

No! Richard felt excruciating pain rip through his shoulder as his arm was wrenched high up behind his back.

'I said *pay attention*,' Peter growled, looming over him.

Fuck! A fresh wave of panic gripped Richard's stomach as the sharp glint of a blade sliced through his peripheral vision. Watching from some faraway place, he realised he'd badly miscalculated. He would have laughed – if his facial muscles had allowed it. He should have trusted his emotions, or lack of. Instead, he'd trusted her. She'd taught him how to love. And now she was going to kill him.

CHAPTER FIFTY-NINE

RICHARD

PRESENT

Richard woke abruptly, hurtled to consciousness by a nightmare so vivid he could smell it, smell his mother's fear as she stumbled around, searching for the medication that kept her black heart beating. Her eyes beseeching, her hand outstretched towards him, '*Please…*' she'd implored him. This dream was different. This time, the scrawny boy she'd stuffed in the under-stair cupboard didn't walk away and leave her to die. This time, she'd caught him.

Christ. Sweat saturating his face, pooling in the hollow of his neck, he tried to move, only to find his arms were numb and trussed high above him. Attempting to alleviate some of the pressure, he shifted his weight on the hard bench he was seated on and squinted against the grainy darkness around him. His first thought was that he had a crippling hangover. His second was that he was in a confined space, and this nightmare was real.

Fuck! Reeling inwardly, his heart slamming against his chest and nausea gripping his stomach, his gaze went instinctively to the slivers of light, which he guessed were filtering through a blind at the window. Disorientated, he tried to focus. His vision was blurred. His memory? Where in *God's* name was he?

Groping for some level of calm, he closed his eyes and swallowed against the acrid taste in the back of his throat. *Chlorine!* The taste registered in his brain. He was in the pool house. Scrambling for some recollection of what had happened, he came up with nothing that was tangible, his tenuous thoughts seeming to slip away like water through sand. He had a few disjointed memories: Becky, making slow, sensual love to him; the soft melody of 'Salut d'Amour' heightening his senses. Coffee? Dripping. Ceramic, splintering. Olivia? Had she been there? *Peter!* That bastard definitely had. Squeezing his eyes tightly closed, Richard tried desperately to remember.

And then he almost had heart failure as a door was yanked open. His pulse ratcheting up, he blinked hard against the blinding white light that flooded the space he was in. The space he was apparently being held prisoner in. Richard tried to quell the nausea now clawing its way up his windpipe as Rebecca walked silently towards him.

Her eyes were flat, emotionless. Her expression hard and uncompromising.

She was a good friend, a dear friend, and I've decided you need to make amends. The words she'd said, the tacit threat, filtered through the wet cotton wool in his head. Her fingers running through his hair, clutching his hair – Richard felt it. Saw the glint of the blade before it moved to his neck and sliced through his flesh.

His eyes flicked downwards and he saw the flecks of blood on his shirt, staining the white fabric a deep crimson. Why was she doing this? Torture? Slow torture. Was she fucking *insane*? Guardedly, his eyes went back to hers as she stopped in front of him.

He flinched as she reached a hand to his face.

'*Shhh*. Keep still, Richard, I'm not going to hurt you,' she said soothingly, her fingers now delicately tracing the tacky track of blood from his neck to his chest.

Richard jerked his head back in a futile attempt to move out of her reach.

'Oh dear, I see you're already not liking the new game. That's a shame.' She sighed, stroking her hand under his chin, and then spun abruptly around to walk away from him. 'I did hope we could play nicely.'

'Where is he?' Richard asked gruffly, his throat tight and sore, on the inside and the outside. The bastard had actually cut him with the blade he'd been wielding. He would kill him for that. If only his hands weren't tied to a fucking coat hook. How ridiculously amateur could this get? If they were aiming to terrify him before finishing the job, they would fail miserably. Richard didn't terrify easily. Didn't she realise that if his *game*, as she fondly called it, was up, then he would welcome death? Relish it, in fact, now he'd found out, too late, that life might have been worth living.

'Who?' Blinking innocently, Rebecca turned back to face him.

'You know damn well *who*,' Richard spat venomously. 'Your cowardly accomplice. I doubt he'll be much use to you, Rebecca – a man incapable of defending his own son.'

Rebecca ignored that. 'In the house,' she said, looking him over coolly, 'playing with your "daughter".'

Noting the quotation marks she made with her fingers, Richard looked away. 'Fuck off,' he snarled.

'That's not very nice, is it, Richard?' she said, her huge lying doe eyes now round with feigned shock. 'Not nice at all, after all that we shared together. Smiling, she walked across to him, her hand shooting to his crotch, squeezing so hard Richard almost choked. 'It might be better not to use such foul language while you're defenceless, *lover boy.*'

Richard dropped his head as a searing pain shot through him, ripping through his abdomen like a knife.

'Look up,' she said evenly, after a minute.

Gasping, Richard couldn't breathe, let alone look up, and she knew it.

'I'm talking to you, Richard,' she pointed out patiently. 'I consider being ignored rather disrespectful, too.'

The warning implicit, Richard braced himself and – with some effort – met her gaze.

'Better.' She extended her hand, causing him to instinctively recoil again, and then ran the back of it softly down his cheek.

Bitch. Impotent fury broiling inside him, Richard watched as she walked casually away. 'What did you give me?' he demanded, his mind going back to that morning, when he'd been too tired to drag himself out of bed. She'd slipped him something then, clearly. How long had she been planning this? 'The drugs, what were they?'

Taking her time, she looked back at him. 'A little cocktail,' she said, her smile inscrutable. 'Some of the Prozac – you know, the drug Nicole was prescribed to decrease her anxiety?' Her expression turning to hatred, she lost the smile. 'I mixed it with flunitrazepam. A risk, but one worth taking, I felt, to make sure you didn't get back up, you piece of shit. It's more commonly used as a date rape drug, but I'm sure you're familiar with it. I can't imagine a man like you wouldn't be.'

Richard smiled caustically. 'I don't need to drug the women I have sex with, Becky, do I?' He took the opportunity to remind her she'd been all too ready to fuck him, and she'd damn well enjoyed it.

Rebecca's expression remained bland. 'Peter provided it, actually.'

'Peter, of course.' Richard shook his head disdainfully. He'd been surprised at his involvement, he had to concede. Up until now, he'd considered him the type of man who would slope away quietly to lick his wounds rather than stand up and fight. He'd misjudged him. That had been remiss of him. But then, from where he was sitting, trussed up like an animal, it seemed as if Rebecca was the one in control, with Peter ready to jump to her command. Now, why would that be? 'You're fucking him, presumably?'

Her smile was back, enigmatic, giving nothing away. 'No, Richard,' she assured him. 'Unlike you, I don't need to fuck people to get them to do what I want. Peter was happy to help. More than, as you can imagine.'

Out of revenge for what had happened to his son, no doubt. Richard laughed with contempt. He might have been impressed, had the man found the balls to tackle him before he'd been rendered incapable. 'So, what are you going to do?' he asked her, thinking he would rather know how they intended to kill him, where they would dispose of him. He could probably give her a few pointers.

'What? To avenge Nicole for what you did to her? To Lydia? Emily? Olivia's mother? *All* of the women you mercilessly tortured and murdered?' Rebecca surveyed him coldly. 'You mean you haven't guessed? I really thought you were clever enough to be one step ahead of me. I'm disappointed, I have to admit.'

But Richard was one step ahead. She was going to kill him, that much was clear. And whatever it was she had in mind for him, it wasn't going to be painless.

'It's not what I'm going to do that you need worry about, Richard,' Rebecca went on, remarkably calmly. 'It's what *you're* going to do.'

'Ah, a little intrigue. No doubt designed to make me consider my punishment while I wait?'

Rebecca cocked her head indifferently to one side. 'And will you?'

Richard smiled. 'Most definitely,' he assured her. 'Point of note, though, not that I imagine it will make any difference: I didn't murder Nicole, and I was nowhere near Lydia when she died.'

Rebecca simply stared at him. In her eyes was a look of absolute abhorrence.

CHAPTER SIXTY

RICHARD

PRESENT

Richard did reflect when Rebecca left him alone, presumably to sweat while he waited. He wasn't contemplating his own demise. On the assumption that she had decided to inflict maximum pain and he would probably die slowly, he didn't care to linger too long on the details of that. His thoughts went instead to Lydia, an old woman, who, as far as he could see, had made it her life's work to denigrate her daughter. Even in front of him, wanting him to imagine her as a sweet, lonely old lady, she'd only ever managed to talk to Nicole with a marginal degree of civility. He'd felt protective of Nicole on one occasion, fleetingly; because of his own suffering at an uncaring mother's hands, he'd assumed.

Nicole should have been glad to be rid of her. That was the plan. He doubted Nicole would have admitted as much, so caring was her nature – to her own detriment – but she was supposed to have been quietly glad to see the back of a woman who'd given her none of the emotional tools she would need to cope with life and relationships. Instead, thanks to Olivia losing her bottle and running when Nicole had turned up unexpectedly, she'd been traumatised. Slipping in the woman's blood wouldn't have helped her state of mind, he imagined. She'd been covered in the stuff – which Richard had found repugnant. She'd also been suspicious, obviously, which had kicked off a chain of events that had pushed him to the limit of his patience and caused him to deviate from his plan. The day Nicole died, the day his child died with her, Olivia had orchestrated things – baiting him, provoking and taunting him. Always daring him to take risks.

And he had. Determined she should know that her role in his life would only ever be one of subservience, he'd given in to his desire that fateful day. She'd known he would. He'd given her exactly what she wanted.

Richard felt his gut twist with something akin to grief and insurmountable anger. If he could have one wish before he met whatever fate they had planned for him, it would be to hear that bitch scream for mercy… assuming she wasn't in on this little charade along with Rebecca and super-fucking-hero Peter, of course.

Jesus! Richard slammed his head back against the wall as a final realisation dawned. Of course she was in on it. She wasn't in here, with him, was she? She'd probably been scheming and plotting for weeks, convincing Rebecca he'd acted alone. How the fuck could he have been so blind? Richard emitted a disbelieving laugh.

She'd played him.

She'd won.

CHAPTER SIXTY-ONE

REBECCA

PRESENT

Rebecca watched him carefully. She'd just informed Olivia of Richard's situation – restrained and at her mercy, prior to getting his just deserts – and left the young woman to consider her own fate. But Richard was still outwardly calm. Apart from his earlier display of aggression when she'd given in to her own base instinct, tempted to part him from the equipment that he imagined made him a man, he'd shown no emotion bar contempt. She hadn't meant to give in to her own emotions so easily. She needed to do what Richard did so well, become the soulless monster he was and stay in control. He was sorely testing her, however, looking at her even now with mild amusement. As if all of this was some inconsequential little game, no more than an annoyance to him.

'What is it that you imagine you're going to force me to do?' he asked her eventually, a brazen smile tugging at the corner of his mouth. 'Take my own life? Is that it, Rebecca? Are you going to offer me more of your lethal cocktail and suggest I do the decent thing, or else?'

Rebecca delayed before answering, keying in a text to Peter instead. 'It's a thought,' she said, hitting send. Noting the cocky, almost couldn't-care-less look in his eyes as she met his gaze, she realised this wasn't going to be easy. In reality, she had nothing with which to convince him he had no choice, apart from the threat of going to the police. Imagining she would anyway, he would be bound to be stubborn on that basis.

'Not quite what I had in mind though.' She gave him a reassuring smile. 'We could always come back to that option, of course. I'm sure that, resorting to your methods, we could easily make your death look like a suicide. And given your nefarious activities, I should imagine the police wouldn't be at all surprised you'd taken your own sad little life rather than face the consequences.'

'Right.' Richard's smile was now openly scornful. 'And you have proof of these *nefarious* activities, do you?'

Rebecca nodded thoughtfully. 'Enough, I think,' she said, glancing nonchalantly from him to the door as Peter came in.

'Ah, here he is.' Richard looked Peter over with derision as he walked across to Rebecca without even acknowledging him. 'Becky's little lapdog, jumping to his mistress's command. Will she reward you with a treat when this is over, *Peter*?' he asked, his voice loaded with contempt. 'A pet or a stroke? A blow job, perhaps?'

Despite his visible anguish when he'd read the letter she'd found in the shoebox, Peter's expression didn't alter as he handed Rebecca Nicole's last two letters, but she couldn't fail to notice the thunder in his eyes as he turned away, heading towards Richard, who watched him with arrogant amusement.

Pausing in front of him – at which Richard looked marginally perplexed – Peter studied him for a second. 'Don't,' he said, without inflection, his hand darting out before Richard could blink. 'Just don't.' Gripping his throat hard, he pressed his fingers into the wound he'd already inflicted. 'The only thing standing between you and me right now is Rebecca. If one more derogatory comment spills from your mouth, I *will* kill you.' He squeezed harder and Richard winced. 'And trust me, I will take great pleasure in doing it slowly.'

After giving his throat one last squeeze, causing Richard to gag, he released his hold, nodded politely in Rebecca's direction and walked calmly back to the door.

'I think Peter has issues with keeping you alive, Richard,' Rebecca informed him. 'Namely, that you murdered Nicole, whom he loved very much, and that you ruined his son's life without compunction. I wouldn't recommend provoking him, if I were you.'

Noting the fresh trickle of blood dripping onto his shirt, Richard's demeanour was somewhat ruffled, at last. 'I didn't,' he said, his voice hoarse, a hint of something near regret in his eyes as he looked back at her. 'Nicole. I told you, I didn't…'

'*These* say differently.' Walking across to him, Rebecca held up the letters in front of him. 'Nicole and I kept in touch. Frequently,' she said, enlightening him of a fact he plainly hadn't been aware of.

A disdainful look now in his eyes, Richard dragged his gaze away.

'Read them.' Rebecca cautioned herself not to react.

'Or else?' Richard challenged her, that conceited fucking smile playing at his mouth, humour dancing in his eyes.

Rebecca stood no chance. 'I said read them!' Her anger spewing over, she slapped his face hard. How dare he? How *dare* he imagine he still had the upper hand. That he could dismiss Nicole's last words so carelessly.

Meeting her furious gaze with an incensed one of his own, Richard seemed to debate and then reluctantly dropped his attention to the letters.

At length, he looked back at her. 'This isn't proof,' he said, a flicker of remorse clouding his eyes, Rebecca detected. 'She was depressed, imagining things, half out of her mind. Her GP will—'

'Where you drove her!' Rebecca screamed over him. *Bastard.* Incredulous, she stared hard at him, and then backed away before she was tempted to stop the lies spilling from his mouth once and for all.

Stay in control. This is what he wants, she warned herself, attempting some degree of composure. This *was* a game to him. If he knew he was getting to her, if he saw that he'd rattled her, then he would consider it a win. To achieve what she wanted, she had to think like him, be as devoid of emotion as him. Instil fear in him. He had to know she was serious. Deadly.

Calmer, after a moment, she pulled her phone from her jeans pocket, selected the audio file she'd recorded of Olivia masterfully acting the victim of incest, which Peter had transferred, and pressed play.

Richard listened, unmoved at first by Olivia's tearful revelations, and then his eyes darkened to grey, his jaw tightening as he undoubtedly considered where this might be leading. 'It's bullshit,' he sneered, when Rebecca paused at an appropriate juncture. 'She's—'

'Not your daughter,' Rebecca finished, as he scanned her face warily. 'I know. I know all of it, Richard. Every despicable thing you've done, all corroborated by your lover and accomplice.' She didn't. She was bluffing now, but he wouldn't know that. 'The women – how many and why: for money, for kicks, for power. Ultimate control over women. You tortured them and finally murdered them, which fuelled your depraved sexual desires.'

'I didn't murder anyone.' Richard's face was a shade whiter. 'None of this proves I did.'

Rebecca didn't comment. She wanted to rip his heart out.

He looked away and back again. 'Is that what passed between us? Depraved sex?' he asked, his tone curious – and tinged with sadness, Rebecca could hardly believe.

She simply looked at him. What did he really expect her to say? It was great? Hot? Let's just forget about the dead bodies and pick up where we left off?

'Why did you try to save her? After you pushed her, why did you go in after her?' she asked, wanting to know, *needing* to know. It would have all been over for him, if Nicole had survived.

'I didn't push her. She slipped!' Richard held her gaze briefly. 'I… can't feel my arms.' His voice was strained. He was clearly in some discomfort.

'Why?' Rebecca appealed to him. 'For God's sake, Richard—'

'She was pregnant!' Richard shouted. 'She didn't *tell* me.' He looked back at her, genuine pain in his eyes. 'She would have made a good mother. She… she should have told me.'

Rebecca watched, stunned, as he bowed his head. He'd wanted *children*? Dear God, he actually believed he was capable of being a father.

'Do you realise how much that child would have meant to her?' she started quietly. 'How long she'd wanted to have a child? How desperate she'd been after her baby died? Have you *any* comprehension of what you put her through?'

'Baby?' Richard's gaze snapped back up. 'She didn't mention anything about losing—'

'Can you imagine what must have gone through her mind, as she sank into that dark, lonely grave?' Rebecca seethed, fury unfurling dangerously inside her. '*Can* you? Can you conceive for one second how she must have felt, knowing her baby would drown with her? You callous…'

Gulping back tears of rage, Rebecca turned away. *Evil.* He was evil personified.

'So, what do you intend to do?' Richard said, after a pause, during which Rebecca attempted to rein in her spiralling emotions.

Tugging in a tight breath, Rebecca faced him. 'We're changing the rules, Richard,' she said impassively. 'Now we're going to play by my rules.'

'What?' Richard's expression was a mixture of uncertainty and incredulity.

Rebecca kept her eyes locked firmly on his, hoping he would see she meant business. He'd better see she meant business. 'You will transfer all the proceeds of your activities into my account. Where we go from there, I haven't decided yet.'

His eyes narrowing to slits, Richard studied her. 'You mean you're doing this for the money?' He laughed in disbelief.

'All of it,' Rebecca said, walking to the door. 'Every last penny. And remember,' she said, glancing back over her shoulder, 'you don't have any other choice.'

'Don't I?' Richard stopped her. 'The thing is, Rebecca, I don't care if I die,' he said, his tone indifferent. 'I've been searching all my life for something that, to me, seemed elusive. I thought I'd found it. And now… I don't care any more. Don't you see? Your threats mean nothing to me.'

Shit. Rebecca cursed. The upper hand, she reminded herself – he would always strive to have that, to take back control. It was who he was: a dysfunctional man who couldn't bear to be controlled. 'I think you do, Richard. You're calling my bluff, and it won't work,' she said. 'I'll leave you to think about it: how you'll really feel when you know you're about to breathe your last breath.'

Flicking off the light – hoping that might help focus his thoughts – she reached for the door.

'No!' Richard said urgently behind her, causing her to jump. 'The light… I…' He stopped, leaving Rebecca bemused, until the penny dropped.

She almost laughed out loud. He was scared! Of the ghosts that might come back to haunt him? She very much doubted that. Of the *dark*. He was scared of the dark. He'd wanted to see her. *I want to see you… Let me see you*, he'd said. The first time they'd made love, he'd switched on the light. She'd been uncomfortable for the briefest of seconds, until he'd stilled her nerves with his reassuring words, his mouth possessing hers.

He didn't like closed-in spaces, intimate restaurants. He was claustrophobic.

She *had* him.

Kindly, she reached to turn the light back on. 'Don't take too long debating your options, Richard,' she suggested. 'Peter has a plan for you, should you decide you don't want to play things my way. I'm not sure you'd be quite so blasé, buried in some small, dark space… alive… would you?

CHAPTER SIXTY-TWO

OLIVIA

PRESENT

'What will you do with me?' Sitting on her bed and wringing her hands wretchedly, Olivia eyed Zach's father with trepidation.

He said nothing, looking impassively at her from where he stood in front of the door, his arms folded across his chest like something out of *The* fucking *Bodyguard*. Was that supposed to intimidate her?

The truth was, Olivia was petrified. The man hadn't taken his eyes off her since that sluttish cow had delighted in delivering the news that Richard was bargaining for his freedom, and in so doing was trying to convince them that she'd somehow manipulated him. Uncertain of how much she was bluffing, Olivia had to admire her cool. She was obviously an amateur compared to enigmatic Rebecca, the master of manipulation.

'It's all lies,' she said tearfully. 'The things Richard's saying about me, they're not true.'

Peter continued to stare stonily at her, causing a fresh wave of panic to clutch at her insides.

'He used me!'

His expression unflinching, still he said nothing.

Olivia's stomach twisted. 'He sexually abused me!' She spelled it out for him, since he clearly wasn't moved. 'I was just a child. He used to come into my room. When he was married to my mother, he—'

'He raped you?'

Olivia faltered. 'Yes.' She wetted her dry lips with her tongue. 'The first time—'

'Like Zach?' he said flatly, his eyes hostile behind his deceptive Mr Nice Guy glasses.

Olivia felt hope sink like a lead weight in her chest. 'He told me to do that.' Perspiration prickling her skin, she looked desperately at him. 'He made me… to ruin Nicole's wedding day. He said if I didn't—'

'It worked.' The man's tone was still emotionless.

'I couldn't stop him. I couldn't stop him doing any of it. He's too strong. I tried to warn Rebecca and he almost strangled me,' Olivia blundered on, attempting to elicit some degree of sympathy. 'I tried to tell Nicole. I—'

'You should know that he's saying it was you who pushed her,' he said quietly, cocking his head to one side as he studied her.

Fear pierced Olivia's heart like an icicle. He was making it up, trying to shift blame from himself, hoping for a lesser sentence. That wasn't likely. Richard knew it. He must know that no one would believe him. How could they? How could anyone imagine that she – a sweet, innocent young thing – would do anything so abhorrent, unless mercilessly corrupted by him? How could he do this? Did he honestly feel so little for her that he would see her grow old, her beauty fading as she spent the rest of her life behind bars? She choked back a sob, feeling more alone than she'd ever felt in her life.

'It's bullshit,' she said, real tears squeezing from her eyes to roll down her cheeks. 'I was nowhere near her. He did it! He was there, not me!'

'He also says you pushed her mother to her death,' Peter added matter-of-factly. 'Did you get a kick out of it, I wonder? Killing a frail old woman? Driving Nicole to the brink of madness? Murdering her? Did you get off on it?'

'No!' Olivia blurted, desperation climbing inside her. 'I didn't. I didn't like it, the things he did to me. I wanted a normal relationship!'

This was getting her nowhere. She could slash her wrists in front of him and he wouldn't blink.

They hadn't tied her hands, restrained her in any way, probably hoping she would. Shakily, Olivia wiped the tears from under her eyes, pulled her hair back and got to her feet. 'A loving relationship,' she said, more softly, 'with a normal man.'

Walking towards him, she smiled tremulously and reached out to trail a hand down his cheek. 'Please let me go,' she said. 'I'll do anything. Rebecca needn't know. You could say I slipped out while you went to the bathroom.'

His mouth curving into a slow smile, his gaze strayed to her lips. Olivia closed her eyes, relief coursing through her veins. 'Anything at all,' she breathed seductively, her hand straying lower.

Peter caught it, clamping his hand around her wrist like a vice. 'I can't imagine a time when I would be desperate enough to go anywhere near something like you,' he snarled, looking at her as if she'd crawled out from under a stone.

Shit! Olivia stumbled back as he released her. 'You're all the same!' she screamed. 'Bullies, all of you!'

He shook his head.

'I'll kill myself!' she threatened. 'I will! I'll throw myself out of the window!'

Peter glanced over his shoulder as the sound of a door opening and closing downstairs echoed through the house.

Turning back to her, his smile this time was heartless. 'Make sure you miss the pool,' he said, turning calmly to walk out of the room.

CHAPTER SIXTY-THREE

RICHARD

PRESENT

She was bluffing. Richard studied her face as her accomplice worked to free his hands. Her expression was impassive, her gaze hard as steel. *Christ Almighty*, she really meant it. Surely she hadn't planned all this from outset: chosen him, the way he'd chosen his victims? That first time she'd met him at Nicole's funeral, had she been plotting then, whilst playing the role of the grieving friend? Was it possible that she was just like him? Richard almost laughed at the irony of his situation. They could have made a great partnership. Not now though. Not with her little lapdog in tow. They would want it all: everything he'd ever worked for.

'Up,' Peter instructed, having finally managed to untie the rope. She was on to a loser with this incompetent prat. Maybe he should enlighten her to that fact, but possibly not now. Seeing the murderous intent in the man's eyes, Richard fancied he might do better to keep his observations to himself.

'I said *up!*' Peter repeated, clutching a handful of his shirt and attempting to drag him to his feet, which was monumentally irritating.

Richard shook his head, unimpressed. 'Do you think I could have a minute?' he asked, wincing as the blood returned to his arms like a thousand burning needles.

'No.' Peter smiled flatly and shoved a hand under his arm, physically heaving him up, which hurt like fuck. His shoulder hadn't fared too well the first time he'd aggressively manhandled him. Quiet, inoffensive Peter was plainly the reactive sort, under the surface, not capable of restraining himself – as evidenced by the wound in his neck, which he'd needlessly inflicted. Definitely a man with issues. No sooner had he managed to get unsteadily to his feet than Peter was yanking his arms behind his back to retie them, which was also extremely painful.

'Are you seriously considering a future with him?' Richard asked Rebecca, unable to believe that she would choose this weak specimen over him.

Rebecca smiled that enigmatic smile she had. Combined with her hitherto hidden qualities, it really did make her enticingly attractive.

Richard smiled sadly back. 'Good luck with that,' he said quietly.

Rebecca dipped her head, as if appreciating the sentiment. An enigma, most definitely. One Richard would like to have explored further. *C'est la vie.* He sighed and shrugged, trying to ignore the wrench in his gut as he thought of the last time they'd made love together. And it had been lovemaking – for him anyway – which had been a novel experience.

Quashing his urge to verbalise what he thought of Peter, he allowed the man to steer him around and shove him towards the door, rather too strenuously.

Giving him a demonstrative shove every other step towards the house was uncalled for, Richard thought, but refrained from pointing out. Already contending with the various injuries he'd sustained at the man's hands, and with nausea still sweeping through him, it would possibly be a bad move to give his persecutor cause to inflict more damage.

'So, what now?' he asked, struggling to maintain his footing as Peter kindly 'assisted' him through the patio doors.

'Now we make the transfers,' Rebecca said, nodding towards the dining area, where his laptop, he found, once guided there, was already set up on the table. She'd been certain he would do this then? Of course she had. What alternative did he have?

'Small problem,' Richard said.

Rebecca eyed him with a mixture of curiosity and suspicion. She was good, he conceded, wondering how she'd ever managed to look at him with such affection in her eyes when she so clearly despised him.

'I won't be able to do much with my hands tied,' he pointed out.

'Nice try.' She smiled wryly and led the way to the table. 'You talk; I type. And don't try to pull the wool over my eyes, Richard. I'm not stupid.'

Sitting down in the chair he was 'assisted' into, Richard smiled wryly back. 'I don't doubt it.'

'We'll start with the UK accounts,' Rebecca said, firing up the laptop. 'And then we'll move to the overseas accounts. If that's okay with you?'

Richard laughed at that, genuinely. He couldn't help but admire her temerity. 'Perfectly,' he said. He would have no use now for the considerable sum he'd amassed and deposited overseas – as she'd shrewdly guessed he had – unless money bought favours in hell.

Obligingly, he reeled the various user details and passwords off, as requested, receiving several curious glances from her and the dynamo that was Peter as he did. He supposed they'd thought he would be more troublesome. Richard had already decided there was no point fighting the inevitable. Given free rein over a man with his hands tied behind his back, Rebecca's 'heavy' could hurt him. Richard didn't particularly want to be hurt any more.

'Is that everything?' Rebecca asked, having cleared out all of his accounts.

'Apart from the money in my wallet, yes. Obviously, you can help yourself to that, if you need to.'

Her look this time was one of amusement. 'I don't,' she said.

'No.' Richard smiled sardonically in acknowledgement of that. 'So, what do you have in mind for me now?' he asked, scanning her eyes curiously. 'Death? Or slow death?'

Rebecca held his gaze. 'The jury's still out,' she said, a flicker of concern in her expression, which offered him some small comfort.

Richard nodded, guessing she'd understood what he meant. 'No doubt you'll let me know the verdict. Meanwhile' – he took a breath – 'do you think I might use the bathroom? I'm feeling rather nauseous.'

'I'm not surprised,' Peter said, the smile on his face somewhere between contempt and satisfaction. Richard had to accept that he himself might not be the catch he'd seemed, but he really had no idea what Rebecca could see in him. He would be no challenge for her whatsoever.

Ignoring him, he looked questioningly back to her, since she was the one making the decisions. 'It's internal, the downstairs bathroom,' he reminded her. 'No windows. I'm not going anywhere.'

'Yet,' Peter added drolly.

It took supreme effort on Richard's part to ignore that, keeping his attention on Rebecca instead.

She nodded her acquiescence. 'Don't be long,' she said.

'Thanks.' Richard took another short breath and got to his feet. 'I, er…' He hesitated. 'I might struggle to…' He trailed off, thinking he didn't need to state the obvious.

The two exchanged glances. Nervous glances, Richard noticed. 'I'm not proposing to drown myself in the toilet,' he assured her. 'So, unless Peter would like to assist me?'

Glancing at Rebecca, Peter didn't look too thrilled at that prospect.

Still, Rebecca looked uncertain.

'I'm not going to fight you, Rebecca. I've nowhere to go. Nowhere to run,' Richard pointed out quietly. 'Retie my hands in front of me, if it makes you feel more secure, just… I'd be grateful if you'd allow me some small dignity before the jury comes back?'

Rebecca took another second, then, 'Retie him, Peter, would you?' she said.

Peter looked warily from her to Richard and back. 'Are you sure about this, Becky? He doesn't exactly rank highly in the trustworthy stakes.'

'I'm sure,' she said, her eyes never leaving Richard's.

'Thank you,' he said again, allowing Peter to do what he had to do, faffing about with the rope for what seemed like an eternity. Rebecca really could do better than him, he thought, finally making his way to the toilet.

Once inside, still unsteady on his legs, Richard leaned his forehead against the comforting cool of the mirror. He was perspiring – profusely, he realised – possibly more to do with nerves than the drugs. The tap was dripping, he noticed, slowly and steadily, each drip like a nail being driven into his coffin.

Would she leave him to die as she'd hinted she would, he wondered, his chest tightening. He didn't think so. He doubted she would kill him at all, which was a pity. If she made an anonymous call to the police, undoubtedly the floodgates would open. Richard's heart rate ratcheted up at the prospect of being questioned in a police interview room. The thought of being held in a cell caused his stomach to clench violently. He couldn't do it. There was no way he would survive being locked in a room no bigger than a shoebox.

Rebecca knew it. Knew precisely how this game would end.

Richard felt repulsion with himself as he remembered the small boy shaking with fear as he sat alone, confined in the claustrophobic dark of the cupboard. It was while sitting there, listening to his 'loving' mother singing soprano along to the radio, that he'd made his decision. Finally, his patience had been rewarded. Killing her had been easy. He hadn't felt anything very much, that day or thereafter.

He was feeling now though: undiluted terror, chilling him to the bone. Closing his eyes, Richard tried to still the nausea churning inside him, and then, a fresh spasm gripping him, he leaned to retch the acidic contents of his empty stomach into the toilet.

Hearing a sharp rap on the door, he straightened up. 'Two minutes,' he called, flushing the toilet and then hurriedly yanking the towel from the holder, his hope to suppress the noise, should Rebecca have a fit of conscience. It wasn't easy looping it over his arm with his hands tied, but desperation, he found, was a good motivator.

Fuck! He cursed as the smashed glass of the mirror crashed into the sink.

The rap on the door this time was urgent. The handle rattled noisily as Richard grabbed the most suitable shard of glass he could find.

'Shit! The bastard's actually going to do it.' He heard Peter's voice close to the door. Several loud bangs on the door were followed by the sound of splintering wood, as he pressed the sharp point of the glass to his jugular. Would they try to save him? Richard thought not, as he drove it hard home.

CHAPTER SIXTY-FOUR

OLIVIA

PRESENT

She'd wondered why they hadn't tried to stop her, hadn't pursued her. They'd seen her leave, she was sure, slipping through the patio doors rather than throwing herself out of the bedroom window – which she was sure Peter wouldn't have tried to prevent her from doing. Perhaps they realised, Olivia thought, that the police, who she'd seen from the fields were approaching the house, would find her. They'd taken her purse, leaving her with no money or any way to obtain any. She had nowhere to go but the streets.

They were concentrating on their goal: relieving Richard of his funds. She'd felt sorry for him, almost, as they'd led him from the pool house, pushing him and shoving him, his hands trussed behind him, blood all over his shirt, his face the colour of death. They would be gone from there now, more than likely. Richard, too, taken away in handcuffs. He would struggle in prison. He'd told her once – confided in her – that he didn't think he would survive it. Had he ever loved her? Did he know how much she'd loved him, she wondered, wiping a slow tear from her cheek. Had he even cared for her? She thought not; knew he couldn't possibly have cared, now that she'd seen him making love with a woman, rather than fucking as a means to an end. She wished she could tell him that that was why she'd written down everything about her involvement and posted the letter through the police station door before she'd come here. She knew he'd only ever viewed her as a means to an end, no more than that.

She'd been nothing to him. Was nothing.

She'd never imagined herself succumbing to a state of emotional abandonment where she lost all rational thought, her sense of identity. Lost sight of her. It happened gradually, subtly and insidiously, until you really did believe the madness was 'all in your mind', as Richard had so often told the women he'd tortured.

She'd tortured.

Olivia knew how that felt now.

She knew from experience that her passing from this life into oblivion wouldn't take long. Her limbs flailed instinctively as she slipped into what would become her watery grave. The water was cold, much colder than the surface air. Hypothermia would set in quite quickly as her body constricted surface blood vessels to conserve heat for her vital organs. Richard had explained it all to her once.

It was happening just as he'd described it: her head began to throb as her heart rate and blood pressure increased. She could hear it, the strange whooshing, gurgling sound, which wasn't the water around her but the sound inside her. Her muscles tensed suddenly and she shivered uncontrollably. Her lungs, bursting within her, screamed at her to draw air. Once she did, of course, her lungs would fill and she would be gone. Her hope was that her core temperature would drop rapidly and that her wasted life would fade to black before that happened.

Her tears of regret mingled with the murky water as her thoughts ebbed and drifted. It wasn't snapshots of her past life that flashed before her. The images that would fade with her were of them together, bodies entwined, tongues seeking each other's – languid, sensual movements as they sought to pleasure each other, gaining pleasure from the knowledge that she was watching. Rebecca, at least, knew she was. As they'd reached the heights of ecstasy, she'd turned her smiling face towards her and whispered, 'It's all in your mind'.

The other women, Olivia saw them too, with their confused expressions, their bewilderment and deep disillusionment, which soon gave way to fear as realisation dawned. They'd been trapped. Butterflies in bell jars, they'd continued to flutter until their colours faded and their fragile wings crumbled to dust.

Wanderer, offering her unconditional love whatever her mood; she saw him, patient and loyal on the hall rug, waiting for the familiar thrum of her car engine, her key in the door. She would miss him. She wished she'd been nicer to him; hoped that they would look after him. Be kind to him.

Pain and sorrow turn to wisdom in time. You should have been more vigilant. Those were Rebecca's last words to her. Olivia wished she had been.

CHAPTER SIXTY-FIVE

REBECCA

PRESENT

Richard's eyes had fluttered open as they'd carried him out. He'd actually smiled. The sad smile of a condemned man, his fate a fait accompli. He would live, the paramedics had assured the police officers attending, who'd in turn assured her that he would be placed on suicide watch once released from hospital into custody.

Sadly, Olivia hadn't survived. Peter thought she'd escaped justice. Thinking about the way she'd chosen to die, Rebecca thought not.

Listening to the last strains of Elgar's, 'Nimrod', Rebecca walked away from the funeral, which had been attended by no one other than herself, and went straight to see Nicole. Would she have minded her being there? Knowing her friend's caring and forgiving nature, Rebecca suspected she wouldn't. Had she been alive, Nicole would probably have attended herself.

There would be an investigation into the proceeds of Richard and Olivia's appalling crimes, of course, all of which had been accounted for – bar any that was rightfully Nicole's, plus a little bit more. 'I doubt they'll miss that amongst the other millions,' she assured her, kneeling to place her flowers on the grave. Not roses. Faded pink just wasn't Nicole. A delicate spray of colourful freesias suited her better.

'The purchase of the property will be completed soon,' she chatted on, taking the wilted flowers from the urn and replacing them with the fresh ones. The property on the high street was an ideal choice, she thought. Richard hadn't completed the renovation, so the apartments wouldn't be quite so luxurious now, each converted into a share for two families – women with or without children – who needed sanctuary from controlling, abusive partners who regarded it as their right to rob them of their lives.

'I thought employing a security guard might be a good idea,' she went on, sure Nicole would agree. So often these broken women were found by their tormenters and felt they had no choice but to return home again. Rebecca wanted her venture to be different, to provide true security in comfortable surroundings until these victims of crime were able get their lives back on track and start afresh. No doubt she would hit snags along the way, be accused of being idealistic, meet the wrath of neighbours not wanting such a project on their doorsteps, but… 'It's a start, at least.' Laying a hand flat on the ground where her friend rested, she hoped she could hear her, that she would be happy that Richard had been punished in the worst possible way for his sins against her. 'From little acorns… I'm hoping this will be the first of many – in time, obviously.'

Rebecca stopped, her attention drawn by a sleek black BMW gliding along the path towards the church. 'That will be Edward.' She turned back to Nicole. 'My new councillor friend,' she reminded her, certain that if Nicole judged her, it wouldn't be badly.

'He's quite good-looking, in a lived-in sort of way,' she went on, knowing that Edward would be happy to wait. She'd seen from the greedy look in his eyes that he was interested in more than a 'professional' relationship the second she'd offered him a bribe to ensure her business went smoothly. Well, needs must. She'd been aware that purchasing the property she'd had her heart set on would be tricky.

'He's older than me, but not too off-putting to climb into bed with. He treated his first wife abysmally, according to rumour.' Rebecca knitted her brow scornfully. 'But I've yet to establish all the facts...'

THE END

A LETTER FROM SHERYL

Thank you so much for choosing to read *The Second Wife*. I really hope you enjoy it.

I would love to hear from you via Facebook, Twitter or my website. If you would like to keep up to date with my latest book news, please do sign up at the website link below. Your details will never be shared and you can unsubscribe at any time.

www.bookouture.com/sheryl-browne

This a story about relationships, some of which sadly turn sour. Sometimes people find themselves in situations that might be abusive in some way. They're never quite sure how it happened and, perhaps for financial reasons or because of low self-esteem, might struggle to find the strength to leave. Some might even feel guilty at abandoning their partner. Controlling relationships are not an easy subject to look at and my fervent wish is for anyone reading this book to realise it is written from the heart. Guilt is such a negative emotion. The message I hope to convey is that, personally, I found it okay to ditch the guilt that came with starting to put myself first in certain situations. Looking after myself was my first step: the diet, the hair, the clothes, the make-up – whether I wore it or not. I chose to start doing that for me. These were baby steps. The bigger strides came later.

As I write this last little section of the book, I would again like to thank those people around me who are always there to offer support, those people who believed in me, even when I didn't quite believe in myself.

To all of you, thank you for helping me make my dream come true.

If you have enjoyed the book, I would love it if you could share your thoughts and write a brief review. Reviews mean the world to an author and will help a book find its wings.

Keep safe, everyone, and Happy Reading.
Sheryl x

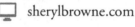 sherylbrowne.com

 SherylBrowne

 SherylBrowne.Author

ACKNOWLEDGEMENTS

I would like to offer a massive thank you to the team at Bookouture, without whose expertise and dedication *The Second Wife* might have been struggling! Special thanks to Helen Jenner for her magical editing skills and tremendous patience throughout the editorial process. I'm thrilled with the results and I hope my readers will be too. Special thanks also to Kim Nash and Noelle Holten, the dynamic Bookouture Publicity Managers, for their hard work and unstinting support. We would be floundering without you. To all the other super-supportive authors at Bookouture, I love you! Thanks for the ears and the smiles!

I owe a huge debt of gratitude to all the fantastically hardworking bloggers and reviewers who have taken time to read and review my books and shout them out to the world. Your passion always leaves me in absolute awe. Thank you!

Final thanks to every single reader out there for buying and reading my books. Authors write with you in mind. Knowing you have enjoyed our stories and care enough about our characters to want to share them with other readers is the best incentive in the world for us to keep writing.

CPSIA information can be obtained
at www.ICGtesting.com
Printed in the USA
LVHW041627200819
628309LV00014B/1103/P